Archipelago

H R Hawkins

This novel is entirely a work of fiction. The names, characters and incidents portrayed in it are the work of the author's imagination. Any resemblance to actual persons, living or dead, events or localities is entirely coincidental.

First edition

Paperback ISBN: 978-1-3999-7251-2

Gull Rock

www.hr-hawkins.com

Part I

Chapter 1

Ren Stares Out of a Window at Dusk

Ren reclined on a worn leather chair, watching a cold dusk descend over the tower blocks. The lingering threads of daylight seemed soaked in melancholia, but that was perhaps just a reflection of his mood, a bleak spirit that had lingered these past weeks since his return. He would doubtless be back in the same chair at dawn, as that had become a ritual of sorts, although he hesitated to call it a routine, for that was one thing he had built a life avoiding. It was, more likely, a simple reflection of his lifestyle and that pitiless plague of insomnia.

The arriving night was not one of dark skies peppered with stars, for that was a rare sight indeed on Marrakesh, a planet eternally shrouded in cloud. Instead, a nebulous glow seeped from the city, lying in puddles beneath and rising up to sheathe the towers whose monolithic forms seemed to hang unnaturally in the mist. Fine rain thickened the air, making it appear as though lit from within by pale neon. He bathed suspended in the nightscape, the sense of immersion heightened by a wall of glass and apartment lights dimmed to a fraction above zero.

Far below, in gaps between hulking towers, the garish parade of coloured lights from Super Paradise pulsed and throbbed. It was not quite a twenty-four-hour party culture, but close enough.

Ren chose to live here – and he could afford more bourgeois areas – because of the honest, raw life that seeped out of the throbbing clubs, pubs, hostess bars and brothels. It was not that he spent his life mired in all the iniquity – well, other than a few favoured bars – but the life of the party around him gave some respite from a solitary and occasionally lonely existence. Many nights he would ride down the forty floors and simply wander through the thicket of drunken laughter, dancers, piss-drenched alleys and shabby street vendors, all bathed in lurid neon. It was all a mind-altering, sordidly intoxicating sensory overload.

Out of the corner of his eye, Ren noted the low red flashing of an incoming call. His implant was on 'do not disturb' so as not to ruin this peaceful, contemplative moment, but the house terminal did not obey all the same rules. The fact that this call had slipped through his filters meant that it was deemed critical by someone reasonably important. That 'someone' could only be from work, but he was still on leave and stubbornly ignored it.

Instead of answering, Ren moved over to a rigidly clean kitchenette, where he ground coffee beans and boiled water. The space was slickly modern but fundamentally bland. It was a show home for busy people with no ambition or care for interior design. Like the foyer of a big chain hotel, it was modestly stylish, but it could be anywhere or anyone's. This was not an area of life where he felt the need to leave a mark. That was for other people, and he genuinely preferred the apartment's profound averageness.

The caller was trying again, so Ren grudgingly abandoned his isolation to check their identity. It was Vola. That moment of beautiful silence was broken, and his thoughts were now clouded.

External Affairs' diplomatic corps was made to understand that a certain type of cruelty was used well when deployed as a temporary measure in the name of a 'good' cause, but Vola Lindari seemed to be the kind of man who felt that that cruelty should be magnificent so as to be absolutely sure of avoiding any future problems that might stem from its original use. Ren couldn't help but think that Vola had a cruel heart, and his job in Special Services provided him with a perfect cover for an innate sadism. It made Ren wonder about his own judgement in counting Vola as a friend, even if he did use the term loosely.

Still, Ren's hands were hardly clean either, and those late nights watching the dawn were a symptom of the Lady Macbeth in him; a lingering, unshakable sense of guilt. The dagger hung before him in the dark. He still believed in the cause but couldn't always stomach the methods. Some demons linger and become hard to exorcise.

He closed his eyes, leaned in, and inhaled the earthy aroma of ground beans. Coffee was a mild addiction and an expensive imported luxury on Marrakesh. The months spent abroad on other worlds each year with work had accustomed him to going without for extended periods, but on finally arriving home after a trip, he would make coffee, right after dropping his bag in the hall.

Vola was calling for the third time, so Ren finally succumbed. He brought up a few select lights and then glanced about to verify that the apartment looked as people might expect. It was neat enough, deliberately mediocre and carefully free of all the things that might make his employers scratch their collective chin. Ren wondered how many other people guarded their private lives so closely. The professional and personal spheres could never meet, mix, or mingle, not because he guarded secrets but because he simply couldn't reconcile them.

In a mirror he appeared somewhat gaunt and unshaven, but that was to be expected off duty, so he allowed the call in.

"Ren, good evening. Sorry to call you on leave, but this is about as big as it gets."

"Hello, Vola," replied Ren. "That's fine. I'm intrigued… pray tell."

"First let me state that this is highly confidential. Your ears only, as they say."

Ren didn't need to be told it was confidential but that was Vola for you: the man who sat in on meetings – smugly – as the intelligence guy, dripping with the grease of his self-importance and saying as little as possible so as to appear smarter than he was.

"Isn't everything confidential?"

"It's the Archipelago," said Vola ignoring Ren's question. "They have sent us a message."

"The Arc?" Ren struggled for words. His mind spun. "You mean the Jericho gateway has opened?"

It was a pointless question, as the Jericho gateway was the only one left alive after that audacious coup decades ago. All connections with Core and the other leagues had been severed, except for the Jericho link, and that had been firmly closed for over fifty years. Since then, the Arc, an eccentric cluster out on the galaxy's rim, had been silent.

"No, it hasn't opened, at least not physically," answered Vola. "We have a single message and that's all."

"And?" asked Ren.

"Well, that's it so far," said Vola. "I haven't seen the message yet, but I thought you would want to know."

"Yes, thank you. I appreciate it. Call me when you know more."

"Will do." And he clicked off without further pleasantries.

Ren stared at his semi-reflection in the apartment window. "The Arc," he mouthed before looking down, holding his head in his hands.

Bewildered and in need of a drink, he rode the elevator down to the apartment complex entrance at level two below. The lobby might once have been a poster boy for a form of faux grandeur, but now it was in irretrievable decline. All was thickly adorned with neo-deco styling: organic and geometric detailing, chandeliers inlaid with pearly glass panels and acres of distressed, crazed mirrors. The lighting, inexplicably locked in a deep, red monochrome, barely illuminated the space. Most sat in murky shadow, helping to hide the filth which filled all corners of a cracked marble floor. Heading out through heavy double doors onto the street, he was assaulted by the sudden contrast of lights, din and whirling chaos.

Threads of music collided and mingled with the angry noises from anarchic traffic, advertising and the countless voices of those beckoning for trade: food vendors, club door touts and street artists, but also the darker voices of madams and pimps selling other people's lives. Ren bought a box of food from a street vendor and ate as he followed a meandering path through the warren of alleys.

Recent arrivals might spend months decrypting just a modest local area, as there were six distinct street levels, all interconnected but in wilfully confusing and arcane ways. Some of the larger venues were multi-tiered, so you might go in on one floor and leave on another. A very long time ago, the definition of true street level had become elusive. Yes, some levels were exposed to the sky, but were then covered up a few paces further on. Other levels were galleried arcades looking down on traffic below. In every direction, at all angles, lay a gaudy collage of illuminated signs in every font known to man, each ruthlessly intent on sucking customers into their particular den.

Of course, with an implant, there wasn't a true obligation to learn your way around. You could opt to have maps and metadata sprayed directly into your consciousness, or select a simple visual overlay with signs and directions. The latter was in some ways less intrusive but in other ways more so. The truth was that Super Paradise was so chaotic, ever-changing and actively deceptive that much of the information was either plain wrong or at best out of date. Ren chose to keep the implant as close to *off* as was technically possible or reasonable under the circumstances. The incessant data feed added layers of distraction that he usually despised, but tonight he needed to be contactable.

This wasn't home in any conventional sense. Ren wasn't from Super Paradise. Hell, he wasn't even from Marrakesh, but he rarely wasted time thinking about Palau, a world some sixty light-years distant, where he had been born and spent his first twenty years. For Ren, Palau represented agriculture, boredom and small-mindedness. He was not the slightest bit patriotic about the place and, without living family, he had precious little motivation to return. Gradually, and perhaps deliberately, he lost touch with the handful of friends from his youth. Ren was the only one to have left, and they now moved in radically different orbits. On the last trip, he had found it to be a dull and obscure backwater, full of mediocrity and simple ideas. These were people who rarely, if ever, travelled off-world. People would ask him questions about his life elsewhere and then glaze over as he answered, already planning how to steer the conversation back to local things. He understood that people regularly asked questions they didn't actually want the answer to or lacked the worldliness to understand even if he gave an answer. All this meant that going home was lonely and alienating, so in the end, he stopped bothering.

He walked the familiar alleys, basking in the chaos, attempting to choose the first of the night's bars. There were familiar favourites that he just walked on past and then, on a whim, turned out of the traffic and into the Silver Arcade. Here it was purely pedestrian and far quieter, with none of the pachinko din of outside. The bars were more personal, but it was also harder to hide – you couldn't so easily sit alone in a corner with a book or just your thoughts. In tiny venues like those, Ren would feel obliged to talk to the barkeeper and perhaps to other customers, but at least that presented a delightful lottery of character, class, gender and background. If the mood was right, that might be what he sought, but if it were not, then it was an unbearable burden.

He chose Only God Forgives, with its antique carved wooden façade, absurdly low entrance door, and name scrawled in a deep, lustrous red neon. The proprietor, Suiiki, was washing glasses and filling the space with pungent cigarette smoke.

"Ren, you fabulous cunt. What will it be?"

"Suiiki, you ugly little fucker. How are you? I'll have a highball – any whiskey."

"You're out early. How much longer you off for?"

Suiiki placed a bowl on the counter full of those toxically coated nuts that nobody ever requests or likes but still feels compelled to eat. Ren scowled at them.

"Officially, I have a few more days, but something has just come up, so that might be cut short."

"I swear you're a fucking spy. Never met anyone who's been to so many planets as you. Some of them I haven't even heard of. You don't even tell me where you've been for weeks on end. Go on, admit it."

"You know what I do, Suiiki. Why do I even respond to your imbecilic crap? It's true, I'll never understand why they gave me the job. It's like making a pyromaniac the foreman of a firework factory."

"Yes, yes, Ren. And I'm the emperor."

And with that, he turned to ramp up the music and attend to a gaggle of newly arrived customers.

Suiiki was not quite a friend. They wouldn't call each other or meet outside the bar, but there was a quiet comfort in his company within this safe little enclave in the Silver Arcade. Suiiki knew full well Ren wasn't a spy, but it was fun to play, and he enjoyed weaving florid stories of his own invention about him for his other customers. And Ren was always disarmingly charming in public with those people, like Suiiki, whom he didn't need to know too well; those he kept just at arm's length, a distance close enough to enjoy company but distant enough that he didn't have to let them into his private domain and so become a burden on one another.

He often wondered whether that level of friendship was sufficient for some people – for him – or if he was deluding himself. Deep inside, he knew it was not enough, but that was a truth he had kept buried for years. Ren wanted real friends and a community but didn't know how even to begin the search for them.

One thing was for sure: the company of strangers could make for the ideal night. You could be a blank canvas without baggage or preconception. So, as always, Ren put aside these thoughts and turned to the newly arrived customers.

Two drinks later, after having left Suiiki's bar, Ren was back roaming the streets. The Silver Arcade was a peaceful haven, but he turned back into the main thoroughfare and just walked, flicking away the many and varied offers of pharmaceuticals or 'company' and trying to blank out the cloying, pleading voices of beggars. There was a darkly cynical art to avoiding eye contact and remaining arrogantly aloof, or at least appearing that way. You had to seem as though you simply didn't give a shit. This was the only way to survive regular exposure to the dispossessed – those who lived on the margins of Marrakesh's underbelly. The reality was that he wasn't a sociopath, and he couldn't remain entirely detached. It all wore away at his soul, inexorably, little by little.

Ren's mind had turned to thoughts of his previous mission. The work on Urubamba had been bleak and draining. Each recent trip had chipped away a bit more at his soul, and he felt increasingly jaded. There was nothing wrong with bringing a dose of healthy cynicism to work, particularly when he was so often facing off against monstrous manipulators of people and truth. But the feeling of inching towards a soulless, belief-free existence was well beyond the outer limits of what one might call 'healthy cynicism.'

He accepted that it was nigh on impossible to conduct his variety of missions without a degree of intrigue. After all, these things had been at the heart of politics since man first walked out of the forests and put on the hats of mayors and presidents. There was a point, though, when intrigue became raw manipulation, when brilliant but callous people started to let their egocentric intellectual games override any true ideology. All was done in the name of preserving the position of the Core Planets Federation. Spelling out the full name made it sound grandiose, maybe pretentious – everyone just called it Core or the CPF.

At work, there was a widespread acceptance that being virtuous would leave you weak in the face of an 'enemy' who felt no compunction to act virtuously or with dignity. This idea led to a practical reality in which almost all ethics were put aside. Even legality was regularly stretched to the limits based on feeble arguments around jurisdiction. Core External Affairs and, even worse, the intelligence arm with its strangely nondescript name, Special Services, were no place for the scrupulous or for the moral idealist.

All this meant that Ren had begun to question his own purpose, bound up as it was with External Affairs' darker activities. He had once been entirely true to the cause, perhaps even messianic, but that old certainty was now riddled with doubt. This in turn meant that he had come to dread the end of his leave and the impending arrival of a new assignment.

A garish, plasticky shop called Party Fun caught Ren's attention. Its ridiculous name was entirely arbitrary and said nothing about its six floors of madly eclectic merchandise. He entered and browsed, without the slightest intention of actually parting with money. The first floor was a sea of trinkets, gadgets and gizmos; things that nobody would ever truly need, but they filled a purpose as witty or ironic gifts that would be immediately put aside and almost certainly never looked at again.

The second floor was devoted to poorly made fancy dress and cosplay costumes, the exotic garb of media stars and fictional characters. And so it went on, with each floor bearing no resemblance to the last but offering an entirely absorbing sensory experience. The top floors were darker and more explicitly sexual. Ren skipped these. The remarkable palate of perversion knew no bounds. It wasn't that he found it morally repugnant, but it wasn't his world. He did not feel the need to gawp or linger.

His mind turned to what he knew was the real reason Vola had called. Both of Ren's parents had been from the Arc but had been on assignments in Core space when the coup occurred. Each had become an accidental and very reluctant refugee in Core when the gateways snapped shut. Depending on your definition of identity, Ren was from the Arc too, but it certainly didn't feel that way. Indeed, the whole notion of the Arc felt surreal, distant and entirely alien.

Frustrated now at not having heard back from Vola, and despite the late hour, Ren called.

"What have you got? Is there any more news?"

"I said I would call. There's little more than rumour at this point," answered Vola.

Ren let the silence linger, inviting him to say more.

"...Just looking at who's to talking to whom and the people on the move, I reckon something big is going down. That's all I have."

"Okay, I'll call you again on my way in tomorrow morning. Thanks."

"Speak then," replied Vola before clicking off.

Moving on through the maze of streets, he stopped at a microscopic bar named Copacabana. It was little more than a handful of stools on the kerb, with the barkeeper deftly manoeuvring within a cramped cockpit. Copacabana was charming in a supremely kitsch way: vaguely beach-themed with bamboo, fake palm leaves, and the crooning music of distant coastal peoples. The land it referenced, with sandy beaches edged by rustic bars such as this, didn't exist anywhere within the colonised systems. Even the music was a fabrication conjured from various sounds and cultural references. None of it was based in any reality, and yet people lapped it up. He sipped a suitably tacky cocktail with a weakly comical name and an entirely unnatural, almost toxic colour. It went with the territory.

It was the perfect spot and a perfect hour to contemplate the legions of merry, pickled strangers staggering from one bar to the next. Small bands of suited company employees drunkenly bonded outside the tight confines of office law. There were a few solitary mega-perverts determined to burrow into Super Paradise's shadowy recesses. Where did they come from? Where did they go home to? Ren could spend hours observing this messy river of humanity.

Hours later, neither drunk nor sober, he returned to the apartment, where he watched the dawn from the ease of his faux-leather chair. The lights of Super Paradise continued to throb, but the bars would shortly close to be hurriedly and half-heartedly washed down whilst police swept the streets for the worst of the night's casualties. They would be open again within an hour, luring the desperate millions coming off their night shifts.

The paradox was that he had never been here as a pleasure-seeker. In truth, he was not a hedonist at all. It was a last resort for a man without identity in a world where no community seemed to fit. This place served as a form of prayer, and he discovered something darkly therapeutic in getting messed up with strangers, off-duty hookers, and desperate souls in a far, far worse state than him.

His was a tale of two cities: the mask of formality at work and the solitary, self-medicated private life. Right from the very beginning, his instinct had been to separate work and private spheres. If he hadn't succeeded in that, he would be in the gutter with the rest of them.

Ren hadn't slept. He wasn't so much tired as weary in his entirety – a weariness that pervades everything and that sleep does little to fix. It seemed possible to believe that the work was necessary and that the methods were justified, whilst simultaneously being eaten alive by self-loathing. Perhaps one was more rational and the other a deeper, resonant response.

It was then that a message rattled in from Astrid. She was

his boss of many years and a friend to boot. More accurately, Secretary Astrid Marinen was everyone's boss, the overlord of External Affairs and thus one of the most influential people in existence. That said, there was little of the master and subject about their relationship.

They both started life on Palau, but this was more of an odd coincidence than something they reminisced about. Perhaps there was something about this shared origin that gave them a bond in the vast chaos of people, leagues and worlds. That, and they were more than happy to go out and get wrecked together, even when work was taxing.

"My office, 10 am sharp. Important."

Her terseness was entirely typical. That was Astrid through and through. At least it confirmed that Vola's call hadn't been based on empty rumour, and now Ren was hungry to know more.

Sobriety would arrive in time via natural methods, but he now needed it more urgently. From a cupboard, he took a small pill and gulped it down with water. While he waited for it to have its desired effect, he stripped and entered the shower. There, in the soothing rush of hot water, the chemicals took hold, and the lingering effects of alcohol were banished. A sharp, bright concentration surged through him, and tiredness retreated. He knew that using these tiny pink pills presented a long-term danger, but they were the glue between his career, which required complete mental alertness, and other aspects of his life, which required medicinal escape.

Chapter 2

Ren Goes by Train to See the Boss

Barely an hour after receiving Astrid's message, Ren was striding through Kukuvo Station's concourse en route to her office in the External Affairs headquarters. There was a spring in his step, something that had been absent for a very long time.

The Station was modelled on some aesthetic from great antiquity on a terrifyingly distant planet. It was deliberately but clumsily retro, seeming more like a stage set than a clever architectural reference. Ren should probably have been thinking about more important things but instead was marvelling at this absurd neoclassical pastiche. The station concourses of Marrakesh served a simple purpose, corralling millions of passengers on their diverse daily migrations. At this, Kukuvo Station succeeded with a violent efficiency. On other planets, they were often grandiose statements of power or celebrations of ancient glory, but here, beyond the basic utility, they occasionally went off-piste with playful designs.

There were a handful of food kiosks and a single, rudimentary bar. These were the bare necessities that the mesh couldn't supply. Anything else – signs, directions, advertising, timetables and ticketing – was quietly delivered straight into the brain through an implant. Ren kept it all largely invisible. A fabulous side benefit of his approach was that grand spaces such as this could be presented raw and undressed – without the clutter of signage or the soul-sapping cheapness of advertising. Advertisers knew that almost nobody remembered their timetable or route, so happily, nauseatingly piggybacked on the delivery of that information. For a brief moment, Ren wondered if there was any lower occupation than theirs, but he remembered that there were lawyers who were easily a grade or two below. Then he recalled his own profession and wondered if he was beneath them all.

Another of Kukuvo Station's quirks crackled through hidden speakers. An antiquated voice in a crude mishmash of Standard and some ancient dialect announced, "The train to Niigata leaves from platform four at thirteen forty-five. Ladies and gentlemen are invited to board now."

This was all a theatrical confection. Niigata was not a place he had heard of. He doubted it existed at all, at least not on Marrakesh. Perhaps it was some reference to an older planet or a story. Platform four certainly did not exist. Nobody had called anyone 'ladies and gentlemen' in hundreds of years. Ren wondered at the efforts people went to for theatrical absurdity.

The platform was a long, angled ramp terminating at a dark hole. Beyond, it plunged down into smoothly burrowed tunnels running terrifyingly deep into the planet's belly. Why clutter the surface of a world with such banal infrastructure when it could lie far beneath? One just set the burrowing machines to work, sat back, smoked a cigar, and waited.

Before boarding, he called Vola, who answered immediately.

"Ren, are you on your way?"

"Yes, of course. What have you got? Anything?"

"Yes, but remember that this is speculation with a sprinkling of facts. I believe that the gateway will open quite soon, and a delegation will be going in."

"I had hoped that would be the case," replied Ren. "When? Who's going?"

"Those are questions I can't answer."

"I have to board," said Ren. "Let's meet when I arrive in Haikou. We'll have a few minutes to talk before the meeting."

"Sure, speak then."

Despite Vola's more loathsome qualities, Ren quite liked him, or at least respected the man's operational virtuosity. Whatever the class of his character, Vola was a useful, often vital, source of information.

Two hours on the train was an eccentric and luxurious waste of time. There were far quicker routes, but he craved a single, uninterrupted journey without queues or transfers. It was better for the soul and dampened anxiety. Privately, he also chose to avoid gateways when he could, even though they were so fundamental to his work. He didn't bother to admit this to others, but for Ren, there was a cold dread around the approach to a gateway. Some aspect of passing through them felt utterly 'inhuman.' He wasn't proud of this failure of eloquence but always failed to articulate it more clearly than that. It was yet another item on the rather long list of things Ren kept to himself. Many forms of sharing made him squirm with discomfort, and the solution was privacy.

The train ride began with a gut-churning drop. For some, it was a satisfying momentary thrill, but to others, it was a hateful experience with stomachs attempting to exit their bodies through their mouths. The capsule fell like a stone, accelerating under gravity alone but gently cushioned against tunnel walls by fields. An adrenaline-drenched start swiftly transitioned to a pleasant semi-weightlessness, with normal gravity returning through the long curve towards horizontal. By then it was a kilometre down and travelling at terrifying speed, barely having burned a joule of energy. The remainder was a more conventional ride with the capsule pulsing forward powered by fields alone.

On a more mundane journey, he would read books, documents or news, or simply people-watch. Today he was afflicted by a strange blend of anxiety and excitement that left him struggling to concentrate.

The journey's final chapter required a modest acceleration to build up speed before the upward tilt. This allowed the capsule to coast upwards, decelerating under gravity until it reached a standstill at the platform. There it was grabbed at the perfect, split-second moment to prevent it from sliding back from whence it came.

This was Haikou District, a mammoth conurbation that had thrust together several older cities into a sprawling administrative centre. External Affairs was just one of a profusion of interplanetary federal agencies based here. Inevitably, with all these came a veritable circus of hangers-on, pressure groups, corporate lobbyists, special interest groups, political factions and NGOs. After all, this was far more than a planetary central government; this place represented the machinations of the entirety of the Core Planets Federation.

Ren left the station concourse and wandered through the immaculately manicured gardens surrounding it. Parks in Haikou District were green and pleasant but always in a rigidly formalised, almost mechanical style. Every bush was trimmed to perfection, and small armies of gardeners patiently swept, organised, clipped and planted.

Halfway across the park, Ren found Vola waiting for him.

"Ren, let's walk together."

They walked on in silence while Ren hunted for appropriate words. "The Arc feels like little more than a legend," he finally said. "All my life it has sat there like a piece of fiction."

"And yet, here it is."

"Could this be deemed a threat?" asked Ren.

"I don't think so, not in terms of the Arc being a threat to Core, but it will stir up the powers that be."

Ren considered that as they continued onwards. Vola was quite correct. There would surely be a frantic scramble for control, both within Core and in the other leagues.

Haikou District was devoted entirely to the unified role of the Federation, whereas Marrakesh's local government was located on a cold, distant, and even rainier continent. Like any other planetary government, they had representatives here. They just weren't in any way influential, because this particular planet was a minnow amongst whales.

Ren was not from Marrakesh, but neither was he here as a representative of his homeworld, Palau. Instead, he was an ordinary, non-partisan employee of External Affairs and had spent his entire career since graduation here. He had adapted well and, he noted with a degree of pride, was often mistaken for a local.

The city was a turbid sea of diversity, mixing planetary identity, ethnicity, language and gender in almost infinite permutation. Some boldly attempted to blend in, but others preferred to scream their identity from the rooftops, often with an absurd exaggeration of whatever parts of their existence made them feel special. Many were here on brief sojourns, but others lived here semi-permanently as career diplomats representing their remote governments. Those who spent long enough in Haikou were guaranteed to be absorbed into the congealed slime of local pettiness. With time, the mindset of expatriates always began to drift. Any original patriotic purpose morphed into banal political double-speak, an absurd language understood only by the clique.

Marrakesh had not been chosen because of its importance. Indeed, quite the opposite was true. It was selected so as not to lend too much credibility to one of the larger, more populous, wealthy or powerful planets. A modest backwater made perfect sense, and Haikou District brought a thriving, much-needed local economy to this humble planet. There was said to be a higher restaurant density here than anywhere else in the entire Congregation of Populated Systems. This was a pointless, unsubstantiated morsel of semi-truth, but nonetheless endlessly embellished and repeated. The restaurants catered to vastly varied tastes and were guaranteed to be brimming with outlandish fashions and peculiar languages. An off-worlder was easy to spot but such an everyday event that, in reality, people barely registered. Furthermore, it was quite normal to celebrate and flaunt your origin, essence and ethnicity in the streets of Haikou.

All that said, Ren often wondered why they had chosen such a steaming shit-hole. It just rained and rained and rained. When it wasn't raining, it was cold and foggy. Marrakesh was flat and dull, completely lacking great mountain ranges or expanses of prime wilderness. It was essentially all pampas-style farmland or interminable urban sprawl. True, there were significant oceans, but they were unappealing, cold and relentlessly ferocious. Even Marrakesh had kinder, warmer and dryer corners than this bleak, high-altitude plateau. Why build Haikou District here? Why?

With a few minutes still spare, Ren and Vola followed a winding route through the gardens.

"Let's be blunt," said Vola. "There's a chance that one or both of us are going to be assigned to this."

"You're jumping the gun," replied Ren. "This is still just a rumour, and people more senior than us might take it on. We have no idea what's going on yet."

"Come on, Ren. This is our type of thing."

"Let's just go and find out," said Ren.

Ren knew that Vola might be right, but quite frankly, he would prefer not to share any more missions with him. He looked bleakly at the surrounding city and wondered at his role in the vast machinery of state.

Core External Affairs had its centre of operations in a chaotic, sprawling campus inhabiting two city blocks, one bordering on the park. It represented the collective foreign policy of all members of the Core Planets Federation. Individual planets and habitats had their local governments there, along with their private but tamed foreign relations departments. In practice, this meant that their individual policies barely existed. That was the cost of membership.

It was the diplomatic arm and outward-looking face of the Core Planets Federation, a league of planets spanning more than four hundred light-years of space and containing fifty properly bonded planets along with another thirty or so 'loosely bonded' entities. CEA handled relations with everyone outside Core including all other leagues, smaller alliances, the unbonded planets and a handful of rogues.

Its headquarters was a vast, solid colossus that appeared to have been hewn by a giant from a single sandstone block. Windows, although large in actuality, appeared from a distance as dark, narrow slits, giving it the menacing feel of a fortress. It stared visitors down, intimidated them, and delivered a deep sense of apprehensive dread. All this was deliberate.

Ren and Vola mounted the steps into a vast lobby composed of acres of polished stone and dotted with those glamorous designer chairs that are as uncomfortable to sit in as they are beautiful. There was no visible security, but it was certainly there in spades behind the scenes. Everyone knew that it was utterly pointless to walk in here unless you were pre-authorised. It was a bullet-proof certainty that any rogue element would not have got as far as the lobby without being challenged. It went much further than spotting an unknown face. Malicious intent would have been detected in eyes, gait, tiny mannerisms, pulse and breathing by a gen-5 that diligently and perpetually policed CEA and, if the truth be told, much of Haikou District. In the same vein, they were able to walk up to a bank of elevators without having to pass through a barrier, despite this being one of the most secure office buildings ever created.

All the while Ren's implant was quietly, almost subliminally, guiding him to Astrid's office on the fourteenth floor. He could find it with his eyes closed, but that guidance always hovered in the background.

Astrid's official title was Secretary-General of Core External Affairs, or CEA as it was more often called. She had held that position for a decade with the help of a ferocious intellect, an unhesitating devotion to duty and masterful control of information. In her younger years, countless fools had catastrophically underestimated Astrid by assuming that her beauty somehow correlated with stupidity.

They arrived on the nose of ten, and Astrid was at her desk waiting for him. Across from her sat a tall man with cropped grey hair and a short, neatly trimmed beard. This was Elia Volse, the head of Special Services and Vola's boss.

"Ren. Thanks for coming in at such short notice," said Astrid.

"Is it true? Is the Arc talking?" said Ren. "What's the story?"

"Ah, so Vola has been gossiping..." said Astrid without amusement.

"You may know the basics," said Volse. "We hadn't heard a peep from them since the last diplomatic cable fifty-one years back, which was just a few weeks after the seizure of the gateways."

Volse had the gravitas one might expect of a man at the helm of Special Services. His voice carried conviction, a familiarity with command, and echoes of a life moulded by harsh experience.

"That is until yesterday," interrupted Astrid, "when the remaining connection – the Jericho link – suddenly sparked into life and delivered a cable to us."

"They're inviting us in," added Volse.

"Us?" asked Ren.

"A delegation," said Volse. "We have been discussing the possible composition of a team along with candidates."

Ren and Vola glanced at each other, both wondering about what he meant. It suddenly occurred to Ren that his background, far from being a bonus, might actually make him a poor candidate. Might they not worry about dual allegiances?

"This *is* big," said Ren as the implications began to dawn.

"Yes, it's huge," replied Astrid with glee. "The Arc has two of the most desirable planets ever found, and one in particular is the most successful terraforming project achieved anywhere. Full stop. When they cut us off, they severed several claims to territory and also effectively walked away from corporate investments of an eye-watering magnitude."

Volse added, "That act stung the Hanseatics and the trans-planetary corporates, and it made a mockery of both External Affairs and Special Services."

"You should hear the text of the message. It's deeply eccentric."

Astrid picked up a sheet of paper, seemed to stare at it for an age, and then started reading.

"Good day!

"Well, it has been a while hasn't it? How are you all? How are the kids?

"After much rumination, we have decided it is time to have a little chat. You never know, we might become friends.

"We invite you to send a diplomatic team to visit us and discuss the future. This team is to include a representative from each of Core Planets, the Hanseatic League, the Old Worlds and Isabella IV.

"The gateway will reopen for a reply in two days and again for the team in ten days, should you accept.

"Kisses,

"Central Control of the Amarok Archipelago"

Ren was stunned. No diplomatic cable in history, particularly of this import, had ever been delivered in such a puerile tone. Were they trying to be funny? Were they just playing or trying to break the ice? Why bother?

Astrid continued, "Look, we have examined this from every angle but all we find is its superficial content.

"I don't think we can derive their intent from the letter. However, we have little choice but to play along, and we have already replied with an acceptance. I think it will be hard to stop the flow of this river once the dam has opened. Sorry, that was a terrible metaphor. We're back in the game with the Arc."

Ren smiled wearily. "Isabella IV?" he asked.

"That's what the message says, but they're out of the picture, obviously. We'll send a second person in their place."

Isabella IV had once been a heavyweight with far more wealth and influence than any member of Core Planets, but over the decades, its power had waned to the point that it was now an irrelevance.

Ren said, "It's strange to hear of Isabella IV in the same breath as everyone else, but I suppose that's how it was back then. How quickly the mighty fall."

"The Arc couldn't know, of course," said Astrid. "That's how I'm justifying a second delegate from Core. It might piss the others off, but this is our party."

"What they don't know won't kill them," said Vola.

"I'm sorry to push you on this, but who will these two be?" asked Ren.

Astrid sent a private communication to him, the message appearing via his implant, not as words that had to be read, but as a fully-formed thought.

"Before I get carried away, would you go if asked? Would you do this one? Would you be up for it?"

Ren paused for a moment before replying.

"It's a lot to take in, but yes, I would go in a shot."

"That's what I thought, but I felt duty-bound to check."

Returning to the public conversation, Astrid said, "We have been battling to choose which CPF entities will be represented. One person from External Affairs is obvious, and that will be you, Ren."

He nodded in acknowledgement and allowed a small smile to flit across his face.

"But there were several candidates for the second seat," continued Volse. "They included Special Services, one of the trade bodies, and UCoM."

Core military, always shortened to 'UCoM' was a messy amalgamation of personnel and hardware lent out on an obligatory quota system by member planets' domestic militaries. Motivations, loyalties and influence were of Byzantine complexity. Thus it was legendary, not only for its raw power but also for its dysfunction.

"In the end, UCoM won the argument," said Volse.

"Sorry, Vola," added Astrid. "I imagine you're disappointed."

"I'm mostly relieved," he replied limply, but his eyes told a different story. He was devastated.

"You will be running the operation from this side, though," said Astrid. "Perhaps that's some compensation."

"One more thing, Ren," added Volse with a hint of a smile. "Since Vola isn't going, you'll have to represent Special Services in addition to External Affairs."

"Whose rules do I play by?"

"There's only one set of rules, Ren," replied Volse. Everyone knew that was nonsense, but it was a necessary pretence.

"And who will the other team members be?" asked Ren.

"No idea," said Astrid. "The other leagues don't even know yet. I should have told them ages ago but wanted to give them as little time to prepare as possible. I'm on my way to see the bastards this afternoon in a magnificently obscure location, far from prying eyes."

"Only you?"

"It'll be me, Volse and General Banz," she replied.

These three were some of the most powerful figures in Core. It seemed inevitable that the heads of External Affairs and Special Services would be involved. Alian Banz represented UCoM, and although Ren could never quite fathom their many ranks and grades, he knew that Banz was the most senior General of them all.

"What about Hobak?" asked Ren.

Astrid just rolled her eyes in place of a reply.

Amza Hobak was the President of the Federation Parliament, which should have made him the most important of them all. But the truth was that the member planets' representatives at court in Haikou District were mostly toothless proxies who answered to far more powerful planetary presidents and premiers. Everyone, everywhere knew Hobak's name, which at least gave him celebrity to compensate for his absent power. It was obvious why he wasn't involved, and Astrid didn't need to explain that to Vola.

"I would have asked you to go home and pack, but you might as well stay here in Haikou. You'll be supplied with everything you need," said Astrid.

"And perhaps a few things you don't," added Volse mischievously.

"See my assistant for accommodation."

And with that, the meeting was done and Ren was dismissed. He returned to the park, found an empty bench and sat there processing the strange facts of his new mission.

A vast, brutalist silo monopolised the park's northern edge with a hostile, brooding presence. Its form was that of a flattened cupola like a colossal pantheon roof, sweeping into the ground with gently curving lines. The appearance of roughly cast concrete was an artifice, as it had simply been made in the style of something from a different age. Urban designers had been instructed to deliver spaces that invoked feelings of awe, power and permanence.

The silo housed the local gateway nexus. This connected Haikou District with ten other locations in far-flung parts of Marrakesh, along with one on the far side of its second moon, Shiva. This last one was the only direct route off-world from Haikou District, adhering to a common safety rule of buffering the interface with other planets. Gateways and hubs were carefully placed in a complex network across the globe to optimise coverage, throughput, journey time and, of course, cost. Co-locating them in hubs helped with 'changing trains' and also meant that a single local power plant could provide the terrifying energy requirements.

Ren could have chosen to travel to Haikou District through the silo, and frankly, it would have been far quicker. The sensible route from Super Paradise involved passing through three gateways, on a path that looked entirely mad in a pedestrian, cartesian representation. The intervening gateways were separated by tens of thousands of kilometres, so to understand the journey, you had to mentally fold the map together. It took a special kind of messed-up brain to comprehend the duality of the journey experienced and those distant points in normal temporal space. The train took three times as long, but he avoided the dread of walking through three bloody gateways. Most of the trip was spent in queues or dealing with humourless, overbearing security protocols. The actual journey time from gateway to gateway was a flat, mind-bending zero.

Ren studied the silo, knowing that the journey that lay ahead of him would begin there, and that he would yet again have to conquer his dread of gateways. But the dread felt small next to a sense of excitement that kept building. Ren quietly hoped that the Arc might help make him make sense of his confused identity. Maybe it would provide the breakthrough he needed, but his cynical side only expected disappointment.

Ren was relieved that Vola would not be present on this mission, despite the man's indisputable skill. He had been pivotal in Ren's last assignment on Epsilon Indi b. Core often referred to planets by the technical notation of star/planet rather than the vernacular of the local people, who in this case called their humble home Urubamba. It was Core's puerile way of trivialising and undermining the validity of the local government or cause. By not using the fond, colloquial name that the local people had given to their world, they were not explicitly recognising that deemed right to self-determination – as if it remained a blank slate that the Federation might validate and name according to their own rules. That seemed to be their standard operating model.

Vola had helped spy on their well-meaning but naïve founders. He had discovered their skeletons, which they were bound to have in one form or another, and then, without an ounce of remorse, they publicly ripped them to shreds with that covertly gathered information.

These were dark and brutal methods, but if people will dance too close to subversive ideas, then they really have it coming to them. Arrogant though it sounded, Core believed it served as the steward of mankind's future. This belief was held with pseudo-religious fervour in some quarters. It was not within their philosophy to allow planets and habitats to find a path of their own. Simply put, the diplomatic efforts of Core External Affairs were all too often a mask to cover their crusade to normalise political systems around something close to a standard model. Urubamba's flirtation with radical ideas, and frankly only slightly radical, had set the sirens wailing.

Special Services had deployed agents and tech, but then hung back in the shadows while Ren did the dirty laundry in the public gaze. It was he who courted the acceptable moderates who would replace those they ruined. It was he who charmed them, inflated their egos, learned their ways, and laid a smooth carpet on their path to office. One thing was for sure: he was not going back to Urubamba on holiday.

This time Vola wouldn't be present, which meant that Ren could captain his own ship. That said, Ren did wonder who UCoM would send and if they might be worse.

Astrid appeared at his side, evidently having followed him out shortly after the meeting ended. She sat down next to him.

"What's going on here?" asked Ren. "Why send military representation?"

"I'm not really being given a choice, and anyway, I mostly agree with the decision. There's a great deal of nervousness about what we'll find in the Arc, and they want someone who can evaluate the security situation and their military capability."

Astrid thought for a few seconds before continuing, "There are things we know and can control and then there are things we don't but still might be able to exploit. The inclusion of the other leagues bothered me at first, but it might be a gift rather than a burden."

"I see," said Ren. "At least I think I do."

He was silent for a few moments and then said, "I know less about the Arc than you might imagine. My parents seldom spoke of it. Maybe it was too painful for them. I honestly have not one shred of Arc identity."

The truth was that Ren's parents hadn't chosen to leave the Arc, and as accidental victims of events, had never quite recovered from the shock of exile. For a few years they waited for the gateway to reopen, but eventually, with monumental sadness, gave up. They found each other and made a life of sorts on Palau, but the rest of their days were imbued with grief for their lost homelands, family and friends. They had forged a life and participated passively in Palau's community, but their hearts were elsewhere. Ren's childhood was drenched in the misery of his parents' grief and alienation. Perhaps that was why he had left.

"I don't think that matters," said Astrid. "My theory – right or wrong – is that it will ease dialogue with the Archipelago.

"Your bigger problem will be learning how to play with the gang of devils travelling with you."

And with that, she turned and strode off, leaving Ren alone considering what might lie ahead.

This was like being invited to go and meet a unicorn in a magical forest, but he might also finally shine a light on his origins and gain some understanding of his enigmatic parents. But something felt very wrong. More was going on than had been explained to him. Of that he was certain.

Chapter 3

A Gallery of Rogues

Astrid stepped out through a gateway's black disc into the searing sunlight of a pretty coral atoll. For a few brief moments, she was alone on this little island, alone in the midst of a vast, dark ocean.

It was like something from the pages of a glossy magazine, with pristine coral sand, scurrying hermit crabs and sweeping, gravity-defying coconut palms, which provided a dappled shade. Between the shore and a distant rim of coral where surf pounded and frothed was a shallow, sandy lagoon. Terns hovered and wheeled over the water, calling to each other in a shrill chatter.

Astrid walked from her gateway towards a clearing of hard-packed sand set back from the shore within a glade of coconut palms. In the clearing, five heavily weathered wooden chairs stood in a rough circle. They were once painted in gaudy colours, but years of exposure to sun and salt had left them as almost bare wood, with only a few flecks of flaking paint to hint at the bright pigments they once bore. Other than the chairs, the clearing contained just a single fallen green coconut, some beautifully worn driftwood and the trails of crabs' eccentric meanderings.

In abrupt, simultaneous activity, two more gateways expanded from tiny discs up to full aperture. They were such a profound black that their spherical nature couldn't be discerned; just impossibly dark, zero-albedo holes set against the bright backdrop of sand and sea.

Astrid watched Elia Volse emerge. He wore an immaculately tailored suit with the jacket slung over one arm. A perfectly white shirt with crisp, starched cuffs gleamed in the sunlight. She knew Volse well and trusted him so far as one could trust the chief of Special Services, a master of the dark arts.

From the second appeared General Alian Banz in full UCoM uniform, with a scarlet armband to mark his rank. To Astrid's eye, a smug arrogance seemed to hang in the air around him. In Haikou District, he would have been in civilian attire, but on this day, on this magnificently remote island, his uniform seemed entirely appropriate.

As they approached the clearing to join her, their gateways shrivelled to the ebony marbles of their dormant state. Two more gateways sat idling beyond the trees, awaiting the final visitors.

The three approached to within a few feet of one another in the centre of the clearing. Each represented a distinct pillar of authority within Core, and there was a comfortable familiarity in one another's presence, but not for a moment did Astrid make the mistake of regarding them as friends. Delegates from the other leagues would soon be joining them, and they were more tangible foes.

As a whimsical nod to the tropical island setting, Astrid wore a simple beach dress with a ruby hibiscus flower in her hair. She carried herself with a rare confidence.

"Astrid. Good to see you," said General Banz. "This is going to be interesting."

"It's good to see you too, Alian. Yes, it certainly will be. You know most of what there is to know about this," began

Astrid, "but there are a few things to discuss before the others arrive.

"Here's the question," she continued. "Why would they stay completely isolated for fifty years and suddenly start talking now?"

"I don't think any of us can know the answer to that for sure," replied Volse.

"And why have we left them alone? Couldn't we have sent a mission?" asked Banz.

Astrid wondered why Banz felt the need to ask such an obtuse question but answered nonetheless. "The Arc is isolated," she said. "We would have to have sent a mission right after the coup to get there, and even then, we would only be arriving now. We didn't know they would be silent for so long, and year drifted into year. There's also the expense."

"There are legal issues too," added Volse.

"True," said Banz. "Without explicit invitation, it's only legitimate to send a mission in a handful of situations, but it isn't so very hard to manufacture a justification. At best it's a grey area."

"But a military mission – an *insertion* – is another matter," said Astrid, casually throwing a grenade into the conversation. "They are both illegal and hard to justify, but it's not impossible."

"Ah..." said Banz. "You must be thinking of the other leagues."

"Yes," said Astrid, "but the timing issue applies to them almost equally, although they would have had a couple of years head start on us, simply based on the proximity of their nearest systems."

Since the Jericho gateway first opened, she had been puzzling over this possibility and couldn't quite get the idea out of her mind, despite the seeming implausibility of it.

"I agree that it's not impossible, but we have zero intel to that effect," said Volse. "Admittedly, they don't play by the same rules as us, but I would be surprised if our intelligence had failed so completely."

"The Hanseatics and the Old Worlds would care far less about the legal aspects," said Astrid, "but it still feels like a low-probability scenario. Still, we have to explore it."

In her mind, she played out the additional words, *so we'll be playing a little game with them.*

With that, the remaining gateways blossomed. A single figure emerged from each, before walking towards the clearing to join Astrid and her companions. Tension immediately escalated.

First was Laynna Mu Rosa, a woman in late middle age dressed immaculately but ostentatiously, like some kind of corporate fashionista. Her garb seemed madly inappropriate on the atoll, but that was part of Astrid's game. Alongside her was Premier Virsenko. In the Old Worlds, formality reigned supreme, which meant that Virsenko was known by that name alone or, when he was not within earshot, by a peculiar nom de guerre, Little Mouse. His unknown first name was reserved for family and the closest friends.

In the entirety of the Congregation of Populated Systems, there were only a handful of souls who could match the power and influence of these five.

Astrid faced Mu Rosa and said obsequiously, "Director, how lovely to see you." Then she turned to Virsenko and continued, "Premier, welcome."

"Astrid darling," replied Mu Rosa. "It's just lovely to see you too." Her tone drenched in patronising venom. Virsenko smiled.

Astrid considered these two rogues in turn. Director Mu Rosa was no autocrat but comfortably the most powerful individual in the Hanseatic League. She was infamous for her ruthlessness, staggering personal wealth and matchless arrogance... and she had the heart of a spider. Virsenko had none of Mu Rosa's swagger, but in its place was a quiet, brooding single-mindedness. He had never been seen wearing anything but the clothes he now wore: an austere, collarless suit with a lapel pin bearing the Old Worlds' insignia.

"Thank you for coming so far. Apologies for the obscure location, but these are strange times and privacy, as you will soon discover, is paramount."

"Thank you, Secretary Marinen," replied Virsenko, somehow managing to sound mocking despite the formality of his words. "This is intriguing."

"The Archipelago has woken from its long slumber," began Astrid. "Fifty-one years after slamming the door in our face. They have opened the Jericho gateway and wish to parley. We – Core that is – are cordially invited to visit."

"Well, well, well," said Mu Rosa. "Why the hell are you sharing this with us?"

"What have they said? What do they want?" asked Virsenko.

"They have communicated little beyond inviting us in, perhaps to reestablish relations. So let me ask you, what might their motivation be? Why suddenly start talking after sulking for half a century?"

"Stop now," said Mu Rosa with a flash of anger. "We're not having a fucking conversation about this without you telling me why I'm here."

"I'm with her," said Virsenko more calmly. "You wouldn't be sharing this with us without good reason. Get to the point, and then we can talk about the Archipelago's *motivations*."

"Fine," said Astrid. "You're correct that I would prefer not to be sharing this. However, I hoped we could do a deal, Laynna. You and Virsenko. You like deals, don't you?"

She had warned Volse and Banz of this play in advance. They were to say nothing about the invitation extending to the Hanseatic League and Old Worlds.

"I like deals when they're good for me."

Astrid continued, "The mathematics suggest that if

someone had acted quickly after the coup, a mission would have arrived by now.

"I thought that if either of you had had the remarkable foresight to send a mission, and were already in position, this voyage into the Arc would be transformed. We could do with knowing more about what we're walking into and an in-system presence might provide an escape route for our people if things were to go to shit."

She was delivering the kindest possible interpretation of a mission, deliberately avoiding the word 'insertion' because that implied naked aggression, and accusing Mu Rosa of that wouldn't help.

"Don't be ridiculous," said Mu Rosa. "If you mean *insertion*, say *insertion*. And no, we don't have one, nor am I aware of one."

Virsenko just shrugged.

Reaching this point was exactly what Astrid had expected. Despite the existence of vague rumours, she knew that an insertion was unlikely. Still, she wasn't quite done with her fishing, so with the assistance of a modest fib, she cast her line once more.

"I had hoped to offer you a deal: join us going into the Archipelago in exchange for access to any in-system presence you might have. If you have nothing, that's fine, but it will be our mission alone."

A burst of private comms rattled between Mu Rosa and Virsenko. It was entirely invisible and theoretically discreet, but tiny lapses in engagement could reveal when someone was distracted by their implant.

"You have wasted our time," said Mu Rosa. "You dragged us out here, toyed with us, implied we had broken interplanetary law with a covert insertion, and generally patronised us."

"That is perhaps the only time in your life you have expressed concern for interplanetary law," retorted Astrid.

Mu Rosa almost allowed a smile.

Attempting to smooth the path, Volse said, "There is

plenty about the Arc's departure that broke interplanetary law, and the gravity of this situation arguably justified an extreme response."

Virsenko said, "There's no insertion. I regret that there isn't, but there you are."

"Are we done here?" asked Mu Rosa with finality.

Astrid had hoped to get more than this, but she surrendered and reverted to the fundamentals of the story. "I forgot to mention that the Arc also extends the invitation to your leagues. I don't know how that slipped my mind."

"Wow. You actually played us," spat Mu Rosa.

"I would expect nothing less from you," said Virsenko wearily.

"It seems you are considered relevant powers." Astrid held up her hands in mock puzzlement.

"We do our best," replied Virsenko, his voice oozing disdain. "This game of yours will not be forgotten, but for now we can move on and talk about their motivations."

"It might be innocent enough," said General Banz. "A society can only remain as an island for so long. Knowing that the great span of the Congregation of Populated Systems is marching ahead without them would cause developmental anxiety. They can only imagine the discoveries and scientific advances, and that must surely make them wonder."

"Perhaps they are weakened by internal strife," suggested Mu Rosa. "Maybe their sociological experiments have failed. It's even possible that there has been civil war, and they are now broken."

"All those things are possible. We can only guess."

"Then again, they might just want to chat," said Volse with a smile.

That statement caused a collective chuckle, but it was a forced and awkward humour. Not one of them, not even for a moment, was inclined to accept the situation at face value.

"We have accepted their invitation. A small diplomatic

group will be going deep into Arc territory for several weeks," said Astrid. "I need one representative from each of you in Haikou District by tomorrow. They will spend two days preparing as a team. Please send details to my office and I shall ensure that visas are ready."

Astrid was not the most senior person present. Absolute seniority was difficult to gauge between these disparate groups. However, she did control the entry point into the Arc, and this gave her a degree of authority that she quite enjoyed but the others were bound to resent.

Mu Rosa in particular bristled against her assumption of command. "You're acting as though you're in charge. It sounds to me as though we're all on an equal footing."

Astrid shot back, "Do you want to come or not?" Mu Rosa smiled in grudging respect. "That is all for now."

And with that, the meeting had been terminated. Laynna Mu Rosa turned and sauntered back to her gateway, which swelled to greet her. She stepped through without pause and was gone. Virsenko nodded, turned and walked towards his exit, leaving Astrid, Banz and Volse alone in the clearing.

"Crap, Astrid. You're playing with fire," said Volse.

"I still think it was worth a try," she replied.

"Maybe," said Banz, "but if we play such tricks, they will feel entitled to do the same."

"They'll play their games whether or not we behave nicely," added Volse. "There's some chance that they do have some form of in-system presence in the Arc but didn't feel the need to tell us."

Astrid was struck by the truth of those two statements from Volse. They were precisely her thoughts, but instead of agreeing, she played it down.

"We should assume nothing. It wouldn't hurt to dig deeper into that, but we have to plan for all branches of probability... let the games begin."

"When shall we three meet again? In thunder, lightning, or

in rain?" asked Volse.

Astrid continued, "When the hurlyburly's done, when the battle's lost and won."

General Banz rolled his eyes.

With that, Volse and Banz walked back to their gateway and stepped through into the dark. Astrid watched them leave and then kicked off her sandals before walking down to the shore. There she stood, scrunching the coral sand and tiny shells between her toes, letting the water lap around her ankles. She felt the warmth of sand and the blazing tropical sun on her shoulders. The air was richly salty and the sounds of the distant surf carried across the lagoon to mingle with the hiss and sigh of sea breeze stirring the palmtops.

Despite appearances, Astrid thought she had played well. Her ploy had not succeeded – at least not visibly – but Mu Rosa and Virsenko had revealed a great deal nonetheless. The forced involvement of these princes of subterfuge had vexed her at first, but now she smelled the vapours from a hot broth of intrigue, and that was undeniably exciting.

The Arc's motivations remained an irritating mystery, but that mystery was now compounded by a new certainty that Mu Rosa and/or Virsenko were hiding something from her. But what?

She spent some moments watching the snowy terns as they hovered and dived, and then sighed, turned and returned to her gateway, leaving the coral atoll empty once more.

Chapter 4

Play Nicely Together Now

R en sat alone in the plasticky booth of a diner, slurping fat noodles from a hot broth. He was shocked and slightly embarrassed by how little he really knew about his parents' worlds. They had rarely spoken of them and, quite frankly, he had not taken an active interest. As he ate, Ren listened to External Affairs' own dry internal summary, delivered in the resonant voice of a kindly, learned and entirely fabricated professor.

The Archipelago was remote by any measure. This modest patch of space towards the galaxy's rim happened to contain a loose cluster of stars that were otherwise quite isolated from neighbours. It was a vague notion and a bit of a stretch of imagination over reality, but the name stuck, and it gave identity to the cluster.

As humanity began to seed the galaxy, it had done so in a spidery, dendritic manner as opposed to a neat, homogeneous sphere. This pattern was thought to be down to primitive human nature, which invariably demanded to go deeper and further. Once one system had been reached, there was a forceful tendency to continue further out on that branch rather than to go sideways and fill in the gaps. This primal impulse wasn't universal, but it had occurred often enough to generate a distinctive pattern.

One side effect was that transit could be awkward between systems in the outer reaches. Circuitous journeys via gateways in the more central planets were often necessary. These might involve fees, visas, permits, tolls or plain old truculence. Some branches were thus both physically and practically isolated. 'Out on a limb' took on an amusingly literal meaning. It was a cause of bitterness and strife that outer systems were dependent on the whims of more established inner ones, so they sometimes stopped begging and chose isolation.

One branch led to this isolated archipelago. The first of the cluster's stars to have been reached all those centuries ago was Amarok. And thus they had their name: the Amarok Archipelago, although it was almost universally referred to as *the Archipelago*, or more commonly, *the Arc*.

This diner had been chosen to ensure some quiet privacy, far from the madding crowd and safe from interruption or intrusion. Diner-style noodle joints such as this were a quirky local speciality, but few outsiders genuinely appreciated their slummy charm. Ren treasured them, but he had a peculiar, dogged determination to 'go local' rather than cling to old habits and ways. For him, such diners spoke volumes about this part of Marrakesh: utterly unpretentious and thick with local gossip. Great clouds of steam blossomed from the stoves, and boisterous chefs laboured noisily. Ren knew of dozens of such places because he had a loathing of eating at a desk, something most staff in the department seemed to think necessary due to busy schedules and deadlines. Escaping for an hour refreshed the dusty corners of Ren's mind and helped stave off the slow afternoon decline and decaying energy of those who 'powered through.'

He had passed two days in Haikou District waiting for the group to gather. It was not in Ren's nature to sit and wait idly, so he passed the time immersed in private research. This, despite knowing that an intense briefing would shortly be hosed into his brain. The simple fact was that he didn't wish to be perceived as utterly ignorant, particularly with his connection to the Arc.

The Archipelago's distinctive fame, it seemed, was down to two things. First was the spectacular success of terraforming projects, all infused with an obsessive focus on ecology. Even their habitats were full of verdant, beautifully rendered caverns, all rich with life. The second element of its fame was a subversive socio-political movement that had come to dominate until Core, with help from the other leagues, stamped on it. Then came the coup, and there the story stopped.

Putting his research aside, he paid and then strolled back over the park towards the messy conglomeration of CPF buildings. In the External Affairs lobby, he crossed to a bank of elevators dedicated entirely to the second floor, a special zone devoted to public events and meetings.

The décor was cheaply utilitarian and unsophisticated. Government budgets did not allow for the luxurious glamour seen in corporate offices. And yet, it was functional, efficient and did all it needed to do. The meeting room sat empty and expectant. Ren poured a mediocre coffee from one of those silver jugs that always seem to be there, always seem to be full and are never more than lukewarm.

Astrid appeared next and immediately slumped into a chair at the head of the table. "Hey, Ren. I could kill a beer."

"You're on..."

He was about to say more, but others began filing into the room and their attention naturally shifted to new faces and duty. First through the door was Vola, immediately followed by Volse, his boss, and General Banz. Then came the usual suspects from External Affairs along with a handful of unknown faces.

The conventional pre-meeting chatter was unexpectedly subdued. In place of small talk, people poured themselves drinks they didn't really want, feigned busyness and searched for confident postures.

Astrid rubbed her eyes wearily, slapped the table and then spoke. "Let's get started. Time is short."

She left a dramatic pause, partly to indicate that the meeting proper had started and partly because that was one of her idiosyncratic flourishes as a speaker.

"You have all been briefed, so I don't intend to waste time repeating the basics. We now have the team assembled and they leave in three days. Let's start by introducing that team."

Astrid looked across at Ren, and he acknowledged her with a little nod.

"Ren Markov will represent External Affairs in ambassadorial duties and détente. He's a career agent, a role usually referred to as 'diplomat' externally. He's a specialist in deep foreign placements like this. Oh, and he has a familial connection to the Arc too."

Ren was not naïve nor overly humble about the reasons for his selection. When asked to perform a job, he always just got on with what he had been asked to do, and he did it well… like some clinically efficient assassin.

Next, Astrid turned to a bearded barrel of a man who, up to this point, appeared to have found everything highly comedic. It was hard to tell if he was overweight or just built like a tree.

"Also representing Core is August Broher. After a long military career, he now works in External Affairs."

That was a lie. August was still in the military, but Ren understood that External Affairs didn't think everyone needed to know.

Ren studied him closely. Who was this jovial old fool? Some sixth sense made him mistrust August as much as the others, despite him being part of the same club.

Astrid continued, "The Hanseatic League has representation through Imiko Kovaelli."

A slight woman at the far end of the table raised her hand

to be identified. She had short, chaotically-cut hair, framing an angular face with high cheekbones and set with intelligent grey eyes.

"Imiko is familiar with External Affairs, by way of a secondment earlier in her career from the Hanseatic League to our 'Special Threats' group. Like Ren, she is familiar with foreign operations through placements on several unbonded planets."

Astrid loathed these secondments into her department but had been forced to accept them via a dictum from above. In theory, it made sense. There were plenty of planets outside the influence of both Core and the Hanseatic League, and some of them represented a shared threat. Thus a degree of cooperation was rational. However, it was akin to inviting a spy into your boudoir. Frankly, it was impossible to have outsiders in the midst of External Affairs' most critical activities, so their operations took place in a dedicated department within a separate building. Even with this caution, the crushingly bureaucratic reality was that there were two layers to her unit's operations: the ordinary, visible one and another that took place more discreetly in coffee shops and bars and on park benches. The whole thing was messy.

The system was a thinly disguised channel for the Hanseatic League to peddle influence. This was self-evident, but Core was complicit and happy with the free labour. Throughout the populated worlds, and particularly in this business, one always had to be on guard for dual or disguised allegiances. Even within Core, there were planets such as Nuevo Mundo and Helsingor that wielded too big a stick. The CPF was meant to be a harmonic gathering of equals, but the presence of planets like those spoke of a deeper truth in which power was imbalanced and balkanised.

Astrid turned to a man seated to Vola's left and said, "Next we have Kani Rosenko representing the Old Worlds."

Rosenko was thin, slight and bony, and wore a suit that seemed a size too large. He had an aquiline nose, small eyes and a sour mouth. Ren felt a hint of recognition, but it could only be his imagination, for there were hundreds of billions of people out there in the populated systems, and his involvement with the Old Worlds had been minimal.

With the introduction done, Astrid switched gears.

"We have exchanged a couple more bursts of communications with the Archipelago. It's not substantial, but it explains some practical details and we now have more clarity about the plan. The four will head through and remain together as a group for an introductory period. Beyond that, there may be an opportunity for independent travel across the Arc worlds. They'll be gone for an indeterminate period but we can expect it to be several weeks."

"Is there an explicit mission or target?" asked Banz.

Astrid replied, "This will form the basis for negotiating a formal relationship and treaty between us. Beyond that, no. They just need to watch and learn. We don't know what we will encounter, making an explicit mission hard to define."

"Do we know the route?" asked Volse.

"We assume that the gateway will take them to Jericho. At least, that's where the endpoint was when it all went pear-shaped, and we have no reason to believe that they have moved it. Beyond that, we have precious little idea of what the team can expect or what is expected of them."

"Can you confirm that there has been no contact at all since the gateway closure?" asked Imiko.

"We sent regular conciliatory messages but never received even a single word in reply. It got boring."

"Thanks, Astrid. Who's in charge?"

"Since Core organised this, Ren will be the team lead," replied Astrid, glancing at Ren to gauge his response.

Ren smirked at the comedy of that. The others would have no intention of marching to the beat of Core's drum. He scanned the faces in the room, attempting to read subconscious gestures, strained mannerisms and those exchanges of eye contact that convey so much with so little.

"Look, have lunch and then we go straight into briefings."

Silence ruled the room. Had Astrid just ended the meeting? She nodded, stood and left without a word of closing pleasantries. A low murmur of conversation built amongst those who remained, as if the knob of an amplifier were being very slowly turned.

After all these years, Ren had an intuition for missing information and for the subterfuge that often went with its absence. This time, his uncanny ability to read people failed. The faces were blank: they told him nothing, and that stirred an emerging pool of disquiet. He still really wanted this assignment, but something about it felt eerily wrong.

Ren decoupled from the wider group at the table and joined his new team that had instinctively gathered off to the side at a window. They shook hands and spoke politely in low voices, not out of secrecy but because they were strangers and somewhat bewildered.

Their characters, motivations and purpose would take time to perceive. Loyalties aside, they were just four people going on an adventure. Not one of them would have refused to go, and some would have happily given a limb to be included. This was their trade, and the Archipelago was an almost mythic thing in their consciousness. They would soon see its legendary worlds and meet its quixotic hippies.

An hour later Astrid pinged him.

"You free? How about that beer?"

"Yes, give me fifteen minutes and I'll see you in Apocalypse Now. Does that work?"

"Sure, see you then."

It is a common facet of those who work in the corridors of diplomacy and intrigue that a manic devotion to duty in daylight hours is easily matched by the desire to escape and misbehave by night. It was responsibility and irresponsibility in an unholy alliance; a corrupt yin-yang.

Ren didn't dare sit down for fear of crashing, so instead of waiting for Astrid in the lobby, he made his way over to the bar. He could wait for her there, where at least he would have a drink in his hand. This particular trashy bar was in an even trashier corner of Haikou District, and that meant crossing a few city blocks. A little walk in brisk, post-rain evening air would do no harm and might even be recuperative.

The immediate vicinity of the External Affairs complex was deeply formal and corporate. Here, the restaurants had tediously obsequious maître d's, crisp white linen, polished cutlery and patrons with signs on their foreheads saying, 'Fuck off, I'm better than you.' He passed glamorous bars – ludicrous places with ludicrous prices – all packed with cartoonishly slick, absurdly beautiful people. They were moguls, magnates, financiers and the accidentally rich, all with their hangers-on, desperately trying to gain position and favour. They sipped their outrageous cocktails, they strutted and posed, and Ren walked on.

A few blocks beyond, the slickness was displaced by a radically different vibe. Restaurants were earthier, less pretentious, more authentic and offering accurate realisations of ethnic foods. The bars became simpler, dirtier and rowdier. Elegantly painted signs gave way to neon. The Apocalypse Now, a dark balcony above street level, was easy to miss if you didn't know it was there. The entrance was a steep, gloomy staircase drenched in a low ruby glow. It felt like climbing into Valhalla. A shadowy interior was dotted with eclectic tables, each sitting in a private puddle of light. Ren took a free spot in the corner of the balcony, switched to 'do not disturb' and watched life with all its vulgarity slide by in the street below. This, he felt, was a forgotten but valuable art: just watching the world go by: ordinary folk going about their business, drunks acting ridiculously, bickering couples, workers scurrying home. It was hugely illuminating and a form of meditation in itself. With a beer ordered, delivered and in hand, Ren settled in to wait for Astrid.

He was accustomed to being cleverer than most, but, like many in this category, he was in awe of those who brilliantly outshone his own intellect. Astrid was one of those people. She was invariably one or two or even three steps ahead in her reasoning and always knew precisely what to ask. More terrifying for those around her was a readiness to hack them down if they presented poor information or incomplete arguments. It wasn't arrogance or malice; she simply didn't know how else to be. This lent her an abrupt nature, and she didn't bother much with pleasantries or with those hundreds of words of 'filler' with which most people adorned their speech. She was direct, efficient and quite brilliant. Ren understood her and they got on well, but others were terrified of her withering, crushing take-downs.

She arrived exactly when she said she would – of course – and slumped into the chair opposite whilst signalling the barman for two more of the same. Some hand signals were universal.

"Ren, you must be tired. I'm destroyed."

"Yes, but it's all right. I can cope... beer to the rescue."

"Astrid, how are you still with Elie? You are always working and when you're not, you're in crappy bars like this with reprobates like me."

Astrid laughed, "The less time you spend with a partner of twenty years, the better. For that matter, why are you still single?"

"Single? Who says? I have... well sort of... somewhere..." he said and smiled.

Astrid wouldn't get anywhere with this line of questioning, but she seemed to enjoy prodding him. It was an act they went through before moving to other topics. No real answer was wanted or expected. Perhaps this ability to leave certain aspects of their private lives at the door was part of their bond. People had these little charades. It was a form of balletic, choreographed banter that prefixed any real conversation.

"Can we just skip talking about the last mission?" asked Ren. "You know how it went on Urubamba."

"Sure… there are bigger cats to swing." Astrid loved mangling metaphors. It was never clear if they were deliberate or accidental.

"Do you have any off-the-record questions about all this?"

"Is anything ever really off the record? But no, not really… Why me?"

"You were requested by the Secretariat, but I would have suggested you anyway so it was kind of easy. You know your character profiling and you know it makes sense."

"Yes, perhaps… but it is a bit mind-bending," said Ren. "Would you have chosen me without my connection to the Arc?"

"Most probably, yes. At least, you would have been on the shortlist. This is going to be quite, quite mad. I'm slightly jealous."

Ren took a long swig, put his glass down and then spoke.

"I thought I recognised Rosenko from somewhere, but then I realised that it wasn't the individual who was familiar but the type."

"I know what you mean. He's the guy we've all met in the lobby of a hotel wearing a crumpled suit and presenting a business card stating something vague, like 'Advisor.'"

"Yes, that's exactly it," said Ren. "He's that thinly disguised intelligence man you find in every embassy.

"Why did you say we should view the presence of the Hanseatics and Old Worlds as a gift rather than a burden?"

Astrid was silent for a few seconds and then said, "Things are not quite as they seem."

"Are they ever? But what do you mean?"

"Either the Archipelago is a threat or it is not. This means you will have to rapidly adapt to what you find there. If they are benign, then External Affairs can behave in its most classical, chivalrous and courteous manner."

Ren nodded knowingly. "I should smile, be cordial and make plans for a pleasant future full of flowers, holding hands, sunny days and cooperation."

"Precisely. However, if they are not benign, then a different version of Ren Markov might have to put in an appearance."

Ren's heart sank a little. He knew what was often expected of him but had naïvely hoped that those dirtier methods wouldn't encroach on this mission.

"I see. I shall go home and sharpen my knives. That said, I don't know how easily I can measure the threat level of a group encompassing several planets in only a few days. Beyond that, how much trouble can I cause on my own in the Archipelago?"

"And so we get on to why the presence of the Hanseatics and Old Worlds might be a gift rather than a burden. They will have their own agendas, which they certainly won't share with you or me. However, they are simple souls and will have little interest in judging the legitimacy of the Arc's sociopolitical system. Simply put, they want their money returned, they want access and they want their corporates back in operation there. And they will stop at nothing to obtain that."

"You're torturing me. Please get to the point."

"Right, sorry. If we judge the Archipelago to be benign then we can expose the scheming aggression of Mu Rosa and Virsenko, and in so doing ruin the potential for the Arc to work with anyone but us."

"Ouch. Never miss an opportunity to crap on the Hanseatic League, eh Astrid?"

She continued, "But if we judge the Arc to be a threat or just deviant, then we cooperate with the others to bring about their downfall and divide the spoils. It's win-win."

"Damn, Astrid. That's a dark plan."

"We do what we do, Ren."

The evening rolled on, beer was drunk along with a

whiskey or two, and they just talked. They spoke of Palau, a subject they rarely broached and when they did, they spoke of it obliquely. It was not a conversation full of fond reminiscences. There was no, "Do you remember when…" or "Did you use to go to…" It was clear that some places had one-way streets out. It would be close to impossible to return to some sleepy town on Palau and reintegrate into local life. However, they still shared cultural peculiarities and linguistic quirks. These things added up to the fact that they could be more relaxed together and confident that the other would understand the metaphor, the drift and the sub-meaning of their words. Conversations with people from different birth worlds were fantastic in their way – and to be clear, both Ren and Astrid generally preferred that variety – but there was a comfortable depth of meaning and understanding when origins were shared.

It reminded Ren that his bond with Palau was both weak and strong. One force pushed him away and another tugged him back. For some, identity and belonging were entirely wrapped up in the place of their birth and childhood, like some old oak tree whose roots plunged deep into the earth to entwine with the rocks. Ren wasn't that old oak, but he did experience pangs of longing for that place he had left long ago with barely a glance back.

As they stood up to leave, Astrid said, "There's more to this than I have shared so far. I'll explain what I can before you leave, but try to get a read on the other team members. All of them."

Ren was intrigued, but he could ask no more. He nodded and babbled about small things as they descended the stairs back to street level.

Chapter 5

Seriously, Are We There Yet?

Commander Palina studied the approaching star. At fifty astronomical units, it was little more than a bright spot set against the galaxy's vast, misty expanse. A cool red dwarf isn't all that bright in the first place – just a baby ember in the grand hierarchy of stars. Yet, fifty AU was deemed to be the perfect distance to start waking up dormant systems for the final approach. It had already been braking hard for almost a year, burning down from half light to the sober speeds required for system entry.

To Palina's eye, the dull smudge of Juliet-II wasn't much to look at, but sensor data accompanying the blurry visuals was loaded with information critical to the next step. He was always awed by moments such as this, when an interstellar mission finally arrived.

Often they were virgin systems, never before touched by humankind, but not this one. It had been inhabited for hundreds of years, and there was no great mystery about the orbital structure or habitability. The usual thrill of detecting new planets and hoping for exciting discoveries was replaced by urgent data-gathering. Where were the human populations? How much hardware was there? What was its capability? Were there listening outposts? Were there military depots? Where were the seats of government? Where were the gateways? Where did the gateways go? It was a long list of questions that could only be answered by snooping, because the terrible truth was that its inhabitants would not welcome this covert insertion.

Discretion was everything, hence an approach that might make the craft seem like a small comet to a meticulous observer but, more likely, remain undetected. Not that Palina and his team were on board, as this was a robotic craft in the final stages of a decades-long journey through the interstellar void. If all went to plan, that gateway on board would soon open, and then they would finally gain access to another star system.

Deceleration was a simple enough process. It required nothing more than an active power plant and basic subsystems for maintaining the flow of reaction mass. The unavoidable by-product was a thick spray of matter pointed in-system, and no comet behaves like that. Physics had evolved but Newton and Einstein still reigned.

Palina had to be wary of detection, but he also knew that a solar system is an almost inconceivably large space, so even the most advanced cultures would struggle to spot a craft that is determined not to be seen. Braking thrust was not the only sign that a determined observer might be on the lookout for. There was also the distinctive radiation signature of the gateway at its heart. The best detectors, well-positioned and looking in the right direction, might also spot that. Luckily for the craft's secretive senders, the gateway could be maintained at a small aperture, sufficient for the delivery of mass but avoiding the theatrical radiation signature of a gateway at full power. Smaller is better.

His organisation dwelt in the shadows between the planetary leagues. They did the jobs that the leagues could not be publicly associated with and they did so with absolute discretion. He was a mercenary of sorts, and he adored the intrigue, the lawlessness and, if the truth be told, the violence too. But Palina had only recently been handed this mission. He was simply delivering the 'action' stage on a clandestine project decades in the planning.

Half a century ago, it had been delivered into the dark, spinning up to over half the speed of light in two hundred days – an impossible task with conventional rocketry. But with propellant delivered from afar via an onboard gateway, they could ignore Tsiolkovsky's classic jet-propulsion equations. They stuck to the rules of physics whilst simultaneously breaking them. After two hundred days of acceleration, and having almost tripled its mass due to relativistic effects, it simply coasted through the interstellar void. And here she was, fifty years into the journey, and in the last days of deceleration. Her vast ablation plate had been jettisoned prior to the deceleration burn and now drifted for eternity through the interstellar gulfs.

The craft's builders had done everything in their power to conceal its origin. Its trajectory was obfuscated by course changes designed to disguise its path between the stars. If it were to be detected, captured and examined, the trappers would find no markings, no components from recognisable manufacturers, and control systems turned to sludge by automatic kill switches.

It was a 'she' only by the accident of a language that gave a spacecraft a feminine pronoun. It was simply dubbed 'Two' to distinguish it from 'One' and 'Three,' her sister missions, targeting other systems. A great deal can go awry on a fifty-year mission. Just a fleck of interstellar dust would rip a craft travelling at such speeds to shreds, despite having the vast majority of its mass in an ablation plate. That is precisely what had happened to 'Four' – a catastrophe, yes, but at least they had the remaining three.

On less secretive missions, there was money to be made on the side. A few fabulously rich but desperately sad egotists paid staggering sums to step through gateways and spend time aboard craft travelling through the interstellar void at more than half the speed of light. They might spend a few years aboard on and off, sleeping, watching old movies and gazing at themselves in mirrors, only to return inexplicably younger than they should be. It was a mind-fuck.

A second screen flickered on, displaying the blurred disk of a distant rocky planet.

"There it is," said Rubos, head of engineering and Palina's number two. "That's Jericho."

Palina nodded and studied the crude image. A half-smile creased his face.

Of Juliet-II's six rocky planets, just this one was of interest. Only Jericho had been successfully converted into a habitable world.

The screens switched away from Jericho to remote imagery of its barren, dusty moon.

"So this is our best option?" asked Palina.

"We're lucky it has a suitable moon and that it's largely empty," replied Rubos. "I would have been happier if it had been tidally locked. That way we could more easily work out of sight, but this will serve."

Jericho was the target but not the immediate destination. This moon would provide a discreet harbour, along with many of the raw materials required for the next stage. They had a base to assemble, but Rubos's technical team would look after that.

"And when the time comes – if it comes – how quickly can we get to Jericho?" asked Palina.

"It depends on how subtle you want to be. It'll be a few hours at high-G, but that sort of arrival would wake the dead. There are more discreet approaches requiring several days."

In the Juliet-II system, selecting a location for the base had been relatively simple, but light-years away, its sister missions had been far more challenging. 'One' had arrived in the Heimdall system many months earlier, so there had been time to find a solution. But now, Palina and Rubos turned their attention to the final mission, which had just finished its journey through the interstellar void. After completing a spectacular deceleration burn, it now coasted through the Hypnos system at a sombre, inconspicuous speed while a target was selected.

As soon as it was close enough, the craft's gen-4 began to map the Hypnos system, identifying planets, moons and asteroids, and scouring the vast space for a place to settle and hide.

Over a period of days, the craft had autonomously selected a shortlist of candidate targets. These now lay before Palina and Rubos.

"I think this is by far the best option," said Rubos, gesturing towards the image of a dark, lumpy asteroid.

"Can't we get closer? Kraken has two moons."

"I believe it's too risky. They're quite heavily used, which makes detection a concern. We also need to balance the need to access both Kraken *and* Typhon."

"Fine. The asteroid it is," said Palina.

Directional thrusters fired. From this point in, all that would be required were a few delicate microbursts as she fine-tuned her arrival. It was so immaculately controlled that final contact on the asteroid's surface was like a feather settling on a cushion. The rock provided a discreet base along with millions of tonnes of nickel and iron, much-needed materials for the next stage.

Palina still didn't know how he could make this mission work, but they had arrived and he almost ached with the thrill of it.

Chapter 6

So What's the Plan, Gang?

Freezing sleet stung Ren's face as he crossed the park in the semi-darkness before dawn. He passed through the External Affairs lobby into an open courtyard which led to the Special Threats building. It wasn't so much that their mission was deemed to be a 'special threat,' but it was simpler to host this peculiar group in a facility designed for outsiders.

Their numbers had been whittled down to the group of four along with Astrid, who stayed only briefly to introduce the agenda. There were to be three long sessions: a compressed geo-history of the Arc, a sociopolitical guide, and finally, the detailed events of the coup including its complex build-up.

The word 'compressed' proved to be the equivalent of converting Proust into a pamphlet. Their presenter, a wizened, bright-eyed professor, hammered through the topics with an enthusiasm and pace that belied his age. Material on the sequence and technique of colonisation could have been coma-inducing, but somehow he made it tolerable, even engaging. He started at the beginning (a fine place to start) with Amarok …

"…which was the first star system on the branch, but without a suitable planet, no permanent colony was left behind.

It remained as nothing more than a gateway junction with a skeleton maintenance crew on rotation. Then came Jericho, the only colonised world around a red dwarf star known as Juliet-II.

"They hadn't actually expected to discover Jericho, as red dwarves are generally poor candidates for colonisation. At the time, the Juliet-II system was considered more of a stepping stone."

Red dwarves could occasionally provide planets in the habitable zone. Of course, that zone was much closer in towards the stellar body than in 'main sequence' stars, so the candidates were often tidally locked and hugging their star's feeble infrared glow.

Jericho, a small but dense planet, sat just outside the 'Goldilocks' zone. Its sister planet, just a little further in, was tidally locked with one side permanently facing its star, giving rise to a broiling, molten surface, whilst the other 'dark' side permanently faced away into the gloom of the universe. Despite a thin atmosphere and reasonable magnetosphere, there had been no prospect of colonising its surface, but there was nothing stopping them from filling the interior with caves and burrows – a life interior, so to speak. Indeed, these *habitats* were by far the most common type of colonised world. Surface dwelling was hard to engineer, even with the very best candidates. It required centuries of labour and vast expense. Even then it might fail.

It was an irritating, perhaps even depressing fact that you might have a habitable zone in theory but nothing of the sort in reality. Why spend decades sending missions to systems with such poor prospects? Often it was nothing more than the simple statistical distribution of common star types: there are a lot of dwarves out there. Indeed, in the early history of The Reaching Out, many of the candidate stars within a few light-years of origin were red dwarves. In the end, they were explored, and in a few, they found ways of making life work.

"Whilst the burrowing of Jericho's caverns started, the

colonising craft continued out – literally out, since they were heading further away from the galactic hub – to a star dubbed Hypnos where they discovered the jewel that is Kraken."

It was odd to hear his parents' home worlds named. His father had been from Jericho, but, with a hint of shame, Ren realised he knew nothing more than that. When it came to his mother's home on Kraken, all he could say for sure was that she had lived by the sea, but the name of the place was long forgotten. He felt an odd mixture of melancholy and shame.

The professor lingered on Kraken. It was, he said, prime galactic real estate over which the trans-planetary corporates had gone into a wild, frothy frenzy. On discovery, it already had an atmosphere of sorts, a healthy magnetosphere and plenty of surface water. They could create a habitable surface in less than a hundred years, and it only required a few of those planet-sized tweaks to achieve it. After all that, they would reap a monumental profit.

"That said, the introduction of life, starting with megatons of bacteria and algae, brought decades of chaos before finally stabilising. There were years of runaway greenhouse warming, followed by further years of ice as oxygen, carbon dioxide and biomass fought out a running battle for an evasive equilibrium."

The process of 'terraforming' wasn't what the word implies, as no bulldozers pushed earth around like macro-landscape gardeners. The reality of this process involved massive processing of atmosphere and ocean to sequester toxins, followed by the slow introduction of bacteria and algae.

"It just sounds like an accelerated version of any terraforming project," said August dismissively.

"That's true, but their impatient pace caused violent swings. Only once they had begun to stabilise could they start wheeling in conventional plants along with the millions of species that make up life in an ecosystem. In the interim, a rocky planet called Typhon was made into a habitat."

"Typhon is where the government was based before they

went dark," said Kani, part as statement, part as question.

"Indeed... During the terraforming period, the Arc was governed from Typhon. The guild of designers and architects in charge of the project was also based there, and thus it was from Typhon that the new political movement sprang."

"Designers and architects or cultish freaks?" asked Kani.

"Or just thieves," added Imiko. Kani pointed at her to make it clear that he agreed.

"In the interim, they continued outwards toward the galactic rim, forming two more colonies on Eleuthera and Bathsheba. The former, a second wonder of discovery, is the moon of a gas giant rather than a true planet. Its development followed a radical technique wherein they burrowed underground and lived there while the surface was made habitable."

August interrupted, "Don't gas giants have radiation belts that toast life, equipment... everything?"

"Yes, but Eleuthera is protected by a magnificent magnetic field." The professor paused and then returned to his monologue. "Bathsheba was a cold desert planet with a feeble atmosphere. It remains that way today. People can breathe its air and roam the surface, but only at the height of day in equatorial regions, otherwise, they must be underground to survive."

The professor continued with unfailing vigour, fuelled by some cavernous store of enthusiasm for his subject. In the end, that was it: five star systems, one planet, one moon, and three habitats. He speculated at length and entirely without foundation in reality about where they might have gone exploring next.

Out of discipline, Ren cross-referenced the professor's words with public sources and with External Affairs' private reports. The beauty of the public data was that it came with a 'QV' or quality-validity ranking. This system was generated over decades through the tireless, diligent data processing of a gen-

5. Its purpose was the estimation of confidence levels around the precision and validity of content. An 'A' rating meant it was largely indisputable, free of any opinion or hearsay, and supported by rock-solid references. An article slipping down the ranks had to be read with a pinch (or handful) of salt. Most available content did not even make the A to D rank, instead lurking in the murky wastes of unclassified material. The CEA text was unranked because it was internal, very private, and therefore not accessible to the gen-5.

Ren was vaguely aware of old rumours regarding some mystery in the Archipelago, but he concluded that it could only be gossip. Rather than make a fool of himself, the matter was quietly added to his private list called "Awesome things that interest me but don't belong at work." Gradually he was assembling a frame of comprehension of the others' characters, in part through the questions they asked and in part by those they didn't. With time, one begins to glean character traits and deeper truths from things others found amusing, interesting or infuriating and also from the little gestures and expressions; raised eyes, exhalations, even just leaning back in a chair at a particular moment. An implant delivered a whole new universe of computational insight in these character analyses, but since everyone had that power, it was somewhat levelling. That said, lying, or at least lying well, required special training.

August found more than he should extremely funny. He had a characterful, infectious laugh that he conjured from deep within. True, there was a certain falseness to his joviality, but this was true of most clowns. Since the beginning of time, comedy had been used as armour by the sad, broken and reserved.

Kani had the classical manner of the intelligence services but without the swaggering arrogance that so often went with that breed. He was cautious with what came out of his mouth, and he maintained a rigidly straight, unreadable face. There was an incredible focus, and he seemed to be in a permanent state of steady concentration. But it was the deadness in his eyes that struck Ren most.

Imiko sparkled with enthusiasm and intellect. In stark contrast to Kani, she voiced whatever popped into her head. Frankly, it was a refreshing change after all these External Affairs folk who rarely said anything straight. They were always playing a game, trying to obtain an advantage or manipulating. Imiko was also a Hanseatic, so that blunt directness was in her cultural nature.

The second presenter was from within the ranks of External Affairs. They maintained a think-tank of researchers, all poised to provide immaculate, polished reports in moments such as this. She was evidently a specimen of the breed that External Affairs pulled straight and eagerly from the best universities, and had almost certainly never known any other job, right down to an internship during holidays. Ren would have bet a month's wages on all of this because he had been one too.

"The emergence of the eventually dominant political movement can be traced back to the earliest colonisation of Jericho, where unusual weight had been given over to ecology, along with building spaces fit for life at large, rather than just people."

"I don't understand why they were so driven to create these biomes," said August. "You can't create a natural ecosystem within a habitat. They'll always be powered and managed by machines and gen-5 minds."

"Right," added Imiko. "And what's real and native on a brand-new world?"

Ren thought of his parents, who had never banged the drum about Arc philosophy, instead choosing to live quietly. He felt sure that they were fanatics at heart but had lost that spirit in Core where their cause was adrift and irrelevant. Instead, they did what little they could managing Malakal's parks, quietly rewilding as much as was possible without attracting attention.

"All of that is worthy of debate, but the fact is that their eco-philosophy existed and was central to the terraforming of these worlds. The Designers Guild was the administrative group running the project. They were obsessives whose plans, it turned out, went much further than their remit and included a sociopolitical blueprint for the planets."

"I don't understand how they got away with that," said Kani. "Was it luck or cunning?"

"Well, it's complicated. In the early days, it was more of an idealistic lobby group, but they nurtured support over many years and gradually gained traction. Eventually, it began to eclipse the conventional political bodies and that's when Core and the other leagues became uncomfortable."

She used a variety of archaic words in an attempt to place a badge on the system, but Ren thought that they sounded odd together. Combining *totalitarian* and *anarchist* seemed like a giant oxymoron. Whichever words best described the Arc, it was this political system that converted its fame into infamy.

"They believed that some problems are too large to be left in the hands of the masses, local governments or nation-states. This is what they called the 'big existential challenge,' again, their expression. To us – to Core, that is – this was a deeply troubling notion.

"They dressed their ideas in simple truisms, such as 'history must learn from the past.' On their own such statements are reasonable, but they extrapolated to strange new territory. It all started to go off in a weird direction and then, as time went on, a troubling one."

Her words were interspersed with media projections, which added colour and detail but also lent an air of reality to something that, for Ren, was struggling to free itself from the shackles of the storybook. There was certainly no shortage of information on the Arc, at least up until the hard stop at the coup. The great mystery was what had changed in that intervening half-century. For him, just speaking the words made it sound like a modest period, but he forced himself to compare life now with that fifty years before, and in that light, the social and technological leaps would be immense.

"Weird and then troubling?" asked Imiko with a raised eyebrow.

"Those words might make more sense as we go on. The next piece of the puzzle is understanding the nature of people who choose to become colonists. Those who are happy and comfortable at home tend not to seek out a life in a harsh new system. Those who do, do so in search of a new life, a new start, to escape persecution or because they believe in something that can never be made to work at home. Statistically, this is the nature of colonists."

"That's certainly my experience," said Ren. "The thing is that although colonists are often idealists, they are often not idealistic in a coherent way."

Kani pitched in, saying, "They tend to be a mess of diverse religions, pressure groups and political creeds, all with a distrust of central government and a potent wish for self-determination."

"That's precisely the chaos we are always facing," agreed Ren.

"I'm not disagreeing with you," the presenter continued. "This is well understood to be both an advantage and a potential tinderbox with new colonies."

Ren had never heard a truer statement when measured against his considerable experience of freshly colonised worlds. But he silently considered the theory that one group's primal desire for self-determination always seemed to conflict with another group's desire for the same. 'Inalienable' rights had a habit of slicing through each other and in so doing proved that the one thing they weren't was inalienable. In the end, it was always realpolitik and horse-trading that got things done. It was not the desperate declaration of rights as if they were written in the stars and born from Platonic forms.

"The designers hatched a plan to solve this conflict. On one hand, there was a clear requirement for some form of central government, but on the other, they wished to cater to the unique desires of diverse groups of colonists. Their solution was to reduce central government to the raw essentials of what was required for the 'big existential challenge.' Indeed, they even chose not to call it government but instead 'Central Control,' an unfortunate choice of words by our standards."

"It might be a curiosity of translation," said Imiko, "or we might be unfairly attributing our specific histories to those words."

"Except you also know they're genuine crackpots," added Kani with a straight face.

"The original remit of Central Control was just as stated – the role of ecological master management – but, little by little, they added things that they felt fit under the category of 'existential threat,' starting with defence and foreign relations."

"And anything else they damn well liked," said August quietly.

"At the same time, they created a system on the surface which, they believed, catered to the core ecological principles plus the disparate demands for self-determination of millions of colonists. This was an ultra-extreme devolution of political life, except for matters covered by Central Control, which was highly centralised and run by an elite clique."

"This was trouble from the outset," said Kani.

Ren added, "Thousands of years of history show us that radical experiments such as this always fail, often at great cost to people."

Kani looked at Ren and said, "And if they don't fail on their own, you help them along that path."

After an awkward pause, the presenter continued, "The surface model involved dividing the entire planet into sectors of fixed size and population. This, they claimed, was optimal for human communities, but our analysis indicates that restricting the sector size was a powerful preventative measure against insurrection."

"I don't get that," said Imiko. "Social and political movements easily cross borders and can gather people up across countries and planets."

Imiko always had questions, and she seemed to have no shame in asking things that might be perceived as stupid. On occasion, that trait could be the sign of somebody smart and, beyond that, confident in their knowledge. The attitude could be summarised as, 'No, I don't know everything, but I'm aware of what I know and what I don't. Nothing makes me look more stupid than pretending more knowledge than I have.'

"To be honest, you will be determining the truth of these theories when you're there. The sectors were free to run themselves as they saw fit unless their ways and methods conflicted with the remit of Central Control. The system was just being born when the doors slammed shut, so we can only guess at what it became."

"You mean sectors can do what they want unless an arbitrary authority tells them they can't," said Kani.

"Well, that's the way it looks to us too. On one hand, we have a sort of neo-anarchy, and on the other, autocracy!"

"So, Core Planets had no choice but to intervene," said Kani. "You poor things. How would the galaxy cope without your moral authority?"

Ren just laughed and the presenter continued, studiously avoiding being drawn into the taunts.

"Well, yes, based on the principles under which Core operated at the time, they put a great deal of effort into influencing the Arc's political journey."

Without it being stated, they all knew what the presenter really meant. Core and the other Leagues in their idiosyncratic ways had used every tool of manipulation available and had gone in strong and hard. The Hanseatic League and Old Worlds had done their fair share of manipulation, just in a different cause.

"When you said that Central Control gradually added to its

remit, what did you mean? What did they add?" asked Ren.

"It was a work in progress when they were crushed. After that came several years with more conventional government until the coup. We simply don't know what was born after that, and we can only guess at what it became. That's for you to find out."

"Honestly, after fifty years, all this might be irrelevant," said Ren. "We know that Central Control still exists, as the letter of invitation came from them, but their role may have been entirely redefined."

"That's right, and it will be fascinating to see what you find there. Happy hunting."

Their final presenter was a grey-suited, nondescript CEA type, probably Special Services.

They had understood far too late that this quiet revolution was not restricted to Kraken. By the time Core woke up, the new system dominated the whole of the Arc except Eleuthera. At that point, Core started a full-frontal ideological war. Physical conflict was not the way of the Core Planets, at least not officially. Indeed, this was generally true of any vaguely civilized league in the Congregation of Populated Systems. Instead, they meddled and undermined. They weaselled and tricked. They threatened with bared teeth through a screen of civilized politesse. They ensured that the Arc was indebted to trans-planetary corporations, which of course they were anyway, but made the implications utterly clear and as laden with threat as they could muster. It had all been going rather well.

Ren recognised the murkier methods of his own work in this description. That meddling and undermining was his trade. He was the Machiavellian bastard doing the same on Urubamba, Helena and countless planets before. This was his wheelhouse, for he was one of their weapons of subversion.

Core appeared to have won, and the Designers Guild, by

then only referred to as Central Control, slipped from view. But the truth was they had not gone away at all and instead began a secret underground movement. Quietly, over months and years, their agents were inserted into crucial positions. They infiltrated all of the key gateway facilities along with embassies and corporate offices. Then, in a single, masterful operation, the gateways were seized and the leagues' security services neutralised. Most gateways were switched off entirely, and in that act, the couplings with their remote twins were permanently destroyed. A few were kept open for the duration of the exodus. Only one was eventually left alive and dormant, ready to be recommissioned at some indeterminate point in the future.

League representatives along with corporate expatriates were given the binary option of leaving forever or joining the Arc as citizens. The majority chose to leave, but a modest percentage stayed. Either way, families, lovers and friendships were torn apart. Within days, leavers had been escorted to the idling gateway in Jericho and then dumped back into the CPF. Just weeks after that exodus, the last few messages came out, and the gateway was sealed. The coup was complete with barely a drop of bloodshed. The Arc fell silent.

Of course, there were two versions of this story: the one provided to the public and that which Ren knew to be closer to the truth. The public story held that they were dangerous revolutionaries whose closure of the gateways was to escape financial obligations to the corporates – a smash-and-grab. The private version of the story was more honest about Core's efforts to disrupt things. It was extremely rare to be so entirely outplayed, and it was on record as one of External Affairs' most epic and embarrassing failures.

Inserting quite so many people into key positions must have required exemplary planning and real doctrinal devotion. This was the work of people who plant trees for the future both literally and metaphorically. What had caught Core out was the presumption that fanatics are always incompetent. Fanatical zeal generally correlated very well with bumbling stupidity, like the terrorist who blows up his bedroom and himself whilst tying his shoelaces.

The account certainly gave Ren pause for thought. He would have to tread carefully with these people, and it would be negligent to underestimate them… but that juvenile letter didn't *appear* to come from serious people.

Finally, the day was done, and Ren's brain was deep-fried. The room stank like a camel and, after a cursory nod towards etiquette, he practically sprinted out the door. A night on the town, followed by ramming an encyclopaedia into his skull, tested the limits of endurance. There were two sanity-saving options remaining: bed or beer. This time he chose bed.

Ren woke to a sullen dawn. He drank coffee and watched rain lash the streets below. His room was in a utilitarian CEA hostel entirely devoid of glamour, but it was clean and offered all he needed. The brashly grandiose hotels of Haikou were well outside the budget of public sector staff. Such hotels were packed full of preening oligarchs and their retinues, the kind of people who rather enjoyed eye-watering prices and didn't look at the bill anyway.

Frankly, he doubted if this punishing schedule made the slightest bit of difference to the mission, but he had no choice but to run with it. Today they had split up, with Kani and Imiko going their own ways, whilst Ren and August received Core-specific preparation.

His first appointment was with Qora Deovski, a professor of linguistics and semantics. She was a full-time academic but occasionally came to Haikou District to provide specialised support to External Affairs. Her speciality was the study of semantic identity, a subject embracing the concept that identity is shaped by a society's language and words.

"I'm here to support your navigation of Arc language. In fifty years it will inevitably have diverged from Standard, and you won't have a connection to our gen-5 to assist with translation."

Long ago, people began to refer to computer systems by their developmental generation. This was not a reference to the era of construction, but to the historic technological leaps that awarded them profound new capabilities. The ridiculous power of a gen-5 would not be wasted on most mundane applications, and only those were deserving of the suffix 'mind.' For example, an implant was typically only a gen-3, whilst a gen-4 had the capacity for semi-autonomous thought and a degree of self-adaption.

Gen-5 minds were reserved for epically hard jobs such as managing the teams of macro-tech terraforming new worlds, or the brains at the heart of habitats, guiding the flow of water, tuning the composition of air, and keeping trillions of fragile creatures alive. They wrote their own software, refined the designs of the many tools required for their grand missions, and sometimes they even developed machines from scratch. Gen-6 had not yet been invented, but the capabilities required to attain that level were well documented and the race was on.

"But I can carry ordinary auto-translation as a local edition, right?" asked Ren.

"That only works for a pair of well-documented languages," she replied. "The Arc's dialects, although rooted in Standard, have been marooned for five decades, and in that amount of time, language can change spectacularly. New words, turns of phrase, and even entire dialects emerge fresh and dripping from the lagoons of isolated populations."

Translation had been the domain of automated systems for centuries. Bots trolled through speech, books and news feeds of all kinds, and gradually built libraries of meaning. They knew metaphor, simile, phrasal verbs, obscenities, irony, sayings, obscure slang, acronyms and dialect. They knew when they heard humour, threat, disappointment and sadness, even when wrapped up in the subtleties of local idiom. All this was threaded into your consciousness through your implant so seamlessly that you could hold a conversation and be only peripherally aware of the assistive automation. The technology meant that he could wander from world to world and talk to anyone without any linguistic training whatsoever. It was unbelievably useful. For a very long time, the only reason to study language academically had been as part of the overall science of semantics and semantic philosophy… or as an eccentric interest.

Unravelling these new forms of language required the mind of a gen-5, and that in turn required a live connection to Core's mesh. Ren hadn't even vaguely considered the implications of being denied this connection in the Arc. They would be cut off from Core Planets altogether, a wholly unnerving experience for people used to being connected literally all the time.

Ren would be sent off with a crappy old static version of Arc translation modules from five decades ago, like a Jurassic insect set in amber. Their time-capsule translation would be guaranteed to get many things horribly, hilariously or embarrassingly wrong (take your pick). Hence the lesson from Qora in language, semantics and semiotics. She could provide the training and tools to help identify the grey areas of meaning and separate known unknowns from unknown unknowns.

Part of the solution to the linguistic challenge was to install a software mod to his implant. This would enable stand-alone translation without a connection and also deliver new sidecar algorithms to study the Arc's soundscape. If desired, Ren's learnings could be cross-referenced with August's, thus giving them a collective adaptive brainpower. Gradually they would process the Arc's languages and improve the libraries whilst on the road.

All this made perfect sense, but it sailed exceedingly close to a huge problem. Core had an unbreakable social rule that a person's implant was their own. Beyond childhood, people managed their own heads, whoever they were and whoever they worked for. That was utterly central to their philosophy of the individual in society. No government or employer could access its data or dictate what software it carried. Requesting a modification to the implant was highly irregular, so it was critical to offer it as a choice. If it were presented as anything but that, it might feel like a violation, despite a gen-3 implant's ability to instantly detect and disable malicious activity.

The problem was that most software was generic off-the-shelf stuff, whereas this was peculiar, bespoke and unverifiable. That said, at least it came from Special Services. Ren honestly didn't care that much, so he received the files and performed a little spring-cleaning to make space for them.

Ren's innate understanding of Arc language was sadly limited. His parents mostly conversed in Standard, only reverting to dialect in private moments, when emotional, or when they wanted to convey a complex idea or deep feeling.

Packing instructions were simple: don't. Ren was given a small pack containing the basics but no tools, equipment or hardware were permitted. That said, he carried an implant inside him, and that could hardly be removed.

A few personal items were permitted, and Ren chose a notepad, a pencil, and a single, heavily thumbed book. Using such antiquated things was eccentric in a world where they generally sat behind glass cases in museums, but he liked the tactile nature of paper and the scratch of a pencil added some purpose and poetry to writing.

Communications would be sporadic and rudimentary, with a single data packet transmitted daily via the gateway: a diplomatic bag of sorts. It was to be raw and unencrypted, thus preventing the transmission of anything complex. To some extent, it would still be possible to encode private messages but in a limited form.

In the afternoon, Ren was summoned to Astrid's office.

"You know this already, but I'm not thrilled with UCoM getting the spare seat," said Ren. "They always see threats, even when there is none, and they always crash about clumsily whilst believing themselves to be subtle."

"I'm sure you know that, in an ideal world, I wouldn't want August on the team either. However, there's more to it than I have explained so far..."

"Yes, you said that last night. Here we go..."

Astrid took a breath and said, "I can't prove it, but I am confident that some other player is already in the Arc. I challenged the other leagues a couple of days ago and they did a fine job of denying it, but I still felt that they were hiding something."

"How do you know?" asked Ren.

"Why has the Arc started talking now? Fifty years is almost exactly how long it would have taken to send an insertion mission. That feels like a big coincidence. They're either already there or screaming into the Arc systems as we speak. The estimated times to all four of their systems are within a year of each other."

"Which is it? The Hanseatics or the Old Worlds?" asked Ren.

"I can't say for sure. Maybe both. Maybe neither."

Ren physically deflated. That one piece of information ruined his understanding of what he had been preparing for.

"So there might be an invasion?"

"Well, that's not certain, but it might be the case. An equally important question is what the Arc achieves by opening its doors now. Motivations seem murky."

Ren sighed, stood and walked to the window.

"From the frying pan into the fire," he said quietly.

"The truth is that a ground invasion from an insertion is a very tricky undertaking, certainly if your intent is not to rain hellfire down on your target. Our devious friends want access and their money back, but those ambitions would not be served by extreme violence.

"If they planned a ground invasion they would have to wheel in a staggering quantity of hardware and personnel. That would get messy and would cost far more than the investments they lost."

"So, what's their intent?" asked Ren.

"I don't know," said Astrid. "I'm not entirely sure that they know either. It gives them a foot in the door and a powerful negotiating position. The Arc can't slam the door again."

"But there have been invasions from insertions in the past," said Ren.

"True, but usually involving a technologically inferior culture and a single well-mapped planet. In the Arc there are five planets that would have to be subdued and three of those are habitats. How do you access the key locations deep within a habitat without using gateways? How do you identify key infrastructure?"

Ren said, "So I will be keeping a close eye on Kani and Imiko."

"Yes, that's right. The truth is, if it all goes to shit, we might be happy to have access to insertion gateways as an escape route. We must therefore avoid antagonising them."

"But if it doesn't, then we have a boatload of trouble because we can't prevent the others from acting."

"Or can we?" said Astrid, smiling widely.

"Oh god, do you ever stop scheming, Astrid?"

"There's a reason you're representing Special Services too. They're going to tool you up. You'll be going in with a swarm of microtech, and you're going to spy on them and torpedo them if they go rogue on us."

Ren's attitude turned. His deflation left, replaced by a thick cocktail of excitement and fear.

"But how can we smuggle that in?" he asked. "The rules on technology are abundantly clear."

"Oh, Ren. Such naïvety. That's the easy bit. Report to Special Services at four to get tooled up."

Ren had been about to leave when Astrid spoke again. "One more thing... not a word, even to August, about your payload."

He nodded and left.

He had a couple of hours to kill which he passed alone, walking miles in the cool air until the 'tooling-up' appointment. His mind could not be calmed.

Deep in a basement he hadn't known existed, reclining in something like a dentist's chair, the med-techs went to work. The squadron of microtech was inserted via his implant port before being powered up and tested. He installed the control software himself. There was no manual, but it was all surprisingly intuitive considering it was such advanced and secret tech.

Through his implant, Ren had a new awareness of the thousands of spore-sized machines he now carried. It was surreal and unnerving. He practised launching them into the space around him, sending destination instructions, and then gathering them up like hens into a coop as night falls. There, with them safely back in their hangar, he could read their data and compile the many tiny fragments into a story.

Night was falling as he walked to meet Astrid one last time.

His choice was a hyper-themed tavern called Forbidden Planet. Its self-conscious motif was the depiction of aliens through the ages. Walls were plastered with posters and artwork portraying toothy, bug-eyed monsters. It was deeply tacky but undeniably fun.

This time Astrid had arrived first and awaited him in a booth formed from the pincered claws of a skeletal alien. They kept the lights turned low to disguise the truth of its crude, plasticky construction and hopelessly amateurish paintwork.

"Ren, what the fuck? Where have you brought me?"

"Sorry. I kind of like it."

"It could be worse. At least I'm not in one of those hateful places full of wealthy arseholes. They need special vents just to prevent the clientele from drowning in each other's arrogance. It flows out the door and forms stinking puddles in the street outside."

"Okay, calm down, Astrid. I hear you."

"Sorry. I've been spending too much time in the company of planet-sized egos. They get my back up."

"I assume I'm not allowed to ask."

She didn't reply, which meant that, no, he wasn't allowed to ask. Instead, they talked about the mission, and Ren shared his half-baked view of his companions.

"Imiko's easy to like. She appears genuine and asks good questions that she seems to actually want the answer to."

"But she's with the Hanseatic League, Ren."

"Sure, but individuals are individuals and don't necessarily carry with them the flaws of their masters."

"I would watch that carefully if I were you. If she has even ten percent of her master's venom, that's enough to take out an elephant."

"Ouch. ...August seems jovial, ebullient and humorous, but there's an edge to it that makes it seem like a façade. Maybe we all have façades though, right?"

"Not like yours."

"Touché."

"As for Kani, it's as though he's just been delivered, packaged and sealed, directly from an intelligence services personnel factory. He's every inch the agent and quietly revels in it. I wonder if the Old Worlds give them some kind of blood transfusion, or just swap their souls for a bag of sawdust."

"Oh, don't trust a soul, Ren."

Conversation drifted away from the mission, and they talked of more everyday things. It was soothing to just drop out of gear and babble about life's smaller matters. For Ren, that never plunged quite to the depths of gossip, sport or the weather, but not everything had to be earnest.

As they stood to leave, Ren asked, "Are you really entrusting me – one person – with this? In a few weeks, I have to decide whether to assist or bring down a league of worlds."

"It will be clear, Ren. If you find billions of enslaved people then your conscience will instruct you. We will also be able to share thoughts, if partially, via the daily transmissions."

Ren sighed, knowing it would never be that simple.

"It is close to certain that the others will be carrying microtech too," said Astrid as they descended the stairs to the street. "Yes, it's conjecture, but we always work in a soup of probabilities. Our best guess is that they have military-grade tech at the sub-millimetre scale. Yours is in a different league altogether: a tenth of the size and extraordinarily difficult to detect. Special Services are good friends to have if you want the very best."

Ren looked at Astrid. Every time she opened her mouth the mission seemed to become more complicated.

Part II

Chapter 7

Road Trip!

The day of departure was smothered in low, brutish cloud. It was a grey and forlorn morning of a type that Marrakesh was infamous for. 'Haikou summer,' an ironic reference to Marrakesh's interminable gloom, was a metaphor for ennui amongst expatriates in the district. A morning like this could often cast Ren's mood in a melancholic fugue, but today it had no power to subdue a genuine and altogether rare excitement. On a personal level, this was a life-defining journey, and on a professional one, it was the culmination of years of unquestioning dedication. A good slice of his cynicism seemed to have parked itself in a distant underground concrete bunker, at least for today.

Thus it started, without a shred of pomp: a little group of seven scurrying over the park to that brutalist silo of the gateway nexus. It was hard to connect this meagre cluster of people in a damp, rainy park with the journey that lay ahead. They would cross continents, travel light-years in temporal space between star systems, and land up at a peculiar new planet, all in time for a late lunch.

The silo's form was that of a shallow, arching dome, as if a vast sphere were buried here with just its crest showing above the surface. The entire periphery was dotted with the gaping arches of entry and exit zones through which thousands of people poured in a perpetual weaving stream. Today there would be no avoiding gateways. Ren wasn't yet sure of the precise route they would be following, but it was certain that several jumps would be required. A knot in his chest testified to that certainty.

The seven souls scurrying across Haikou's park included Ren, the three other team members, Vola, and a pair of rigid military types whose purpose was unclear. They had almost nothing to say, a common trait within the ranks of special forces, from whom they had certainly been drawn. Silence inflates gravitas and amplifies implied strength.

Rain was falling in an irritating mist of micro-droplets. It was the variant of rain that you barely see, but somehow still manages to soak, even under an umbrella's protection. Marrakesh was pulling out all the stops in delivering as miserable a send-off as it could muster from its thick catalogue of meteorological torment.

Ren and Vola spoke in low tones.

"What's your take on my companions?" asked Ren.

"Superficially, Imiko is the Hanseatic version of you, and Kani is the Old Worlds version of me."

"Right, so utterly trustworthy," said Ren flatly. "No skeletons?"

"Neither has great mystery in their past, although Kani was far harder to trace."

"And August?" asked Ren.

"He's only spent part of his career in UCoM, with the rest in his home planet's military. That part is murkier."

In truth, Ren was only making conversation to relieve some tension. He probably knew as much about the other three as Vola did, but he was in danger of anxiety getting the better of him.

Inside the dome sat a vast concourse, impeccably designed

for fluid movement between the eleven gateways. There were elaborate queuing systems and an invisible but omnipresent passport control. Identity was checked on the way in using cameras and then double-checked using sniffers, thus automatically assigning travel permissions.

The first ten gateways sat behind modest pressure doors. Atmospheric pressure was always subtly different across Marrakesh's continents and zones, and there was no desire to trigger gale-force winds howling through a gateway. This was one of the many things that had been learned the hard way, sometimes with amusing consequences but also with occasional tragic and destructive outcomes.

In one event many years before, the absence of appropriate pressure management had caused all the objects, furniture, and people within two hundred metres of the gateway to be gathered up, smashed together and spat furiously out of the other end in a mess reminiscent of that left behind when a tidal wave subsides. On another occasion, they somehow forgot that the other end of the gateway was in hard vacuum. At power-up, all the air was dumped into the void, along with the flash-frozen corpses of fourteen people.

Physicists hated this technology with a cold fury. There was nothing in their theoretical toolbox that explained a gateway's function. Gateways broke every fundamental rule of physics, undermined their theories, and made ordinary people think physicists were a bit clueless. Conservation of energy – forget it. Conservation of momentum – nope. Entropy – problematic. Put very simply, entering a gateway at the bottom of a cliff and exiting its sibling at the top required no energy input to justify the change in potential energy. Conversely, going in the other direction involved energy loss, but where did it go? All this was true of kinetic energy too. Stepping through a gateway on a planet to one on a spacecraft travelling at half the speed of light was a damn big change in kinetic energy and implied infinite acceleration, at least when judged in orthodox terms. The difficulty for physicists was knowing that there was a massive, gaping hole in their worldview and having no idea how to bridge the gulf to gain understanding.

Vast amounts of energy came and went, appeared and disappeared, and all people could do was wonder. Where did it go and where did it come from? Nobody knew. Nobody had the faintest idea. It was much, much easier to turn your brain off and just accept it all or view it as a modern form of magic. Indeed, the latter was a popular perspective on gateways. Where no science exists to explain something, mysticism quickly steps in.

"Which is August's home planet?" asked Ren.

"Helsingor," replied Vola. "Same as the glorious General Banz."

"Is that not an odd coincidence?"

"Not necessarily. Banz was likely to pick a deputy he could trust. Anyway, you and Astrid are both from Palau. Others might be suspicious of you for the same reason."

Ren couldn't argue with that, but of all full members of Core Planets, Helsingor was the thorniest. Palau was a political irrelevance.

They were heading for gateway #3, the Haikou District :: Long Beach line, where a couple of hundred people were backed up awaiting their turn. As always, the diplomatic channel was open, and on this day they had special permission to march through, arrogantly bypassing the main queue. Then it was through the pressure doors and into the cool darkness of the gateway bunker. Here, in sight of the dark sphere, Ren's pulse ramped up sharply, and the hairs on the back of his hands prickled. He despised the loss of control that accompanied an irrational fear, but no amount of will in the world can conquer a deeply set phobia. He was a master of hiding it, which meant that his plight remained a solidly private affair. Why they had to make gateway complexes so intimidating remained a mystery to him. They were draped in an inhuman harshness that seemed entirely unnecessary. What was wrong with a bit of colour, some art, or perhaps a touch of subtle, inventive design? But no, it was raw concrete and flat, functional lighting. Function, function, function.

Ren and Vola switched to their implants so as to continue their discourse in silence.

"Are they clean? I mean, are they discreetly carrying any tech?" asked Ren.

"It's against the rules," replied Vola. "We simply can't examine them too closely without causing an inter-league diplomatic incident."

"Come on, it's us talking."

"Ren, just assume that they are. Assume that they possess every tool in the box, and keep your eyes open."

A trail of passengers was funnelled down to a gantry that stopped just shy of the gateway's black disk. It was like a surreal sheep dip. Nothing else known to man, except perhaps those strange and distant black holes, had no reflectivity at all: an albedo of absolute zero. Every single last photon that struck the surface of a gateway simply vanished. They did not pop out the other side, as that would imply that gateways 'shone' with some distorted image of the far side. They just went... somewhere... not a soul in existence knew where. The brain struggles to process an object so purely black. There is no prospect of resolving the spherical form except by walking around one and determining its true shape from logic. Instead, observers perceived a circular void of indeterminate distance, the eye having no capacity to focus on it. It was like flying over a vast snow-covered ice cap with a pristine, solid whiteness beneath but with no possibility of judging scale or distance.

"August's presence still bothers me," said Ren.

"Agreed," said Vola. "It's not a decision that has been sufficiently explained."

"Astrid was vague, but I think that her hand was forced."

"I'll keep digging and will send word if I uncover anything... and if Astrid allows me to."

The gateway was approaching, and the sick feeling in his gut ended the conversation. Anyway, from now on, he would have to pay more attention to the rest of the team.

They were down to single file by the time they crossed the gantry, and then they stared directly into the gateway's face. Figures immediately ahead slipped from sight as though sinking into tar. Most just strolled through normally, but a few dipped their heads, tensed up, or exhibited some idiosyncratic nervous quirk. Occasionally people found it too hard to walk face-first into blackness, and their solution was to turn at the last minute and back in. For billions of people, this was a regular daily journey and was no different to getting on a bus. It was just part of the fabric of the world and transportation.

Ren found himself last in line, bar the rear escort. He watched his colleagues shuffle through one by one ahead of him. With each approach came a curious reality distortion as they traversed the last few centimetres. This was challenging to describe in ordinary physical terms, as it was such an unearthly effect. The periphery of the traveller became incoherent, blurred, and their form distorted as if partly stretched across a hemisphere. Then it was Ren's turn, so with a deep breath and an elevated heart rate, he stepped through. This was the bit he hated – an acute sense of disembodiment, just for a fraction of a second. It was a feeling of having no bodily form and being absent from the physical world as if ever so briefly in a different place with alternate geometric rules. All travellers experienced this sensation in one form or another, but Ren found it far more unnerving than most.

And there he was in Long Beach, thousands of kilometres from Haikou District within an almost identical pressure silo. The reality wobble was dissipating and that tight knot in his stomach was beginning to unwind. He turned and glanced at the two streams of passengers, one going in and the other coming out, a jarring effect as the brain expected the same people to exit on the near side as were going in on the far side. Of course, those exiting were arriving from Haikou District, and those entering were on their way from Long Beach. Quite why they didn't bang into each other inside the gateway was unknown, but then again, nobody had the faintest idea about what the hell was inside. It was generally doubted that it had anything to do with familiar notions of spacetime. Man's relationship with gateways was like a caveman's with fire. He had rubbed two sticks together and somehow created the stuff, but had no idea what combustion meant or that it might be anything but a gift from the pantheon of ancient gods.

Like passing through an airport as a transit passenger, being in Long Beach's nexus didn't mean that he was in any meaningful way visiting Long Beach. And that was a good thing, as Long Beach was shit. The name, which surely must have been ironic, presented an expectation of warmth, a boardwalk, ice-cream parlours, and glorious sandy beaches with the happy shrieks of children playing in the water. Instead, the long beach in question was a stretch of coast on an arctic sea, covered in black volcanic boulders and lumps of stranded sea ice. Constant southern storms lashed the shore, and churning grey waves beat relentlessly against the rocks. A swimmer would have survived about eight minutes in the frigid water. That is, if they avoided being smashed to a pulp by the waves. Most coastal towns faced and embraced the sea, but Long Beach had its back to it for a reason.

They were in the concourse for all of eight thrilling minutes. From there it was two more gateways to San Cristobal on Nuevo Mundo, some fifteen light-years from Marrakesh. This jump had an additional biological screening step, a fairly standard procedure when moving between worlds. Pathogens, weird new diseases, parasites, and infections could, and often did, propagate catastrophically across dozens of planets without controls. The screening was far from perfect, as it certainly didn't catch and stop everything, but it was a barrier of sorts. Some worlds had an open-door policy, which meant that they treated themselves as a single planetary unit, a sort of pathogen bubble. It made a huge difference to easy trade and the free movement of people, and reduced the cost and bureaucracy of travel.

Nuevo Mundo was an exceptional and influential place in the grand scheme of the Core Planets Federation. It was in the select group of the first five planets colonised, now the only one of that group not a member of the Old Worlds. Strictly speaking, this was a habitat with a barren surface, but whatever you called it, Nuevo Mundo was wealthy, powerful and laden with giant trans-planetary corporate offices.

Within moments they had been shepherded outside San Cristobal's gateway concourse into the bustling base of a chasm whose precipitous walls rose a full kilometre above their heads. Far above was the glint of glass and the deep radiance of a feeble star. The cleft's distant ceiling was sealed with a clear material that allowed a little sunlight in, enough to seep weakly into the upper levels, soaking them in a thick, blood-orange glow.

Looking up was a giddying, disorienting experience. This was a city folded in two and smeared against the sides of the chasm. A fantastical cityscape continued as far as the eye could see in both directions, eventually slipping into atmospheric haze about three kilometres on. San Cristobal hugged and coated the entirety of a natural cleft brought into existence by violent tectonic shifts so ancient that stars had been born and died since its rupture. It continued for three hundred kilometres and was a marvel of architectural invention and shameless excess.

Outside the concourse at street level, a sleek, discreet ground car awaited them with doors ajar. It was simple, austere, and entirely lacking the gaudy opulence typical of Nuevo Mundo's glitterati. Of the four, only Ren had been to San Cristobal before. The others gawped in unashamed wonder at this corporate Babylon and its hanging urban sprawl. Their car sped away from the concourse, into a tunnel, and then accelerated up to speed – immeasurable to the passengers except for the blur of the tunnel wall as it swept past.

August said, "I have wanted to come here for as long as I can remember, but all I get is this passing glance."

"I understand," replied Ren, "but I don't think this is the only wonder that we'll have to rush past on this journey. Maybe you can take the tour on our return…"

"Whenever that will be."

As if addressing herself, Imiko added, "It's like following a coastline on a train. All you want is to be out there on the sand, exploring, touching… and yet you are a prisoner to the journey. A beautiful thing becomes a frustration."

"Why San Cristobal in particular?" asked Ren.

"This is the original, definitive cleft city."

Ren didn't disagree with August. He loved cities, even some of the messy, broken ones, and this one certainly had no parallel. It was a quirk of geology converted into an utterly unique place, with mythical energy and the solidity of a city that had stood for a thousand years.

An hour later, the car left the tunnel and burst out into the bright light of a space quite unlike the natural chasma of San Cristobal. Here they found themselves in a machine-sculpted cavern, strutted for structural strength. It was like standing within a giant ribcage.

After a deceptive entry zone that looked for all the world like an exclusive country club, the cavern confessed its true nature: a military base with all the charm and beauty that one tends to expect of barracks and arms depots. An old-fashioned red-and-white weighted boom blocked the entrance. Helmeted guards in beige and khaki combat gear stood on, their garb a peculiar anachronism, since man-to-man combat was centuries defunct.

The boom swept up, and they were waved through. A sports track lay to one side of the road and a barren, gritty parade ground to the other. Barracks followed – functional, almost wilfully ugly squat blocks. Beyond were hangars and a fleet of craft festooned with the combined insignia of UCoM and Nuevo Mundo.

Whenever Ren was in the presence of the military, he was

left with a lingering impression that nothing changed or would ever change. It seemed that there would always be a harsh, dehumanising gradation into rank and regiment. Soldiers were soldiers, generals were generals, and a parade ground was a parade ground.

The car swept into an entrance in the cavern's back wall and came to a stop on the polished concrete within. So far, they had been on the move for just two hours, half of which was the car ride, and yet they had moved between points amounting to almost two hundred trillion kilometres. Not a soul in existence could truly comprehend those distances. It was beyond the capacity of the psyche to process, and madness surely lay on the road to grasping it.

Kani scrunched up his nose and said, "What a send-off," his voice laden with sarcasm.

Ren added, "Yes, and there was me expecting trumpets and ceremony."

Neither Vola nor the relentlessly mute escorts smiled. The hangar was a cavernous space devoted to the basic function of manoeuvring craft into peripheral gateway chambers. Most were sealed off behind heavy airlock doors, but one stood open, guarded by a group of spiritless soldiers. The airlock was formed from colossal blocks of steel that slid together from left and right to form a central seal. A matching pair lay firmly closed at the chamber's rear. The group of seven seemed small and forlorn in this heavy chamber designed for gunships.

Behind them, dark doors slid closed with a silence that belied their massive weight. Somewhere within were buttery-smooth bearings and slick mechanisms that allowed a lump of steel weighing tonnes to glide like shoji doors over tatami mats. Pressure neutralised, lights turned from red to green, and doors at the opposite end slid open. In a second chamber beyond the airlock, a gateway was already coming to life. This was the final hop within Core territory, from the military base to Kiki, Nuevo Mundo's moon.

Kiki felt jarringly different. A violent drop to 0.2 G

delivered a sudden bodily lightness along with a radical change in the rules of personal motion. Imiko and August were sprawled like broken umbrellas, but they laughed. Moving between worlds also brought sensory confusion as the traveller adjusted to changed pressure, brightness, the light's hue, exotic aromas and a host of more subtle factors. On Kiki, there was no smell at all. The arrival facility was bleak, industrial and forbidding, with lighting devoid of a designer's touch. It didn't even attempt to emulate the modest niceties of civilian terminals. Considering what Ren thought of the civilian ones, this implied a new league of brutality. It was not unknown for him to pass through such facilities en route to some of his more obscure mission destinations, but it was far more usual to stick with civilian or diplomatic channels.

"We keep the location of the Jericho gateway secret… I think for obvious reasons," said Vola. "Evidently, it is here on Kiki, but there's one more leg remaining to the opposite side of the moon. We'll take ground transport from this point."

Ren understood immediately. Gateways to unfriendly or 'complicated' worlds sometimes carried great risk. An aggressor could simply drop a nuke or biological weapon through and then close the gateway from their end. The only way to protect against this was to place them in remote locations, such as the far side of a moon like Kiki. In more extreme circumstances, it could be in the outer reaches or even in an uninhabited system. There were other reasons for discretion: covert missions, illegal private gateways, and discreet diplomatic channels.

The rail terminus was a sea of steel and concrete drenched in angry mechanical sounds. More joyless soldiers manned the entrance. Had their grandmothers all died on the same day or was misery a prerequisite for joining the military? The train capsule felt like a minecart with crude, shiny plastic seats and airlock doors that didn't look as though they would prevent mosquitos from getting in, let alone the harsh vacuum of the moon's surface. The crappy interior was deceptive though, as its motion spoke of solidity as it ploughed forward at a startling pace with barely a jolt or vibration.

With the train's passage, little clouds of dust erupted from the lunar surface and then settled unnaturally slowly. Moons were often hauntingly beautiful, and Kiki was no exception. It was peppered with craters, small and large, but also crisscrossed with fracture lines in ordered rows. It looked as if a giant wolverine had scored its surface. Ren could only guess at the geological process that had generated this peculiarity. Minerals stirred from deep underground lent the surface a distinctive colouration of ochre, burnt umber, sienna, and topaz all in a continuous mottled banding. It was the palette of an artist depicting an autumnal scene.

Through thick windows, they watched a beautiful, desolate surface slide past. Silence reigned; a sign of elevated tension, sensory overload, and the simple fact that they remained strangers to one another. These were the final few moments of their journey, and beyond lay the unknown.

The arrival was marked by a gradual deceleration before plunging into a pitch-black tunnel carrying them deep into Kiki's interior. The train paused, the tunnel sealed behind them, and then came the hiss of atmosphere returning. A handful of soldiers and technicians were present to greet them at the platform. Gone was the spiritless lethargy of their colleagues at the other end of the track. In its place was an edgy buzz of excitement and a babble of animated chatter.

There was one tiny, ticking hour remaining until departure, and then they would be thrust into the great unknown of Arc space. Ren couldn't help but marvel at the fact that they had travelled quite so insanely far but with such efficiency that an hour to spare was considered plenty.

A regiment of specialists had taken up position here since the gateway's reawakening ten days before. Each had been obliged to sign an epically harsh non-disclosure agreement but had done so happily for the thrill of involvement. There were lab-coated technicians, communications specialists, and happy geeks operating equipment designed to detect anything odd travelling in this direction from Jericho. They were poised to sniff out weapons, toxins, radiation, spy tech, and a dozen other dangers. The room was crammed with jury-rigged monitoring equipment, all connected by thick cables which snaked messily across the floor.

Heightened tension accompanied the nervous chatter that was always present at a countdown. The remaining minutes were spent fidgeting and pacing whilst sipping unquestionably awful canteen coffee.

Ren observed and documented his colleagues' nervous quirks. People leak emotion even when they believe they are maintaining rigid facades. He could not read minds, of course, but easily detected the little signals that betray stress, unhappiness, mistrust, and a host of other sentiments. This was a frustrating talent because the thought processes behind their emotive signals remained unknown. Furthermore, there was no possibility of broaching things that people were determined to cover up. All it did was provide him with a little packet of insight into other people's state of mind and an intuition for the presence of lies, and that was a handy talent.

All three were leaking like sieves. They betrayed surprising levels of anxiety for people who were doubtless selected for resilience in addition to their talents and loyalties. Ren wondered at the significance of such raised stress levels.

With ten minutes remaining, they entered the final stages towards the gateway. Ren had never had to pass through a transit complex quite so well protected as this. Five stages of decontamination followed, each leading deeper into the moon's regolith. The final chamber had blast doors thicker than the trunks of ancient redwoods. It contained the essential gateway equipment, along with sensors supplying data to those roomfuls of equipment. It was cold, musty, somewhat surreal, and a very awkward place to stand around.

The hour came and went, and the gateway remained resolutely closed. Seconds became minutes, but still nothing. Ren leant back against the cavern wall, needing something to calm his nerves and tame his restless mind. Then, at last, a full quarter of an hour after the scheduled departure time, the gateway swelled, and that diabolic hole in spacetime stood ready before them. All that remained was a brief handshake from Vola, and they were on their way.

This time Ren went first. It seemed appropriate to have the team lead actually *lead*, so he put aside his instincts and strode forwards. A strange calm enveloped him, and for the first time in years, his gateway anxiety failed to materialise. He stepped through towards Jericho.

The inevitable reality wobble washed through him, but as it subsided, he found himself in a simple, boxy room without any features other than the gateway behind him and a tunnel leading off from the far wall. The others stumbled through after him, all experiencing a momentary anti-climax. After standing there blinking for a few moments, there seemed nothing else for it but to follow the tunnel. A few steps in, a hidden blast door swept down from above, sealing the path back. This repeated itself every few steps until several had closed behind them, at which point they reached a hub chamber with tunnels like spokes leading off in several directions.

A dull light glowed above one of the tunnel entrances, and without anything to instruct them otherwise, it was taken as a signpost, and that path was followed. As before, blast doors swept closed and sealed behind them. This continued until the final set of doors, which remained shut.

High in the wall, discreet apertures hissed open, each releasing a brief puff of aerosol. At first, the jets appeared as inert, dusty clouds, diffusing under the influence of random molecular collisions. But this was no ordinary dust, and the clouds began to move expressively, deliberately, and with a common purpose, collecting themselves into ordered squadrons. These were miniature armies of microtech, each under the command of a drone no bigger than a fruit fly. They flowed across the chamber to target the four travellers, diffusing across their bodies and melting into clothes and hair.

'Decon' was standard practice when travelling between worlds, but the alarming part was this weird approach and its supporting exotic technology. If Ren's microtech were to be detected, that would certainly mark the end of his journey. But the process finished, and the doors hissed open to reveal a chamber identical to the one where they had first arrived. A gateway lay open, practically beckoning them forward, and they continued through without pause.

Chapter 8

Welcome to the Rabbit Warren

A lifetime of travel to a gallery of exotic worlds had not even vaguely prepared Ren for his emergence into Jericho. Hundreds of such journeys had taught him to expect concrete, steel, and the bleak, impersonal grimness of passenger-processing terminals. In fact, the vicinities of gateways were renowned to be some of the most hellishly brutal human creations ever conceived, devoting their entire focus to functionality and security with not an ounce given over to beauty.

On Jericho, he stepped straight into a wide forest clearing dappled with sunlight. Paths wound away through the trees in all directions as if he were standing at an animal watering hole in the midst of a savannah. There was not a single man-made thing other than the obsidian sphere of the gateway, which stood microscopically above the ground without gantries or supporting machinery. Even the forest paths were unmarked.

The air immediately assaulted his senses: warmly tropical, laden with moisture, and heavy with the pungent spice of vegetation, along with a hundred things his brain could not yet identify or process. There was certainly no familiarity in the atmosphere of this place. Why should there be? But Ren had quietly hoped for some thread of association with his father's world.

Behind, Imiko, Kani and August emerged and gathered behind him. All stood dazed and blinking in the sun, regaining their calm after the jolt from one reality to another. The gateway's perfect sphere immediately began to shrink, and on reaching the size of a fist, it halted briefly, as if thinking, before shrinking again down to a barely visible dot.

A lone woman stood at the edge of the clearing, and with a brief prayer motion, a bow and a nod, she strode confidently towards them. She was barefoot and wore a long, light, swaying dress with simple beads about her neck and ankles.

On reaching the group, she began to speak in thickly accented Standard. "Welcome. I am Oso-Rae Tsi, and I am your guide and companion here on Jericho and in the Arc."

Leaping in first, Imiko said, "I am Imiko Kovaelli, Hanseatic League." She then gestured towards Kani, a clear and deliberate snub to Ren's status.

"I'm Kani Rosenko from the Old Planets. It's a pleasure and an honour."

"I'm Ren, Core's ambassadorial representative and team lead. This is August, also from Core External Affairs."

"I'm delighted to meet you – team lead – and welcome all you here. This is such fun… and unprecedented. We have a great deal to discuss. Please follow me."

A slight smile crossed her lips, deftly defusing her gentle mockery of Ren's slightly pompous introductions. And with that, she turned and started walking down one of the forest paths towards the tree line, continuing to talk as she went. There was no ceremony, nor were there ranks of uniformed officials, nor any sign of the intimidating military presence that usually accompanied the entry into a non-league world. Flaunting military power in the face of an off-world visitor was a juvenile intimidation tactic. The comedy of it was that the 'don't mess with us' attitude almost always correlated with a real weakness or vulnerability. Humourless military police, like a pack of Dobermans, were designed to terrorise, but in reality, conveyed pathetic insecurity.

And yet here, in the most important encounter of his career, there was a single, casually dressed person and a bloody forest.

Without warning or explanation, she switched to one of the Arc dialects, and the translators immediately kicked in, subtly layering in Standard on top of her words so that the speech could be understood without losing the timbre, tone or spirit of the original. All other natural sounds were unfiltered and clear. A bird's call and an insect's buzz landed in the brain in high-fidelity stereo as if there were no audio processing in-between.

"We have a short walk of about half an hour to our destination. This is the Rose Cavern, one of Jericho's more modern creations. The oldest was started 270 years ago."

The word *cavern* reminded Ren that he was *within* rather than *on* a planet, and his gaze swept upwards. And there it was, despite having been invisible to him until he thought to look. Far above lay a smoothly white ceiling so entirely lacking in surface features that it was impossible to gain focus, so giving it a nebulous sense simultaneously like and quite unlike a natural sky. Other than that peculiar ceiling, there was a spindle sun in the middle distance on its daily migratory path down the length of the cavern. On reaching the end, it would dim to create an artificial night to counterpoint its artificial day, and then migrate back in the opposite direction at dawn. Thus, cavern dwellers were accustomed to alternate days in different directions. For new arrivals from planets lit by the suns they orbited, this oscillating day-night cycle was oddly disconcerting. But, like everything in life, given time, it became the new normal. Humans adapt. Species adapt.

"We have a bigger journey ahead of us than you may realise," said Oso-Rae. "You will be passing through several worlds so that you can see what we have built. We can use the journey to talk about both the past and future of our relationship. It is important that you gain some understanding of our creations and the philosophy that underpins them."

The path wound forward, lined with thickly leaved plants and intricate flowers of unlikely colours. Broad tree trunks reached into the sky with vines and epiphytes dangling from their branches. It seemed to be a form of cloud forest: somewhere between deep tropical and temperate. Everything lived in, on, and amongst everything else with lichens, trees, shrubs, orchids, and a host of peculiar plants outside Ren's lexicon. Armies of black ants moved in ordered columns from trees to unseen nests. Butterflies of a dozen colours flapped their way on their eccentric paths, alighting here and there on a flower to drink or on a leaf, for reasons that only a butterfly might know.

Here and there, a stream passed under the path, each straddled by a simple, rustic bridge. The streams bubbled and gurgled over rocks fringed by thick mosses and filigree ferns. Ren wondered where these came from and where they went; after all, this was an artificial cavern without a water table or destination sea. It seemed like a huge artifice but an admittedly beautiful one. He was accustomed to caverns on other worlds where they contained cities, farms, and a little parkland, but not this.

One of the streams emptied into a small, dark lake a few metres off the path, and here Ren stopped for a few moments. He was at the back of the group, and the others continued forward, leaving him alone by the water. Dragonflies danced and shimmered amongst the reeds at the pond's edge. Water swirled, hinting at the presence of fish below the surface.

Oso-Rae appeared at his side and said, "Beautiful, isn't it? I can watch the water for hours."

"Yes, it is. I'm more accustomed to farms, formal gardens and parkland. This is different... it seems wild."

"Much of this was created long before we became 'the Arc,'" said Oso-Rae.

"I suppose that's true. When the machines moved in, this planet was a new discovery and under the control of our leagues and the corporates."

"That's right, but that was a long time ago," said Oso-Rae. "The Archipelago's principles appeared gradually over decades. What we have done in our splendid isolation is protect, refine, and make the curation of ecologies like this our central purpose."

"Your central purpose is gardening?" asked Ren, teasing.

She smiled, recognising the intended humour. "It's a little more than gardening, Mr Markov."

"Please, call me Ren."

Oso-Rae smiled. "We know who you are, Ren. Your father was from Jericho... not so far from here as it turns out, and your mother was from Viola Bay on Kraken, as am I. We are distant cousins, believe it or not."

Ren was speechless. Other than his parents, he had never met a blood relative, nor had he ever thought he would. It was exciting but troubling for someone who had long ago written off the notion of family.

Oso-Rae put the bombshell aside with a wink and a smile before returning to the previous conversation. "In truth, this is a highly managed ecosystem. It wouldn't survive without tuned processes to pump, heat, light, balance and control... all operated by a capable gen-5 mind. Our greatest and fondest work is to be found on planetary surfaces. They offer greater potential and more challenges in equal measure."

"I look forward to seeing it all," replied Ren.

"And see it you shall, cuz."

With considerable relief, Ren noticed relief that his anxiety had subsided. In its place was a new, tingling excitement.

They left the lake and continued along the path, gradually catching up with the others.

"Why would you not put the gateway in a better-connected place?" asked August. "I don't understand the purpose of making people walk when the gateway could be anywhere."

"For us, the journey itself is important. Instantaneity prevents you from seeing what's around you. We also want visitors to see Jericho for what it is before they set foot in one of our urban centres."

"In other words, to annoy visitors and for propaganda," said Ren.

She looked at him sharply.

"Sorry, maybe it's too soon for jokes. I suspect there may be a bit of playful eccentricity in your designs too."

"Ha! That's insightful. I think that is true. We like to be playful. We can't abide stern philosophies that leave no room for laughter, dance and irreverence."

Their path meandered on its way to higher ground via a series of long bends, and there, towards the top, the trees thinned to offer a view down the cavern's length. In parts the ground was flat, stopping abruptly at the cavern's edge, but in others, it curved upwards to form a smooth asymptote with the wall. These flatlands, hills and vertiginous slopes provided diverse terrain, which supported various microbiomes along with innumerable tree species. On higher slopes, the ranks of green were replaced by gravelly scree dotted with jagged boulders.

From this high vantage, they could see that there was an overall incline to the cavern, allowing water to flow gently under gravity, searching out its inviolate course.

"Where does the water come from, and where does it go beyond the cave?" asked Imiko.

"It's a vastly complex system of pumps, pipes and channels. Some of the water systems flow for hundreds of kilometres, but others are local to individual caverns."

In the far distance, the many streams merged to form a modest river, and at its terminus, a broad lake sparkled. Only there, far off on the lake's fringes, did they begin to see the signs of human activity and habitation.

Oso-Rae explained, "Rose Cavern is distinctive, as it serves to welcome guests and to host meetings for people from all over Jericho and beyond. Most caverns blend wilderness with farmland and habitation, always in a strict ratio, but here there is no farming, simply because of its special role. There are other caverns with similar purposes and several which have no humans at all."

"Why no humans?" asked Imiko.

"To provide for the species that shy away from mankind and to allow apex predators places to roam… and just because."

"I think I understand."

Twenty minutes further down the path, they approached the lake nestling at the Rose Cavern's foot.

Pointing upwards, Oso-Rae said, "You can see dwellings up in the walls. We try to leave the cavern floor largely free of construction to ensure a more natural space. Cities are the abyss of the human species, so they say."

"Mine is fantastic in a slightly brutal and chaotic way," replied Ren, thrown by the harshness of her words. "I think there can be great beauty in urban spaces, just as in nature."

"Indeed, they can be beautiful, but they always harbour a horrific human experience, particularly for the poor and forgotten at the bottom of the pile. In nature, you can be poor but free of those urban horrors."

Ren didn't wish to antagonise so soon after meeting her, but he was tempted to remind Oso-Rae that the billions of people on Marrakesh, and on the many worlds like it, simply couldn't be housed without their cities. Yes, they brought their share of social dysfunction, but they were a simple necessity for populations of such staggering scale.

The wall was riddled with openings as if some colony of giant termites had gone to work. Many of the openings were just a few metres above ground level, whilst others ranged higher up towards the ceiling. Some appeared to be little more than roughly hewn holes protected by a simple railing, but others were more substantial with jutting terraces, gardens and dangling creepers.

One of these openings in the cliff wall was destined for them. Oso-Rae led them to a wide entrance, unadorned and unmarked on the outside but gradually expanding within into a bright lobby.

"We will be staying here, and I'll show each of you to your rooms. There will be a reception on the terrace later. Until then, you may rest."

She explained how to hook into the local mesh. Engineers on both sides had devised the protocols for accessing each other's systems in the few days running up to their arrival on Jericho. It was a truly rudimentary data feed but sufficient to navigate locally and send messages amongst the team.

An hour later, Ren sat on the little balcony of his room and wrote notes on the day's events as the distant spindle-sun slowed and faded into simulated dusk. Instead of a real sun slipping over a horizon and shifting towards red through thickened atmosphere, the sphere of a spindle-sun slowed to a standstill in the sky and ramped the colour temperature down through shades of ochre and garnet, whilst gradually dimming. This method was partly to keep the wildlife happy, but it was also beneficial to the human psyche. It created a sense of evening that stirred primal emotions deep inside the hearts of people. For humans hadn't left the surfaces of planets long enough ago to have yet adapted. These same forces were what made a natural fire waken the inner palaeolith, engendering feelings of safety and of comfort. Basic instincts.

The dispersion of his earlier anxiety came as a great relief to Ren. So far, they had not faced anger, threat or intimidation. Indeed, quite the opposite was true.

Gradually, more lights appeared, in the manner of stars slowly revealing themselves with encroaching night. The luminous glow from within interior spaces left warm puddles of light, punctuated here and there by the sharp pricks of exposed lanterns. The distant cavern wall was mottled with a haze of orange shades. Birds clustered in the safety of treetops, where they gossiped happily while settling in to roost.

Finally, Ren decided that this moment was as good as any. He delved into the darker recesses of his implant, summoned the recently installed routines and woke a fraction of the slumbering swarm. Within seconds they were on their way. He could detect nothing physically to prove that the swarm had left his body, but a status panel confirmed that the job was done. And off into the night they sped.

The rudimentary mesh connection gave Ren sufficient fragments of information to operate locally. Instructions for water, lighting and the subsystems of daily life were all clear. More critically, it assisted with local navigation, agenda and destination. This enabled him to wander out through the swing-door of his accommodation precisely on the nose of the seven minutes required to get to the reception.

Labyrinthine tunnels wound their way up, down and around. Without landmarks or points of reference, it was impossible to keep track of his path, leaving him entirely at the mercy of his implant's guidance. Panel lights in the ceilings provided enough light (and presumably the right wavelengths) for dark mosses and shade-loving plants to emboss the walls. It struck him that even here, in the connecting spaces between human living areas, they had made room for life. The tunnels were rough and uneven, although carved steps revealed the truth that it was highly engineered. It all walked a delicate line between natural chaos and something explicitly designed for humans. The ground beneath his feet was paved in parts, sandy in others, and all interspersed with mosses and tightly cropped grass.

The tunnel opened out onto a spreading balcony some hundred metres above ground. It jutted beyond the wall like the buttressed half-disc of a fungus clinging to the trunk of a tree. From this vantage, a panoramic vista presented the whole of the Rose Cavern. Ren could just spy segments of the path they had walked earlier. Plants and smaller trees adorned the terrace, but here it was managed, trimmed, and manicured around tables and alcoves. The spindle-sun at the far end of the cavern was now just a dull ember. It delivered the remnants of an artificial dusk and, in so doing, cast exquisite, rich shadows.

Oso-Rae was there waiting, smiling, relaxed and radiant, along with three other Arc'ers – if that was the collective noun – in her immediate group and a couple dozen more standing back on the periphery. August and Imiko had arrived before him, whilst Kani appeared just behind. Oso-Rae introduced the three as Saki, Ychi and Eler. Just the one name was proffered, and no surnames or aggrandising titles were added.

"Saki works with me in foreign relations. Ychi is a technologist and Eler is a local sociologist. It was hard to know which skills to bring but we tried for a sensible spread. I suspect we are all polymaths of a sort anyway."

"I'm Ren, a long-serving diplomat in External Affairs. I wouldn't call myself a polymath or anything close to that. Our society seems to have lost that concept long ago."

He paused before turning to introduce the others. "This is Imiko Kovaelli of the Hanseatic League, Kani Rosenko of the Old Worlds and August Broher, also from Core.

"You requested a representative from Isabella IV, but a great deal can change in fifty years. Unfortunately – or fortunately – they are no longer relevant."

"Please explain," said Saki.

Fifty years before, Isabella IV had been a heavyweight with far more wealth and influence than any member of Core Planets. There had been a period during which they had courted both Core and the Hanseatic League over possible membership. In the case of Core, they had bristled against the many rules, along with their obsessive ethical monism. With Core, right and wrong were never open to interpretation by planetary societies. Acceptable ethics only took one form: theirs. The Hanseatic League would have welcomed Isabella IV with open arms had they not demanded too much. Their arrogance insisted on too many seats at the High Table, so a deal was never done.

Instead, they went their own way, which to them was not such a tragic outcome, since they were rich and had always danced to the beat of their own imperious drum. The problem was that in their isolation they began to believe more in their specialness. Increasingly militarized, militant, and stoking the fire of nationalism, the possibility of league membership withered. They became a pariah, and Core, being Core, subtly assisted in their downfall. Now they were nothing more than a dusty backwater – an unbonded planet with a pathetic junta and a strutting, bemedaled general in charge.

Ren delivered a compressed and slightly sanitised version of this complex story. Other than a raised eyebrow, Saki and the others in the Arc contingent seemed unperturbed.

The Arc people were dressed in simple clothes, seemingly of linen or some similarly coarse fibre. There was a subtle elegance in their muted colour palettes and modest prints. Cuts were uncomplicated, and they came across as neither grand nor formal. Ren compared this to the dozens of welcome receptions he had attended on other worlds. They always featured flamboyant fashions, grandly tailored clothes and hideous extravagance. Such events were the domain of the exquisitely manicured and were often a lunatic exaggeration of human vanity and pride. Not here.

Oso-Rae flicked a fingernail against her glass and, in a louder voice, said, "Saki has prepared a little speech to celebrate the arrival of our alien friends."

At that, Saki, a small man about a decade older than Oso-Rae, stepped forward, and a wide arc formed about him. His voice had depth and gravitas, which came unexpectedly from his diminutive frame. As he spoke, he turned to make solid eye contact with each person present. The selective use of hand gestures added emphasis in just the right places and accorded an air of confidence. This man was an experienced speaker.

"I would like to warmly welcome our visitors from Core and the leagues to Jericho, one of our humble homes here in the Archipelago.

"We have not had visitors from afar since I was much younger... a child. Most of you were still playing with toys or adding two and two at school. A few of you were not yet born. It feels like some fictional past to me.

"Back then, when the gateways were closed, our relations were drenched in animosity. There was a smog of anger and bitterness, and enough resentment to power a gateway on acrimony alone.

"We live in a brave new world now. The Archipelago is strong and deeply established. Our borders are defended. There is no longer a reason to stay isolated from the other leagues, as humanity's fate is ours together.

"Today opens a new chapter in mutual understanding and respect. Please share your experiences, lives and innermost thoughts with Ren, August, Kani and Imiko during their stay. This is about building bridges and closing old wounds.

"Thank you, and skol."

Drinks were downed, and there was a form of applause involving clicking fingers. Some traditions continue through the millennia unbroken. Societies came and went, planets colonised, languages appeared and disappeared, whole people lost to genocide, and yet a toast at the end of a speech continued as an unchanged cultural artefact throughout recorded human history. The strangest traditions were preserved whilst others that seemed far more important at the time simply faded into oblivion.

The group dispersed into clusters and moved to seating areas around the platform. Oso-Rae took Ren by the arm and guided him over to a cushioned area under overhanging branches. Linking her arm through his was an extraordinarily intimate gesture by the measure of Core, but he could already see that they were naturally tactile and unencumbered by rigid decorum. For her, it was nothing more than a natural gesture.

Ren sipped a peculiar spiced drink and sank back in his

chair. All around them, little coloured lanterns hung in the branches, casting intricate knots of shadow across the balcony. There was a background thrum from distant cicadas and the occasional croak of frogs, accompanied by a thousand disparate sounds of nocturnal life. Some faintly glowing insects fussed around a dark pool of water, and bats silently swooped and dived about them. He couldn't deny the idyllic perfection of the moment. Nor could he help but contrast it with his apartment in the concrete jungle of Super Paradise. There seemed to be something quite wrong with loving them both, and yet he did.

"You know I work for Core External Affairs as a diplomat dealing with special off-world situations. What about you? Who do you work for?" asked Ren.

"I work for Central Control, which is based far from here. I don't have a job title you would recognise, so let's call me a diplomat too."

"What's Central Control?"

Ren tried his utmost to pretend that it was an honest question and that he genuinely didn't know anything about it. It was important not to come all the way here only to deliver his preconceptions back to her.

"I'll be able to explain more as we go, but in essence, it's a minimalist central government that only handles a few core areas of political life. Other aspects of government are delegated and decentralised. I'm sure your briefings taught you that!"

"Yes, they did, but our information was very old and quite possibly wrong. Oso-Rae, may I ask you a question? I understand the story of how you cut yourselves off, at least our version of it, but in your own words, why did you do this?"

"Man, straight in there, eh?"

"We could talk about the weather or something…"

"Well, it wasn't me, it was my ancestors, but either way, we shut ourselves away from Core Planets because you saw our system as a threat and tried to undermine it. Your saboteurs seemed to gain a sick pleasure from their cruel, subversive games… and then had the nerve to dress it all in the clothes of noble purpose. It seemed that your singular desire was to destroy an ideology that didn't align with your own. So, it was a natural decision to cut ourselves off, mainly for self-preservation but also to give ourselves time to solidify and build strength. And don't get me started on the Hanseatic League." A closing smile from Oso-Rae somehow succeeded in converting her harsh critique into something much lighter.

To Ren, elements of that speech sounded like stock answers. There was something a little too decorative in the words she chose to describe the CPF's behaviour. In truth, there was nothing surprising there, except perhaps the part about building strength, which Saki had also made reference to in his speech. He wondered what that meant and filed it away for future investigation. It was a relief that her vitriol was not aimed at Core alone.

As if sensing she had been too aggressive, Oso-Rae changed key.

"But don't get me wrong. Core was just behaving as Core does. It was entirely in character and therefore expected behaviour. That made your moves easy for us to predict. We didn't even really resent it because it is your nature."

"Well, that's a little patronising, but okay."

"We feel that getting angry with Core is a little like getting angry with a cat for bringing home a dead bird. You can if you want, but it is pointless to be outraged by an entity's very nature. It is wiser to manage your expectations of such animals and moderate your behaviour accordingly."

"So, we are comparable with a cat?"

"Yes, I would say so."

"Is this view of Core a personal view or widely held?"

"I would say that it is very widely held since it is taught in schools," replied Oso-Rae with another laugh.

"I don't see myself or my colleagues in your description of people taking a sick pleasure from their work." He winced, thinking of Vola's cruelty, and then continued, "We have a heartfelt purpose to protect mankind's long-term wellbeing. Do you really not believe we are well-intentioned?"

"We think you have good intentions, if blinkered, but much of the evil in history has been enacted by people with good intentions. It simply isn't enough to be well-intentioned.

"So, it's your turn. Tell me, Ren, what do you believe in? Call it ideology or whatever you will, but what is Core's modern purpose? Have you changed at all?"

Ren paused for a moment to decide how to answer. Some music had crept into his consciousness. It was, to his ear, an unearthly tribal sound; beautiful in its unfamiliar forms and hauntingly strange, but still adhering to recognisable forms.

"Our ideology has not changed. We still celebrate the five ideals of freedom, knowledge, reason, tolerance and individuality."

Oso-Rae bent over with laughter. "That mantra sounds like something from another century. You are held hostage by your little list."

"These are universal ideals, not just Core's. We didn't invent them and they should apply to everyone, everywhere. If Core Planets and External Affairs did not uphold them, I would not in good faith do what I do."

Ren winced again internally. He was repeating words that no longer carried the certainty they once did, but he was startlingly good at sounding compelling when he voiced those doctrinal gospels. That was the skill that marked him out from others – the disarming charm with which he delivered Core's sermon.

Oso-Rae countered, "The problem with ideology expressed as a list is that you get stuck in semantics. No list of words can ever represent the wondrous complexity of the human condition."

"Do you pretend to have no ideology?"

"It depends what you mean by that. What do these words

represent and, in particular, what do they convey in different languages and societies? How does their meaning stand up to translation, or for that matter, to the mutation of context and understanding over centuries? They have never stood the test of time or remained relevant through history."

"I get the semantic issues, but saying that the most important ideas are entirely vague and lose meaning over time is just false."

Ren knew there was more truth to Oso-Rae's challenge than he could readily admit, but he could not perceive of an existence without a clearly stated ideology, credo or whatever else you might want to call it. It seemed that her problem was with the word itself.

"Why do you call other people's systems 'ideology' and your own not? Do you have no principles?"

"An ideology is a set of words open to interpretation. We have a base tenet of existence that is immutable and beyond debate. We don't over-extend, and we let the rest of human existence bubble away without imperious, centralised dictation of rules, law or ethics."

Ren didn't know what to do with that. Her whole speech seemed nuts: simultaneously dictatorial and passive, but he chose one part to begin.

"Immutable and beyond debate? That's spectacular arrogance," he said.

"Not really," she replied, "because it only covers one central idea; that is, we must preserve an ecology in equilibrium and that humans are just one small part of the myriad species that make up our worlds. We don't word it legalistically because the spirit of it is what counts."

And there she was, already talking about the natural world. Ren noted a pattern of standard, practised dogma in her speech, but then again, maybe the same was true of his.

She added, "Every attempt at building a society based on a singular ideology will fail."

"We haven't failed, Oso-Rae. Core has been around for hundreds of years."

"You will eventually... Anyway, tell me about this ideal you call 'individuality.' What's that all about?"

"In our society, all individuals have a basic right to believe, act and express themselves freely, regardless of sex, gender, race, tribe or creed. If you express an unpopular view, there is no coercion, except when it steps outside the realm of legality."

Oso-Rae was smiling at him. She seemed to be toying with the exchange rather than treating it as an urgent intellectual battle to be won.

She launched her attack. "I understand you *claim* to value individualism, but you only value it when it plays by *your* rules. You only value reason when people agree with you within narrow limits. Those in your society with notably alternative views struggle under the tyranny of the majority. They are marginalised and politically neutered. If anything, Core disrespects the individual because it's your way or the highway."

Ren thought she sounded like an angst-filled teenager who had just discovered politics. Perhaps that was exactly what the Arc was.

"Says the woman who happily works for a totalitarian regime," laughed Ren. "Anyway, how do you know all that? You have never been to a Core world."

Oso-Rae pretended to look wounded but smiled and said, "Does a leopard change its spots? I see that you enjoy trying to get a rise out of me. I would also advise you to be careful with badges like 'totalitarian.' They won't serve you well here.

"To be honest, we think you place individualism on too high a pedestal. Individuals don't exist as islands outside their villages, towns or clans. Human decency and wellbeing are wrapped up in that of our immediate and wider community."

Ren wondered at that. He was an island as far as one could be without becoming an ascetic, but it came at a cost. Why did he always turn away from community?

A larger group joined them, defusing the intensity of the moment. Ren and Oso-Rae were pulled into the wider conversation.

She closed with the words, "I would like to continue this chat, but another day. What do you say? Remember that in order to forgive, we have to understand one another."

"That's why I'm here."

For most of the exchange, Ren's translator had chugged along fluidly, perhaps because their dialect had only moderately drifted away from Standard. There were solid, common linguistic roots. It had flagged up a handful of words and phrases that had uncertain meaning in context, but Ren tried not to pay too much attention to the translator's warnings, as it interrupted the fluid flow of conversation.

Drinks were drunk, the group relaxed a little, and conversation turned to family, friends and life's many pleasant little things. Ren's tendency was towards earnest discussion, but he knew there were moments to put that aside. Still, he always avoided the most banal end of small talk of the kind people employ when they truly have nothing to say to each other.

He was relieved that the Arc did not shun alcohol; he had never quite trusted people without vices, and alcohol was the surest way he knew to defuse tension and engender a deeper honesty in human relations. He was also relieved that these people were easy conversation, which was not always the case, particularly with some of the more peculiar cultures outside Core Planets. There were societies with so little in common that conversation became horribly stilted and punishingly awkward. Oso-Rae and her colleagues had a lightness and eccentric humour that he had not expected. They laughed a great deal, took offence at nothing, and delighted in poking a little gentle fun at their visitors and themselves. There were echoes of his parents in their manners and humour. It was simultaneously joyful and melancholic, illuminating the memory of people long dead.

As the evening drew to a close, Ren noticed Kani standing

apart on the platform's lip. He had been quiet and emotionally removed all evening, and now stood with his hand on his chin, gazing out across the cavern, lost in thought.

Back in his room, Ren prepared a brief message for Astrid before dropping it in a special repository for transmission home. It was like taking a steam ship in an age of interstellar travel. He described the Arc'ers and their eccentric manners and noted the unfathomable blend of light-heartedness and earnest severity that threaded through every conversation.

Then finally, as the night drew to a close, he brought up the swarm's status panel. Many had travelled far afield and had not yet returned to roost, but a handful had stayed local, fishing around August, Imiko and Kani and the cave complex. And, voila! It was hazy data, but there were signs that someone else had begun to spin their web. Ren was not the only one here with microtech.

Tiredness stole over him, so he prepared for this first night in Jericho's warren. There were curtains and a screen that could be pulled across the opening onto the cavern, but Ren left it wide open and crawled into bed, allowing the thrum of nocturnal activity to pull him down towards sleep. Insects hummed and chirped in the forest canopy below. Frogs croaked in their dark pools, and mysterious beasts called to one other in shrieks and ghostly howls.

Chapter 9

Let's Do This Our Way

A roughly hewn, monolithic stone platform rose twenty stories from a ravaged plain. The billiard-smooth upper surface was tattooed with six identical sets of markings. These denoted nothing more than landing points, but along with this pedestrian function, they were also things of beauty, like accidental artworks. An orange windsock puffed out in the relentless wind, accompanied by acorn-sized drops of torrential rain. In one corner of the platform stood a rudimentary hut built of raw concrete and topped by a simple, corrugated roof. It existed only to protect occasional visiting technicians from the weather as they awaited transport.

One of the landing points was occupied by a bullying brute of a VTOL craft. It appeared to hug the concrete as if guarding its underbelly whilst broodingly surveying the terrain. Its engines were angled down for vertical takeoff, and its squat wings lay half-folded. There was no attendant pilot or crew, as both functions were handled by a gen-3 control system.

Captain Palina was early, as those he was due to meet were not the kind of people one kept waiting. So he sat in the hut upon a rudimentary metal chair, which made an ear-gouging scraping noise against the concrete every time it was moved even an inch. To pass the time, he surveyed the scene below. It was one that few humans ever had the chance to witness – that of an autonomous terraforming mega-tech team at play.

Ranks of vast machines were being constructed by squadrons of more modest flying drones. These ranks extended far off into the distance in increasing states of completeness. Cloud and rain killed visibility at around two kilometres, but construction extended far beyond. The machines were bulky, inhumanly ugly, but ultimately functional. There was no role at all for aesthetics, since humans were not required for their construction nor involved with their operation. For that matter, humans never inhabited the same spaces, other than for occasional site visits. This was the only purpose of the stone platform on which he sat.

These armies of machines were designed, refined, built, and controlled by other machines. Those had themselves optimised and improved the designs over centuries, resulting in remarkable examples of gen-5-driven evolutionary modification. Some of the miniature drones had roles that the humans who built the very first examples would never have guessed at. Swathes of new technology had appeared through iterative learning, a few happy accidents, and millions of hours of trial and error.

All that was required to begin this process was a single, modest seed machine that was small enough to pass through a regular gateway. That seed machine was more brain than brawn but was able to initiate the collection of raw materials for the manufacture of the coming army. A mobile gateway would hop from point to point on a planet's surface, dropping seed machines as it went like an ovulating queen ant.

Each seed machine surveyed and cunningly adapted to the common and exotic minerals available to it locally on the planet's surface. Before long, it would have built plenty of diverse new machines along with power plants for their fuel. At that point, growth became exponential, and the operation started to crawl across the planet's surface like a robotic alien pestilence. For a few decades during which this process was at its peak, it seemed nightmarishly dystopian. The planet appeared ruined, ravaged and poisoned, but little by little the atmosphere cleared, greenery was seeded, and the machines began to dismantle themselves, returning to piles of raw minerals, which in their turn became new landscape features.

The terrifying scale of these legions of leviathans in action was a sight that transformed those who witnessed it forever, just as people are changed when they go into orbit and look back at the pretty, fragile marble of a planet they call home. It was a similar feeling of minuteness and pathetic irrelevance in the face of vast forces.

A second VTOL craft swooped in, its engines rotating and tilting down, converting forward thrust into lift. Wings began to fold, and it settled on dampened legs before powering down. From the craft stepped a single figure, that of Premier Virsenko, who walked across the concrete to join Palina.

"Premier Virs....," started Palina before his voice was drowned out by bellowing engines of a third craft dropping through the cloud base.

Within seconds it was upon them, banking as its wings folded. The vast power of its thrust sent puddles of water flooding off the platform, accidentally creating a dry path for its passenger, Laynna Mu Rosa, to walk from its now-open doors to the hut.

"Hell, could you have chosen a shittier spot for us to meet?" asked Mu Rosa as she entered.

Ignoring her question, Virsenko said, "Astrid's ploy almost worked, didn't it? It's a good thing we were on the guest list already or we might have had to go crawling back to her."

"She's a controlling, destitute bitch," said Mu Rosa angrily. "She lives for her little moments of theatre and she can have them. However, she should not forget that I am vengeful and bear legendary grudges."

"At the end of the day, it was a good play," said Virsenko

more calmly.

Palina had no idea what they were talking about, but it was not for him to interrupt them. He was rarely intimidated by *anyone*, but these two – his temporary employers – demanded respect and a degree of humility on his part.

He quietly wondered at what it meant to have Mu Rosa and Premier Virsenko in the same room, cooperating on a covert operation. Superficially, their two leagues had much in common. Both were commercially focused and used trade as the foundation of their external relations. Both were traditional, hierarchical and favoured the influence of families that had always ruled. However, Mu Rosa had no patience for the Old Worlds' singular, monolithic and inflexible religion, from which the entirety of their ethical (or otherwise) conduct was derived. The truth was that ethics wasn't something that kept her awake at night. If pressed, she would say that morality was the domain of the individual and leave it at that.

The strain worked both ways. Virsenko could not abide the Hanseatic League's teleological and consequentialist approach to life. He found it shallow and it irritated him.

These two made for tense bedfellows.

Palina was clad in a dark, austere uniform, but absent were the markings and insignia of a planetary government or anything else that might brand him as Hanseatic or Old Worlds. And that was perfectly accurate, since Commander Palina was a mercenary and his organisation worked in the shadows doing the dirty work of governments and trans-planetary corporates.

"Commander, thank you for joining us," said Virsenko.

"Of course, Premier, I'm at your service."

"How about an update? What's the latest score with this little scheme of ours?" asked Virsenko.

Palina took his cue and said, "We have been in the Heimdall system for several months, and we're now well-established in the vicinity of Eleuthera. We only arrived in the Juliet-II system very recently, but we're already in position on

Jericho's moon. Of course, we have had to move very slowly to ensure discretion. As for the Hypnos system – that's Kraken and Typhon – we are arriving in-system as we speak, and there's a great deal of work ahead."

"How much does the loss of the fourth mission affect us?" asked Mu Rosa.

"It's not ideal, but we were fortunate it was the Karakorum mission that failed, because Bathsheba is the least important and least populous world in the Arc. If we could take and hold the others, they would have to capitulate."

Palina was in his element. He knew his job, knew his data, and revelled in the attention.

"How long until we can act?" asked Virsenko.

Palina didn't know what their true intention was. There was one scenario in which their job was to intimidate the Arc and nothing more, but there was a second where they might use force. This was what he had been asked to prepare for, but he somehow doubted they would ever pull the trigger.

"There isn't a single date. The longer we get, the more prepared we will be. Until a few days ago, I would have said it would take years to be ready, but now, with your agents on their way into the Arc, everything has changed."

"How long?" asked Mu Rosa impatiently.

"It depends on what you mean by 'act.' The current model is to focus on Kraken and Eleuthera as, being planets, the infrastructure is mostly on the surface, so we can drop out of orbit and quickly immobilise them. Jericho and Typhon are habitats, which means that the infrastructure is all deep underground. There's much less we can do there unless you want to crack them open. It's doable, but fighting our way in would be messy."

Palina almost said 'catastrophically messy' but didn't want to put them off too much. A messy invasion might be fun.

"What do we need to happen?" asked Mu Rosa.

"We need data, we need movement across the Arc, and we

need our people to plant beacons," said Palina. "Everything depends on whether the team stays on Jericho or travels to the other planets."

"Of course," said Virsenko. "If they stay on Jericho then all this will be a long game."

"Or no game at all," added Mu Rosa.

"But if they go to the other planets, we will learn the locations of gateways, military sites, key infrastructure, power plants and so on. Of those, the gateways are most critical. If you control the gateways, they can't move, and you have them in a stranglehold.

"All that said, there's no clear solution to penetrating the shells of Typhon and Jericho. We can certainly act much sooner than anticipated, but that remains a barrier."

"This isn't looking great from my perspective," said Virsenko. "We need everything to go our way. We need the beacons to go live. We need impeccable data gathering. And even then we don't know how to access the habitats."

"We could probably defeat them by taking just the planets in an initial attack," replied Palina. "After securing Kraken and Eleuthera, we take our time burrowing into the habitats. It's not ideal, but we could make it work."

Virsenko turned to Mu Rosa and asked, "What's your biggest concern?"

"We can't ignore the timing," said Mu Rosa. "The fact that they are opening up now, exactly as our insertions arrive, either means that they know about them, or that they know to expect something in this timeframe. I wish I knew which it was."

Palina worried about that too. The timing was indeed odd.

"Let's regroup in two days," said Mu Rosa, bringing the meeting to a close.

Mu Rosa and Virsenko returned to their respective craft and, in a rather elegant coordinated movement, they rose together, dropped away from the platform gathering speed, and swept forwards, accelerating hard towards distant gateways home.

Palina considered the subtext of Virsenko and Mu Rosa's words. They had shown a hard determination, and that might make them throw caution to the wind and act impetuously. One could only hope.

Leaving the hut, he entered his own VTOL craft and settled into a padded seat. Engines roared, the stubby wings tilted, and acceleration pressed him back as it gunned forward. The hut stood empty, and rain continued to hammer down, coursing off the platform in rivulets. Beyond, the machines prepared to forge mountains, excavate oceans and exhale a new atmosphere.

Chapter 10

Oso-Rae Drinks Tea and Reports In

In the Rose Cavern, Oso-Rae woke early to the riotous symphony of the dawn chorus. She dressed and spent a calm moment looking out over the canopy with a steaming tea in hand. A large bird of prey with slow, sweeping wing beats soared and wheeled over the forest. Heavy masses of vapour rose up, gradually dissipating in slow, twisting spirals.

She gazed at the scene, moved by its serenity. In terms of natural wonder, it did not stand up to comparison with her home world, or with Eleuthera, of course, but she allowed herself that morsel of planetary pride. Her clansfolk would have chastised her for expressing such immodesty, but it was a private thought, and her clan was far away and remote from her now in so many ways.

She put the cup aside and wandered down through the warrens and out into the open. The path carried her down a gentle slope to the banks of a mirror-still lake. Waterbirds with upturned bills and bright-blue eyes stood preening at the water's edge. They emitted sorrowful cries that carried low across the water to rebound a moment later in an off-key echo from the cavern wall. From the trees poured the excitable hubbub of birds preparing their day. Cries from larger macaws and parrots blended with the more delicate melodies of songbirds.

She followed a stone walkway along the rim of the lake before turning in towards the forest on a meagre, uneven path that followed a gushing brook. Some five minutes along this path brought her upon a pristine, mossy clearing sprinkled with fallen leaves.

Saki awaited her, seated on a fallen log, his hand on his chin. Next to him was a surreal, almost solid projection representing the figure of a third person, Nako Moon.

The figure spoke. "Morning, my fabulous friends."

"Morning, Nako," they replied in unison like obedient schoolchildren.

"Tell me, what's it like meeting heathens and wraiths... these ghosts from our past?"

"It's a strange mix of disappointing and satisfying," said Saki thoughtfully. "Disappointing because I expected something darker, more hateful and alien. Satisfying because it's somehow better to know they're nothing more and nothing less than people."

"I agree. They are disturbingly normal. It's even tempting to see them as well-meaning." Oso-Rae waved away the beginning of an objection. "Don't worry, I know that's naïve. But, like Saki, an undeniable part of me wanted them to be gorgons in dark robes. It would have fit better."

Nako couldn't let it go. "You would be wise to assume they are still the gorgons you imagined, but wrapped in human skin."

"Even Ren?" asked Oso-Rae. "After all, he's one of us in a way."

"Even Ren," replied Nako. "People tend to be products of the societies that raise them. Genetics and history have little to do with it."

Oso-Rae wasn't so sure, but she had no intention of debating the point with the great Nako Moon.

"So the plan remains," said Saki. "We'll take the slow road to Hypatia."

"Yes. Follow your training. Conduct your work with a purity of purpose. However this ends, we will need *some* form of contact with the leagues."

"It's the tourist road then," said Oso-Rae. "Let's show Ren where he comes from."

"So far, we could not have hoped for a more constructive start." Saki turned to Oso-Rae and she nodded in agreement. "They are reciting lines we could practically have written for them."

Oso-Rae pondered the instructions drummed into them over the preceding weeks. There were some things about the Arc that had to remain secret for the time being and then only be leaked in controlled ways. This was not out of a sense of guilt or shame, at least that's what Nako said, but because these outsiders were not capable of comprehending some of the more radical facets of the Arc's system. They could not afford for the visitors to latch onto the radical before they had had a chance to absorb more moderate ideas. Some things you have to build up to gently. She knew the drill, and the route had been immaculately designed to entwine with the gradual presentation of ideas, but even so, many things were unpredictable and chaotic.

"What about their psych indicators?"

"We monitor body language and the minutiae of facial expression. There are clear stress markers, but that is only to be expected for people thrust into a strange land. We see evidence of them hiding information, but some to a far greater extent than others."

"Yet again, as expected."

"That's two reasons why this has to play out slowly," said Oso-Rae as if to remind herself.

Nako closed the meeting abruptly. "Let's get to it. See you in Hypatia in a few days."

That was the end of the meeting. Saki and Oso-Rae turned and wandered to the edge of the clearing, where they performed a ritual. Kneeling at the thick base of a tree, they closed their eyes, clasped their hands in a cup shape in their laps, and leaned their foreheads forward onto the gnarled trunk. This little ceremony was finished in a few seconds, and then they were on their way back, skipping and hopping like children down the path back to the lake's edge.

Saki continued alone, whilst Oso-Rae paused for a moment on a wooden jetty jutting into the lake, supported by wooden stakes. She sat at its tip and dangled her feet in the cool water. Tiny blue butterflies and iridescent dragonflies explored the reeds and bulrushes at the lake's edge. These sensory moments – the delicious feeling of water on skin, the warmth from a winter sun, sea spray in an open boat – did far more for her well-being than any amount of debate.

She looked at the elaborate tattoos on her forearm. On a normal day, she barely noticed them, since they had been part of her being for so long. She only thought of the markings now after having explained them to Ren. These were the brands of her identity – Kraken, the Neosho Sector, the little town of Viola Bay, and, last but not least, her clan. All were represented in these artful symbols inked in black, white and blue on her inner forearm. At that moment she wondered what identity meant and if these symbols represented her collusion in some vast, distorted system of repression. She felt torn between duty and home.

The spindle-sun was approaching full power and had begun its march down the cavern. Around the lake, birds were settling in to their day's routine when Oso-Rae finally rose and walked back. A million cicadas took their cue, and the forest began to throb with their rasping hums.

Chapter 11

The Slow Train to Maputo

Ren was roused by the daybreak. There had been no chance of sleeping through that rebellious dawn. Although wide awake, he felt no urgent need to leave his bed, choosing instead to lounge and watch the light metamorphose from cold blues through peaches and pinks before arriving at the mustard hues of day.

With the colours turning, he hauled himself from the gentle envelope of his sheets and moved to the balcony, where he stood surveying the forest canopy below. After a time, he saw movement along the edge of the lake and saw that it was Saki and Oso-Rae returning from the forest. There was no reason to think that unusual or odd, but he did wonder what had drawn them out so early. For a time she sat, seemingly lost in thought, at the lake's edge. Then, from the path that led back towards the cavern's centre, he saw Kani emerge from the forest too. Ren smiled to himself. The intrigue that Astrid had promised him was already spinning up. He resolved to keep a close eye on Kani.

At the tail end of the previous evening, Saki had made an enigmatic comment about them 'going travelling' the following day. Ren was puzzled but amused by Saki's mischievous vagueness. So, with the allotted time approaching, he dutifully made his way to the foyer where a small Arc contingent waited, ever courteous and with zeal at maximum.

The group followed an overhung path running alongside the cavern wall in the direction of the lakeshore. Minutes later, they emerged from the trees onto flat ground set back from the water's edge. There, on a neatly trimmed patch of grass, stood a train, waiting patiently. Three magnificently crude wooden carriages rested on iron chassis, which in turn rested on simple rails. Each carriage was painted in pretty pastels: powder blue, cotton candy pink, and a dusty yellow. Ren was familiar with old-fashioned trains from his childhood on Palau, but this was more than that. It was so archaic and achingly whimsical that it seemed contrived.

Saki gestured towards the train. "All aboard," he said before bounding up the steps himself and taking a seat.

At a stretch, Ren could have kept up with the train on foot. On one side the lakeshore slipped past, and on the other, only inches from the carriage window, lay a wall of forest. With an outstretched hand, he brushed his fingers against the leaves as they passed. 'Window' was a generous word for what was nothing more than an empty, rectangular aperture. A cavern, being what it was, had little need for sealed windows. There were no storms to hide from, and, at least here, it was always warm. When rain fell, it fell straight down and streamed off the roof without affecting passengers.

The train lurched forwards towards the Rose Cavern's tip, en route to a still-unnamed destination.

Oso-Rae said, "We have some distance to cover this morning, so asking you to walk might have been a stretch."

"I might as well be walking at this pace." Ren smiled to be doubly sure that they understood he was being flippant.

The bigger question was, why they were on a train that would have fit better a thousand or more years before. Ren had spent less than twenty hours on Jericho, and in that time, they had walked a rustic path and were now on this absurd, rickety contraption.

"Yesterday we were on forest paths, and today we travel aboard this piece of theatrical nostalgia," said Ren. "And yet, you evidently have scientific competence... you travel between the stars."

Despite the absence of a clear question, Oso-Rae understood what he was asking and replied, "We walked yesterday simply to enjoy the journey, and to introduce the flavour of Jericho's cavern life. To understand us at all, you must first see our culture and nature, not our engineering. We don't shun technology, and we are not Luddites who dream of a return to tribal prehistory. That would be absurd because Jericho could not exist without the application of technology on a staggering scale. Nothing here would work."

"So, where do you draw the line? When do you choose the forest paths and when do you embrace technology?"

"That's not easy to answer." Oso-Rae paused to think and then continued. "I suppose we are sincere about living life as members of a habitat, reducing reliance on tech where possible, but accepting it where it's required. Our policy might seem hard to navigate at first, but we think there is method in our madness."

"For us, the journey can be as important as the destination," added Saki. "We often deliberately slow things down, because it is good for the soul, and because few things are genuinely so urgent that you must take the fastest route."

Ren considered debating this but then remembered his own route from Super Paradise to Haikou District. He often chose the slow road too.

"There is another aspect," said Oso-Rae. "We think that humanity should be entwined with an ecosystem... we don't stand removed. Technology provides the framework for the fundamentals of heat, light and water, but the less we do to interfere with the details, the better."

"How do you define a viable ecosystem in a cave?"

"We make room for all the species of animals and plants that would naturally interact and share a space. It's complicated because you begin by emulating an ecosystem that works elsewhere, but it quickly becomes its own thing. Whatever it becomes, it must find equilibrium.

"Each cavern has a balanced carbon cycle. Each is at a crustal depth such that the combination of ground heat and the spindle-sun keeps it at an appropriate temperature. The mathematics are phenomenally complex."

August joined the conversation. "None of this works without spindle-sun tech. That keeps it all alive. It is nothing without those key technologies."

"Yes, of course," said Eler. "And in turn, those require vast amounts of power. Similarly, the water cycle requires desalination and desilting. It is not the purest system, but we try."

Oso-Rae continued, "I think you are trying to say that there is a flaw in us calling it a natural world when it is maintained by machines and gen-5 minds."

"True, I'm wondering about that," said August.

As Oso-Rae prepared to answer, they reached the cavern's terminus, and the train thrust forward into the murk of a roughly-hewn tunnel. Ren was suddenly aware that they were leaving the Rose Cavern, and that his swarm was incomplete. Some remained out on patrol, and they would be lost now unless they returned here. If the journey were to be long, the attrition rate would be high. Lesson learned. In future, he would be more sparing.

"We accept the intervention of technology," said Oso-Rae. "It's necessary for our mission. That doesn't prevent us from seeking sustainability and equilibrium.

"In this vein, we don't maintain clusters of human life in cities entirely separated from nature... a humanity clueless about the origins of their food, water and raw materials... a humanity oblivious to the destination of their waste." She was agitated.

"What, you all chop wood, gather berries and roast squirrels?" asked Kani. With a different tone, his question could have been amusing but instead, it was thick with ridicule.

Pretending that she hadn't registered his poisonous tone, Oso-Rae laughed and said, "Not quite. If every human had to be self-sufficient in food, then there would be no room for science, art, or thousands of other forms of specialisation. All this would die."

"You don't like cities, do you?" asked Ren.

"I like them from a distance, but not up close. I see beauty in architectural creativity and also in the potential for social design. Perhaps I would need to spend time in one to comment, but we are taught that they are humanity's worst invention and that they are at odds with nature."

"Well, 'humanity's worst invention' is ridiculous hyperbole," replied Ren, barely containing his exasperation.

Oso-Rae smiled weakly and then pouted with airy mock petulance. The conversation dwindled.

After a time, Imiko said, "Look, this isn't so unique. We have planets devoted to the natural world in the Hanseatic League too."

"You have theme parks for the rich," spat Saki. "Ordinary people know only concrete and steel."

"They live well enough, thank you very much," said Imiko, casually batting away his aggression.

Light loomed ahead, and they exited the tunnel into a new cavern. A cool, damp wind, heavy with the scent of pine and heather, streamed into the windowless carriage. There was little to see, as the cavern's rock wall stood on one side and an impenetrable forest blocked the view on the other.

Eler cut through the conversations and said, "Our route takes us past the Antipili Falls, the start of a water system that threads through dozens of caverns. From there we will continue downstream, passing through several caverns on the river's path. First stop in ten minutes."

Oso-Rae added, "Eler is the only one of us born and bred Jerichan, so he will be answering the more specific local questions. Or you could ask me, and I'll just make something up."

"Oh, and Ren, we're going to meet your ancestors," said Eler with a cheeky smile.

Ren just stared at him.

"Well, more accurately, we will pass through your father's home pod but not his cavern. It would be quite a detour, and they aren't quite ready to learn of your existence. It's all a bit much and they need time."

Ren was quietly relieved. He wasn't ready to meet them either, particularly with the gaze of this group on him.

Ten minutes was not always ten minutes, at least not exactly. Each world had its own natural cycles and synchronicities. Some turned on their axis in a few hours, some over several days, and a few not at all. There were those that orbited their star in days but others did so in years. A few had a moon that delivered a daily and monthly cycle of tides along with other more subtle influences. Others had no moon, or perhaps several, each with its sway over the mechanics of the world and those who inhabited it.

The established norm was to devise a local time system that made sense for each planet. These would have subdivisions relating to their local stellar orbit, rotational spin and lunar influences. However, within that, there was no escaping standard units of time like seconds and minutes, since so much of science required this. Nor could they escape the fundamental biological need for a waking-sleeping cycle that allowed for shockingly little flexibility. The fact was that some planets just glued on some fraction of an hour in the transition through midnight, and others had a local version of the hour, minute and second. Making all of that fit together neatly meant squashing or stretching things, so an hour was about an hour and a minute was about a minute. For someone touring between many worlds, circadian rhythms would certainly go to hell, causing nausea and general feelings of unwellness. It was a form of jet lag in triplicate.

Ren turned back to Oso-Rae. "How did you come to work for Central Control?"

"Oh, it isn't a job you apply for exactly. Children are identified at around eleven years old and put into a fast-track schooling system. They don't always stay in that stream – many drop out. It's an intense education, and you have to excel but also find belief in the central principles. You could be the smartest person in the room and still fail if you aren't there, heart and soul."

"And if you don't make the grade at eleven, is there any way of joining later?"

"There is a way, but it's difficult, because standard schooling moves at a very different pace."

"And then?"

"Then you are moved from your cavern, in Jericho terms, or sector, in Kraken terms, to a C-C university. Leaving your clan is a massive life change, and in many ways, we never return to them in the same form."

That sounded close to home. It made Ren remember his early life on Palau and the impossibility, or so it seemed now, of returning permanently. Perhaps that was what she meant; perhaps it was something else.

"So, at that point, you leave your sector?" he asked.

"There are a few sectors on Kraken – I'll speak about Kraken because that's where I'm from – given over to C-C activities. Several of these are almost entirely set up as universities, along with vocational academies.

"I studied foreign relations, but there are a multitude of other disciplines. That said, many courses of study that you might associate with university are not represented at all.

Medicine, architecture, most civil engineering, and so on are not relevant to Central Control, as they are not part of its remit. These studies exist, of course, but are operated locally."

"It does sound as though you move into an elite, learned class," said Ren. "Is it not an intellectual aristocracy – very much a 'them and us'?"

"You can paint it that way if you want, and in a way it is, but it's a model that works for us. Let's see how you feel about it after spending time here and getting to know us. We have both been taught to expect things of each other."

Ren didn't need to argue. Her response was reasonable, and it would all take time to unravel. It would take even longer to separate the official dogmatic lines from any deeper truth. That is what he was here for and what he genuinely sought. The conversation withered as the train slowed on its approach to Antipili's station, a place of simplicity and quiet discretion.

The station vicinity was enveloped in a copse of tall deciduous trees, heavy with lichen and epiphytes. Water was everywhere, dripping from leaves, running off branches and coursing in rivulets down the cavern walls. This space seemed mind-bendingly immense, even to those accustomed to habitat worlds. Its ceiling was an unreal canopy dizzyingly far above their heads. A waiting guide joined the group, diving straight into a practised monologue in the wooden style of those who repeat the same stock phrases day after day.

A steep path dropped away through the trees, beckoning them towards the thumping roar of water. Commentary was delivered in a local brogue that caused the translator to trip and fumble: an odd blend of dialect, new words and obscure humour. They understood enough to learn that this was, by a hair, the tallest waterfall on Jericho, tumbling over a kilometre and a half from the cavern roof. The resulting river snaked through dozens of downstream caverns, losing height as it went and so generating an unhurried natural flow. Far away at the river's terminus, a gateway gorged on the flowing water and spat it out back here, high up in the cavern roof. The lion's share was piped into the belly of a hydroelectric plant deep within, whilst a fraction thundered down for dramatic purposes and to help this damp microclimate prosper. This provided just enough power for the gateway and some excess for the habitat's systems. Energy for nothing. Of course.

Moments later, the path emerged from the trees, abruptly revealing the falls along with a view over the cavern's expanse. Thousands of tons of water tumbled vertically down to crash into a boiling, frothing pool at its base. There, the bedrock was stripped bare and the channel was worn into elegant curving swirls. Greenery clung on just feet away, eking out an existence in absurdly marginal clefts and ledges. Life was resolute.

Continuing down a winding path towards the river, the guide explained that the flow was seasonally modulated along with randomised adjustments to provide downstream ecosystems with natural cycles and undulations. Life thrived better in a cyclical and chaotic system. Perfect constancy seemed not to be the way of things.

Ren addressed a discreet question at Oso-Rae. "Is an ecosystem still an ecosystem when designed, guided, patrolled and managed by humans?"

He was struggling with her arrogant attachment to this core idea that she had called 'immutable and beyond debate.'

"What we do here isn't ideal, and yet it would not exist at all without intervention. We do what we have to do to keep it alive, but we leave as much as we can for nature to figure out on its own. Believe me, there are factions in the Arc that see this as some kind of deviant menagerie."

Ren dwelt awhile on that. So, there were factions of opinion and disagreement in the Arc. That was something.

"Isn't the truth of all this that you administer a giant vivarium?" asked Kani with predictable indelicacy.

Oso-Rae looked into his eyes but chose not to reply. He seemed more interested in stirring than obtaining an answer.

An awkward silence followed until Ren said, "Yesterday

you told us that Central Control has a limited remit and that you let the rest of society bubble away and do its own thing… or something like that. Why do you so loathe conventional government?"

"Being governed is an alienating experience for anyone in a minority," replied Oso-Rae. "You feel utterly unrepresented, and this is made doubly bad by the perception of those in the bland majority that it is fair and just. Furthermore, governments corrupt because power corrupts. This has been repeated for millennia, and we all know it to be true in our hearts."

There were two quite different points there and Ren wasn't sure which to start with. Both sounded an awful lot like textbook doctrine rather than personal opinion. It was an absurdly severe rebuke, but he had already come to expect hyperbole from these Arc'ers.

"You say that power corrupts, but it doesn't have to if you design the system well and ensure people can't endure in power. Yes, politics attracts those bigger egos, and the system is wrapped up in the battles of giant personalities. However, these people generally have good intentions in their hearts – people are fundamentally ethical. Power is not incompatible with good. The system works."

Oso-Rae appeared to listen but then seemed to go off-piste.

"It was once said that man was born free but everywhere he is in chains. Those who think themselves the masters of others are the most enslaved of all." She paused and turned to face him. "I haven't got the words quite right, but the gist is that there is a deep ethical corruption and self-delusion in those who see themselves as masters. The leaders, simply because of their popularity and position, give themselves the right to preach ethics, censor unwanted ideas, command all to their clumsy ideology, whether or not they have the intrinsic wisdom or virtue to match… Look at this flower."

That was Oso-Rae through and through. One moment she was in the midst of an impassioned speech and the next she seemed to have forgotten about it and was talking about flowers.

August pitched in, having been listening quietly on the sidelines until this point. Oso-Rae's intent had been to park the topic but he either hadn't detected that or didn't care.

"You have a dim view of people who seek power. I am surrounded by impressive people doing noble things for the constellation of systems. Yes, there is politics, but those fearless, arrogant leaders at least get things done."

Oso-Rae coiled and attacked. "Your leaders are chosen at a puerile auction – a banal talent show in which the skills required to construct a state do not feature. They are talkers and flatterers instead of philosophers, sociologists, scientists and economists."

"And yet it works better than anything yet devised by mankind," said Ren more calmly. "Anyway, you do have a government, so I don't understand why you pretend you don't. Perhaps you have the worst kind – one that pretends not to govern but behind the scenes is totalitarian and controls everything. It is the stuff of nightmares."

"You do like to wield that 'totalitarian' word freely. We have Central Control, which is not the kind of authority you might be accustomed to. It's more of a bureaucracy than a government. It administers the fundamental minimum that we can't do without or do locally. We shall see if you still think us to be autocratic when you have learned more."

With that, their feisty conversation lost steam, but Ren was sure that was not the end of it. Yet again, she had delivered her lines in an odd blend of academic formality and playfulness. It wasn't at all clear what she believed beyond the practised lines, but then again, it probably wasn't all that clear to her what he actually believed either. Shit, *he* barely knew. At any rate, that uncertainty mattered little, as they were both here to toe their party lines and to sound genuinely thrilled about it.

Their path followed an angry, frothing river as it descended steeply from the plunge pool at the waterfall's base. The water was milky and riddled with powerful eddies, but further on, the ravine flattened out and the river eased into a serene channel. At its edge stood a dock with a simple clinker boat tied up fore and aft. It was narrow in beam and flat-bottomed, with rowlocks for oars which lay flat inside. A boatman with leathery, calloused hands and a deeply creased face awaited them.

Eler turned to face them and said, "From here, we will follow the river. Please…"

And with that, he gestured them aboard.

Hessian ropes were cast off bollards on the dock and then coiled neatly. The boatman shifted to the stern and took up one of the oars, slotted it into a special rowlock over the transom, and pressed it into service as a rudder. They were heading downstream, drifting with the current. The boatman's only task was to maintain a course in the centre of the river. Not one word came from his mouth for the rest of the day.

Antipili was a special cavern, for reasons that extended far beyond its remarkable waterfall. Not a soul lived here, and other than the station, there were no buildings at all. This was a pristine, delicate boreal taiga biome. Away from the path were lynx, wolverine, silver fox, snowy owls and a few caribou and moose. Many of these creatures had a deeply uncomfortable relationship with mankind. They preferred to live in the depths of wilderness and scurried away at the slightest vibration from a human foot. Beyond this minuscule area on the cavern's margins, nobody trod.

"Purists find Jericho's wilderness zones problematic," explained Eler. "Our hands are tied when it comes to accommodating the more exotic species, as there simply isn't room for packs of wolves, roaming bears, sea eagles and migratory salmon. Planets like Kraken do provide such possibilities, but Jericho never will. We are forced to mould the food chain around alternative apex predators."

Forest tumbled down through boulder fields to flat, boggy ground where silver birch thinned to gnarled stumps. Higher up, the birch blended with spruce and pine along with dead trees lying at messy angles. In a clearing stood a moose next to a calf so young that it still wobbled on awkward, slender legs.

Eler continued, "We are in late summer here, and the spindle-sun is already dimming for the coming winter. Snow will come for almost half the year."

"What?" asked Imiko. "You spray the place with ice and pretend it is natural?"

"We all fill rocks with air and call them home, don't we?" replied Saki. "In a way, we are all in zoos of our own making. We are not complicit in some subterfuge."

"Are you not playing God?"

"I don't really know what you mean by 'playing God,'" said Eler. "We can either do this or allow species to perish and be consigned to the phalanx of the extinct. To us, the distinction between 'playing God' and custodianship is clear." He practically spat the words out to show his distaste for Imiko's question.

"What are the limits of intervention?" asked August. "Is there population control? Do you sustain species that struggle to keep their collective head above water? Do you suppress disease?"

"When we are obliged to intervene in any of those areas, we see it as a failure, and yet we certainly have to… more often than we would like. On the other hand, we have to remember that these species appeared in very specific niches long ago in response to exact local conditions. We haven't given nature time to adapt to all these new worlds and find its place. There is rapid evolutionary adaption but 'rapid' in evolutionary terms is still the scale of centuries… or even millennia."

They had drifted downstream for some kilometres, but now approached the cavern's end wall. Rounding a bend, the trees gave way, the river narrowed, and on a strengthening current, the boat plunged into a hole in the rock face. They were carried into the dank semi-darkness of a tunnel but soon returned to the intense brightness of a new cavern.

Eler turned back to his running commentary. "This is the start of the Kandahar Cavern system, and the first ordinary habitat you will see on Jericho. Here there is a mix of human life and nature in a ratio dictated by Central Control. At least half must be given over to wilderness, a quarter to light-touch agrarian and forestry, and a quarter to more intensive farmland and dwellings.

"Here, the hub is at the top – it's usually one end or the other – to put some distance between people and the wilder parts. The cavern wall is also a natural truncation point."

They swept past a shield of trees screening the river's exit, before rounding a bend into a hub of activity. Low ground near the riverbank was scattered with conical buildings raised on stilts. Their structures were formed by bamboo inlaid with woven panels, and each was encircled by a terrace. Roofs were formed from overlapping pads that spiralled down from an apex. Grassy open ground was studded with small ornamental trees and interwoven with a network of paths.

The backdrop was a chaos of interconnected boxes, cupolas and arches, all clinging to and seeming to tumble down the cavern wall in adobe style. Everything was whitewashed in perfect alabaster, with window frames and doors painted in lustrous blues and greens. Steep paths wound between the buildings and up into the precarious heights. Beyond, they threaded their way into the rock to a network of tunnels within.

Dozens of people went about their business, oblivious to the passing boat and its cargo of off-worlders.

Detecting the question in Ren's gaze, Oso-Rae said, "No, this is not where you're from, but I'll be sure to tell you when we get there.

"This is a fairly typical settlement for Jericho, although building styles are varied, as are the types of communities they house. The fundamental piece of social structure here and in the other planets and habitats of the Arc is the 'clan.'"

"What's a clan?" asked Ren. He knew of the concept from his parents but wanted to hear the formal answer.

"Your societies focus on the nuclear family in which children are raised and sheltered by biological or adoptive parents. In ours, people live collectively in a clan containing fifty to a hundred individuals. Members of a clan live amongst one another in a highly comingled way. Children are raised collectively and roam freely around the clan houses. We believe that this approach is more attuned to the primal instincts of humanity and provides a far richer environment for children."

"Where did this come from? It can't have self-evolved."

"It only took a little push to make it happen, because people are attuned to that manner of living from our tribal pre-history."

Ren had never bought into the notion that humanity was fundamentally palaeolithic and hadn't moved beyond that. Why would we have stopped evolving? Why should we romanticize that epoch?

"If you say so."

Ignoring the doubt in Ren's voice, Oso-Rae continued. "Meals are prepared and eaten collectively. This forms part of the clan's bond but also helps with sourcing food and managing waste."

Ren's mind leapt to thoughts of failed communes and their obscure, cultish ways. It seemed implausible that a society might quickly and naturally adopt this form of living. How could it be so natural if every other planet chose a conventional path? It was a puzzle, and it didn't connect with his understanding of human nature.

"Forgive me, Oso-Rae, but I need help with this. Earlier you said that, outside the narrow influence of Central Control, communities were free to organise themselves as they see fit, but a unified system of clans and communal living seems to be a world away from that anarchism."

"Firstly, I never used the word anarchism," said Oso-Rae.

"You just threw it in there... why, I'm not sure. All I did was describe the failure of your system in representing minorities and the dysfunctional way you choose leaders. Secondly, they are free to organise themselves as they see fit, within certain boundaries."

"Fair enough. But how can the clan be a standard model of society when people are free to structure themselves however they want? How can billions of people suddenly choose to re-order themselves on this model, in the presence of this spectacular liberty?"

"We didn't forcibly transform communities," she explained calmly. "The physical and social aspects were designed over a long period of time. When people finally moved in, their lives naturally wrapped around those structures. There was no revolution. In truth, it used to be more diverse, but over time society has coalesced around a few fairly standard models."

Ren found it hard to accept that so many people would consistently choose to live this way without coercion. It wasn't the time to make that accusation, so he parked the thought and instead asked a related question.

"There is an old saying from prehistory: I against my brothers. I and my brothers against my cousins. I and my brothers and my cousins against the world."

"I have heard something like that before," said Oso-Rae.

"The adage has survived for millennia because it contains a simple truth. We are defined by these concentric rings of loyalty. Ours (in the CPF) goes quite quickly from family to nation to planet to league. What's yours? Is it clan – cavern – planet – Arc? Where in all of that is the rivalry? Where is the conflict? For it seems to be an immovable truth that mankind cannot exist without those things."

Oso-Rae replied, "There is a little friendly rivalry between clans but rarely more than that, as they have to cooperate in so many fundamental areas of their daily lives. Occasionally we witness social collapse due to conflict, and in those situations, we help manage splits and migrations. The principal rivalry is between caverns and pods – that's a collection of caverns – in areas such as sport, resources and so on. Competition between planets within the Arc doesn't exist at all. We ensure that the structures are balanced and of a size that makes war difficult and pointless.

"We believe that nations and nationalism are spectacularly stupid. They are arbitrary things propagated by governments to coerce their populations – they keep the populace dumb and distracted. Nothing in history has generated such staggering amounts of wasted human effort. And don't get me started on wars and entrenched poverty."

"I agree with you to some extent," said Ren. "It's true that governments use nationalism to distract the masses from more important internal strife, but people need a sense of cultural belonging. We don't exist in an infinite sea of human ubiquity."

Oso-Rae countered, "But nations are in a false state of competition because a nation of two billion people will always overwhelm one of five million. There is no balance at all, and bullying becomes the accepted norm. It's just a numbers game."

"Well, these structures aren't pre-defined. They appear over the course of millennia and are instructed by ancient ethnicity, religion, conflict and language. We can't just redraw the map on a whim. Firstly, no country would just sub-divide, and secondly, it would leave isolated and disenfranchised communities. You can't dictate identity."

"Oh, Ren, we are going to have some fun with this, aren't we? I particularly look forward to you converting your people back home when I have finally won you over."

"Ha! When pigs fly."

"The translator copes well with your strange metaphors."

And she smiled, as always. This was confusing because she could seem so severe in mid-sentence and then defuse it all with a cocky grin at the end. What did this woman believe?

Food parcels were distributed. Each was wrapped in a palm

leaf and tied with string. Within were delicately pretty morsels. At least the flavours and textures were accessible, so Ren did not have to suffer the wretched nastiness of some planets' culinary output. There was plenty of citrus, modest spice, and vegetables he couldn't place.

"This is delicious, thank you," said Imiko. "I have to ask, though... do you eat meat?"

"I do not personally," replied Oso-Rae, "but I think that you meant the collective 'you.' Oh, this gets complicated, Imiko. How long have you got?"

"Isn't there a short version?"

"Not really, but I'll try to compress it. Sectors and pods are diverse in their attitudes. Some are militantly vegan, and this can create a cultural wall with those that are not."

"What does Central Control have to say about it?" asked Kani.

"Central Control doesn't dictate a policy because it's not within their remit."

The township was dissipating as they continued downstream on the current. Beyond were farmed lands, but not of the type they were accustomed to outside the Arc. In place of the large fields of monoculture found on Palau and Marrakesh were highly diversified plots. Small patches of root vegetables lay between capsicum and tomato, some overhung by sparsely planted fruit trees of cherry, pear and peach. These were just some of the species that Ren could make a reasonable guess at, but there were dozens he had no idea about.

"This cavern feels different," said Imiko, "...warmer, and the plants and trees have changed. Are these abrupt transitions normal?"

"Yes, this cavern is temperate," replied Eler, "and the previous one was taiga. With caverns, you can make each unique. It's usually a more gradual transition but still much faster than on a planet. The difficulty is the river, as water temperature changes very gradually. We end up with a disconnect between the water life and the land life, but who is to say what is normal anymore? So long as life thrives."

"I'm surprised to hear you say that. I would expect you to be obsessive about matching them."

"There are factions of opinion on that."

Cave habitats were not some unique invention of the Arc, so they did not need a tedious explanation of how they were burrowed and formed. The difference was that not one within the Core Planets Federation put such intense focus on the natural world. Most were a teeming morass of humanity with only a few areas of meagre parkland. The majority of food was either imported, vat-grown, or derived from intensive monoculture.

Without an abrupt, fenced line between farmland and forest, the crops blended gradually into larger fruit and nut trees, which in turn transitioned into forest. Even past the point where it became wilderness, it was not the end of human presence. People roamed the forest paths, foraging, picking wild fruit, or occupied with a host of other errands. On the water, a handful of fishermen cast throw-nets from their canoes.

This peaceful, meandering journey continued, with the boat simply drifting on the flow. Everyone was at ease. August reclined, his face arched up to the spindle-sun. Imiko chatted casually, avoiding strong opinions or entrenched Hanseatic positions, at least for now. Kani, a man who never appeared all that relaxed, seemed lost in the moment too. His brow unfurrowed a tiny bit.

Ren had noted several words that the translators had given up on, but a conversation was often enough to tease out their meaning. Many turned out to be newly coined, some with an easy equivalent, but others, dense with cultural meaning, evaded clear translation.

He recalled the words of Professor Deovski, who had said that only by enmeshing yourself in a society and learning the language natively can you gain a true understanding of these seemingly untranslatable words. She described that magical moment when they finally click. According to her, cultural identity and even the perception of reality were entirely wrapped in the language used. To understand a people, one must understand their language.

On the left, a large river merged to join the main flow, and a little further on, another came in from the right. The tributaries' upstream paths led to apertures in the cavern's side walls. These gaping holes, easily a couple of hundred metres across, were windows into neighbouring caverns.

Following their gazes and sensing questions forming, Eler explained, "Those are connections to other caverns in the Kandahar pod. A single space can support a population of under five hundred, so that's five to ten clans. We therefore connect something like a hundred and forty individual caverns into clusters called 'pods.' These provide collective populations of about fifty thousand – a sensible number for administration and services."

"And small enough to prevent political mobilisation," muttered August quietly to Ren.

Eler continued, "Caverns are limited in size, simply due to the structural limits of the rock and the possibility of collapse. We heat-treat the entire periphery to create a strong shell, but in the end, inviolate physics dictates the maximum length and breadth."

"How big are they?" asked Ren.

"Typically, about eight kilometres long by two wide. That's a roughly standard format. Antipili is as large as it is only because of the local integrity of the rock.

"The pod structure is on a twelve-by-twelve grid. Most are populated like this one, but we allocate a fraction to pure nature, large lakes, power generation and industry. Since they are openly connected, they are always of a common ecosystem."

"We're following a line through the middle of the grid," said Saki. He gestured to the left, adding, "Up that way are more conventional caverns along with a gateway hub." Then, turning to the right, he said, "And up this way there's a small industrial complex and a military facility."

It was time to go fishing, so Ren let loose a fraction of his swarm. He could almost feel the tiny machines leave his body and head out into the cavern. He wanted to know if physical reality matched their description. Little lies might imply that there were bigger lies.

As the day progressed, they were carried through more of Kandahar's caverns. Each was separated by a gaping window, just like those forming the lateral links.

Eler returned to his commentary. "The narrow tunnel we passed through on leaving Antipili is standard between pods, as it provides isolation between one ecosystem and the next... and between human groups or cultures."

Finally, at the bottom of the fourth cavern, the river emptied into a wide lake where, freed from the stronger current, the boat slowed. Moving forward from his steering position in the stern, the boatman began rowing towards a settlement fringing the lake. He pulled hard for a few strokes before coasting in to rest at Maputo's jetty.

Its structure followed a now-familiar pattern with a few houses around the lakeshore, backed by a rising, tumbling adobe core. As with all of Kandahar's towns, the buildings were whitewashed and trimmed with colour. From a square by the lake, steep cobbled paths wound upwards into Maputo's heights.

This was the end of the day's journey, and they were to rest for the night at a guesthouse right on the square. It was a simple building without signage, staff or any of the other embellishments that might mark a hotel. The ground floor was a seating area with a kitchen set around a covered courtyard. Upstairs were bedrooms and a communal washing area, all accessed from a balcony overlooking the central courtyard.

Towards evening, August and Ren walked back across the

square to a park near the dock, where they sat by the water on a rickety bench. The townsfolk kept a respectful distance, and beyond a few quizzical glances, they were left in peace. The visitors were a source of mild fascination, but they were not grand celebrities. What struck Ren most was a universal meekness and humility.

"That was one for the bucket list, wasn't it?" said Ren. "At least I'll have something to tell bored barmen. Not sure what the hell is going on though."

"Me neither," said August. "I suppose they're revealing themselves little by little. There's nothing stupendously radical about this." He gestured around at the space. "Caverns have been burrowed this way for a thousand years. Spindle-suns aren't that remarkable; they just require huge amounts of power."

"Superficially it seems that they want us to understand their culture and society, and cease to see it as a threat. But there must be more to it than that," said Ren.

What he was thinking was, *It's alright for you. I have to decide whether the Arc represents tolerable eccentricity or subversive danger, and act accordingly. You're already on your path, whatever that may be.* Would his axe have to come out for the Arc, or was it destined for another purpose? He wondered at the absence of any automatic loyalty to this place in the name of his ancestry. Would it have been possible for his parents to keep that identity alive without the wide support of an expatriate community? Did the biology of birth matter at all?

"Some red flags were raised today," said August. "Central Control is evidently an elite ruling class, despite their pretence that it isn't. And who the hell organises themselves into clans voluntarily?"

Ren chose not to reply. He knew that August might be right, but he had to come to his own conclusions, and it would not help matters to feed the fire of August's suspicions.

He continued, "After fifty years of isolation, they take us

on a train ride and a boat trip. Fine, they want us to see them for who they are, or at least paint a romantic portrait of that identity. But what's next? What's the game?"

Ren suspected that August's purpose was misaligned with his own, but he could not even begin to guess at what that purpose might be.

"We have no choice but to take it at face value and continue the tour. Our duty is to be open-minded, question without being overbearing, and seek the truth."

"I suppose that's true," said August without conviction before standing and taking his leave.

Ren remained for a time, listening to the flow of water and leaves stirring in a light breeze. A path followed the river downstream, disappearing into darkness a hundred metres distant. Two figures emerged from the gloom, talking earnestly. He recognised Kani and Imiko from their gaits long before he was able to see their faces. On the fringes of town, instead of walking into the public spaces of the square, they ducked into a side street that led back towards their rooms. They were not behaving like two people from rival leagues who only met days before. This *was* interesting.

In his room, Ren sat and pondered the situation. What were those two up to? They were evidently colluding in something. He knew in that moment that Astrid's instincts were right. There *was* an insertion, and both were involved.

He turned his attention to the conversation with August. The truth was that they were broadly in agreement. The practised, rigid credo of the Arc'ers was, without doubt, a red flag. In his experience, such dogma was often a feature of societies that had stopped thinking and had no capacity for change. But there was a quirky playfulness to their tone that helped to paint them in a softer light. He sent a message to Astrid, briefly summarising these observations. Encryption or no encryption, it was a simple matter to disguise his thoughts in ordinary words.

Just as sleep started to beckon, the drones he had sent out earlier began to reappear. There was no physical sensation to mark their return, but the control panel displayed the news of their arrival. And they showed precisely what the Arc'ers had said they would. Deep inside the Kandahar caverns was a gateway hub, a small industrial complex and what appeared to be the entrance to a military base – nothing more and nothing less than they had been told.

With their data digested, he quickly repurposed them to scour the forest in the direction of Kani and Imiko's outing and sent them back into the night.

Chapter 12

Mu Rosa Drinks a Margarita

Laynna Mu Rosa was lounging by the pool with a margarita, awaiting a surprising and intriguing visitor.

Her yacht, *Anger Management*, was at anchor. She was listed as a 'pleasure craft' in the vessel registry, as were all non-commercial or military vessels. It was a largely pointless category, since all vessels here were pleasure craft except for a few tour boat services, along with some game-fishing launches for those who could afford such archaic and extravagant pastimes. The problem with the semantics of this category was that it gave no hint at the grandiose monstrosity of the ship. At almost three hundred metres in length and two hundred in width, it was the largest in service on Cervantes, and that was saying something, since this planet existed for one purpose only: as the playground of the Hanseatic League's rich, powerful, arrogant and entitled.

She required four satellite hydrofoils to rise out of the water and so achieve her full cruise capability of sixty knots. At lower speeds, these retracted to hug the hull, enabling her to cruise into shallower waters. The ride was as smooth as butter, even in a big swell. It was entirely possible to hold a full martini glass without spilling a drop whilst caning the engines at full

151

power.

The vast deck was a hotel in itself with several restaurants, a cinema, sports facilities and a nightclub. Staff quarters, rigidly separated from the rest, provided accommodation for over a hundred cleaners, waiters, chefs, butlers, maintenance staff and crew. For the sake of appearances, her owner had been advised against the chosen name, but frankly, she didn't give a crap. She gave fewer than zero craps.

Today she was at anchor in Peaceful Bay, a stunning natural harbour garlanded by wooded hills of juniper and cypress. The bay was on an island named Constanta, one of tens of thousands in an archipelago that stretched over a quarter of this planet's sphere. Its patchwork of interconnected seas, channels and islands made it ideal for this form of leisure. And leisure was the entire economy of Cervantes, a planet that sat firmly in the Hanseatic League's dominion. Their principal planets had a tendency towards staggeringly large populations, making land too valuable for parks, forests or scenic holiday destinations. The solution, one that really only made sense to the Hanseatics, was to dedicate a few planets to just this purpose. Don't eat where you shit. Of course, this also made them ludicrously expensive, so only the uber-rich had any prospect of coming here. The poor... well, who cares? Let them eat cake.

Mu Rosa was director of Genesis, the largest trans-planetary corporate in existence by a mile. Indeed, it was the largest company that had ever existed and had clung on to this ranking for four hundred years. Genesis's influence hung over many planets in the Hanseatic League, but its notional headquarters was on a planet called Orinoco, a backwater run as a private fiefdom.

Deep in the bowels of the ship, a gateway came to life, expanding to admit a lone visitor. Of course, individuals were not generally permitted to own private gateways, but this was the Hanseatic League, this was Genesis, and this was Laynna Mu Rosa. She could do whatever the hell she wanted. The visitor was Alian Banz of UCoM, and this was a rare visit by a

Core General into Hanseatic territory.

He was escorted to the deck and delivered to Mu Rosa's poolside by an almost mute servant who backed away, bowing in excruciating humility.

Banz, although accustomed to a degree of luxury, was astounded by the obscenity of Mu Rosa's excesses. Not that it mattered. Today he was putting those sentiments aside in order to come here and strike a deal with the devil herself on her ridiculous yacht.

"General Banz, how lovely to see you, darling."

Mu Rosa called everyone 'darling,' but there was not a shred of endearment in the word. She had a dark heart and the social delicacy of an angry leopard.

"Well, this is rather grand, isn't it?" said Banz, gazing around. "Why can't Astrid arrange meetings in places like this?"

"General, you called this meeting, not me. Anyway, that miserable scheming bitch can meet where she wants. She patronises and plays me for a fool," spat Mu Rosa. "Come on, Alian. I haven't got all day, and this margarita will not drink itself. What brings you here?"

"I have a proposal you might find appealing."

"How intriguing. Shall we disable implants?"

Implants brought startling benefits, but discretion was problematic. Anyone might be recording anything, frankly. A 'disabled' status was locally broadcast, allowing words to be exchanged more freely.

"I am aware that you have insertion missions in three of the Archipelago's systems and a fourth to Bathsheba that failed."

Quite how Banz had discovered this, he didn't reveal, but this time Mu Rosa didn't bother to deny it. The precision of his information made it pointless.

"And..." said Mu Rosa.

"Astrid is making a mistake in trusting this to dialogue," began Banz. "We need to be ready to take control of the

Archipelago. There are times when gunboat diplomacy is the only way."

"Oh, we aren't planning military action, Alian. Even if we were, what could you possibly offer in support?" asked Mu Rosa.

"I know that a successful, clean invasion requires several factors to come together. One is excellent coverage of all the relevant planets, and on that front you may be in a strong position so long as your people gain access. Then you require ultra-precise targeting based on solid ground intelligence. I imagine that Kani and Imiko are carrying a boatload of tech, and that will help. The third is that you'll find it difficult to subdue the habitats without gateway access to their interiors."

"Go on..." said Mu Rosa.

"You have your insertions, and I have my man, August, and the tech he carries with him... tech that could transform the situation."

Mu Rosa seemed unconvinced. "What tech could you possibly have that we don't have?"

"We have miniaturised idle gateways to the sub-millimetre scale. At that size there's no detectable radiation signature. August carries around two hundred with him."

Mu Rosa's eyes widened, the implications immediately clear to her. If this were true, it gave them access to the interiors of Jericho and Typhon. That made an invasion not just possible but achievable, and within weeks.

"And how are they powered? There's the inescapable fact of their power requirements."

"We have two possible approaches. One is to seed them next to existing Arc gateways. In the right moment they become parasitic and steal power... hiding in plain sight, so to speak."

"And the second?" asked Mu Rosa.

"That is to put them somewhere discreet, and over time they build their own power plant. It takes around two weeks."

"That's genuinely impressive, Alian. And what do *you* get

from this?"

"On one level, I don't need anything more than the satisfaction of knowing it is the better course of action." Banz was quiet for a few seconds and Mu Rosa let the silence run, sensing that he hadn't finished.

"...But there's more."

"I thought there might be," said Mu Rosa, a smile creasing the corner of her mouth.

"You know me as a General of UCoM," he said with some pomposity, "but that is just a position, and my primary allegiance is to Helsingor. We no longer see our future with Core, and I propose switching sides to the Hanseatics."

Divided loyalty was a flaw within the Core Planets Federation and the bane of UCoM's existence. Banz's presence here was a shining example of that dysfunction. His loyalty to UCoM was a trivial thing when compared to that of his home planet. Core had no military of its own. Instead, it was lent units by member planets under a form of feudal fealty.

He continued, "How would the Congregation of Populated Systems look with the Hanseatic League beefed up by Helsingor and the Arc? Do the maths. The balance of power would be rewritten."

She stared at him for some seconds and then laughed. "Darling, I didn't see that coming. We would be detonating a political bomb."

"Core is winning, Laynna... Little by little your influence is reduced."

She knew the situation. Helsingor was one of the more powerful entities in Core, but the irony of CPF membership was that it contained and constrained the accrual of further power. They strove for balance and an equality of sorts between planets. Helsingor's government had started to feel held back and resentment was building.

"And you would want a seat at the High Table..." said Mu Rosa. She was negotiating now, and Banz knew he had her attention.

"I think two seats would be fair," he said.

The Hanseatic League was administered by a handful of its most powerful entities. Some were corporates, others were planets or habitats, and in some cases, those two things were hard to distinguish. The High Table was where the elite of the elite convened and ruled.

Mu Rosa threw it back at him. "You're fucking kidding me. You don't get two seats. You're on crack."

The merger couldn't occur without representation at the High Table. Why suffer the chaos if only to become a junior member of the Hanseatic League?

"Fine, one. But if I bring Colomba and Alegre with us, it's two."

These were close neighbours in a loose alliance with Helsingor. Where Helsingor went, they might well follow.

With that, it all clicked into place for Mu Rosa. "You have a deal, General Banz. I will convene the High Table for a formal decision, but you can assume it's done. Select parts of this will need to be conveyed to Little Mouse, so as to justify your involvement. I'm looking forward to seeing Astrid's face."

"Hell hath no fury…" said Banz. "We should sell tickets to that show."

"You will have to come and stay on the yacht as my guest when it's all done."

"That would be lovely."

It was garbage, of course. She was not actually inviting him, and Banz wouldn't dream of coming. They were empty words. Mu Rosa waved him away with a cheeky, arrogant little flip of the hand. As he returned to the gateway, *Anger Management* weighed anchor, coasted out to the channel, and then let the engines rip.

Mu Rosa had cocktails and a dinner appointment on a friend's yacht, and that meant burning down the gulf to Thaki, a neighbouring island of unparalleled beauty. Conventional hulls were restricted to twenty knots to prevent their wash from damaging beach houses and disturbing children at play in the shallows. The wonder of this craft's hydrofoils was that they generated little wash, so she could open up the throttle once out in the channel. Being allowed to travel at three times the speed of ordinary mortals suited Mu Rosa just fine.

While the yacht manoeuvred, she summoned Commander Palina.

"Get here immediately. The mission has changed."

Chapter 13

Under the Spreading Banyan Tree

Ren sat at the riverside waiting for the day to start. He watched mesmerised as a tiny, semi-translucent grasshopper crawled along his sleeve. It stood out like a bright green jewel against the white fabric. From the forest beyond came the grating, unmusical screeching of bickering macaws.

This morning it was immediately and abundantly clear that he was immersed in a haze of melancholia. He had suffered from this seemingly unstoppable cycle for as long as he could remember, so to an extent, it was his normal. That said, acceptance didn't make the moment any easier. His condition was not truly debilitating, but some days took on a starkly desolate shade. There was no rhyme or reason to it – seeming to correlate with nothing else in his life – but it seemed unnecessarily cruel that it should arrive now.

Ren's new mood left him with a problem, as it did not fit well with discovery, debate, negotiation, or sober analysis. He would have to dig deep to find the diligence and enthusiasm required, and deeper still to find his signature charm and disarming smile – those tools that helped make hard words sound kind.

Archipelago

This morning there was a journey to continue, and at least that might offer some reprieve from the affliction of this bleak spirit. Today's journey, he was told, would also take him home, or at least to what his father once called 'home', but for now, he remained entirely emotionally detached from that fact.

The drones had returned from their nocturnal hunt without finding anything conclusive. Hints, yes. Smoking gun, no. For now he only had his suspicion.

At the dock, the slender wooden boat and its gnarled boatman had been replaced by a larger craft. They clambered aboard and in almost complete silence, it surged forward into the lake, leaving a gentle wake behind.

Eler explained, "We have several lakes to cross and require a powered boat, as the flow is gentle. We are heading through to a downstream pod called Kawazu."

The lake's distant edge butted right up against the cavern wall, where it shelved off to invisible depths. There was a single, narrow aperture – the only blemish on an otherwise sheer, uninterrupted wall. Barely slowing, the boat approached and then surged forward into the murk of a tunnel, just like the one that had carried them from Antipili to Kandahar.

They powered through and soon punched out into the dazzling daylight and heavy tropical humidity of Kawazu Caverns. Soaring hardwoods with buttressed roots grew right down to the water's edge. Creepers and epiphytic ferns hung from branches over the river. Neon kingfishers darted about, occasionally with a flash of silver in their beaks. A few stick-thin palms shot up high above the forest canopy. This was mature tropical rainforest.

Oso-Rae looked over at Ren and said, "Welcome home, Ren. The Kawazu pod was your father's home."

Ren had no ready reply and turned away so that the others could not see his face or read his emotions. He gazed at the jungle and searched for familiarity. Could he really find identity here?

Eler spoke again. "This is a radically different ecosystem to Kandahar. We are now in a tropical arboreal habitat. There are only ninety kilometres from here to the falls, but with caverns, the biological gradient can be steep."

"You may not have noticed it, but as we went through the last tunnel, we passed through an emergency screen. There is always some remote possibility of catastrophic structural failure – perhaps a meteor piercing the crust to depth, or even a deliberate attack. We thus require the ability to protect neighbouring caverns. In such an event, the screen would drop, sealing the tunnel and the river."

"Has this happened?" asked Ren. "Have you had to use them?"

"Only once, several decades ago. It was due to flaws in the rock strata that hadn't been properly stabilised. The roof caved in, and its atmosphere was lost in a moment. It blasted through the pod like a hurricane, stripping the land bare. Thousands died, and an ecosystem was ruined… frozen. We learned."

In the Kandahar pod, the town usually came first, followed by farmland and then a stretch of wilderness. Here it began with the wild part, so for the first stretch of their journey in Kawazu, they cruised past a screen of impenetrable forest. Spider monkeys played raucously in trees at the river's edge. Flocks of hyacinth macaws streaked past overhead, and the insects of the forest screeched, chirped and whined in a ceaseless cacophony.

A scattering of mirror-flat oxbow lakes lay to each side of the river's main flow. These had not been formed over time through natural, weaving erosion. Like so much here, they were an artificial creation catering to the needs of an ecosystem. Quiet pools provided a refuge for the many species of fish that only thrived in dark, peaty waters such as these. A host of birds nested, hunted and roosted in trees around the lakes. The snouts of black caiman protruded from shallows.

The first signs of human activity came with breaks in the forest where coffee plants grew between groves of cacao. Modest plots of corn bordered squash, cassava and citrus.

Towards boggier ground, papaya flourished. With a connection, his implant would have identified the other crops, but without he could only guess. Plots of maize filled a few dozen square metres; it could not be further from the monoculture of Palau where fields stretched to the horizon and beyond.

Further along, a scattering of buildings appeared, gradually developing into the cavern's town. In place of Kandahar's colourful flair were muted browns and greens. The buildings were airier and lighter, with slender flying buttresses and delicate arches.

As they gazed at the clusters of houses, Ren asked, "Who owns property here? Is it the clan or the individual? Tell me about how all that works."

"Ha! I barely know where to start with that question," said Oso-Rae. "First of all, clans are a social structure as opposed to a legal entity, so they don't 'own' anything. Furthermore, since the clan system is not universal, it doesn't work to have them as legal bodies.

"But more importantly... do you really not know this? We completely reject the ownership of land, of space, and of rock and soil, all of which seem to us to be both ridiculous and dangerous."

"You what?" said Ren.

"It's strange to think of things that are intrinsic to us and alien to you. If you bother to stop and think about it, property ownership is absurd. I wonder who first enclosed a patch of land, called it their own, and found people simple enough to accept it. Whoever it was, they set a ball rolling that has swept across the planets, leaving a trail of misery, war, horror and environmental destruction."

Ren looked at her, trying to determine if she was serious or playing. It was extraordinarily hard to tell with Oso-Rae, but she continued in the same vein.

"We have seen its absurdity and corruption for what it is and thrown it away. How can land belong to one person when the world belongs to us all and a myriad of creatures who have no say and no voice?"

"Come on, property is the foundation of a highly functioning society," replied Ren. "It delivers economic prosperity, security and resilience. It can provide a ladder out of poverty, food security, and it helps motivate those who work the land. This is a profound human need and has been an anchor for society's development."

"Well, you asked, and that is our view of private property. It is a terrible human arrogance."

"Okay, I get it," said Ren. "Well, I don't, but I accept your explanation. But how does housing work? How do you acquire a place to live? Who pays for its construction, maintenance and repair?"

"There isn't much construction anymore. The burrowing of most caverns was completed a long time ago, so most of the time they are just doing simple repairs. Pods can access burrowing machines, leased from Central Control at a modest cost. These things are self-replicating and inexpensive, but we avoid waste by centralising it."

"So that's another thing that C-C does. So much for the existential minimum."

Oso-Rae said, "Sure, but it's difficult to create a workable system without central planning. It would be chaos without. If you are planning centrally, then it makes sense to allocate machinery in the same way."

"If you say so."

She continued, "With a static population, it boils down to the replacement of worn elements and some rebuilding, generally using local materials.

"I don't want to give the impression that we have swapped private property for collectivism, because that is not the case. Individuals can pay for a better dwelling and to improve existing homes, so long as it fits in with the overall strategy for the cavern. They pay a form of rent for the right to use that space and live there. That rent is essentially a form of taxation, and no individual or group owns it."

"It is human nature to strive to be successful," said Ren, "and with that success, you purchase privilege. For us, that means buying a nicer house, in a better area, with a superior view or a bigger garden."

"You can pay more for a better place to live, but you also have to remember your place within the clan and society. People here don't live in isolation or worship at the altar of the individual. But, at the end of the day, some clans and some individuals are wealthier than others, at least by our measure... probably not by yours."

"So, owning property or not owning property seems to be almost the same thing. It sounds like smoke and mirrors."

"Perhaps, but the difference is fundamental to us in terms of our attitude towards the spaces we inhabit and the rights of other species within it."

Ren was confounded. It fit no category and the accepted political classifications seemed not to apply. He knew it would be wiser to put aside the labels, but it was more problematic than that. People didn't just choose paths like this. They were imposed.

He let the exchange fizzle out and switched his attention to Kani and Eler, who were deep in conversation.

"I think you said that a pod was around fifty thousand people. That suggests that around six or seven hundred people are born and die each year."

"That's about right."

"That, in turn, means that approximately that number enter and leave school each year. It doesn't sound like enough to support specialisation: medicine, teaching, and so on."

"You're quite right. Populations of this size are enough for teaching common trades but not for specialised vocational colleges. For this reason, pods are themselves clustered into super-pods of around twenty with the specialisations spread between them. One big institution covering everything is difficult to accommodate in a cavern system."

Kani asked, "What if you want to go somewhere completely different to study… or live, for that matter?"

"The only way you can go far away to study is if you're in the Central Control stream or another highly specialised domain. Otherwise, it isn't a common thing. You can leave your cavern or pod, but it requires an application to be accepted. Reasons might be a falling out, a romance, or a particular passion for another pod's environment or speciality."

"Speciality?"

"It's the same as with education," replied Eler. "Some things are too specialised to be represented everywhere. So if you build trains for a living or design computer systems or work on a rare illness, then you will almost certainly need to migrate to achieve this."

"But if you're a carpenter and you want a new start?"

"You can make your case and hope you are accepted."

"And if you want to move to Kraken or Typhon?"

"There are migrations, both individual and larger units, but we don't have a highly mobile population in the Arc. People become very attached to their local environment. Such moves are quite eccentric."

"And what if you just walk out one day and take a gateway to another pod?" asked Kani. "What stops you from just going?"

Eler looked awkwardly at Saki, who stepped in, saying, "People just don't do that in the Arc. They wouldn't. They couldn't. It would be weird, subversive, and it's simply not socially acceptable."

They had left the boat and were resting in the shade of a spreading tree in the town square of Wakaba. Ren was out of sorts. A part of him felt an immediate connection with this pod, but he knew that might be nothing more than the psychology of expectation. It was a stunning place and easy to like, but that didn't mean there was some intrinsic bond.

Ren took his leave from the group and spent time wandering the winding, cobbled streets. He listened to the lilt of dialect, absorbed the pungency of market stalls and looked deeply into people's eyes. A group of old men sat at a café's outdoor table, grumbling and arguing in the way that old men do. He could just about picture his father sitting amongst them, but he could not imagine the same of himself. *If I'm not from Palau, not from Marrakesh or here, where am I from?*

It was hot, and Ren retreated into the shade of their hostel. The group was due to gather later, and until then, Ren passed time in the calming enclave of his terrace with only a cool drink and his thoughts. Wakaba's accommodation was modest, but his terrace presented a view over the town's rooftops and the mass of trees beyond. A shadow of ennui was all that remained of the morning's deeper melancholy. It had been a miraculously short-lived episode.

He spent a while assembling a gallery of the first days of his journey. Ren favoured these visual records, as they were far more effective than the written word for locking ambience and sensation into the slippery world of memory. Some might be used in his reports, but the truth was that it was a private activity and this place was special. He didn't share his creations with others or spend much time browsing galleries from the past because it was the act of making them that was most important. It helped seal his vision and understanding of a place.

Next, he summoned the swarm's status, some of which had now travelled far and wide through Jericho's cavern systems. Their collective data allowed him to assemble a crude map extending far beyond their official path. But there were no grand revelations, just a network of caverns without hidden spaces or anything that contradicted the Arc's story. Now that they were installed in Wakaba, Ren once again turned his swarm on his companions. Tonight he would be ready to trail Kani and Imiko.

It was a curious thing to be lounging outdoors on soft furnishings in the copper light of late afternoon. If External Affairs had been running this show, it would have taken place within the rigid confines of a conference room, and it would have been drenched in decorum and formality. Here there was no boardroom table, nor fancy chairs to boost height and ego, and there were none of those other little trappings that modern statecraft had imported from the corporate world.

They assembled as evening approached, making their way out of town along the river. As they walked, a gaggle of filthy, snotty and barefoot children burst through the undergrowth, stopped and stared at these foreigners in their strange clothes, and then ran shrieking into the woods, continuing with whatever game had been occupying them the moment before. Ren was mystified by this vision of barbarian children.

Detecting his puzzlement, Oso-Rae explained, "In their first few years, our young ones are encouraged to run, explore and be part of nature. They get lost, break bones, get stung by hornets, and wash only occasionally. These are their foundational years, and there aren't too many rules, but they do grow close to one another and their cavern. There is plenty of time to socialise and educate them later, and we achieve little by starting that process too young."

"They don't live at home?" asked Ren.

She blinked at the seeming stupidity of his question and said, "Yes, of course they do. It is just our version of play and growing up."

Ren thought of that day at age four when he started school, quivering with nerves in his absurd little uniform and struggling to release his mother's hand. Yes, it felt too young then, but they had to start early to get them through that vast educational journey to a job like his in External Affairs.

Their destination was a patch of flat ground beneath the vast spread of a banyan tree. Amongst its branches lay an enclave draped with cushions, and there they settled.

"So, what are we here for?" began Saki. "I know that we have been slow to get to the point, but there is a reason. If we are not to repeat the past, it is critical that you first understand a little of who we are and what we have built."

"The ball's in your court," replied Ren. "You broke off contact and then summoned us here."

"True. The question of re-contact has been a debate that has bubbled away in Central Control for decades. This decision finally came with a changing of the guard. We had to let the founders grow old and die, and then let the group that came after them do the same. Only with a fresh generation was the bitterness of our past mistreatment put aside."

"*Your* mistreatment? *You* are the ones who threw us out. It was *your* coup," snapped Imiko.

Unfazed, Saki continued, "The young guns believe that we should be part of the Congregation of Populated Systems. Just as we think that mankind is wrapped up in nature, we think that our lives should be wrapped up in yours. The second aspect is strength. Historically, we were bullied and manipulated by your Leagues, but now we're strong and established enough to stand up to you."

"What do you mean by strong?" asked August.

"Militarily, we evolved and now have an established defensive capability. Sociopolitically, we have a deeply engrained system that would be hard to undermine. We feel safer now. When the gateways were first closed, we were just beginning and everything was fragile.

"The final reason is that we would like to influence the philosophy of colonisation outside our own little Archipelago. I don't mean by aggressive proselytising, more by being exemplars and sharing our knowledge."

"And what are we aiming to achieve here?" asked Ren.

"Mutual respect and understanding," replied Saki. "We each carry preconceptions partly based on emotion and malicious misrepresentation. For example, our default position is that Core bullies planets into compliance with a standard political system, whereas the Hanseatic League forces them to bow to their commercial dominance.

"It's evident that you perceived – and perhaps still perceive – the Arc as somehow politically deviant and therefore a threat."

"Don't paint us with that brush." Kani tended to say little, but this had irritated him. "It's Core that worries about all that. We care about the theft of our investments. Will there be reparations and will our corporations be allowed back in? We need to know if there will be free movement of people. Will there be trade? Will there be embassies?" Imiko nodded in agreement.

"Well, you tried to bring us down too, whatever your reasons. Either way though, we can discuss the things you raised, but some of it will take time. Let's first establish if we understand each other enough to even begin. Let me relate our view of history."

"Can I heckle?" asked Imiko with a smile.

"I reckon you will, whatever I say," he replied, laughing.

Saki began, "Many decades ago in our little archipelago, we created a brand-new system for a new epoch of interstellar life.

"We wanted the Arc to be guided by learned masters rather than corrupt officials who want nothing more than personal power, or worse, to line their pockets. We believed that the most talented philosophers, ecologists, sociologists, educators and economists should congregate and combine the best of their ideas. It could be made to work, so long as the system was protected from absolute rule by an individual or domination by a tiny cabal."

August interrupted saying, "Put differently, you created an autocratic uber-class and kept the rest of your people in a zoo, like so many animals."

Saki rolled his eyes dismissively and continued. "To us, and by 'us' I mean the original designers of decades ago, it didn't make sense that a pepper farmer in Kandahar Cavern should have insight into the mechanics of statecraft. Why ask this farmer for his opinion on ecological master management, optimal population size, or foreign policy if he can barely understand the concepts?"

"To us, that is terrifying arrogance." These were the basics for Ren, and it was almost weird to have core tenets questioned. "You have no right to isolate that pepper farmer from the political system. Beyond that, history has shown that it is impossible to keep a benign oligarchy just that... benign."

"Well, that was precisely the view of Core back then, and it was supported by the Hanseatics and Old Worlds. There wasn't even room for debate. You despised our system and went in for the kill using bribery, blackmail, and fostering splinter factions. All you could see was that the system did not represent government in some banal and familiar form, so you became judge, jury and executioner in an insidious witch trial. You pushed us aside but didn't count on us playing a long game."

Jumping to Core's defence, Ren said, "All experiments that can be conducted with society and political systems have been attempted, and most have failed. There is nothing left to try. For this reason, we guard against radical divergence and isolationism. We are certain that dialogue, open borders, and coherent societies are the secret to safeguarding the future.

"At the time, we felt as though we had no choice but to act."

Oso-Rae finally spoke. "And would you again? Is that still Core's nature? If so, perhaps we should return you to the gateway now."

"Some of the things you accuse us of may have happened... probably happened," said Ren. "I can't easily speak for people who acted fifty-plus years ago. Many powerful bodies influenced events, and I wouldn't put it all at the door of the Core Planets Federation. I don't doubt that considerable pressure was applied."

This elicited a collective scornful snort.

"That doesn't answer my question," said Oso-Rae patiently.

"These days, I think that Core is the least of your worries."

Ren immediately regretted his words. This was not the time to be slinging mud at the Hanseatics or the Old Worlds.

Saki continued, "As you know, we found a way to protect ourselves, and the rest is history. We had to be cunning and inventive to defend ourselves against antagonists so much more powerful than us and so quick to use all manner of subterfuge. We know that the Hanseatics and Old Worlds were neck-deep in this too, perhaps for other reasons but guilty nonetheless.

"Now we're back, and we are here to stay, so it's up to you to decide how to work with us. If you maintain your aggression, then we'll have to hold you at arm's length."

With that, Saki finished and gestured to Ren to counter. He had not had the opportunity to prepare, but could easily draw on rehearsed speeches from years in External Affairs.

"Humanity is in the midst of a staggering and unprecedented diaspora. With that, we perceive a grave future danger, and we are resolved to guard against that.

"Despite the gateways, there are colossal gulfs of spacetime between us. Gradually, cultures will diverge and beings will adapt to their new homes. Humanity will stop being one thing and start to become many distinct species. Given a few thousand years, that divergence will become so profound that we will no longer be able to communicate meaningfully, and planets, habitats, federations of worlds and leagues will start to fight. This is inevitable unless we prepare and guard against it.

"As it comes out of isolation, the Arc will have to make ethical judgements about the people they choose to associate with. Do you really think you will be laissez-faire? Surely you will struggle to work with societies that put no consideration into the care of ecosystems. The greatest evil of all is done by those who stand by and do nothing, right? And what if you are invaded and your gardens torn up? Can you defend yourselves against that on your own? In the end, these questions tend to bring about political alignment. It isn't possible to have deep cooperation with a self-styled monarch or dictator."

"It really isn't for you to tell us how we should interact with others," snapped Saki. "You patronise us."

"Hallelujah," added Kani quietly.

"So yes, the Arc was a problem. It has always been part of our duty to encourage alignment, for the greater good of humanity. This isn't about power. It is a noble project."

"Oh Ren, you're all going straight to heaven," laughed Imiko.

"We agree that with the diaspora, divergence is certain," said Saki. "Indeed, we cannot hope to stop it. Instead of trying to enforce your hegemony, why not just allow it to happen? Is it so certain that ugliness will come of it? You have little faith in humanity."

Ren shot back, "And *you* have such little faith in humanity that you think your pepper farmer can't make reasonable decisions about how to be led."

Ren felt uneasy and a little nauseous. It was not the first time he found himself repeating official lines and failing to find the internal conviction to match them, but this time he felt entirely empty of belief. Still, he had the capacity to sound compelling and was a master of keeping his doubts concealed. It was not as though the Arc'ers had convinced him of anything, and there was nothing else other than emptiness competing for his faith.

Oso-Rae seemed happy to allow Saki to do most of the talking, but now stepped into the fray. "Everything you say is anthropocentric. It's all about the diaspora of 'humanity,' whereas in our language and thinking, we never look at humans in isolation. Even our bodies are oceans of billions of interacting bacteria and archaea. So whenever you speak of your obligations to humanity, we have to translate those thoughts into the equivalent for all living things. I'm not saying that they are unrelated, but we should remember our differing perspectives."

Imiko pounced. "That may be so, but we are humans, and whether you like it or not, we are unique in the arch of biological existence. How can you give equal credibility to a toad or a fungus and a human? What if one has to die to save the other? What do you do? The answer to that question is straightforward."

The conversation continued, but Ren felt that all were delivering lines that had not yet been tempered by new knowledge or experience. They would continue like this, with entrenched positions and age-old opinion, until something forced that to change.

Dusk was upon them and lights began to gently glow in the surrounding branches.

"Let's head back," said Eler. "Tonight is the Festival of the Woodsman in Wakaba. It's quite a show, and people come from all over the pod to participate and watch."

"What is the Woodsman?"

"A sprite who inhabits these forests. His spirit, they say, lives within the trunks of medlar trees."

This crackpot line was delivered in a matter-of-fact voice without a hint of irony or humour.

"O-kaaaaaay…" said Imiko, completely stuck for how to respond.

"It's just a festival. There are animist threads to belief here, with spirits in the rocks, the trees and water, but really it's an excuse for a party."

Oso-Rae and Ren left the banyan tree's shade and began to walk back towards town together.

"Do you believe everything you said?" she asked. "Must we all be identical?"

"Not identical, no. But I do believe we must guard against dictatorship and the many forms of autocracy. Even those who begin with noble founding principles will gradually put them aside in favour of eternal power for the few, who take on the status of demi-gods. It's such a standard pattern it isn't even slightly funny."

"But we are not that."

"I was speaking about the more general view of Core," said Ren.

"No profound change has ever been brought about without a revolution of thought or of insurrection," said Oso-Rae, now on the warpath. "Historically, all great steps towards enlightenment have emanated from the minority, and not from the mass. To achieve leaps in science, politics, liberty and philosophy, we rely on occasional brilliance and a few energetic groups that make things happen. You weren't even willing to listen and demonised us in a determination to cling on to a dysfunctional status quo."

Ren snapped back, "All revolutions fail. The quicker and more violent the event, the harder they eventually fall. Your hypocrisy is to put your own revolution on a pedestal but suppress all new radical thought."

Oso-Rae had calmed herself and said more quietly, "Some of the language you use to describe us is wilfully, aggressively, and almost absurdly over-the-top. Maybe we should tone it down."

Ren nodded in agreement and said, "I have also been told we were 'judge, jury and executioner in an insidious witch trial,' which is equally hyperbolic. But yes, it's better for us to calm it down."

"The Leagues overreacted to some modest socio-political engineering and then tried to rip us apart. We have an imperfect but noble and high-functioning society."

"Most societies think that of themselves," replied Ren.

"It seems that you have no concept of a gradual march towards a more enlightened existence. You believe that we have already reached some kind of apex of achievement that we cannot surpass. Your only job now is to protect this congregation of dysfunction. Why have you given up on improvement?"

Ren said, "There's scope for improvement, but it's extraordinarily hard to believe in revolution if you look at the long arc of failure spanning thousands of years."

After a pause he continued, "We are still exchanging ideas forged by other people long ago. To get past this, we will need to be more candid. I need direct experience, not theory. The only insight has come from the mouths of you, Saki, Eler and Ychi. We need empirical evidence, we need to speak to ordinary people, and we need to see Central Control in operation."

"I understand," said Oso-Rae. "There is more to your visit than this journey, but as Saki said earlier, it is critical that you gain a flavour of ordinary life on our worlds. You simply won't understand it without direct experience. Believe me when I say that there's plenty more coming. We have our reasons for treading softly and restricting the pace. I even think that this discussion tonight would have had a different tone without it."

"So, what's next?"

"Tomorrow is tomorrow, but I can promise you some big changes."

"Are you seriously not telling me?"

"Don't worry. It'll be fun," she said and smiled mischievously.

A crowd had descended on Wakaba, filling its square and surrounding streets.

"People come from all over the pod and beyond to watch," explained Eler.

A hushed silence enveloped the town until a single drum struck up a metronomic beat, its sound carried down from the heights. The rhythm became more elaborate as further drummers joined and began to descend the steep streets. Then they appeared: a troupe dressed in white with flashes of elemental pigments, softened like Buddhist prayer flags. Alternate rows wore double-ended drums slung across their chests.

On approaching the square, the troupe paused, and the drumming briefly returned to its metronomic origin before exploding into boisterous noise. In practised unison, the troupe launched into a complex, energetic dance. Vocals were layered in, starting with a single voice but followed by the wider group in a call-response style. They continued down, looped the square, and then began to rise back up again towards the heights.

More troupes followed, each uniquely dressed, their music chaotically overlapping as one built and the other decayed. They were interspersed with costumed figures in green wearing deranged masks. In time, the passing troupes withered, the music fizzled out and crowds began to disperse.

"Was it a carnival or a religious festival?" asked Imiko.

"A bit of both – they can be hard to separate – but I doubt that religion means to us what it does to you."

"I heard that you ban religion," said Kani.

Saki stepped in, saying, "We don't ban it, you silly goose. That said, what your worlds call 'religion' is little more than another power structure… just another hierarchy with property, leaders and dogma… another patriarchy… another tool of coercion."

He was taunting the Old Worlds for their humourless zealotry. Ren sensed where this conversation was most probably going and, wanting nothing to do with it, moved apart from the group.

For Kani, Saki's words were like a red rag to a bull. "Oh, please! Our faith is no more a choice than is breathing. We don't choose it… it finds us in the dark. Do you banish faith from the mind of man?"

And they're off, thought Ren. He would not get involved with this exchange but couldn't resist listening from a safe distance.

"We don't interfere in the private sphere of individuals," said Saki. "A person can believe whatever they want, but we don't allow faith to create power structures or become political. Religion in government creates an apartheid for those of alternate faiths."

"This is not some hobby for our spare time," said Kani, agitated. "It's impossible to restrict it to the mind and home." Then, more calmly, he said, "Religion dictates the very foundations on which a moral life and decent society is built. How can you then ask us to leave faith out of politics, which surely has the job of delivering a society that reflects the most profound moral tenets of its members?"

"Well said, but the problem remains for those from a minority faith or no faith at all," said Saki. "They don't even have the opportunity to debate those ethical precepts, because they don't derive from logic but rather from scripture.

"We stand for the liberation of the human mind from the shackles of religions whose purpose is to control, coerce, and repress philosophy. Spirituality here takes many forms, and perhaps you will see some of it during your stay. Today you learned a little about the sprites of the woods."

"You'll discover something else too," added Oso-Rae. "We love humour, irreverence, and laughter. We poke fun at ourselves, but all those old-world religions are austere, solemn and humourless. That's not our spirit at all."

"The old religions are vile things built on rules and fear," continued Saki, seemingly unable to divert away from this pointless debate. "They are soaked in self-righteousness and hypocrisy. Truth is not conditioned in heaven and doled out through priests and books. Truth is not fixed and eternal, but fluctuating, like life itself."

"Pah!" said Kani before walking off, scowling.

Ren had dodged the exchange, but he heard enough to know that in this the Arc seemed muddled. Their ecology was coherently argued if deluded, but this was messier. Central

Control doled out 'truth' in the same patronising manner as the religions they so loathed. He wondered how the Arc might have gone about eradicating the old religions. What kind of persecution might have gone with that?

"Are you religious, Ren?" He hadn't quite gotten away with it.

"I'm not going to speak about myself. Some members of Core Planets grudgingly tolerate, others respect, and many participate in religion. We generally accept that it has been an iron rod through history, giving people stability and a sense of belonging."

"That doesn't seem to match what you preach politically: one system for all under singular, monistic ethics."

Ren knew that Core's approach was no more coherent than The Arc's. Indeed, in this each league appeared equally muddled, but rather than say this aloud, he moved on. "How about you?"

"I'm not keen to speak about myself either, but you will find a broad spectrum of faiths here. People here are not generally theists, with a conventional god or pantheon of gods. The notion that without a divine power there is no morality, no justice, honesty or kindness is problematic to us. Justice, truth and fidelity are woven into the fabric of nature."

This sounded like yet more of those standard, practised turns of phrase as if drummed into them from an early age. In casting aside the old gospels, had they simply adopted a new one?

"Honestly, that sounds equally dogmatic," he said. "As far as I can tell, these things just grow organically. What are you going to do, lock people up if they don't behave?"

"Education and social guidance steer people away from inadvisable paths," said Saki with more mystery than explanation.

The crowd had dissolved around them. A few happy, bubbling groups tumbled down to the river, where they would carry the party into the night in a famously drunken melee. The Arc'ers and visitors said their goodnights and drifted off into the town. Ren watched his companions move towards their hostel but, instead of entering, they walked past and turned into the winding streets behind. His heart suddenly beating faster, Ren hung back in the shadows to watch and wait.

Half an hour later, with patience running out and tiredness winning over, he stood to leave, but at that very moment he spotted them walking in the direction of the banyan tree. It was a scene not too dissimilar to the previous evening, only this time August was with them, and they were going somewhere, not returning. Ren followed at a distance.

Once free of the town, the three turned to face each other and began to converse in low tones. Ren couldn't make out the words, but their body language was tense and their faces anxious. It genuinely hadn't surprised him to discover that Kani and Imiko were up to something, but now August was involved too. He was supposed to be on Ren's side. He was supposed to be with Core. What the hell?

Alone in his room, Ren put together an urgent report for Astrid. She wouldn't stand for fluff or banalities, so it had to be succinct, factual and considered. Yes, she was a friend, but that didn't mean he could bypass her rigid protocol. With that in mind, he focused on the urgent topic of August's scheming with the other two. That done, he turned to the Arc and its people. He quoted phrases such as *social guidance* and *inadvisable paths* and made clear his suspicion that there was more in these words than the nuance of language.

Ren felt a muddle of emotions. The intrigue was undeniably exciting, but he was far from sure who he should be rooting for or who to protect. He knew that they were up to no good, but Ren was becoming strangely comfortable in the company of his companions. Even Kani seemed to have softened.

With the report sent, he crawled into bed, overcome by a wave of exhaustion. Within minutes, he was dragged deep into the cocoon of sleep infused with the soundscape of croaking frogs, nocturnal insects, and the soft hoot of a distant owl.

Chapter 14

Asteroids and Pesky Drone Swarms

Palina and Rubos spoke quietly in a corner of mission control's main theatre.

"The mission has changed," said Palina. "New partners have provided another agent on the ground in the Arc. That person is in possession of a couple of hundred micro-gateways, which are being seeded across the Arc as we speak."

Rubos, wide-eyed, simply said, "Wow."

"This is radically new technology, and it transforms what we can hope to achieve. It means we have a way into Jericho and Typhon."

"We can take the Arc," said Rubos, gradually making sense of the implications.

"If so instructed," said Palina, gently chiding the rashness of Rubos's words. "We will bring the gateways' siblings on site gradually as they are seeded and awaken. We don't yet know the team's route across the Arc planets, so we can only deliver them when we know which planet they're planted on. Frankly, we can only expect a fraction to be successfully seeded."

"This is a game changer," said Rubos, still processing the implications.

"Yes. We urgently need to generate a new plan and

reallocate resources. There's a chance we will be asked to act far sooner than we expected."

"We'll get on it," said Rubos.

Craft 'Three' had settled on the dark, lumpy asteroid and was now fully retired from her interstellar career. That retirement was not to be one of golf, bridge or gardening, as there was now a small town to build. In truth, the original ship was now just an inert carcass on the asteroid's surface. Its gateway and gen-4 brain had both been removed, and that was akin to sucking out its soul. It would lie there, dusty and useless, for the rest of time, but its identity had now morphed into that of the captain of a burgeoning city.

Power was key. Keeping a gateway open to the diameter of a coin was all that was required for the delivery of reaction mass, but expanding that to the aperture required for people and machinery was a whole different box of frogs. The measly onboard powerplant that had fuelled her journey across the void was no longer sufficient, so a brand-new juggernaut had been built and was ready to be switched on.

Palina watched nervously as the timer ticked down towards the critical moment. Things rarely went wrong, but there was always some degree of risk.

This process had been practised for hundreds of years and was now exquisitely refined. There was no guesswork, few risks were taken, and nobody tried to be clever or inventive. The power plant followed a standard design using practised, proven technology. Long ago there had been errors, and those were not just costly but often catastrophic. A modest manufacturing error might cause a kilometre-wide blast, thus torching a mission of vast cost after years or even decades of effort. Parts were cast, cut, printed, etched and bolted together. These were supplemented by the gateway delivery of small, specialist components along with essential exotic materials. It was all perfectly devised.

With fuel delivered and safety checks completed in triplicate, it was lit up. The torus glowed, power surged into the gateway, and the tiny black sphere inflated.

Palina sighed with relief and looked across at Rubos, who smiled back at him. Applause rippled through mission control.

No sooner had the gateway reached full aperture than Rubos triggered the next step. The construction of hangars and airlocks would begin soon enough, but something more urgent needed to be done first. A fleet of small drones emerged through the gateway and immediately zapped off into the dark. These were scouts and sappers, paving the way for the coming cavalry and artillery.

A cluster of the drones fanned out so as not to appear as a single, large object before homing in on an ordinary, some might even say dull, yellow-brown planet called Typhon. Its thin atmosphere was just sufficient to support giant dust storms that swept around in ordered latitudinal bands, streaking the sphere in subtle shades of burnt sugar, hazelnut and copper. From a distance, these looked like neat stripes, but closer inspection revealed them to be chaotic, intertwining and co-mingling. Even closer inspection revealed a strange, churned-up surface of spoil heaps and crushed rocky waste. It was curiously sad that the cloud tops of this modestly pretty planet disguised a carbuncle on the surface. Far below that ruined, inhospitable skin lay millions of cubic kilometres of caverns, which provided a home for hundreds of millions of people along with countless other species.

Palina knew full well that the drones, indeed the whole mission, would be deemed an unwelcome arrival. Of course, that only mattered if it were detected, and the inhabitants of this system would have to look very closely to notice such a devious entry. They would be certain to call it an 'invasion', but Palina preferred the word 'insertion.' Semantics.

A larger drone cluster fanned out towards a radically different planet. Kraken, the jewel in the Arc's crown, was mottled with blues, greens, whites and yellows – the signs of water, continents, life, clouds and ice. It was a startlingly beautiful marble of delicate colours. Polar caps extended deep into temperate zones on long, twisting, mountainous arms. These were nothing more than an odd coincidence of geology. Two giant mountain ranges ran from pole to equator, their altitude extending the polar ice, injecting threads of permanent winter almost to the deserts.

Kraken had been beautiful for millennia, but the greenery had only started to appear in the last two hundred years. With it came changes to the cloud systems, an increase in blue and a reduction in ice cover. It had swapped one embroidered shawl for another.

With the fleet of drones dispatched, equipment began rolling out onto the asteroid's surface. Caverns would be excavated deep enough within to provide shelter from radiation: high-energy protons and heavy ions, along with a few irritatingly energetic photons.

Palina turned back to Rubos and said, "You were right. We *can* take the Arc. I'm certain now that we'll be given the green light."

Rubos nodded and smiled back.

Chapter 15

Deserts, Divers, and One Last Boat

A vibrant Oso-Rae walked them to Wakaba's station, chattering as they went. She possessed some deep reserve of cheer that never stopped fizzing or ran dry. Their destination remained a mystery, but Ren somehow knew that they would be saying goodbye to Jericho.

A train, no more modern than the first, carried them onwards into Jericho's vast network of caverns. The first few were within the Kawazu pod, but from there they transitioned into a temperate deciduous forest. Ren gazed at the view, conversing occasionally. He was relieved to have a break from Oso-Rae's earnest lectures.

They talked fluidly despite the gulfs of language and society, both amplified by long isolation. Maybe this was testament to human nature overcoming these barriers. Or perhaps it was nothing more than the natural pleasure found in the company of a kindred spirit.

"Yes, I'm from Palau, which is basically an agrarian backwater. I couldn't wait to get out, and I'm in no rush to go back."

This was a rare candid moment. It was uncommon for him to speak about his home world, particularly at work. It was simpler to paint his identity as belonging to Marrakesh. Oso-Rae had a knack for making others relax and for loosening tongues.

"I have heard of Palau but know nothing of it beyond the syllables of its name. I can't imagine feeling so completely separated from home. True, I'm a little distanced from my sector and clan too due to my life in C-C, but I still yearn for home and return regularly. Like you, I feel somewhat alienated, but the children, the food, the aromas and wildflowers draw me back."

She continued, "So tell me, do you feel an innate connection to this place? Is there familiarity or is it entirely strange?"

"I can't say I do..." started Ren. "At least, I don't think so. I mean, how could I? You can't be familiar with a place through genetics, can you?" He wasn't certain and his incoherence must have been obvious to Oso-Rae. She smiled.

"And yet expatriate communities do keep their culture alive despite their remoteness, often in an exaggerated form."

"That can be true," replied Ren. "They sing their anthems more loudly than they had at home. But that requires a community. All I had was parents who seemed to try very hard to forget their past."

Cavern after cavern of forest passed by outside the window. The train wove in and out of tunnels, for the most part clinging to the rock wall, but in some sections, it traversed the cavern base.

"I don't think I was born for a life on Palau, and I was desperate to leave from my mid-teens. Life on Marrakesh suits me better, although it's hardly a tourist attraction either. I swapped endless fields of wheat for rainy pampas."

"That's fair enough. We have people who simply don't feel they belong and become anxious to move to a new sector. A few feel highly isolated."

"What happens to them?"

"That depends. Sometimes they just live a frustrated life, but occasionally we offer re-education or an emigration path to a new pod or sector. People often believe that the grass is greener on the other side and that elsewhere there will be an opportunity to start afresh. Sadly, they often find the same frustrations in their new homes too. Either that or they find fresh things to grumble about."

"Ummm, re-education? Central Control's choice of phrases makes it sound almost comedically villainous. It's as though you put them in a dark cellar with electrodes attached to their privates."

"Oh, it just means trying to get to the bottom of their dysfunction and helping them integrate better."

Oso-Rae was wilfully digging a deeper hole for herself, but she seemed oblivious to the implications of her word choice. Ren wanted to press the point, but at that moment, the train plunged into a tunnel and began to slow. Moments later, it exited the darkness into the blinding light of a spindle-sun on high power and a wall of blistering, oppressive, dry heat.

Eler said, "This is the Taskala pod and we're approaching the town of El Borj. This is the final ecosystem we will be showing you on Jericho before moving on. There are so many more and it was hard to choose, but Taskala is distinctive and was a genuine technical challenge."

El Borj proved to be a low-rise town of dusty sandstone rendered in brilliant light and dense shadows. They came to a halt just off the main square, where a man in loose robes waited to greet them. Striding forward, he presented himself with hands clasped together in a quarter-bow, just as Oso-Rae had greeted them that first day in the Rose Cavern.

Saki said, "This is Anaik Meties. We need a local guide here because desert pods are quite specialised, and I'm no expert."

"Welcome to El Borj and to Taskala. I have --- asked to --- you a little of our town and ---. I was born --- and have never --- further than Taskala and the surrounding ---."

As Anaik spoke, the translators fell into a panicked overdrive in an attempt to descramble and extract sense from the chaos of his words. His dialect was a peculiarly musical variant with short vowel sounds and silent endings. The translation was delivered as a choppy, inaccurate mess. Many words and phrases were flagged as either unclear or completely unknown.

Laughing at their confusion, Oso-Rae said, "I know his dialect is challenging, so I'll help translate."

Anaik continued, "Let's have a ---- walk across the ---- and continue on foot down ----."

Ren's translator simply gave up on half of the sentence. With time and with data it would surely catch up, but for the time being, it just flailed around.

In the square, a bustling open market was in full swing. Stalls were screened from the spindle-sun by acres of billowing canopies, all in broad blue-and-white stripes. The fabric was worn, faded, and riddled with partly mended holes, all revealing the strain of exposure to intense sun. Beneath, an artful pattern of diffuse sunlight marbled the ground.

Stalls were heaped high with fruit, vegetables, nuts, dates, olives, and a hundred other things, all in a riot of colour. To Ren's eye, the town had the air of a surreal fabrication. It was as if they had assembled a stage set full of actors playing the role of happy indigenes clothed by an overzealous designer with an exaggerated eye for the ethnic.

With Oso-Rae translating, Anaik explained, "Some of this produce doesn't grow in this climate, so it has come from further away. The basics do all come from Taskala, but almost everything else is from Taskala's super-pod."

Imiko asked, "All I see is desert, so how do you grow anything? Where's the water?"

"Desert pods have wadis, which are either upwellings of groundwater or exposed running water. Around these, there is intensive localised agriculture. They are little blooms of green dotted through the desert. A river runs through it all but mostly underground. Rivers are like an umbilicus through almost all caverns."

Eler added, "If you ever see a three-dimensional view of the river systems on Jericho, it looks for all the world like a network of blood vessels. It's creepily biological."

The locals were aware of the foreigners' presence but avoided eye contact, kept their distance and maintained an immaculately polite decorum. Had they been coached? Why were they so meek?

Further stalls were piled high with clothing, carved trinkets, jewellery, bread, grains, and fish on ice: a mix of scaly, silvery pelagic and brightly coloured demersal or reef species.

Anaik said, "The desert ecosystem produces a modest fraction of the food we require, thus making us quite dependent on the sea."

Beyond the town, a rocky desert rolled away towards distant hills. The only signs of life were scattered low, thorny bushes and a bored goat.

August asked, "Since all this is a manufactured system, why do you deliberately create harsh environments? I mean, the heat is uncomfortable, and I guess it supports a lower biological load with fewer species."

Oso-Rae picked this up. "Well, that ends up being quite an existential question and answer. We see it as our duty to accommodate species adapted to specific environments, humidities and temperatures. When combined with the principle that human life should not exist in isolation from nature, you arrive here. We are part of a rich tapestry of species that have evolved together over aeons."

Anaik continued with Oso-Rae patching up the translation gaps, "And what is the definition of a harsh environment? We live comfortably here, and our houses have their feet in bedrock, making them naturally cool. We design them and our lifestyles to work with the heat."

"And yet people can and do live happily in isolation from nature," Ren said. "We have habitats that don't support life in this way. Importing food is easy and inexpensive. There are parks with grass and a few trees. People live well enough."

"Sure, but to us, that is an anthropocentric arrogance. I recognise that this is unconventional thinking, but we live and breathe these ideas."

This topic had started to annoy Ren because he liked his urban life. It wasn't this grand horror that Oso-Rae liked to suggest. Furthermore, he saw no way of putting people on the same level as nematoid worms or lichen. As a member of the human race, it simply didn't add up logically... or perhaps emotionally. All of a sudden, he wasn't sure which it was.

August asked, "Why don't you just chill the air in your houses? After all, you use gigawatts for the spindle-sun."

Ychi said, "That's a matter of attitude. We do without what we don't truly need. I think this is a hard concept to convey to people who do not live according to a code like ours. Simplicity is important in itself. Simplicity is the most beautiful virtue."

Beyond the market square, they followed a steep road spiralling downwards around the hill over which El Borj was draped. As they walked, a view down the cavern's long axis was revealed.

Puddles of green dotted the expanse of desert. These were the wadis where Anaik had said food was grown and where little fish, songbirds and frogs found isolated islands of existence. An expanse of sea sparkled at the bottom of an incline about a kilometre distant. It was calm but shimmered in the harsh light. Invisible breezes mingled with the turbulence of hidden currents to stir the surface, creating mottled patterns that weaved and shifted. The sea stretched far into the distance, eventually disappearing into a haze with the cavern wall barely visible beyond.

Ren was genuinely dumbstruck. He had never seen or even heard of seas within a habitat, let alone an entire cavern. It seemed strange that things like this existed without him having been aware. It couldn't be new; it was impossible that all this had been created in the fifty years since the coup.

Saki said, "We thought this would be a surprise."

Anaik said, "The sea takes up one-third of this cavern and about half of the total pod. We have coral reefs, forests of seagrass, and even deep-water environments with some parts descending to eight hundred metres. This was one of the most challenging habitats we have attempted anywhere in the Arc. The undersea world is so vastly interconnected that you need all of it to work in perfect synchronicity. And corals. Don't get me started on corals.

"We fish it modestly, but even with that to supplement our crops, Taskala can only support about half of the population density of other pods."

They had left El Borj and descended a long path towards the seashore, sweltering in the late-morning heat.

Anaik said, "We keep the ultraviolet part of the spectrum constrained, so you are unlikely to burn. Some UV is necessary for life, so it is not entirely suppressed."

Looking closely, it was clear that the desert was far from lifeless. Brown-green lizards darted in and out of the rough rock wall that lined their path. Dung beetles marched past on their mysterious journey somewhere, for something. Neon bee-eaters waited patiently for prey in the upper branches of spiny bushes. To some eyes, this would be nothing more than a barren, dusty wasteland, but Ren found beauty in the bleak, austere terrain.

The salty zing of sea air met them as they walked. A marina lay at the end of the path, and within, fishing boats painted in canary yellows and electric blues bobbed. The marina was separated from the open sea by a low rock wall.

The water had a pristine clarity, with visibility comfortably penetrating fifteen metres clear down to sand and corals. Fussy crabs scuttled across the exposed rocks, and the black scars of sea urchins studded the shallows. Nets dried next to ragged lobster pots.

Ren said, "Let me guess. Another boat trip?"

Oso-Rae replied laughing, "Yes, but it's the last one."

Awaiting them was an open-sided passenger boat set with rows of wooden benches. Anaik greeted the boatman in an impenetrable burst of dialect that neither the translators nor their Arc guides attempted to decipher.

Soon they were gliding across the open sea at a solid thirty knots with just the sound of water and a splashing wake. A silent propulsion system was at work somewhere below. Startled by the boat's passage, flying fish fanned out from the surface, sparkling in the light. Spreading wing-like fins, they glided impossibly far before dipping back below the waves.

Within minutes, they approached the gaping hole of an intra-pod cavern connector. The launch slowed noticeably as it fought against a current that surged through the gap towards them.

"How is there a current?" asked Ren.

Anaik replied, "The sea connects in a big loop which allows a small but desirable Coriolis effect to come into play. You notice it here because it is forced through a narrow aperture. We also use daylight programmes to generate temperature gradients, which in turn create breezes that blow between the caverns."

They were through into the pod's second cavern and accelerating once again. This one was divided along its length, with the sea in a kilometre-wide strip down one side and land rising on the other. The gradient was gentle near the shore but became increasingly steep and ragged further back until finally merging with the wall. Patches of green studded the lower reaches.

Ren asked Anaik, "Tell me about your sense of identity within your clan, cavern and pod… and to Jericho and the Arc. Which elements define you most?"

"They are all layers of an onion, but some layers are much thicker than others. The clan is ultra-personal. We bicker and fight, we love and procreate, we eat together and bathe together. This is an unbreakable feeling, and although you may leave your clan for a dozen reasons, you certainly don't forget it. The cavern is more of a home than a piece of your identity, which instead comes from the pod, since that represents your collective ecological uniqueness, your produce for trade, and most cultural traditions.

"My loyalty to the Arc is quite theoretical. There are no situations when I have to stand up for it or represent it. I respect its work, its principles and its protective layer. We are all proud when a child from the clan is selected for C-C."

"So, to whom do you feel patriotic?"

Anaik looked across at Oso-Rae. He was puzzled by the question and uncomfortable.

She replied, "That's not a fair question to Anaik. He has never known your concept of patriotism, which implies the nation-state. For him, you are referring to a historic artefact. So, if you don't mind, I will answer that one.

"Patriotism is anathema to us. It is a dangerous superstition and a dark art that leaders use to coerce their populations. They draw a line on a map, create a false narrative of historic importance wrapped in racial or linguistic specialness, and then use that to control minds, or worse, go to war and bully weaker nations."

And she's off again, thought Ren.

She continued, "Nationhood and patriotism are fallacies created and sustained through lies and misrepresentations of the past. It was once said that it's a superstition that robs people of their self-respect and dignity, and increases their arrogance and conceit."

Ren said, "Okay, here we are again. Are your caverns, pods and sectors nothing more than arbitrary lines on a map too?"

"You could say that, but there are some fundamental

differences. One is that they were never drawn through existing communities – never manipulated for a leader's gain. People moved onto Kraken and into Jericho, straight into these spaces. The second is that they are of balanced size, so there is no opportunity to bully and repress others. Finally, they are not in competition for resources or power, so there is little tendency towards conflict."

Ren replied calmly, "I have said before that nation-states serve us well. The system is ugly at times, but it prevents other types of political horror. It remains up to you to prove that the Arc is not what we have been taught to think it is. Theory and experience suggest that it can only have become one terrible thing – repressive and totalitarian."

"Ugh. Will you please stop with those words? You seem determined to brand us, and in so doing find fault. Was your mind made up before setting foot here? We have built something new, and if you refuse to even look at it, we will fail. Anyway, how dare you tell me that I have to prove anything to you."

The other Arc'ers laughed at Oso-Rae, mocking her impassioned style. She scowled back at them and then flashed a smile and touched Ren's knee, and in that instant completely defused any sense of conflict. Anaik looked confused.

They sped on, and within half an hour had passed through three desert caverns, each with a different relationship with the sea. The previous one was mostly water, whereas this one was dominated by land. Some areas had the dull darkness that hinted at great depth beneath them, and others the translucent turquoise of shallows.

On the shore ahead lay the cavern's town. To the right was a rocky outcrop down which a waterfall dropped fifty metres into the ocean from a hole in the cavern wall. Sea birds, only visible as distant white specks, wheeled and dived around the turbulence where river pounded into sea. The boat set a course towards a dock at the foot of the falls.

Anaik explained, "This is the riverine termination from a

neighbouring pod called Opobu. Some pods have self-contained water systems, but others flow through several. This is fresh water that dumps into our sea. We then desalinate and return the water way back up-system."

At the dock they bid farewell to Anaik, adopting the Arc'ers' half-bow used for both greeting and parting. He turned the boat around and sped away with a wave.

From a dizzyingly high platform, divers pirouetted and plunged into the waters on the falls' fringes. Light applause from onlookers accompanied each dive. A steep path, paved with cleverly joined flat rocks, led up the side of the waterfall, past the jumping point, and then a little further before turning in towards a large shelf standing between the falls and the bedrock behind. Within was a cool space with a shimmering, translucent window formed by falling water. Shifting threads of sunlight penetrated, painting a marbled pattern within.

Towards the rear, the enclave contracted down into a rough tunnel leading deep into the regolith. At the tunnel's end stood the dark disc of a gateway. Without pause, they marched through to a nexus hub, much like the one between Kiki and Jericho. A pressure door hissed closed behind them and a second blocked onward progress. As before, ordered squadrons of microtech appeared and swarmed over them.

Ren had seen little in the way of visibly evolved tech in the Arc, but this process bore no resemblance to the decontamination processes elsewhere. Isolation was bound to cause technology to diverge, and as the years passed, the more it would deviate and the more distinct it would become. The Arc had clearly not spent five decades sitting on its arse, communing with nature and stagnating. Instead, they had created this peculiarly distinctive and eerily capable microtech.

Ren watched August evaluate the situation. He could now read the strain beneath that immaculate, jovial façade. Indeed, Ren now had to be careful not to study August too much. It would show. Despite having passed this step once before, Ren wondered if his microtech would be exposed. He would hate for the journey to end here and to be marched home. It was surely possible that they were being played. Secret or not, he would now be cut off from the fraction of his swarm left behind on Jericho, but it had served some purpose and might still be of use down the line.

Saki said, "It's far from perfect, but it can detect and remove the tiniest of insects along with a wide range of pathogens. Some bacteria, spores and viruses are harder to contain, but this step simplifies the process."

Ren asked, "Does it tell you what it finds and contains?"

"No, not usually. If there's a specific contagion of concern, there's an additional medical step, which can delay departure by some hours."

With that, the motes of microtech disappeared back into their garages, and the second pressure door glided open.

"Let's go to Kraken!" said Oso-Rae.

The gateway did not carry them straight there. Of course not. Instead, it was to another set of concrete corridors, just like that first facility between Kiki and Jericho. Its physical location was unclear and was most probably a well-guarded secret. They were in an active hub with dozens of other people in transit. In Jericho's communities, people had been meek and discreet, but here they were greeted more confidently. Ren took little pleasure from the attention. He was not one to appreciate celebrity.

Up one tunnel and down another. A pressure door. Crowds. Chaos. Then they were in a small queue advancing towards a final gateway before stepping through into blue sunlight and a cool breeze.

The air, light and acoustics were all suddenly and jarringly altered. This place had a radically different aspect and pungency. Some corner of the subconscious seemed to know instantly that they weren't in 'Kansas' anymore. Given a few hours, the brain would adapt and make it the new normal. Brains were good at that.

They were in the centre of a large, paved square at the heart of a town, nestled between imposing snow-capped mountains. Buildings carpeted the entire bowl of the valley except for a central lake. At the fringes, buildings continued, clinging on more tightly as the as the incline grew, before finally dissolving into scree and rock. The mountains rose on three sides, and on the fourth, the terrain dropped away to invisible lowlands.

Mountain peaks stood in tiered ranks beyond the town, their height hard to guess, but the tallest spoke of inhospitable cold and thin air bordering on vacuum. High-altitude winds swept snow from the packed ice between the peaks, sucking ice particles into pirouetting streams.

After Jericho's settlements, this town, a village by Ren's standards, felt like a teeming metropolis. It had an incongruent aesthetic blending rustic, alpine simplicity with hypermodernity. The air was cool, crisp, and exaggeratedly transparent. The bluer tints of Hypnos, Kraken's star, lent everything a strange hue at first, but just like donning tinted sunglasses, after a time, the brain adapted to the new colour scheme.

Oso-Rae turned to them with a massive, beaming grin and said, "Welcome to Kraken. You wanted to see Central Control, and here we are.

"This is Hypatia, one of several Central Control hubs on Kraken. They are spread around the planet and have different areas of speciality. You are free to go where you want and speak to whoever you wish. There are no secrets here, and we'll wash your cynicism into that lake and down the river to the sea."

Saki added, "This will be our base for a few days, but we will be travelling to a few other places. No more boats, I promise.

"Oso-Rae and I are both based in this town, although we spend about a quarter of our time back in our home sectors. Our paradigm requires balance between duty to Central Control and clan life. It prevents a loss of cultural identity and avoids C-C becoming disconnected from day-to-day life in the sectors, at least in theory."

They were thrilled to be back here, bursting with pride and eager for the visitors to appreciate their home. Ren wondered if these Arc folk were genuine or putting on an elaborate act. It did not seem like a veneer covering some hidden truth, but he knew that might be naïve on his part. They certainly appeared sincere, but sincerity was also present in the deeply indoctrinated. One person's truth is another person's brainwashing. Indeed, there wasn't always the clearest line between these two things, and the best way to ruin dialogue was to accuse your counterpart of not having the capacity to think for themselves or that their beliefs are based on social manipulation. He would have to navigate carefully around these reefs and shallows.

They walked along a wide, tree-lined avenue set with benches and the soft forms of stone sculptures. Trees were bare and scattered autumnal leaves hinted at the season. Down the avenue's centre ran a canalised stream with waters as clear as the very best vodka. Small fish hovered amongst hornwort weed swaying slowly in the current.

There were no large or high-rise buildings, which seemed odd for a centre of government. Instead, the town was dominated by steeply roofed, mountain-style buildings ranging from the size of a house to that of a modest hotel. There was little decorative excess, with the exception of ornately carved balconies. The overriding impression was of a sensible, functional town that shunned theme park tweeness.

Ren had become so accustomed to Jericho's paths and waterways that he had missed something crucial. It now struck him that here, and on Jericho, there were no cars or flyers. Indeed, there were barely any powered vehicles at all except for those ridiculous trains.

"We walk, we take trains and, as we are all aware, a few boats and gateways. What I don't see are roads with vehicles or flyers."

"Oh, we usually prefer to walk, and when it isn't viable, we have the other methods you have seen. We use flyers for a few things, but they are not so common."

"How do the elderly and differently-abled get around?"

Oso-Rae replied, "That depends on the situation. The very elderly don't stay on in Central Control zones beyond their working life. They retire back to their clans in their home sectors. Care for the elderly sits firmly in the clan community.

"Most citizens with disabilities are given augmentations, so making their lives quite ordinary. A few embrace their uniqueness and reject bionics, instead choosing old-school methods to get by. We are not at all afraid of technology and use it where it makes sense to us. That said, there's a strong spirit of shunning vehicles unless absolutely necessary. This state of mind is fundamental to our way of life and you must absorb it if you are to understand us."

"And who decides when it makes sense? Who draws the boundaries?"

"It's a collective mindset."

Ren understood the emotional root of this motivation. He often walked when he didn't exactly need to. He also took slow methods of transport when faster ones were possible. His reasons were his own, but it meant that he was at least open to the idea. The Arc philosophy more generally would take time to unpack.

Their accommodation proved to be a small house just off the main avenue. It was given over to them in its entirety, and they had leave to come and go as they pleased. Oso-Rae explained how they could obtain sufficient data access to navigate the town and to determine the purposes of the many buildings. She put markers down for her, Saki's and Ychi's locations, along with a few landmarks.

Oso-Rae highlighted map locations as she talked.

"If you keep walking up to here, you will get a fabulous view across the town. There is a rough path here that goes higher up to the col, and from there you can look across an ice field stretching over to the foot of Cerro Quizapu, our second-highest mountain."

Continuing to mark up the map, she said, "You can get food here, here, and here. The town knows of your presence, so just ask for whatever you like. All of these buildings coloured in green are open-door. Feel free to walk in and have a look around. The others are businesses, private accommodation, or confidential operations.

"We'll see you here later."

"Thanks, Oso-Rae. Just one thing … we travelled very light, and it is damn cold out there. Is there some warmer clothing we can use?"

"Absolutely. Look in the side hall. See you all later."

And with a little wave, she was gone.

Ren was still adjusting to the jarring contrast between Jericho and this mountain town, but it was more than the physical aspects of gravity, atmosphere and geology. There was an important principle that he had been in danger of forgetting. It is complacent to think of something even as small as a nation as a single socio-cultural-political-religious entity when in truth they always contain spectacular diversity. It is even more complacent to think of a planet as a culturally coherent thing since they contain yet greater diversity. Here they were not considering a nation or a single planet but the Arc, which was a league of planets, so he had to stop thinking of it as one thing.

In a cosy corner, Ren sat with a blanket knitted in autumnal shades and gazed at the distant mountains. This was the first time he had seen terrain on this scale, with peaks so high that snow and ice disappeared towards the summits. The pinnacles projected through the tropopause into the stratosphere – practically reaching up into space.

This thankless mission was playing on his mind. Astrid had given him an impossible job, and a decision would become urgent sooner than he would like. More information was desperately needed. With that thought, he resolved to accelerate the pace and let loose his swarm into Hypatia.

He dozed for half an hour, but his dreams were weird and unpleasantly lucid. On waking, he felt frustrated, groggy and utterly unrefreshed. The others gradually appeared from their rooms, and once gathered, they set out to explore Hypatia.

For a time, they walked without destination. Hypnos was low in the sky and cast long shadows whose crisp blackness was sharpened by the high mountain air. The temperature was plunging fast.

Ren said, "Does anyone want to have a stab at explaining what we are doing here? What have we accomplished and what are we achieving right now? What do they really want from us?"

Nobody rushed to answer, but after a generous pause, Kani finally spoke. "Superficially, we are being invited to see the supposed beauty of their habitats, planets and society – they seem supremely smug about all that. Quite when we begin dialogue is another question."

August said, "In any other situation, this would be dealt with using a large-scale delegation of ministerial, trade, and corporate reps, perhaps in some neutral territory. They are at pains to show us that their people are not repressed or coerced, which usually means that is exactly what they are."

Ren said, "And are they? It doesn't feel right."

"They must know that the Hanseatics care less about their politics and society." Imiko turned to Kani in search of approval. "All this is aimed at Core. They know what we want but don't address it."

"Fair enough. We will have to force them to talk about that too. But just on the topic of coercion, beyond Saki, Oso-Rae and the others in Central Control, we have only spoken to a couple of hand-picked guides."

Imiko added, "And even with those guides, there was the air of master and subject."

August said, "It's conjecture, but I got the same vibe."

Ren had started the conversation but now wondered why. It was pointless to make a meaningful collective plan, so he reverted to banal platitudes. Privately, he resolved to crack the veneer of this carefully constructed scene. He didn't believe that the exchange meant anything at all to Imiko and Kani. They were most probably on their own paths and acting out a public role. That might apply to August too, but his purpose was irritatingly evasive. It was clear that he would have to act alone and so he framed an excuse.

"Let's divide and conquer. We are more likely to get dialogue going as individuals rather than as a marauding gang."

Imiko said, "Yes, that's a good plan. I reckon that they just want to be respected and loved. It's a simple human need that often manifests at the level of the state."

With the dropping temperature, they went in search of food. The chosen venue wasn't a restaurant in the sense that Ren was accustomed to. Yes, they served food to strangers for a fee, but it felt more like a canteen than a restaurant. Seats were taken at long, collective tables, but no menus were brought. In choosing this place, they had also unwittingly chosen their menu. To avoid faux-pas, they watched the locals and cloned every move.

Night had fallen by the time they began their walk home. The sky was decorated with stars, and the milky smudge of the galaxy glowed overhead. Back at the chalet, the Arc'ers were waiting for them, lounging like cats.

Saki said, "Now that you have seen Hypatia, a seat of Central Control, do you have any new questions?"

Ren said, "It would be useful to go over your main activities... the 'existential minimum.' Can you explain what they are and why they are centralised? On the other side of the coin, we should consider some things you aren't involved with that a central government normally would be."

Saki said, "Sure, sounds fine."

He projected a list of Central Control activities. Some were unsurprising, such as foreign affairs, ecology and defence, but one in particular stood out. At the bottom of the list, dark and ominous, was 'suppression of subversive influences.' Ren could barely believe that was a publicly declared role. Most governments merrily get on with that in the shadows but none own up to it.

"Surely we can brush over some of these," said Ren. "There's little to debate in 'defence from external threats,' since that always requires planetary or league-level management."

August added, "That's true enough, but I do have a couple of questions. To start, how big is your military, and what form does it take? Secondly, what threats do you perceive, and who are you protecting yourselves from?"

Saki replied, "Look, we aren't ready to talk about our military capability. We have some way to go before gaining that level of trust."

"Fair enough."

"The question of the threats we perceive is easier to answer. Frankly, you remain a threat, and by you, I mean all three of your leagues in some measure."

Imiko smiled and said, "Who, us?" and then feigned being mortally offended with a hand to her brow.

Saki smiled and continued, "Sometimes military strength is required just to avoid being bullied. We see threats on all sides because we have Kraken and Eleuthera and simply because there is chaos out there in the non-league worlds and in the more general unknown of the galaxy."

Ren said, "We all have our militaries but war remains rare outside the confines of a planetary society. They're usually internal affairs – rebellions, civil wars, religious strife, and so on."

August added, "On occasion, we still need to bare our teeth."

"My point exactly," replied Saki.

What he wondered was if they might have something that required special protection... that rumoured secret, perhaps. He wondered what modern weapons they might have conjured from their research labs. A single invention had the capacity to entirely subvert established centres of power.

Inter-planetary relations was another obvious role for centralised government. That said, it was a peculiarly theoretical activity in the Arc as they had had no external relations. Central Control had spent decades without experience or practice, developing ideas in a vacuum. It was like an army sitting on its hands during a five-decade gulf between wars. All they could do was develop principles whilst maintaining infrastructure and personnel. Two of whom, it turned out, were Saki and Oso-Rae. *How strange to have a theoretical occupation*, thought Ren.

He asked, "So you get put in the C-C educational stream in your sector and then what? How do you end up in a specific department?"

"We choose our department quite early, usually while at university, but in some cases, it is effectively chosen for us based on the specific skills and talents exhibited. There is some movement between departments, but usually early in your career. Some cross-pollination is advisable or it becomes cliquey."

"And you then move up some kind of hierarchy within the department?"

"Yes, although we aren't a particularly hierarchical society, so it is more about learning and experience. Department heads are elected by members of that department. We have micro-democracy within Central Control's departments."

"And what's at the top?" Ren threw that question out without expecting a useful answer.

Saki said, "At the top, we have the Bureau, or the 'Gang of Twelve' as we like to call them. There isn't a single leader, and these twelve make all final big-picture policy decisions."

That was the big reveal. It was bold, direct, and began to divulge the top-level governance of Central Control and thus of the Arc itself.

Ren quietly cringed at *the Bureau*. Perhaps it was an accident of dialect that he was reading too much into, but it mirrored the language of dictatorships and insidious police states. He knew it was semantics and that they were just words, but the cumulative effect of all these phrases weighed heavily. But he also considered the name they had given to their capital. *Hypatia* was that ancient vanguard of classical enlightenment over dogma, and surely the choice of name said something positive about their nature.

Saki changed tack. "I think we're wasting time. The big-ticket activity for Central Control is ecological master-management. Our planets and habitats were derived from blank canvases, and building worlds simply isn't achievable without a holistic, planet-wide approach. Plus, the gen-5 mind that delivered the master plan, and now refines it and maintains equilibrium, has to be operated centrally.

"This is true within and outside the Arc. For us, the extension of this universal truth is the detailed planning and administration of ecosystems. We dictate which go where and constantly monitor them to ensure their robust health. We maintain studies of species, examine population explosions and crashes, and study the appearance and mutation of phyla, classes, orders, families, genera and species."

Ren said, "Look, this is hardly going to be a sticking point. Any concerns are far more likely to come from the areas where this intersects with human existence and liberty."

A spiky Imiko said, "Or our investments. Let's not forget that we paid for the development of these planets."

There was nothing unique about the Arc in taking this approach. Terraforming had always been a planet-wide enterprise. It was naive to think that continents and zones might establish their own ecosystems in isolation. These worlds were manufactured over centuries by slowly bringing things into balance at a planetary level. Carbon and water cycles, atmospheric currents and algal blooms were all connected in a vastly complex whole. The health of a forest in one corner of a planet was influenced by ocean currents on the other side, and a stable temperature required all to be in tense, semi-chaotic equilibrium.

Ren said, "For me, it's less clear with habitats like Jericho and Typhon. Theoretically, it doesn't need to be a planet-wide strategy, because the cavern systems can be isolated from one another."

Saki said, "That's partly true, although it helps to coordinate air, water and waste. However, the spindle-suns generate a lot of heat and we have to think of global temperature gradients. Planets like Kraken and Eleuthera are far more complex."

Ychi added, "That, and we also weren't willing to wait the decades and centuries that it takes for a planet to naturally stabilise before occupying it, so we established communities while everything was still in a state of flux. Frankly, it's still unstable, although we're getting closer. Even now, without a gen-5 gently coaxing things in the right direction, we would have unsurvivable chaos."

The truth was, these challenges were universal. Throughout the Congregation of Populated Systems, planets had been terraformed only through the massive application of technology watched over by brilliant gen-5 minds. Planets were artificially maintained in a strained balance, with technology constantly fighting off chaotic extremes. The holy grail was self-sustaining equilibrium, but that was an extraordinarily rare achievement anywhere.

Humble Palau was close to equilibrium, but only through its dullness and the application of simplistic monoculture. On Ren's rather boring planet, there was none of the Arc's genetic diversity or that startling network of ecosystems. It was an area in which the Core Planets fared poorly, hence the Arc's fame. The trouble was that the CPF ethos didn't allow any real choice in this failure. There was no political capital in dictating land use or population control, so they had to make the best of it. In Core, human life always came first, and that was even more true in the Hanseatic League. There, it wasn't seen as a failure because it was a reflection of their defining value systems.

It was evident that their intent that evening was not to beat the list of C-C activities to death. This was a conversation, not a debate. The words dried up, the gathering fizzled out, and Ren retired to his room.

He was desperate for sleep, but there was a duty to perform first. Shortly after arriving in Hypatia, Ren had dispatched his swarm into the mountain air. The fraction that had reported back showed that the town was already littered with microtech.

His companions – each one of them – had gone to work here, a clear ramp-up from Jericho. What was August up to? He was evidently working with the others, and what did that mean for Core? They must be connected to an insertion mission. Any doubt about that was evaporating by the hour. Ren could almost sense the invasion hardware staring down from orbit.

Chapter 16

Oso-Rae Questions Her Loyalty

Saki and Oso-Rae walked together in silence along Hypatia's main avenue. They were arm-in-arm. This was not a romantic gesture, but rather a display of long-held platonic affection. They nodded at a handful of familiar faces as they passed, but exchanged few words. Both seemed serenely relaxed, and no great urgency drove them forward. Above them were the skeletal forms of plane trees in winter mode, their branches pruned back to gnarled stubs. Sheets of their peculiar moulting bark scattered the ground amongst fallen leaves.

At its upper end, the avenue terminated at a shadowed and mossy public garden. There they waited on a weathered stone bench and watched perky snowfinches hunt for breakfast at their feet. The garden was a sea of green with cushions of moss and a scattering of boulders adorned with distinctive phenocrysts. Some were low and smooth, whilst others were tall and angular, but all had been selected for their unique forms. These were local to the valley's indigenous igneous geology and had been placed in a meticulously considered arrangement.

Slow-growing pines dotted the expanse of the park, few more than human height. They had clusters of olivine needles so long that they drooped under their own weight.

Whilst they waited, Saki asked, "What's the ideal outcome? What relationship should we have with the many-headed beast that is Core... and the other leagues for that matter?"

"I want to see an open door. I want cross-pollination of ideas. I want to avoid us becoming an endlessly persecuted pariah. I want us to be part of the community of planets. More than that, I want us to influence how new planets are colonised."

"And how might this affect Central Control?" asked Saki.

She looked back at him to make clear that she wanted him to answer that dangerous question first.

Taking the prompt, he said, "I hope that contact will encourage reform. You know I'm not at war with our system, but every year the purity of the original purpose is corrupted that little bit more. Every year, the remit of C-C is subtly adjusted. We are collectively blinkered by the system."

Saki was preaching to the choir. They knew full well what each other thought, but rarely did they have the courage to voice ideas like these.

"What is subversive?" asked Oso-Rae. "What is seditious? Why stifle debate so entirely?"

Nako Moon entered the park, joining them on an opposite bench. They had last spoken in a forest clearing on Jericho with Nako connecting from afar.

"Welcome back, my wonderful colleagues."

"Thank you, Nako," replied Saki. "It was an exhausting tour of Jericho's beautiful caverns. Frankly, I need a cocktail and a lie-down."

"Yes, you'll have to take a long holiday. Perhaps visit a spa and get a massage, you poor dear."

Nako paused and the humour in his eyes disappeared. "I'm sorry to change gear abruptly, but let's talk about who these people represent, what they are capable of and why we are here. The truth is that there is more to this than meets the eye. A few weeks ago, we detected some strange comms in the Heimdall system. Spotting it was a lucky coincidence, but hell did it get sirens wailing in the Bureau."

Oso-Rae and Saki glanced at each other. It was a momentary connection of eyes containing a full essay of content. Those who know one another extraordinarily well have this almost psychic ability to convey an ocean of thought and emotion with a simple look.

Nako continued, "We only have that one encrypted snippet with a data structure at once familiar and strange. We can separate the header, body and tail, but it doesn't help us identify its origin or content. It could be some rebellious domestic element, but that's unlikely. The implication is that something is present near Eleuthera... and maybe elsewhere in the Arc.

"It could be a rogue transmission from ancient hardware left behind, but it might also be something more insidious... like an insertion."

In that moment it dawned on Oso-Rae what was going on and why the visitors were really here.

"By *insertion*, you mean an uninvited, backdoor entry into a colonised system, or an invasion in normal words. And the only possible senders are our visiting friends."

Nako replied, "Precisely. There has always been some possibility of the leagues doing this, but we had assumed that from the date of the coup, it would have taken some years to make a decision to send a mission of this expense and magnitude. To be there now, they must have acted almost immediately. If it is an insertion, they didn't even bother to wait a few years to see if our silence was just a petulant tantrum born from the coup.

"So, please do not pretend for a second that this is purely the innocent foundation of dialogue. We must watch them like hawks and wait for a mistake."

Oso-Rae was blindsided but finally found her voice. "I

have about eighty questions, but to start, why are you sharing this now? Can I also say that I am very disappointed that you kept us in the dark? It makes me feel ridiculous."

"Ditto," added Saki.

"We always meant to share this with you, but it was critical to get an initial interaction with the visitors unencumbered by preconception. I think you will understand that in time."

"I don't see what kind of mistakes you're looking for," said Saki. "The team may have nothing to do with any in-system presence. We invited them, so they may have no knowledge of it. If they're already here, can't they just invade if they so choose?"

"I doubt that they would just invade. Admittedly it might be a mistake to underestimate the magnificent aggression they are capable of, but a straightforward invasion would be staggeringly messy and complicated. I think that they'll use threat or seize something strategic. At this point, they don't know what is strategic, but their team might help determine that."

"And do their psych markers support the idea that the visitors are involved?" asked Oso-Rae.

"On the whole, yes, but some more than others. If you look deep enough into people's eyes, you can always detect the presence of deceit, even if you can't read what that deceit is. They all show evidence of this, but it's difficult to unwrap."

"So all our conversations and efforts had no purpose. We are just watching them and trying to trip them up?" Oso-Rae fumed.

"No, the debate is genuine. If we can avoid an invasion, we will still need dialogue with these leagues. Furthermore, it could be any one of them behind it, or none. I also need to remind you that an invasion would be very costly, so they would want to avoid one if they believe there are other options."

"I get it," said Saki. "We have to suggest to the Hanseatics and the Old Worlds that there is a chance of reparation and corporate representation, and to Core that we are socially and politically salvageable."

"Very good, Saki. That's precisely right. This helps to delay action. We need time to trace the signal that brought us to this point."

Nako brought an end to their meeting. On a normal day they might chat or reminisce for a while before taking their leave, but today nobody was in the mood. He stood, performed a bow and left.

Oso-Rae was scowling. "I feel dirty."

"Great threats require extreme measures, do they not?" said Saki.

"Within the boundaries of decency," she replied quietly.

Eventually, they too stood, embraced, and then walked away on separate paths, leaving the park empty but for the snowfinches.

Oso-Rae walked the streets alone for some time, lost in thought. She loathed the fact that she had approached this mission full of spirit and on the back of a lifetime's training, only to have the rug pulled from under her. It brought a boatload of issues into question. Her loyalty required trust and a belief that those above her were not aloof concealers of the truth. Nako's light-hearted, comedic manner now felt false.

She walked down through Hypatia's deserted main square and then on to the rim of the town near the moraine's lip. The river crashed violently down a precipice, its form reappearing in the valley far below. In the far, far distance, just beyond sight on the edge of a great ocean, lived her clan, her family. Her identity was torn between the lofty intellectual peaks of Central Control and that earthy existence of her childhood. Keeping both alive was far harder than she could admit to Ren.

Chapter 17

Clans and Surprising Conversations

A flyer soared over the lip of Hypatia's precipice, accelerating as it rose. Its glassy passenger pod dangled beneath a canopy of rotors. The craft was bulbous, inelegant, un-streamlined, and frankly quite curious-looking. A minimalist interior contained little other than eight seats. Each could pivot from forward-facing to a side-on position that presented a breathtaking view through its transparent fuselage. It was neither built for speed, efficiency, nor cargo volume. Instead, its singular purpose was to provide a jaw-dropping view, and with that came an adrenaline-soaked experience. For some, it was a scintillating ride, but for others, it was pure, unadulterated terror.

Aboard were the four visitors, along with Saki, Oso-Rae and Ychi, leaving one seat empty. It was entirely automated, without even a dedicated pilot's seat. Instructions for its course were quietly delivered by Saki's implant.

Instinctive, unmanaged sectors of Ren's brain insisted that he was certain to drop out of the sky and be smashed to a bloody pulp on the rocks far below. He summoned a calming routine from his implant, and with that, the fear subsided. It was a trick to be used occasionally, as its effectiveness shrivelled with over-use.

"I told you that there would be no more boats… probably. This is fun, isn't it?" asked Saki.

"Honestly, we don't get to do this often. Having foreign visitors makes it an occasion with special privileges, but it's also far easier for us to show and explain this planet from the air.

"When we designed Kraken, we had the concept of sectors in mind from the outset. The entire planet was divided into a pattern of hexagons fifty kilometres across, of which a little under 50 percent were on, or partially on, land."

As Ren watched the forest roll past below, luminous red lines began to glow in his visual field, marking the intersection between sectors. These were thanks to a local feed providing metadata to match Saki's commentary.

They would have had to be in orbit to have sufficient altitude to properly reveal the pattern. All they could see from the flyer were three red lines marking the boundary between local sectors. As if predicting this difficulty, a peripheral visualisation displayed a globe divided into neat hexagons.

As they flew onwards from the sector boundary, additional markers were added to show a town and the junction between urban, cultivation and wilderness. All this was thanks to improvements to the data interface between the Arc and the visitors. Technology and data structures had diverged, but the engineers had found ways to make it work. With each day, the interface would improve, and more data would become accessible.

"We have a land area of two hundred and forty million square kilometres, of which three-quarters could be called habitable. That excludes savage mountain ranges, polar extremes, and a few deep, inhospitable deserts. Of the remainder, half of the hexagons are given over to pure wilderness, and the remaining ninety million square kilometres are what we call 'habitable sectors' where people can live."

As he spoke, the simulated globe panned and zoomed to

display the region in more minute detail. Sectors were colour-coded to match his description, with the uninhabitable areas, wilderness, and populated sectors all colour-coded.

It was hard to digest quantities such as 'two hundred and forty million square kilometres.' Measurements on such scales became intangible, and Saki might as well have said, "a bajillion deci-furlongs." Still, the ratios did tell a story. In all, less than 40 percent was given over to sectors that might contain humanity.

"The populated sectors are in clusters of seven, four, three, or sometimes two, and very occasionally just one on its own. We aim for seven, but sometimes the interface with coastlines or uninhabitable areas makes this impossible. You can think of a sector as comparable to a pod on Jericho and the clusters as something like a super-pod. Self-sufficiency within sectors in terms of basic foods and natural resources is fundamental. Beyond that, there is trade with the neighbouring sectors.

"Areas of wilderness are connected to allow for migration routes and to help make life possible for the truly wild animals that require vast territory."

All of this was replicated in a vivid animation that moved and adapted to the commentary. Zooming in to a section of coast, it became clear that the whimsical form of a natural coastline feels no compulsion to conform to rigidly imposed hexagons. The solution was to avoid treating the chosen shapes as some kind of profound magic, but instead to permit distortions around complex areas of natural geography. A river close to the boundary of a hexagon might as well become that boundary. The entire global model had been computed, refined and optimised long ago by a gen-5 mind.

"In all, there are a little under thirty thousand sectors, each of which has a theoretical maximum human population of thirty-four thousand. Some have lower numbers, particularly if there is some special local factor such as land that's marginal for agriculture, or where there is significantly less land area due to sea, lakes or 'difficult' landscape.

"As with the caverns on Jericho, there is a strict allocation of land use within the sectors, with half given over to wilderness, and the remaining half divided between agriculture and urban."

Ren calculated. They were down to less than 20 percent for humanity, including agriculture, and less than 10 percent for urban or semi-pastoral use. That was unheard of within Core Planets.

Kani asked, "So, what happens if a sector disagrees with the central strategy and decides they want to drop your population controls or reallocate land as they wish?"

"We talk to their leadership to ascertain what kind of damaged thought patterns are at the heart of it," explained Saki. "It might require the reconditioning or transfer of a specific leader or group. Alternatively, we might perform an education intervention, but that takes a few years."

Ren's heart sank. He wanted to like the Arc, but words like this were making it difficult. He said, "You must know that those are disturbing ideas for us in Core."

"We don't wield that power casually, and in reality, we hardly need to use it. All we need is the knowledge of its presence, like weapons of mass destruction. It's easier to manage when we are dealing with populations of fifty thousand or less."

"Is that not the real reason you restrict sectors to that size? Is it not to control rebellion? C-C remains unassailably strong when measured against a population cluster."

"I wouldn't say that's our reason, but it helps with stability." Saki smiled to close down that line of questioning. He was keen to get back to the commentary.

"Typically, each sector has only one significant town along with a number of villages. Also note that there is a two-kilometre-wide rim on the periphery of each hexagon given over to wilderness. This gap is a safety net for migratory or roaming species, but it also prevents conurbation across sectors and helps to maintain distinct population units.

"All-in, we find Kraken can support a little over a billion people in reasonable coexistence with the natural world."

"Isn't that number a bit arbitrary though?" asked Ren. "Arguably, it could be any number. Surely, to some more extreme ecologists, that would be far too high, and for others, you might have an obligation or even a moral duty to try and support mankind in larger numbers."

"That's true enough. It is somewhat arbitrary, and the founders tied themselves up in knots debating it, but this is where we landed. Still, we do believe that any attempt to maximise human planetary populations is absurd, whether or not you consider the possibility of continuous expansion further into the galaxy."

They had left Hypatia far behind, but the hulking mountain range remained visible through distant haze. Ahead was a complex, rugged coastline of fjords and islands. On the inner lip of a headland, where fjord met open sea, lay their destination: a sheltered bay. The flyer was already losing altitude on an approach vector. A town lay around the bay's edge, continuing back from the water for a mile or more. As in Hypatia, buildings blended tradition with modernity, but here there was stone and slate in place of Hypatia's wood. The waterfront had an antique and ornamental quality, whilst further back, a more modern aesthetic flourished.

On a bluff between the bay and the open sea lay a patch of bare ground where the flyer settled. The spread of rotors decoupled, landing separately a few metres away. Leaving the craft behind, the group walked towards the town along a narrow, wild path. It followed the ground's natural undulations, weaving between rocks and tracing contours like an ancient animal track. They were surrounded by the autumnal colours of heather and blueberry. Dropping further into the lee of the bluff, stunted trees grew. With each step, they became a little taller and straighter, such that by the time they approached the town, they walked amongst the stark figures of tall, straight silver birch.

Archipelago

The air was at once familiar and alien. There were recognisable aromas of heather and sea, but these blended with other layers of scent that were harder to place. This sensation of the familiar mingling with something deeply odd was an expected sensation on a new planet. All it took was a marginally different atmospheric composition or some invisible local biochemical process to trigger these feelings. Little markers from smell, sight and touch fed the subconscious in ways that were impossible to fathom, dissect or trace. At that moment, Ren felt it intensely. The rich fragrance of earth and heather plucked the strings of deeply buried memories from early childhood on Palau. Or was it more? Was it possible that Ren was experiencing a genetic memory of this place?

Approaching the first buildings, Oso-Rae said, "This sector is called Neosho, and the settlement is Viola Bay. Welcome to my home. Welcome to your mother's sector! Do you want to meet some relatives?"

Things had suddenly become personal, and Ren was caught off guard. Why did they so love last-minute surprises? His visit to the fringes of his father's home on Jericho had left him without any fresh sense of identity or any notable feeling of belonging, but this time they were getting much closer. Would he truly meet family? Ren felt sick with anxiety.

A gaggle of children playing on the town's fringes spotted them, recognised Oso-Rae and excitedly ran over to greet her. They hugged her legs and blabbed in yet another dialect that the translator blanked with a petulant silence.

"These are the children of my and a neighbouring clan. I have been away for a while, and we miss each other."

"You said that you spend a quarter of your time back here," said Imiko. "What's the rotation, and what do you do when you're back?"

"It's not a rigid routine, and it can depend on how far your C-C base is from your sector. Typically I spend a week per month here, but sometimes there are longer gaps. When I'm home, I often continue my work remotely, but at other times, I do local things helping with clan meals, childcare, and so on.

"All this keeps members of Central Control grounded and reminds us of our bonds and duties towards our sectors, communities and clans. It is a fundamental part of preventing the elite clique you worry so much about and keep telling us we have."

Imiko rolled her eyes.

They continued into the town, following streets that wound eccentrically between white-painted stone houses, all with slate roofs encrusted with mustard-yellow lichen.

"Here in Viola Bay, there are a few people who live outside clans, but it isn't all that common. There is no obligation for clan bonding, but it's the norm. It makes life so much easier caring for the young, the elderly, and those who can't care for themselves. It spreads the burden of life in uncountable ways, and it provides automatic community and friendships. There is less worry about old age or serious illness because we have the clan's safety net."

"Okay, but people fight… often seriously," began Imiko. "How does that work in the context of a clan?"

"Yes, people fight, but time cures most things."

"Not always."

"Sure. Occasionally there are fractures that cause people to join another clan or even to live alone. Choosing a solitary life is more common with certain psychological traits that benefit from solace. Children almost always stay in the clan, whatever the parents decide, and that provides motivation for separated couples to figure something out."

"And what of serious crimes? Surely it's impossible to stay in a clan after a murder or some other crime of that magnitude has been committed."

"True, but such crimes are rare here. Our system makes it impossible to commit such acts without detection, so it's only acts of passion or desperation, where people know they will be caught but don't care. This requires the monitoring of implant data, but it's only done in strictly controlled circumstances."

Ren did a double-take. *Monitoring of implant data* sounded ominous. Admittedly, it could mean several things, but the most probable meaning had massive implications. Membership of Core was accompanied by a rigid set of rules, many of which were in the domain of personal liberty and the role of the state. One rule in particular was paramount, and that was the status of an implant, which always belonged entirely to the individual. The sea of data from a device literally entwined with your brain had vast potential for misuse by a rogue government. What if the Arc had decided to walk away from this rule? How would they ever reconcile? He returned to the conversation's thread.

"Is it not hard to protect your child from abuse?" asked Imiko.

"We believe that children get a more balanced upbringing surrounded by diverse adults. But the psychic tendency towards abuse is something we identify in people at an early stage. Once flagged it becomes… manageable."

They were now at the waterfront and following a granite sea wall worn smooth by the elements and by time. Boats were tied up at moorings, bobbing gently behind the triple protection of the bluff, the cove's narrow mouth and an inner harbour wall.

Ren and Oso-Rae were now walking alone some distance behind the others. They sat for a while to watch herring gulls and boobies swoop and dive across the bay.

Ren had been silent for some time, overwhelmed by the situation and what lay ahead. His brain was busy connecting this real place with the image he had built up from his mother's description. They were two very different things but were now coalescing into one.

As a coping mechanism, he returned to his list of questions and asked, "I have been thinking about the sectors and the clans. It isn't just conventional family structures and nations that you have thrown out. The Arc seems to have rejected all of the systems and institutions that make our classical societies function. Some of these have existed for centuries, even millennia."

He continued, "You seem to care little for the huge swathe of human history that predated the Arc's foundation. You see it as some kind of dark age before emerging into the light. When we examine history, we only see the craziest of miserable, misguided revolutionaries who tried to delete the past. Some burned books, many demolished historic buildings, and a few actually rewrote history to suit their ideology."

"There was no book burning and, by definition, there were no historic buildings to demolish," said Oso-Rae. "We don't rewrite history. In fact, we refer to it a great deal. There are plenty of great thinkers from the past... but believing that all great thought has already been thought and that all great social ideas have already been considered, tried and tested is utterly defeatist. It's really sad."

"But you wipe away all our ancient institutions, which provide a bedrock for society and progress. You wipe it all away and pronounce millennia of human history irrelevant."

Oso-Rae pounced. "Things are not good because they are historic. And anyway, we didn't wipe anything away really. It's one thing to foment revolution in an existing planetary society. It's quite another to start with a blank piece of paper as we did with these planets. Why would we wheel in cartloads of dysfunction from history? Why would we emulate a model that fails and kills and destroys whole ecosystems? That is madness."

After a pause, she continued, "No great idea in its beginning can ever be within existing norms. How can it be? The norms are stationary or stagnant."

Ren groaned at Oso-Rae's prepared tautology, regurgitating what he felt certain were stock phrases from Arc doctrine. It felt impractical and entirely abstract. His world was about ancient, established systems and the application of realpolitik to the galaxy's ugliness. Their idealism was laughably naïve. Human existence was too complex to be forced into this singular frame.

"Here's the problem. Just a few decades ago, a small group of planetary designers threw away centuries of thought and became trapped on their own island of doctrine. They thought they could rewire humanity, throw away tradition and institution, and forget the deep history of human progress."

"Which of your ancient institutions would you have us adopt? The church? We have discussed that. Your republics and your parliamentary democracies? We have discussed that too. Your property law? ...I could go on. At what point do you stop hauling dysfunction through the centuries? At what point do you stop and say, 'we could do better?'"

Ren laughed and said, "One day I'll catch you off guard, and you will speak from a more personal account. You can't possibly believe that the whole of Core is a shop of horrors."

"Oh, I don't think that at all. The problem is the opposite – that you see the Arc as some kind of cancerous growth on human progress."

"Well, we will figure it out, won't we?"

"Yes, I do think we will."

After a pause, Oso-Rae added, "Look, I'm not as dogmatic about this as I sound. To an extent, I'm just doing my job in defending it. This isn't perfect, and I do think that the founders of the system threw much of what was good out with the bad – the baby out with the bathwater, so to speak. I can accept that."

"I too am doing my job, but I'm not as determined to find fault with the Arc as you think," said Ren. "There are many noble ideas, but I have to be sure that they are safe and that there is not a façade obscuring an alternative truth."

"You know what we have in common, don't you? We are both good at delivering received wisdom and making it sound as though we believe it right down to the soles of our shoes. In different circumstances, we two could have more interesting conversations."

"The broken idealists club?"

Re-joining the group, Oso-Rae led them back from the

seafront along quirky, winding alleys. The buildings were a collision of angles and forms – the inverse of those regimented rows that typified so many towns. This could only be a deliberately stylised confection since the street pattern had not arisen organically from millennia of habitation, but from relatively recent and explicit design. Somewhere there was a line between clever urban planning and the self-conscious emulation of folksy ancient townscapes.

"This is for Ren, but you'll all find it interesting," said Oso-Rae. "Are you ready to meet the clan?" He wasn't in the slightest bit ready but nodded nonetheless.

They paused at the wide doors of a heavy stone building and then, without knocking, she ushered them inside to a large communal space. It was scattered with eclectic, mismatched seats, cushions, and long dining tables. One corner was set aside as a play area for younger children, whilst another had a suite of vaguely familiar games – variants of things played on dozens of other planets. The space could accommodate fifty or more, but today there were only a dozen people present.

Eyes darted between the two groups, both searching for some shred of recognition. Ren could identify some familiar features, but there was no profound or cathartic moment.

"This is your mother's clan... your clan if you choose to look at it that way." Then, turning to face the crowd she said, "This is Ren, Tassi's son."

Opposite was a woman shrivelled by age but with bright eyes shining in the deep folds of her face. Gesturing towards her, Oso-Rae said, "Oandei, this is your nephew."

Oandei turned to Ren, took a couple of steps towards him, and looked directly into his eyes as if searching. She maintained this stare with the group standing in silence until her frown passed and a sad smile surfaced. She took Ren's hands in her own and said, "Tell me of my sister. When I knew she wasn't coming back, my heart broke a little."

Ren answered kindly and told her a little about his

mother's life and her passing all those years before. But they were being observed, and this spoiled any chance of bonding more deeply. Ren resolved to return and meet her again without these many eyes watching. Oandei stepped back into the folds of her clan group and melted into a soft chair, her eyes now far away and her face shrouded in sadness.

Turning to the wider group, Oso-Rae said, "I invite you to talk and ask questions. This is an opportunity to learn about clan life, and the answers you get will be direct and unedited."

They gathered in the cushioned seating area, and endless introductions were made. The mundane practicalities of remembering names and faces were all taken care of by implants. Without that, Ren would have been entirely lost.

An awkward silence reigned until August finally spoke. "Okay then. I'm divorced, and it was extremely acrimonious… the bitch. We now despise one another with a special venom, and there isn't a snowball's chance in hell of us continuing to live together. How do you handle that?"

His deadpan humour was the perfect opener. They looked at each other, deciding who would reply. In the end, an older woman with a creased face and bony hands took up the reins.

"We don't 'marry' in the antiquated sense that you imply. Our society does not discourage life-long monogamy, but we also don't put it on a pedestal. Here, beyond emotional upset, there is little to fight about. There is no property to battle over, as private wealth will always be with the individual.

"Then there are the children, who are not the chattels of their parents but members of the clan. This means that parents have no opportunity to dispute custody as they might in the old ways."

"So that's it? People just carry on and forget about it?"

"No, there are houseplants and rugs to fight over." She smiled but then returned to the point. "Emotional upset can be overwhelming. If people can't get past it, then one or both might move clans or even further afield. There's a degree of ordinary traffic between clans, but you are likely to move anyway if you form a new relationship. That said, it's traumatic to leave your clan's warm hearth, particularly under a cloud of bitterness."

"I have a really simple question," said Imiko. "How do you arrange food preparation rotas? Who does the work? How do you make it fair? What if, like me, you hate cooking with a primal passion?"

This time a younger man spoke. "You mustn't think of this as a rigid system. Within a clan, there isn't a single, strict model, and there are as many ways of handling it as there are clans. Sometimes a few individuals take care of it and are paid for that role. In other clans, there is some kind of rota, and if you hate cooking with that primal passion, then you might pick up one of the other domestic roles."

"How does childcare work?" asked Imiko.

"It's not so different to food – it varies. It suits some members to take it on as a full-time role, but others use a rota system which allows parents to pursue careers whilst raising families. There aren't usually that many simultaneous babies or toddlers in a clan."

Ren had listened to these innocent questions and decided to throw a grenade into the conversation. "What is the worst social crisis you have had in your clan in the past few years?"

They hadn't expected such a thorny question, but after a little whispering Oandei answered. "There have been a couple that stand out. One was a young woman, much loved by us, who became deeply frustrated at her repeated failure to be selected for pregnancy – we are at maximum here in Neosho. She started to resent friends, family, clan and the whole system. In the end, she emigrated to a less populous sector. We lost contact.

"The second was a young man, Deko, who was flagged up by Central Control's H-Pop department as having deviant tendencies and being a danger to those around him. He resented the system's capacity to flag him in this way, and that aggravated the problem."

"What do you mean by deviant?"

"They were not specific. He was taken for reconditioning but returned as a shell – embarrassed, strange, and awkward. It proved impossible to remain in the clan so, of his own volition, he left to live a solitary life.

"It's extremely distressing, not just for the person taken away but also for their family and friends. You might know in your heart that it was for the best, but you have to trust that the appraisal was accurate. In the end, we have to accept that it protects against the worst forms of abuse and harm, but it can be hard to believe in a crime that never happened."

Ren was speechless. Dumbstruck. These two simple tales had opened a Pandora's box of disturbing ideology and practice. Selection for pregnancy? Monitor minds? Reconditioning? It had all come tumbling out. Had the Arc team anticipated this question and its answer? Had they arranged for these ideas to be delivered in just this way?

There was material in there to fuel a month of debate, but now was evidently not the moment. He had no wish to cross-examine these innocents and instead allowed the questions to continue. The Viola Bay locals asked a few questions of their own about life within the leagues. It was all good-natured, and their naïve questions revealed as much as their previous answers. The whole thing was both heartening and disquieting. There was a beauty to their innocence but an increasingly ugly-sounding layer of dictatorial malevolence sitting behind it.

On the walk back towards the flyer, Oso-Rae said, "There's another distinctive thing here in Neosho. It hosts an important company called Novo that employs a fifth of the sector's population. They design and create gen-4 and gen-5 minds. It's one of those areas that is impossible to achieve without scale."

"So, this is the headquarters? Are manufacturing facilities and operations in other sectors?"

Saki seemed momentarily puzzled as if he had forgotten that this might not be blindingly obvious. "Oh no. A company can't span sectors. That's not allowed. Most of the staff are in R&D, design, and administration. Manufacturing is largely robotic and hidden underground. It is one of the specialised industries that has the whole of the Arc as a marketplace. Other industries, like food and natural resources, are more localised."

"This is the thing I can't wrap my head around," said Ren. "With gateways, *local* means almost nothing. Why is it so important to you when there is effectively zero distance between two points in Arc space?"

"It's about taking care of your backyard. You reap what you sow, you create what you need, you go without what you don't need."

Maybe they weren't so far off when they referred to these people as those "eccentric hippies" of the Arc, thought Ren. There was an absurdist element to their insistence on localism. Palau, his home world, was agrarian, and just a few gateways allowed it to feed population clusters on dozens of other planets and habitats. He wasn't a fan of Palau, but he still felt they performed a great service to the Congregation of Populated Systems. How could that be such a bad thing?

"So, theoretically, could one company employ an entire sector?"

"Sort of," replied Oso-Rae. "But they would also have to cover all other human needs: agriculture, trades, shops, services, amenities… it's a long list. In practice, a fifth is approaching the maximum, because there are so many other areas of human activity that make a sector function."

"In Core, and even more so in the other leagues, the tech industries are trans-planetary titans, often employing hundreds of thousands of people. A few employ millions. That sort of scale is required for evolved innovation and manufacture. I don't even remotely understand how you can achieve the same without that scale."

"I would bet that those corporations are diversified conglomerates and do many things, which frankly only benefit their directors and shareholders. But you're right to some extent. A few of our companies are permitted to pool resources for R&D or theoretical research. A few industries are, to a limited extent, permitted to share data and manufacturing techniques."

By noon they were back in the flyer, jetting their way back towards Hypatia. On Jericho, their days had been spent on languid tours strangely devoid of urgency, but here on Kraken, the tempo had changed. Not only was the pace picking up, but the broad-brush impressionistic start was being replaced by more tangible detail.

Astrid's instructions were preying on his mind again. *What can I do with the grenade I am holding? Shall I let the insertion go ahead or leave the Archipelago in peace and drop the other leagues in the proverbial crap?*

Back in Hypatia and without an agenda, the group seemed afflicted by collective introversion. Saki and Ychi made their excuses and scurried away into the town's alleys. August, Kani and Imiko almost brusquely took themselves off on private matters. This left Ren and Oso-Rae alone, so they wandered the town's cobbled streets together.

They walked in silence along the main boulevard before turning outwards to explore the network of steep, weaving lanes that climbed towards the town's upper limits. There, the buildings petered out and cobbled lanes became stony paths. Oso-Rae chose the most heavily trodden route leading up to the col. This was the excursion suggested to them on their first evening in Hypatia, and now they were walking it as if guided by some secret psychic agreement.

Ren ventured a question that had been building in him. "What moves you personally? What drives you, and what do you fight for? What makes you want to get up in the morning?"

"I'm not as diligent or as earnest as you think, Ren. You ask what I fight for and what drives me, but those words are the wrong ones to describe my motivations. My life is as much about having fun as it is about devotion to work. I listen to my inner rhythms, and I follow them."

She continued, "I ask you what the point in all this is if you can't dance, laugh with friends, visit lovers on a dark night, make tea, swim in a cold sea, and watch the dawn. I refuse to be part of a humourless cause that perceives everything through a lens of misery. I won't represent an institution that thinks those who seek pleasure and joy are betraying their impassioned cause.

"I mean, what is a life well-lived, Ren? It is a life that gives back to your clan, gives back to your people and guards the natural world. It is a life that allows you to live and love fiercely."

Ren smiled at her sweetly impassioned speech, but his more cynical side thought that people who spoke that way usually lived a life as ordinary as anyone else. Very few people truly burned like those fabulous roman candles of literature.

"I don't claim to live fiercely," said Ren, "although my life is more erratic and diverse than most. But, yes, I am motivated by the desire to better myself, learn, and gain wisdom. Surely that pursuit is the better part of us. It is our clear distinction over animals, and if we are to evolve into the universe, we should strive, above all, to perfect the mind."

"I think it's meaningless to live by the dictates of reason alone," replied Oso-Rae. "Characterising human beings as a processor inside a head, with a bunch of dumb meat connected to it for performing tasks, is a poor representation of identity. We are not designed to live by rendering cold logic into actions.

"The reasoning mind is a thin veneer over the top of a teeming mass of instinct. We tend to use our logic to post-justify what our wider being already knew through instinct.

"Don't get me wrong... We should strive for intellectual and ethical improvement, but it has to embrace our messy humanity. Education is a foundation of our society. Ignorance is a destructive force."

Oso-Rae turned away, and in so doing shut the conversation down. She had had enough, and the topic had begun to vex her. Ren suspected that it might be a bone of contention between her and others in her circle. They were coming up to the viewpoint of the col, and once again they lapsed into silence for the final stretch.

Finally, the view was upon them, and they gazed down at a giant river of cracked black and turquoise ice as it snaked from the foothills of Cerro Quizapu, past its sibling peaks and then onwards down a vast valley. It required a mental leap to accept that a river of glacial ice was actually flowing. The truth of this was revealed by snaps, pops and bangs forged deep inside the ice as it wrenched itself past obstructions and around corners.

Mountain peaks rose steeply from the ice in sheer, unclimbable walls, ridges, spurs and horns. Ren had never witnessed natural geology on this mega-scale before. It was humbling.

Furry animals hurried about nervously at a safe distance. Ren was astonished by these creatures' ability to find a foothold in this harsh, barren mountain col.

Oso-Rae turned to Ren, suddenly serious and with sadness gleaming in her eyes. "I fear for us in this, Ren. I don't see many outcomes where this ends well. In the long term, how can the Arc stand up to forces so much bigger than it? Instinct tells me we are being played."

"You're right to question the situation," replied Ren. "I'm used to knowing the game and playing it well based on known rules, but this is different." His words dried up, because to go further would incriminate himself.

"I am saying this because I believe you have a more honest purpose than the others. Sure, you're private, but you wear your heart on your sleeve, so to speak. It might be that you four are working against each other."

Ren's professional instinct told him that he should not trust a word that Oso-Rae was saying. His most basic training flagged this up as a classical ruse. Gain confidence, be charming, and then use your opponent's dropped guard to smite them. And yet those rules of the game didn't seem to fit at all. Rather, he felt horrible guilt, for it was the others who had a clear purpose, whilst he played games.

Finally reaching a decision, Ren said, "If you're right, we will have to cooperate to prevent powerful people from doing stupid things."

Conversation withered as they lingered at the viewpoint, both lost in thought. Finally, they turned and picked their way back along the path towards town. For a time Ren and Oso-Rae continued in silence, but when back on the main thoroughfare, they linked arms and talked of more pedestrian things. Ren described where he lived; the spectacular, noisy chaos of Super Paradise; and his strange adoration of the underbelly of life on Marrakesh. Oso-Rae talked of her clan and the peculiar idiosyncrasies of a life divided between provincial simplicity and the bleeding edge of political life in Hypatia.

It was late afternoon, and Hypatia's temperature was plummeting. The sun had dipped behind the mountains, and a biting wind descended from ice fields beyond the col. Ren was indoors with a fire burning in the grate of their living room. He puzzled over the weird and troubling comments he had heard that day. There were the conversations in Viola Bay but also things he had unearthed independently through conversation and observation. Exploring Hypatia's streets had revealed people who were eager to communicate. They had been kind, courteous, and delighted to share. It was almost as if they had been instructed to talk, particularly about their area of speciality. But, without exception, they became evasive around issues such as policing, the use of force and the suppression of dissent. They would politely demur or suggest that it wasn't something they knew much about. He would have been happy to stay there all evening, but the Arc contingent appeared, this time with a new face amongst them.

"May I present Nako," said Saki. "He works with us in foreign affairs but more directly with the upper echelons."

By way of greeting, Nako bowed to them each in turn. "So where are you with your discussions? What's up next?" he asked.

Kani leapt in. "I want to talk about gateways. Who owns and builds them, and what are the rights of movement through them?"

"We manage them. We build them, and we license their use," said Saki. "They are a C-C monopoly. It's simple."

"Okay, so you don't use companies to build and finance them?" asked Imiko.

"No, but all components are supplied by third parties. We fund C-C by charging for their use, along with a couple of other monopolies."

Officially, state monopolies went against the rules of Core membership, but Ren knew that the rule was sometimes ignored. It hardly marked them as renegades.

"So, as long as the tariff for their use is paid, is there freedom of movement through them across and between planets?" asked Imiko.

"Not exactly. Is there in your leagues?"

"Not exactly, no. Fair point."

Kani stepped in again. "So how would our corporates be able to operate in your worlds? You restrict the size of companies, and key technologies are state-owned. Are you ready to talk to us at all?"

"I'm sure we can find some middle ground," replied Saki.

"Our corporates would also want access to waste export and mineral import activities. How would that work?"

Ren groaned. Had the debate stooped to garbage management? But the conversation that followed unmasked some new facets of the peculiar Arc psyche. For centuries, the issue of planetary waste had been solved by simply wheeling it all through a gateway and dumping it on a lifeless moon. In some systems, waste was dropped into a gas giant's atmosphere, where it would sink to unimaginable depths, liquefy, and mix with the chemical soup at thousands of degrees and gigapascals of pressure.

Conversely, with raw materials it had become unusual, even eccentric, to mine metals and minerals from an inhabited planet. Why bother when you could ravage an inert asteroid or barren moon at less cost? It was a no-brainer.

True, the Arc did these very same things, but intriguingly it was a factional dispute within their ranks. There was an influential body of people who believed that even moons should not be despoiled and that humanity should leave them as virgin wonders. For some, nature included the inanimate, so uninhabited, lifeless places might be worthy of protection. This faction was not strong enough to prevent the practice altogether, but it held enough sway to restrict it. Within the Arc, there were moons, planetoids and asteroid fields under a protectorate, like national parks.

Ren saw some eccentric beauty in this idea of leaving no footprints, but the accessible part of the galaxy was now unimaginably large. Nothing was permanent. At some point, stars would go supernova and wipe away every shred of human impact. To him, the permanence and balance they craved didn't seem so profound or real.

August said, "You hollowed out Jericho and Typhon and in so doing generated gigatons of rocky waste."

"Petatons," said Ychi.

"Okay, whatever. Petatons... you spread the waste over their surfaces rather than removing it and dumping it elsewhere."

"Jericho and Typhon were mostly complete by the time the C-C principles became dominant. It's true that their surfaces are now brutalised, but we would never do the same again with a new habitat. That said, there is a huge cost that accompanies the building of gateways with sufficient capacity to export the volumes we're talking about."

Cutting off the conversation, Nako spoke properly for the first time. Ren was struck by a level of confidence and gravitas in him that hadn't been obvious at first.

"You have now seen two of our humble planets, and tomorrow you begin free travel to destinations of your choosing. These can last up to two weeks, and then you will return here before heading home."

Oso-Rae added, "You will be given mesh access for most of what you need, and one of us will accompany each of you, although we will happily stay out of your way if desired."

"August, what's your choice?"

"I'll be going to Eleuthera first if that's okay. I'll see how I get on there and then maybe move on."

"Ren?"

"I'll stay here a couple more days. I'm not quite done with Hypatia and I also hope to see some of Kraken's wilderness. I'm tempted to visit Eleuthera too."

"I think we all want to see Eleuthera, but I'll start with Bathsheba," said Kani. "As a group, we should cover as much as possible."

"Agreed," said Imiko. "I'll go to Typhon and then see where my feet take me."

"That's perfect," said Saki. "It doesn't mean that you will not see other places. These are just starting points, and it allows us to allocate guides. You'll have freedom of movement and can return here at any time. As you have seen, gateway traffic is largely unrestricted."

"Some sunshine for me! It's too cold here. Ha!" said August.

The meeting was done, but once again they had dodged the more sensitive and troubling areas of Central Control's activities. But Ren also knew that those conversations were pointless. They would paint 'suppression of dissent' as both innocent and necessary. They would say that all societies have boundaries, which was true, and they would say that theirs were reasonable and necessary. Everyone says the same. What mattered was what he saw, not what they said.

Ren was staying on Kraken for reasons he hadn't shared. One was the strange tingling of a bond with those people in Viola Bay. He wanted to know if there was any substance to it, and if not, at least share more with Oandei. The second was that the information he needed was more likely to be found here than on a brand-new planet. A more open form of conversation was evolving with Oso-Rae, and he was sure that the key to progress lay there.

In his room, Ren checked the swarm's status. On Kraken, without the barriers of a cavern world, his latest batch had spread far and wide. Most were busy tracing his companions' own hardware. Others were snooping around Hypatia or making trips further afield. The trouble was that this town was isolated, making it hard to strike a balance between covering ground and getting timely information back.

One batch of data was peculiar: unlike anything he had seen before from micro-tech. Since it emanated from a location in Hypatia itself, Ren left on foot to investigate. Maybe his eyes would reveal something where the data failed to. He made his way down to the square, past the gateways, and continued on to the flat ground leading towards the precipice, gradually being steered towards the data's source.

At first it was hard to make out in the twilight, but by kneeling and peering at the ground, he spied the unmistakable form of a tiny black sphere floating marginally above the ground. It could not have been larger than a pea, but he immediately knew what it was.

"A gateway?" he asked himself out loud.

His mind raced as he thought about the implications of

this. Planting beacons for an invasion was one thing, but gateways were quite another. August was not just scheming with the others, he was in deep, and Astrid needed to know.

Chapter 18

Astrid Puzzles Whilst Laynna Plots

Astrid sat in her office on the fourteenth floor of the sandstone behemoth of the External Affairs building, drumming her fingers on the desk and staring without focus into the middle distance.

In the right light, her office was almost glamorous, as might befit a person of her standing, but looking more closely, it was forlorn and somewhat crumby. Neglected plants had long needed a gardener. One had been dead for over a year, its soil a desiccated lump. The cheap, veneered surfaces of her furniture were tired and scuffed. Floor tiles were stained and heavily worn on the most travelled routes. Everything could really have done with a makeover; indeed, it could have done with this some years ago. The view from her window would have been fabulous had there been anything to look at, but instead, it displayed streaked grey skies and haphazard rooftops.

Humans can become accustomed to almost anything. Given time, they can start to see beauty and find comfort in the most surprising places. Astrid considered her office to be a soothing den, despite its stained tiles and ragged plants. She might well have been upset if someone had arrived to give it a refit, although such an event seemed unlikely on External

Affairs budgets. That pile of papers belonged just there, even if she hadn't touched it in two years. A stack of books on the meeting table was exactly where she wanted it. Not that she ever referred to them, but she liked the possibility of doing so, and occasionally she liked to be reminded of the existence of writings that had helped form her. Astrid's chair was the wrong height but she enjoyed slouching in it. The blinds were all bent and the strings in knots… but it was her dominion.

Ren's communique had caught her off-guard. It wasn't so much the news that August and, by proxy, General Banz were in cahoots with the other leagues. That was the sort of intrigue she was always on guard for. The real surprise had been these new gateways, because that transformed what they were capable of. It turned an almost impossibly messy invasion into something they might actually pull off. Indeed, it became something she might not be able to stop, even if she wanted to. This new nugget of information was at once terrifying and deliciously puzzling.

It was that rarest of things, a partly sunny day in Haikou District, but the broken blinds of her office had lost the battle to fend it off. They hung ashamed and ruined, perhaps wondering what remaining purpose they had in this world. It's not that she hated the sun… far from it. But, like the sharp focus of a camera's lens on an aged face, the bright sunlight was not kind to her office. Everything seemed doubly knackered and worn. Dust was everywhere, and her screen was smeared.

The Hanseatics and the Old Worlds were up to no good, which was utterly predictable and expected. However, she still didn't know why Banz had climbed into bed with Mu Rosa and Virsenko. Was this about UCoM or Helsingor?

The sunlight in her eyes was a distraction that did nothing to help her concentration, so she left her office, walked out to the elevators, and sailed up to the roof garden just a few floors above. It was a serene, leafy space – a surprising and eccentric extravagance on the part of the building's architect. The most baffling aspect was that barely anyone made use of it, so Astrid was almost alone. Sitting in the shade of a willow next to a shallow pond thick with lily pads, she sought new clarity.

Astrid spun out a data request through the most secure External Affairs channels. It was a risk because requests of this nature left a trace. Querying someone's movements could have implications. A careful investigation might reveal evidence of the original data request. Worse than that, she still might not discover their precise movements, because there were ways of hiding, and location could be obfuscated. Next, she messaged Elia Volse and requested an urgent meeting.

An hour later she was in a hotel room in Long Beach, booked under the name of Jane Doe, or some such like. The manager knew the routine, so she entered through a service entrance, avoiding any prying eyes that might notice her passing through the lobby. Haikou District had more than its fair share of spies and journalists who never ceased to gossip and swap favours. It wasn't wise to feed that toxic broth without reason, so it was simpler to meet here, far from prying eyes.

This hotel's singular point of interest was that each of its guest rooms had a wall of glass facing the sea. It was the inverse of almost every other view in Long Beach, which consciously faced inwards as if hiding from the cold. A view like this was certainly a niche taste, but for some it had an ethereal, frigid beauty. Guests could watch the dark water churn and hurl itself against the rocks. They could gaze at glistening blocks of sculpted ice that lay stranded on black, volcanic sands.

A knock at the door announced Volse's arrival. As he joined her on the couch, a large wave broke, sending spray high enough to spatter the room's window.

"I never have understood why you choose this place, Astrid."

"If you don't get it, you don't get it," she said. "Elia, there's a problem. I have evidence that UCoM, or at least General Banz, is working with Mu Rosa and Little Mouse. There's no longer any doubt that there are insertions, and somehow Banz is involved."

Volse absorbed the information without expression or surprise. "How do you know this?"

"Ren has sent a message that made their collusion clear. All of them are loaded with microtech. In the past few minutes I have discovered that Banz left Core space once in the run-up to the team's departure and twice since."

"Ah," said Volse. "What's his game?"

Astrid said, "I don't know for sure, but August Broher is assisting the other Leagues in the Arc. If he's under instructions from Banz, which he surely must be, it might implicate Helsingor more than UCoM."

"Is there any mileage in challenging him and forcing Broher to stand down?" asked Volse.

"I don't think so. Similarly, it would serve no purpose to challenge Virsenko and Mu Rosa. If they wish to act, they will do so. It seems that the only tool we have at our disposal is Ren," said Astrid.

"It's true, we're highly limited in what we can do. Challenging them would be counterproductive. It might even accelerate an orbital drop-out and leave less time to prepare for it." said Volse.

"I hate feeling this useless. All we can do is prepare to contain Banz and Helsingor's government."

"But Astrid..." began Volse. "Why do we need to stop it? Why not let them invade and then be ready to step in to support the innocents afterwards?"

Astrid stared at him for a time. He had a point. If they acted to try and stop an invasion and failed, then, as an act of retribution, the other leagues would carve Core out of any future association with the Arc. If Core actively helped, that would clearly break their ethical codex. However, if they turned a blind eye... well, that might be a plan.

"Yes, maybe you're right," said Astrid. "I need to think about that."

She wasn't sure she agreed, but she didn't wish to

contradict Volse before thinking it through. On one hand he was absolutely correct. If they tried to stop the invasion and failed, then Core would lose everything.

The counter argument was that whatever the Arc's dysfunction, they should, if at all possible, prevent the invasion. They could deal with the Arc later. If Ren did this right, and she had chosen him for a reason, he might succeed in making it appear as though the Arc foiled the plot on its own. But UCoM's involvement would be hard to explain, and the Arc might lay the blame on everyone in equal measure.

Volse took his leave, but Astrid waited ten minutes before making her own way out. She walked to the window, where she gazed out at the low, scudding clouds and squally rain. She knew it was an eccentricity, but she found this view comforting.

The reality was that despite her power, she was no celebrity, and here in this crappy backwater of Marrakesh, nobody was likely to recognise her. But the stakes were high, and she couldn't take chances. She both loved and loathed her lack of celebrity but recognised the conflict of ego in that sentiment. Outside, the pitiless rain continued to fall.

***

Light-years away on Cervantes, Laynna Mu Rosa was having a spectacularly good day... so good that she was celebrating early with a stiff Bloody Mary. It was only four in the afternoon, but what the hell. Her yacht was at anchor a couple of hundred metres offshore, and she sat in the canopied shade of a beach bar, watching her beloved grandchildren at play on the sand. Many would have assumed Mu Rosa to be incapable of love, and frankly it was useful to let them believe that. The truth was that she felt it deeply, but for only a handful of people: her immediate family and a couple of old friends. But her empathy stopped abruptly there. Everyone else could go fly a kite.

Her extraordinarily good cheer was down to the latest news from the Arc and from Commander Palina. The insertions were perfectly poised, and uplinks from all three planet surfaces were going live. Over thirty micro-gateways had been successfully seeded. In just a week or two Palina would be ready and able to act. The Arc would be torn from Astrid's hands.

It was somewhat personal. Astrid was overly cocky about Core's dominance and too smug in her manipulation of people and planets. Mu Rosa grudgingly respected Astrid but would nonetheless take pleasure in her downfall. It didn't exactly paint her morality in a glorious light, but like so many things in this world, she didn't give a crap. For her, ethics were the domain of individuals and had no bearing on the conduct of business or state. Eat or be eaten.

A chime announced the imminent arrival of her visitors. On cue, she walked down the sand, past the excitable gaggle of children, and boarded a waiting launch which whisked her back to her ship, *Anger Management.*

Virsenko, Palina and Banz arrived seconds later and were escorted to meet Mu Rosa under an awning near the pool bar.

"An update please, Commander Palina." Mu Rosa couldn't be bothered with opening pleasantries today.

Palina said, "Of course, Director. As you are aware, the unit in the Heimdall system – that's Eleuthera – has been ready for some time. The other two were more recent arrivals, and we have been racing against the clock to become established. You'll be pleased to know that we are almost ready to go and will be able to perform orbital drop-outs within a few days."

"So we're ready to pounce," said Mu Rosa.

"Not quite," replied Palina. "The beacons are only beginning to come onstream, and we still have to process their data and prioritise targets. The micro-gateways are also being seeded, but they take longer and we need better coverage."

Mu Rosa asked, "How much longer?"

"It depends on when and if your people get to the other

planets and habitats that have yet to be seeded. Once they have, the bare minimum is a week, but ideally more."

"You don't get more."

Banz asked, "What's the likelihood of them having been detected?"

"I think it's unlikely but not entirely impossible. We have been discreet keeping our distance. We have been very careful indeed."

Virsenko asked a naïve but necessary question. "And could you act in Jericho and Kraken first and trigger the remaining planets later?"

"That wouldn't work, as it would leave too many centres of power and gateways under Arc control. They could hunker down on Typhon, Eleuthera and Bathsheba and we would have a stalemate." Palina had thought this through in some detail.

He continued, "There's also the fact that our agents in the Arc have to cover a huge amount of ground in order to pave the way for this. We have statistical estimates of the fraction of gateways, military installations and power plants we need to control, but it is gateways that we need most. Every day more beacons spark up and we get better information. The most fundamental data is around interplanetary routes because if we control those, we have them in a vise. That is key to a bloodless operation. Without them, we have a big old war on our hands."

Banz said, "That is a well-understood strategy. It's useless to clinch just a fraction. We only hold the cards if we control traffic entirely. That's why the presence of the team on the ground is critical to this operation."

The others looked at Banz as if to say *thanks for stating the obvious. You can shut up now.*

"We aim to act in a week. Go prepare, Commander."

Mu Rosa dismissed Palina with a flick of her head. He nodded and departed, leaving the other three alone.

"That brings us to the decision point. Are there any scenarios where we back down?"

"To my mind, we aren't here to negotiate. We act as soon as we are able to," replied Virsenko.

Banz asked, "Is there a final warning to try to force their hand?"

"Absolutely not. Surprise is fundamental."

It was not that these three trusted one another any further than they could throw each other, but they shared a common purpose for the time being. They were like a makeshift squad in a Battle Royale who cooperate until near the end and then fight to the death.

Mu Rosa looked at Banz and asked, "Do we have anything to fear from Astrid? Might External Affairs or Special Services be on to us?"

"I'm confident we're ahead of her," he replied. "She surely knows about the insertions, at least suspects they exist, but I can't believe she knows about this little club."

Virsenko said, "It's dangerous to underestimate that woman. She'll be watching us closely."

"I think she's almost irrelevant in this now," said Banz. "It's not as though she can stop us anyway."

Chapter 19

Whales, Smoking Chimneys, and Sedition

Oso-Rae, forever punctual, stood at the door in comical mittens and a whimsical woollen hat.

"Shall we go on a little trip, Ren?"

She wore a small pack and held a second in her hand, which she passed to him as they wandered down towards the square.

"We are heading to Kirigueti, a continent on the other side of Kraken, so we must resort to gateways, I'm afraid." Somewhere along the way she had figured out Ren's discomfort with them.

Overnight, a storm had blown through, and Hypatia now lay under a thick layer of snow. An unobtrusive hum issued from a squadron of drones diligently clearing thoroughfares. The town looked serene under this pristine blanket.

The snow underfoot scrunched and squeaked happily as they went. Speech was muffled by the snowscape's peculiar acoustics, which allowed some sounds to carry far and clear whilst simultaneously attenuating others. Each breath produced vaporous clouds that coiled into fractal shapes before dissipating.

Snow was not some rare, exotic treat for Ren. Marrakesh certainly got its share, but there it entailed a pure, unadulterated misery of sleet, slush, howling winds and frozen feet. The cold wasn't deep or long-lived often enough for him to own clothes truly appropriate for winter, which meant that on those slushy days, he was always underdressed and shivering.

He had said wooden farewells to August, Kani and Imiko, who were readying themselves for their journeys to other worlds. Ren felt conflicted about his companions. In many ways, it was a relief to be free of them as there was no communal purpose, and their many secrets made each conversation deeply artificial. That said, he had grown to like them as people, even Kani. All showed genuine curiosity for these worlds, even if some of their questions were designed to make a point rather than learn. Questions as statements.

Ren felt no great urgency to visit the other planets, partly as his mission was his own and partly because there was plenty still to resolve on Kraken. On this day Oso-Rae had offered to show him the planet's deepest wilderness. This trip had a dual purpose: one was to elaborate the ongoing propaganda of Arc achievements, but the second was personal. Ren's mother had been a marine biologist specialising in cetaceans. Indeed, it was that job that had taken her out of the Arc when the coup occurred and marooned her. He was to see her work first-hand.

In the main square, five spheres marked the active gateways. Their midnight black stood out sharply against the brilliant white of fresh snow.

Free-standing gateways floating in the open were a quirk of the Arc. It was evident that they had a deep aversion to putting engineering on display, so they hid the supporting apparatus away. Around them, there was nothing more than basic access ramps. Security and pressure management were handled within the intermediary nexus hubs. It actually made a lot of sense.

"How do you manage permissions for these transits? Are we being monitored?" asked Ren.

"Ha! Not exactly," she replied. "The Arc has a liberal approach to gateway traffic. Because we have such strict rules in some areas of life, we compensate by being libertarian in others. There is nothing to stop an average citizen from going from Jericho to Eleuthera as a tourist without permission or visa."

"Is our movement not tracked and monitored?"

"Generally not in a human sense, although a gen-5 monitors everything for purely practical reasons. Don't forget that C-C is a fairly tiny percentage of the population, so there are many areas of life that we don't bother to police."

"Anywhere?"

"There are restricted zones, such as military sites and the vicinities of big power plants. Any society has the capacity to create rebels, unbalanced saboteurs, and terrorists. We all have our delusional mujahideen."

"It's so odd…" said Ren. "Where we have liberty, you have control, and where we have control, you have liberty. I wonder what that means."

She thought for a moment and then replied, "You know that liberty is best served by carefully taking little bits of it away. You do that with a web of laws. We do it our way."

Without queues or security, they were through to their destination in the time it had taken to exchange those few words. The last of three gateways deposited them on a broad, flat area of immaculately trimmed grass surrounded by forested hills stretching to infinity. About the grass stood a hundred or more parked flyers. Some were like the glassy copter they had taken the previous day, but others had obscurely technical functions with clusters of cameras and equipment.

"This is an ecological monitoring site. All these flyers are used to track populations of critical species, sample, photograph, count, categorise, and occasionally tag. They study the development of diseases and pests. In addition, they monitor new genetic mutations and investigate evolution in action. The data allows us to maintain a holistic model of the ecosphere."

The air was fresh and cool, but bright flowers and budding

leaves implied a different season, and that could only mean that they were very far from Hypatia. Kraken's tilt was only fifteen degrees, so seasonal variations were more modest than on some planets. The lottery of tilt had a massive impact on the viability of ecosystems. If the angle were large, then seasons became extreme and life struggled to adapt. If it were low, then there were no seasons, but life might still be successful. It was yet another example of the extraordinary number of diverse factors that collectively dictated the viability of colonisation.

A cheerful technician showed them to their allocated flyer before returning to his chores, whistling. Oso-Rae removed her mittens, hat and coat, stowing them in the pack she carried, and then swung into the pilot's seat. Ren followed, taking one of the two remaining seats, just aft and to the right of hers.

"So, you can fly this thing?"

"You don't fly them in a way that requires skill, dexterity and practice. Instead, you define a route and let the machine get on with it. You can intervene and change course or stop here and there, but it will prevent you from doing anything stupid. I'll show you as we go."

The flyer surged upwards, its rotors tilted forward, and it began to accelerate. At about a thousand metres, the climb eased, and the ground sped past below. The airfield was soon just a distant patch of green; a postage stamp of clear ground amid an ocean of trees.

They were coasting above a mixed forest of deciduous and evergreen trees. To the right, the land gradually rose to meet a remote mountain range, whilst to the left were boundless rolling hills dotted with jagged, rocky outcrops. Ahead was a shimmering expanse of water. Beyond that lay a narrow neck of land, open to the great ocean at the bottom end but joined to the mainland at the top. This isthmus created a vast, sheltered gulf.

As they flew, Oso-Rae explained Kraken's marine ecology and the stupendous challenge of creating ocean habitats. Sure, Marrakesh had an ocean, but largely barren and devoid of life:

a giant mass of frigid water with some algal blooms and simple plankton. It had a humble role in the planet's carbon cycle, but largely through physical rather than biological processes.

Kraken had oceans teeming with life across the spectrum of marine ecosystems. There were abyssal plains with their strange, alien fish, tube worms and crustacea, all feeding on organic detritus from above. There was the vastness of open ocean with photosynthetic plankton, predatory pelagic fish, and vast shoals of silvery sardines and anchovies. There were even sharks along with pods of orca and whales. This had been his mother's work, but he knew little of it because she spoke so rarely of her lost life.

Then there were deep-sea corals, shallow atolls, kelp forests, mangroves, estuaries and shallow polar seas. All this was not some lucky accident. Creating such oceans had required extensive seeding, which had come at great cost prior to the coup, when the Arc was not yet 'the Arc' and trans-planetary corporates or 'transpacs' were still gleefully pumping obscene quantities of money into the project.

One such corporate leviathan was Genesis, a company so large that not one planetary economy in existence could match it. Genesis had put up plenty of risky capital during the first interstellar missions, and this early adoption, combined with an unholy appetite for risk, had made them extraordinarily rich.

The Hanseatic League pretended to be a guild of planetary governments, much like the CPF. However, the truth, only barely concealed, was that it was actually a cabal of trans-planetary corporations. The entire identity of their host planets was wrapped up in those companies, and the directors' influence trivialised that of governments. Those token politicians were the pathetic administrators of daily bureaucracy, but all serious power and decision-making was far, far out of their hands.

One planet they had chanced upon in those wild early years of exploration was dreamily perfect in all ways except one: there was no land. Well, there was a bit, but it was a tiny fraction of the surface, and certainly not sufficient to justify colonisation. The genius of the Genesis board of directors had been to see its potential as a marine farm. So they dubbed it Proteus and began to seed it. Now, almost a thousand years later, it contained ten billion cubic kilometres of supremely healthy ocean, and for an eye-watering fee, they could provide several services. One was to allow millions of cubic kilometres of water to flow to a barren planet through a giant gateway, providing seeded oceans thick with plankton and fish. A second was to leave sub-surface gateways open between Proteus and client worlds in order to allow life to migrate via gentle osmosis. Finally, they supplied specific species to client worlds, and they were the only distributor in existence of large marine mammals. Many of these would have been extinct for hundreds of years without Proteus. And this whole business was nothing more than a side line for Genesis.

Kraken had been the recipient of most of these services up until the coup, and the Arc was most certainly in debt to Genesis. The truth was that the dread of reparations had been some part of the reason for keeping the gateway firmly shut for all those decades.

Out over the gulf, their flyer slowed and dropped until it was hovering just a few tens of metres above the ocean's gentle chop. Oso-Rae scanned the surface, searching for something. And then, as if on cue, a whale breached, twisted sideways, and slammed back into the water. In the following minutes, other members of the pod surfaced. An audio feed from the water below filled the cabin with the hiss of foaming blowholes and their yearning, impenetrable conversation.

As they breached, Ren observed their two-toned, wing-like fins and strangely gnarled chins. He could not have imagined such grace of movement in animals so large. For him, awareness of these creatures was so distantly theoretical that he might as well have been witnessing a troupe of Jurassic velociraptors.

"These are dojo whales, effectively a new variant. We have a population of only a few hundred, but it's growing. The situation is similar with several other species of Cetacea. We have watched them discover migration routes and pass those on to successive generations. We also have pods of orca, along with dolphins and porpoises too. If we ever have the chance to re-establish relations with the Hanseatic League, we would love to seed more species here."

"Don't hold your breath."

"I fear you may be right. They're a bit grumpy with us."

She smiled a wide smile, somehow showing that she didn't much care what the Hanseatic League thought.

The flyer descended further until they were only a few metres above the waves. A whale surfaced beneath them, breathed, and then rolled to one side, its giant, gentle eye observing them.

Looking into that eye, Ren felt certain he was in the presence of a benign intelligence. Instinct fought against logic. It was just an eye, and he knew it was lethal to anthropomorphise or read too much into an exchange of glances. He was annoyed with himself for getting carried away, but couldn't deny the power of the moment. With it came some tiny new shred of understanding of his mother, or at least it felt that way.

"Shall we move on?"

"Yes, of course. Where next?"

"You'll see. I enjoy surprising you."

"And I'm getting used to your surprises."

The craft rose, accelerating back towards land at a broad angle between their starting point and the distant mountains. A squall rolled through, and their flyer was briefly streaked with rain and buffeted by turbulent gusts.

"I know why you brought me here, but how do you feel about this?" asked Ren as he gestured at the surroundings.

"I feel utterly humbled by it. I am thrilled that we have created a biosphere that persists in such rude health. It makes me feel that for all the failings of the Arc, and I admit there are many, we still have a noble purpose.

"I am expected to believe in all aspects of our project, but frankly I do not. However, I do believe in this. Nature never deceives us; it is we who deceive ourselves."

Ren's usual instinct was to debate with Oso-Rae, but there was nothing in her words that demanded immediate challenge or riposte. For the moment he put aside the arbitrariness of the ratios and rules that the Arc'ers obsessed over. He put aside the dangerous peculiarities of their society and considered how those creatures represented the essence of their project. They continued in silence until Ren ventured a question.

"So, which aspects of the Arc project don't you believe in?"

"It's no single thing," she said. "Central Control can be overbearing and secretive. Sometimes I think that our purpose would be better served by creating vast reserves and leaving them entirely alone. This desperation to place humanity at the centre of it all can feel like a false harmony. It feels absurd and contrived at times."

"As an outsider, I can see some clarity of thought in the idea, even if I'm not a believer. Your philosophy requires that you are immersed in it, and that isn't a problem in itself. For me, the trouble come from the levels of coercion towards that lifestyle and the intrusions into personal liberty." Ren paused for a moment and then added, "I also can't quite get past your hatred of cities. That's all I know."

"I have much to learn about the outside before I can rebalance my ideals. That said, it's not that hard to imagine a society that encapsulates many of the Arc's principles but modified by the better ideas from elsewhere. I know that's vague. Sorry."

On reaching the coast, the flyer passed over a steep, pebbly storm beach backed by rising ground blanketed in dunes. High above the shoreline, marram grasses sheathed the dunes' sandy ridges, and behind they dropped away into a stagnant, brackish lagoon. Beyond lay swathes of boggy ground. In the drier patches, birch trees found a meagre foothold. As the land rose higher, the bog was replaced by natural meadows peppered with spring flowers.

The flyer kept climbing, and Oso-Rae explained, "What I will show you next, we take care not to disturb."

With every passing kilometre, the trees shrank a little more until they became wizened dwarfs: the combined effect of increasing altitude and latitude. The terrain morphed into tundra with low brush, reindeer moss, and great frigid rivers. Passing over a col between two peaks, they plunged into a river valley, and in that moment, Ren detected sudden, chaotic motion. It took a few seconds to process and then focus on what he was seeing, but then it was clear. Tens of thousands of caribou roamed the expanse of tundra below, roiling in movement like a vast shoal of fish.

After a long silence, Oso-Rae spoke again. "This is another example of what we think of as deep, ferocious wilderness."

"Deep and ferocious," repeated Ren as if weighing her choice of words.

"These are things that we could not achieve on Jericho or Typhon. A herd of caribou could not exist in a dainty aviary like the Rose Cavern. The real achievement is that we can now stand back and allow it to run itself. We barely set foot here anymore, and it took special permission to allow you to visit."

"Does it run itself, though? I thought there were gen-5 minds sustaining and maintaining it behind the scenes."

"That's true, but they intervene less and less with every passing year."

The flyer swept forward towards the mountains. Deep U-shaped valleys topped by ragged granite pillars slipped past beneath.

"These are glaciated valleys. Have you heard of that?"

Ren had to query his implant before answering, "It's not something I have come across, but I know what it means. I may have been taught it years ago because our schooling has a dubious obsession with the history, geography and languages of distant lands and old powers."

"Kraken had no history of glaciation before we got here. Our first attempts at taming the planet and introducing a biosphere were chaotic. It leapt from extreme to extreme, and what you see here is the result of an early hiccup which resulted in a brief ice age."

At that moment, Ren realised something. After many days of exposure to Oso-Rae and her compatriots, his translator no longer fought with her words, correcting, guessing or substituting. He had begun to understand her peculiar variant of Standard. The most common quirks and sayings had already seeped into his consciousness. Now, the translator was stepping in only occasionally to help with metaphor and adage. Every now and then, it picked up on sarcasm, irony or humour that he would not otherwise have detected, but it was good news because it meant he was understanding her purely, without much intermediary processing.

"I have noticed that my translator isn't working so hard anymore. Is the same true for you?"

"Yes, I think so, but I reckon that your language is quite close to what it was fifty years ago, so we are well conditioned to understand it. There is something about the reality of your hundreds of billions of people that sustains a more static language. Our little archipelago was more likely to diverge."

And then smiling, she added, "All that said, I still have no idea what you're saying half the time. Particularly when you drone on about ideals and democracy and blah, blah, blah."

Ren laughed. The flyer began losing height, homing in on a small cleft between three peaks. It was a barren, grassy area with a shallow lake, offering a view in all directions. They landed on the edge of the tarn before stepping out into a bracing arctic wind. Ren hurried to retrieve his stowed clothing.

They walked to the brow of the first lip, which offered a view down towards the basin teeming with caribou. A bald eagle passed overhead, oblivious to the humans below.

A thought had been gradually crystallising in Ren's mind. Astrid had left him to make a decision but it was not really *his* decision. He was a proxy for Core and she was asking him to make *their* decision. If he were to be true to that purpose, his only choice was to support the insertion and bring down the Arc, but that wasn't his instinct. True, the Arc was politically troubling, deviant even, to the extent that he would normally have comfortably acted against them. Another week or month would not reveal the truth more clearly. He took a deep breath and leapt.

"Oso-Rae, are our conversations discreet? I mean, can I speak openly?"

"Not always, but right now, in the middle of fucking nowhere, yes, unless you're worried about the plovers and snow buntings listening in. This sounds fun."

"I don't know what you lot have figured out already, but this isn't straightforward. I'm aware that you might be steps ahead of me on this, like Astrid always is, but…"

"Astrid?"

"Never mind. Why did you summon us now? Why now after fifty years?"

"We told you," said Oso-Rae. "There has been a regime change, we feel stronger, and we can't be isolated forever."

"And how do you think that Core and, more importantly, the other leagues would have responded to your coup all those years ago?"

"I imagine that they were furious for a while, but that anger belonged to the affected individuals who are long gone. People come and go, and fifty years is too long for grudges."

"Come on, Oso-Rae. These people are brutal, controlling and determined." He continued, "Listen to me carefully. There are league insertions right now in Arc systems. Is that not why you brought us here now?"

Oso-Rae was silent. She walked a few metres away to

process this bombshell. Glancing back at Ren and gathering her calm, she said, "By 'insertion' you mean that there's hardware in the skies above us, against all law and decency?"

"Correct."

"Who …?"

"It's the Hanseatics and the Old Worlds in an unholy alliance. Core has no involvement that I know of, but August is also clearly mixed up in it, and I don't know how to explain that."

Ren knew he had gone rogue. That morning, he had received a cryptic message from Astrid. Superficially, it was a bland, ordinary communique, but between the lines, in a code unique to them, there was another message. She had given him the choice to intervene but only if he was certain that he could succeed. However, she also made it clear that this was not an action certified by the Secretariat. If he were to act, he would have to do so as an unsanctioned agent of chaos. It would be something they never spoke of again. This was his choice alone.

"Ren, thank you. The truth is we had an inkling that something was afoot. Some weeks ago, we detected a rogue transmission near Eleuthera. I have only known this for a couple of days myself. If I'm being honest, I am furious that it was kept from me."

"Welcome to my world. I feel played all the time."

"From one moment to the next, everything we are doing here has changed," said Oso-Rae. "I feel ridiculous spending a career learning the nuances of diplomacy when this is how things really work."

"Now, why are we here?" asked Ren.

"Come. Watch."

He followed her to the second brow and then looked down into an empty river valley, rimmed by low forest. Ren was not sure what he should be searching for, but then a sudden movement against the forest caught his eye.

A powerful animal burst through the trees, running at full

tilt. Just behind, another eight followed. Long legs, greyish-brown pelts and muscular frames meant they could only be one thing: wolves. Ren had only a dim understanding of species such as this, as they now only existed on terrifyingly few planets. He recognised them not from nature but from their age-old representation in storybooks and fiction. They might as well have been trolls or a pack of goblins riding out of the trees.

Oso-Rae said, "As with whales, we think of wolves as one of the most potent weathervanes of thriving wilderness. This pack requires around four hundred square kilometres of territory, just to support the nine of them. Apex predators need the myriad layers beneath to be healthy if they are to exist at all.

"They simply can't co-exist with human populations, and also need large gaps between pack territories so they don't rip each other to shreds.

"Sorry. I'm babbling about wolves... I'm processing."

"What's next?" asked Ren.

"I'll have to share your information with my group in Central Control. It will go straight to the top in moments." Oso-Rae paused as if calculating. "I have to figure out how they will use the information and if I should intervene in some way to prevent a rash, knee-jerk reaction."

"What are they most likely to do?"

"Kick you out and close the gateway. Then they'll hunt down the hardware, and go for the kill."

"And the main risks with that are?"

"That it will become a fully-fledged war. I don't doubt that these insertion units carry with them vast military capability that they might suddenly feel obliged to use."

Ren said, "If the Arc starts hunting, they will do so clumsily because they don't know what they're looking for. The hunt will be obvious, and the insertion teams will go to battle mode... a bull in a china shop."

Oso-Rae continued, "We must prevent powerful people from doing stupid things on both sides."

"Bravo to that."

The wolves were gone by the time they rose from the eyrie. Speeding forward once again, their path carried them over a shallow, braided river that tumbled out of the high mountains and now snaked its way down a shallow valley in deep, sinuous curves. The river split, bifurcated, branched, and re-converged around dozens of islets. In the deeper pools, its water was that milky turquoise of meltwater. In the shallows, it was breathtakingly clear.

Brown bears stood in the shallows where cobbly braids dropped into deeper channels. Salmon pulsed through, ancient instinct forcing them towards breeding grounds still further upstream. With sweeping paws, bears caught the leaping fish and gorged, fattening themselves for the coming winter. These solitary creatures tensely shared prime fishing spots, at least for a few weeks during the salmon run.

The flyer surged higher, cresting the valley's rim, passing over low peaks, and then slowed to a hover as it looked up the expanse of another river valley. In the distance stood a clearing, and smoke rose from a fire at its centre. A cluster of crude huts was assembled around it. They were too far away to see things clearly, so Oso-Rae raised a scope to magnify the view. Distant figures could be seen at work and play amongst the huts. They were dressed in crudely stitched cloth and animal skins.

"What the hell am I looking at?" asked Ren.

"This is an odd fact about Kraken," said Oso-Rae. "A very small number of people take the ethos to a radically new level. They check out of normal society and begin a tribal, almost prehistoric form of existence in the forests. Their life is without technology beyond what you might associate with a stone-age society. They hunt, fish, gather berries, and build homes from rocks, wood, bark and moss."

"And this is encouraged?" asked Ren.

"Central Control permits it in modest numbers. Frankly, I think that some of the ecological planners see a role for clusters of humans in wilderness sectors. Perhaps people have their place here too.

"Back on Jericho at the falls, August described our project as an elaborate zoo. At the time I thought he was being absurd and hyperbolic, but I admit that this complicates things. I understand that people choose this life of their own volition, but then I think of our scientists observing these camps with their telescopes. It does indeed start to feel like that zoo... at least to me."

"And what of the children born to these communities?" asked Ren. "They are not here through volition. Do they not have a right to choose?"

"That's a good question, and in truth, I don't know how it works. These communities aren't often talked about, and their management is secretive."

"And what would happen if their numbers were to grow too large?"

"That's another good question, and the more I think about it, the less I see the possibility of a pleasant answer. Come on, let's head back."

Ren thought of the ancient nomadic saying, 'What kind of mad man builds houses that last for centuries when everyone must die in such a short time? Are we not taught that human beings have no permanent home on earth?'

The flyer rose again, gathering speed as it left the mountains behind. There was a long silence until Ren spoke. "We need a plan, Oso-Rae."

She smiled bleakly, nodded, and brought the flyer down on a wild beach piled high with littoral detritus. On a flat rock amongst seaweed and bleached, skeletal driftwood, the two sat and talked. Puzzled seagulls eyed them from a cautious distance.

Their problem had two parts, both critical but difficult to glue together into a single, coherent plan. One was to subvert an insertion, and the second was to avoid a return to the old status quo, with an Arc isolated for another fifty years and brand-new insertion missions setting forth to wreak future havoc.

"Do we know the motivation behind these insertions?" asked Ren.

"Superficially, but none of this seems worth starting a war over. Yes, we defaulted on contracts with the leagues, but they operate through the courts, not by the sword."

"They have their militias… well-paid private armies. If there is no court available to them, then they resort to other means."

"I can't see them bothering with a vendetta of fifty years," said Oso-Rae. "In that time their motivations must surely have morphed or dissipated. Perhaps there is no intent."

"That's possible, but a project of such cost is never a whim. It's not a safe base case. I suspect we are at the epicentre of a power game."

"So, what are the insertion units up to, and how do we deal with them?"

Ren said, "A military intervention from orbit requires intelligence and pinpoint precision. One planet is a vast area, and five planets are, well, five vast areas. Securing the entirety of those would require a military operation the likes of which we have never seen – a veritable armada. However, with good ground intel, they can focus on critical sites and an invasion becomes possible."

Oso-Rae picked his thought up and said, "So the others are gathering data and have some way of communicating with the insertion teams. Could it be going back through the Jericho gateway as part of the daily cables?"

"No, those comms are rudimentary." Ren paused for a moment to gather the courage for the words that would follow. "The truth is that nobody came here empty-handed. All of my colleagues – I use the term loosely – came into the Arc with microtech. The planets we have visited are now swarming with beacons, transponders and surveillance."

"Great. Wonderful," said Oso-Rae with all the sarcasm she could muster.

"Sorry, but microtech is easy to carry discreetly. Unless you know precisely what you're looking for, you can forget about detecting it. Frankly, it was naïve of the Arc to assume otherwise."

"You have implicated August in this too," said Oso-Rae, "which implies that Core is connected to the insertion. What's going on?"

"August is up to something that does not fit with Core policy. There are layers of intrigue here that I don't yet understand. For now, you should assume that he doesn't represent Core Planets."

Oso-Rae's scowl made it evident that his explanation raised more questions than it answered.

"So, they've probably already established communications," said Oso-Rae. "I had no idea such technology existed."

"It's worse, I'm afraid. There's more... Last night I discovered a tiny, dormant gateway in Hypatia. I'm ninety percent sure that August planted it there. Frankly, I didn't know that technology existed either, and the implications are scary."

Oso-Rae was wide-eyed. "Just one? How many are there?"

"I don't know," said Ren. "If there are many, it could give them access to the cavern worlds. It changes everything. The only card we have is that they need power, which will make them easier to spot and easier to kill than the beacons. I reckon we also have time on our side, as all this microtech takes time to spin up. It has to grow, evolve and build tools. That takes weeks."

"You think, but you're not sure, are you?" asked Oso-Rae. "We have to find the beacons and gateways immediately. How do we know what to look for?"

Ren stood and walked down to the water's edge. "I can help with that." He turned to look at her with an apologetic smile.

It took a few minutes to explain that he too carried microtech and that he had been tracking the others as best he could. The difficulty lay in the vast areas covered and the impossibility of tracing it all. Oso-Rae took it with good grace, seeming more relieved about the possibilities this offered than irritated by Ren's behaviour.

"We can start actively searching the locations I'm already aware of," said Ren. "Beyond that, we will need to track their movements since we separated. I can give guidance to your technical people, at least enough to help them know what to look for. If we discover enough of the tech, then we can probably royally screw up their plan."

"I have a fun conversation with Nako and Saki coming up," said Oso-Rae wearily.

"I can't help you with that," said Ren. "You won't beat the Hanseatics and Old Worlds with accusation alone. We must force them to act and bring their scheme out into the open, publicly exposing the insertions for what they are. Then we deliver our coup de grace by killing their gateways, leaving them trapped and unable to retreat."

"The problem is that we don't know when they will act. What if we're too late?"

"I know they're not ready yet," replied Ren. "Done well, we can control when and where they pull the trigger. With a bit of disinformation, they can be made to attack in the wrong places."

"It could work," said Oso-Rae.

With a plan constructed, their sense of helplessness leaked away. They shook hands – Oso-Rae adapting to Ren's ways – and prepared to leave.

There was something magical about this spot that fed a previously unknown need. In part, it was the simple, transient pleasure in seeing footprints wash away into oblivion, but there was also an ethereal beauty in the leaden sea and the driftwood's soft, skeletal forms. He wondered at the mind's capacity to find grace in the oddest of places.

In the flyer, Oso-Rae sat in silence for a time before turning to Ren and speaking.

"You took a leap of faith today and I will do the same. My purpose is to ensure that the Arc will not be able to walk away from dialogue with Core. After this is done, I don't want us stuck in some new isolation."

"Where are you going with this, Oso-Rae?"

"There's a planet in The Archipelago we haven't told you about... the Rub' al Khali... It's special."

Ren was dumbstruck. "You have kept a whole planet hidden from us? What makes it so special? Why the secrecy?"

She turned to look at him and said, "It's best to show you. Returning to Core with a first-hand account will carry far more weight than a third-hand story."

"Can you not just explain?"

"Not yet, no," said Oso-Rae. "The secret – the discovery – could be made to work in our favour. It would make it more difficult for Core to dictate terms and also prevent the Arc from running away to hide yet again."

"Give me something, Oso-Rae."

"I need a little time to figure it out. If I can't convince Central Control to follow this path, then it's irrelevant. That's my next step. I'm probably digging a big hole for myself to die in."

In Hypatia, the blanket of snow persisted. With a falling sun, the day's snowmelt hardened to form a crust which crackled and crunched deliciously as Ren walked back from the square. He was alone in the house now, thankful to be inside by a warming fire. The others had ventured off on their travels... and that was just fine. He wondered about their destinations. There had been a pretence of drawing straws – as if each of them was happy to go anywhere, but that was surely far from the truth.

Ren spent the evening drafting a short but critical message to Astrid. He was on his fifth edit. It had to be right. It had to sound relatively innocent and natural, but it was also crucial that Astrid recognised the intent behind his words.

The editing slowed, he hovered for a moment and breathed deeply before sending. Officially, this was for Astrid's eyes only, but he could not chance interception. Astrid would have to read between the lines, just as he had with her message.

"I am alone on Kraken now. My companions have their own motivations and have departed on missions to other worlds. I remain here, at least for now, as I have established useful dialogue with my Arc counterparts, and I would like that to bear fruit. This would not be served by acting rashly.

"Core's purpose is not aligned with the other Leagues, so I will stay here to work on our relationship with the Arc. With luck, the outcome will suit us, but it might well be less amenable to the Hanseatic League, the Old Worlds, and perhaps other players.

"Yours, Ren."

Chapter 20

The Gang of Twelve Convene at the Villa

Deep inside the burrows and hidden spaces of Typhon lay a cavern; an eccentric obscurity like no other. It contained a single building that sat in the middle of a patch of immaculate lawn. On one edge, the grass swept down to the fringes of a swamp where broad buttressed trunks reached up from the water. All around, the lawn was ringed by mature live oaks and magnolias. The sinuous curves of their branches spread widely – gravity-defyingly – and interlocked, knotting their fingers together. Spanish moss hung in great mounds, whilst lichens and mosses carpeted every branch. Each was like its own miniature humid biome; a tiny bug's-eye forest.

A thousand cicadas strummed their guitars, and frogs croaked from their hiding places in the swamp's green water. In concert, the wildlife forged a wall of sound. To the few who frequented this spot, it was a calming, familiar melody as opposed to some irritation. An alligator's toothy snout peeked through duckweed, a callous eye watching. A second basked on a muddy bank in the shallows near the lawn. Patches of swamp milkweed were in bloom, showing off their perfect umbrellas of pink and mauve flowers. Monarch butterflies, their wings like stained-glass windows, flitted from flower to delicate flower.

The solitary building might be technically described as an extensive house in archaic plantation style. Its wooden clapboard façade was ivory in colour, and ornate balconies ran around the entire periphery over three floors. Black-slatted shutters were folded back against the clapboards, for today people were in residence. It could go weeks without being occupied, and during that time, the garden and house were diligently maintained by a gang of machines. A life amid this swampy humidity should have ensured mildewed panels and peeling paint, but instead, obsessive maintenance lent the house a curious, stage-set perfection.

Only twelve souls were permitted entry here, to what was known as the Lafayette Cavern. It was strictly off-limits to the Arc's ordinary mortals, and as such had become a private kingdom for the Gang of Twelve. They galvanised the mystique of this enclave because the opportunity to grasp its keys motivated many to strive for the top. There were no grand financial rewards, only kudos and the semi-deification of entering this Parthenon.

The singular point of arrival was a gateway standing on the lawn, halfway between the house and the swamp.

The ground floor was dominated by an open terrace set with wicker furniture. On the ceiling, lazy fans turned, just delivering some semblance of a breeze. The twelve were all present and in the middle of a calm but impassioned debate. These were the doyens of Central Control, that secretive clique at the heart of the Arc. If this was the autocratic oligarchy that Ren spoke of, then here were the oligarchs.

Each represented a specific department in Central Control's affairs, which meant that each had their unique social, technical or scientific speciality. They arrived at this point by gaining mastery of their field and then being elected to the Bureau by their peers. Once there, the appointment was permanent until reaching a designated retirement age. This forced retirement was an odd convention designed to avoid the pitfall of having the Arc administered by an ancient cabal without energy or fresh ideas. Helpfully, it also put a natural cap on members spending too long at the tiller and becoming overly accustomed to their captaincy. Very few had ever been removed from office, other than on rare occasions when an individual's mind was no longer capable of the task.

These twelve were practically gods amongst mortals. Each had a special form of implant that connected them directly to a network of gen-5s. Their minds could see across the entirety of Arc space. Staggering volumes of data were processed and delivered directly into their brains. Every citizen of the Arc could be accessed at will, although there were rules about misusing this power. Even so, their augmentations transformed the Gang of Twelve into something far beyond conventional humans.

Mostly they had known one another for a very long time and were not competing for supremacy. That said, the matter they were debating was as urgent as any they had had to discuss, and that brought a sharper edge than was usual.

"I can't think of a better plan, although having it handed to me on a plate by a visitor from Core smells rotten. We have to put our faith in someone we have no reason to trust from a league we certainly don't trust."

"We could just wait and see if they actually do anything with the insertions. Worry about it only when we have to worry about it. In the interim, we scour the Arc systems."

"That feels complacent."

"I agree. Every day that we wait, the more hardware they can pump into the Arc."

"What do we gain by sharing Rub' al Khali?"

"I don't think we can look at it as gaining something. It's more accurate to say that there's an inevitability, particularly now that Oso-Rae has spoken of it."

"She will have to answer for that."

"Perhaps, but now we must accept the fact that it can't remain a secret. Oso-Rae is correct that this could become a powerful bargaining chip... if we get through the next few days and weeks."

"And we aren't exactly sharing it... yet."

"With great secrets comes great power."

"I thought that went 'with great power comes great responsibility.'"

"I prefer my version."

"This way we write the terms and get to set the debate and the pace for years to come."

A quorum was eventually reached, and the group began to disperse. They fell into scattered side conversations before drifting down to the gateway, returning to their homes, lives and offices on Kraken. For that was the real seat of power, and this enclave on Typhon was a quirk of history. This was where the designers had busied themselves before Kraken became habitable. Coming here was a tradition, and it reminded them of the Arc's original purpose. It was also a highly secure space where they could be quite certain of privacy.

Nako Moon returned to Hypatia, hurriedly bundling into a thick coat as he hit the cold mountain air. The mossy park where he had last met Saki and Oso-Rae now sat under snow, so they agreed to meet at a quiet tavern.

"Well, they are on board, to an extent," said Nako before turning to Oso-Rae. "Your name is now well-known in Central Control, but probably not in the way you might have hoped." She smiled weakly. "We'll create a story around one of our existing gateways, which we can pretend leads somewhere important, but it will be a dummy, a feint."

"So, what are our instructions?"

"You will lead Ren on a tour of Eleuthera and pretend to stumble upon it. In so doing, you will appear to have let slip some wonderful nugget of a secret. Ren will then relay that to the others at an urgently arranged meeting."

"This doesn't prevent an invasion," said Saki.

"True. It doesn't stop them from hitting us, but they are

likely to rush in before they are ready and will allocate most of their resources to a location with zero importance."

"Tomorrow you leave. Trace August's route and we'll do the same for Kani and Imiko. A tech team will join you to begin scanning for beacons. Ren's swarm will be more effective, at least initially, so he's coming too."

"Good luck to you both."

"Thank you, Nako. This is terrifying but exciting.
"

Part III

Chapter 21

Now You're Just Showing Off

The arrival on Eleuthera blew Ren's mind, and it was abundantly clear that it had been designed to evoke this response. Everything about the gateway's location, angle and setting was hell-bent on aweing those setting foot here for the first time.

Ren knew, as a technical fact, that Eleuthera was not a planet, but rather a moon in orbit around a gas giant. It was quite another matter to emerge from a gateway and witness this overwhelming reality right in front of his face. Indeed, he barely noticed Eleuthera itself for the first few seconds, because almost half the sky was filled with the water-coloured artistry of the gas giant Orcus, cut through by the fine line of its rings.

Orcus was a thousandfold more beautiful than any artist could have conjured with a brush and easel. Its colours were a palette of whites, creams and delicate browns. Terrifying atmospheric storms appeared, at this distance, as delicate puddles of buttermilk, flax and porcelain. Streaking jet streams of methane resembled picot ribbons in shades of honeycomb, almond and vanilla. On the junctions between the streaming bands and storms lay fractal whirlpools edged by yet smaller eddies, and so on down to infinity. It was a serene scene reminiscent of melting ice creams of many flavours stirred loosely together. The apparent serenity was an artifice of distance. It was hard for the brain to connect with the bone-crushing, violent reality of Orcus's cloud tops almost half a million kilometres away.

Eleuthera was so close to being on a perfect ecliptic that the rings appeared as a bright line across the middle of the planet. One would have to fly far off the plane of its orbit to witness their full form and so appreciate their majesty.

As Ren's eyes dropped from the pastels of the gas giant, he took in the surface panorama. The gateway had been positioned on a high cliff with the singular purpose of presenting this perfect view, stretching to a horizon some twenty kilometres distant. All this was for show.

Eleuthera had a complicated past: a difficult childhood, a tumultuous adolescence, but now enjoyed a calmer middle age. The tidal friction and heating caused by the tug of Orcus's immense gravity had ensured that its childhood had been a molten, volcanic mess, with a surface formed, melted and reformed a thousand times. The modest cooling of adolescence had coincided with an orbital drift that took it further away from its overbearing parent. Millions of years of gradually falling temperatures allowed the crust to solidify more permanently, but Orcus's powerful forces continued to bend and stretch the moon. New tectonic plates smashed against others and were thrust up, down, and through one another, slowly generating immense cracks and broken shards. Little by little, it cooled more, and Orcus lost its sway over the form of this little world, but by then it was a tectonic and geological marvel. It was not dull, and neither was it flat.

Great shards of crustal plate stood at eccentric angles. Some jutted vertically out of the surface, somehow flipped on their side and now glued for eternity into these unnatural positions. Others stood at acute angles with the surface, forming great cliffs and promontories. A few seemed precariously balanced – a kilometre-thick shelf hanging over a valley. Between the shards were plateaus created through the action of ancient lava rising through fissures, cooling and then setting in place. It was an outlandish combination of billiard-table flatness and splintered chaos. There was nowhere even slightly like this moon anywhere in the Congregation of Populated Systems.

Eleuthera was also teeming with life. Its surface had been seeded long ago and now, at this particular mid-latitude spot, lay a grassy savannah. Acacias and bushwillows dotted the plane, and in the distance stood groves of peculiar, thick-trunked baobabs. Savannah clung to the gentler slopes, coating them in grasses and low brush. Waterfalls fell from the heights, creating local oases of deep green.

Antelopes with silken two-toned coats of brown and cream grazed in a state of twitchy anxiety. A pride of lions sprawled in the shade of a tree, their cubs rolling and fighting. In the distance, elephants wallowed in the mud of a water hole.

Ren was silenced by all this wonder. Oso-Rae watched him, smiling.

"Okay, now you're just showing off," he said. "I had seen pictures of this place, but the reality of it is something else."

"Yes, it's special. I don't think that the Arc would be what it is without this place... and Kraken, of course."

They were accompanied by a technical team that followed at a discreet distance. Ren had coached the technicians before departure, providing them with as much insight as he could into the nature of their search.

That work had started in Hypatia, where Ren's swarm already had a lock on several of the budding beacons. It hadn't taken long to locate the rogue tech. Near the gateways in Hypatia's square, a small device was discovered embedded in a crevice. It had been consuming minerals from the rock and was in the process of morphing into something new, although precisely what was unclear. They had to act fast but discreetly, for it could not know that it was being observed. After a brief, close examination, they retreated and satisfied themselves with subtle remote monitoring.

They at least knew what to look for elsewhere. It was enough for the Arc technicians to continue the search themselves on Kraken and the other planets.

Ren released his swarm. Simultaneously, the tech team let loose a handful of their own drones, none greater in size than a bee. These swept away in a coordinated, balletic pattern. Some hovered minutely above the ground, whilst others crisscrossed at altitude, patrolling.

From the arrival point, they followed a gently sloping path leading downhill. Behind them hung the spheres of three open gateways, one of which had carried them here from Hypatia.

Now that he was on the move, Ren became aware of the shift in gravity. He felt noticeably lighter than on Kraken, and he bounced along the path in giant, floating strides. It was an instant sensation of strength, youth, and fitness.

"You look as though you're trying to dance," laughed Oso-Rae. "It's 0.8 G here. Forgot to mention that."

"And there was me thinking I was being graceful."

"Sure, Ren, sure."

Low gravity was one of the countless facts about this moon that Ren had been force-fed during pre-departure briefings, but even at the time, it had all started blurring together into a single, congealed morass of data. What else should he be remembering?

A tall woman with dark eyes and tightly cropped hair stood waiting for them. She was sheathed in vibrant, patterned fabric, all folded about her as if formed from a single large sheet.

"Please may I introduce Iora Laiini?" said Saki. "She's with Central Control on Eleuthera and will be with us for the time we spend here. She and her team have been tracing August's movements, so she can take us on a more efficient version of his path."

Ahead, a porphyritic granite stairway descended into a

gaping, shadowed hole in the rock. The steps had an annoying cadence, entirely out of sync with the human stride, causing an awkward, staggered descent. A colony of rock hyraxes frolicked amongst low, thorny bushes near the path. High above them, black kites slowly wheeled… searching, waiting.

Iora began a running commentary in her lilting, musical voice, thick with a local patois. The translator was struggling again, but if the rest of their Arc experience was anything to go by, it would not be long before it found its feet and decoded this new variant.

"Eleuthera is a unique world in countless ways. Its ability to support life on the surface is down to a powerful magnetosphere which protects us from Orcus's radiation soup. Despite the liveable surface, most human life is underground. Our model here is entirely different to that on Kraken and Jericho. Human interaction with the natural world follows an alternate design."

"Why the difference?" asked Ren.

"Partly because of the unique physicality of this moon, but also because it followed a design and development path independent of the group that formed the Arc. We joined the party later, once this world was well on its way to completion."

"So, it was developed outside the influence of the designers on Typhon who created Kraken?"

"Exactly. Eleuthera eventually fell under the influence of Central Control, but as an evolved partner. We already had our own uniquely expressed society and distinct ecological mission. Only then did the Arc become a cohesive entity."

"How did it come under the influence?"

"It was a marriage of convenience. In the congregation of planets, a solitary world can feel weak and exposed. Central Control was a unifier with a light touch. Remember that C-C is not some central government on Kraken that rules the other worlds."

"This is something I haven't figured out," said Ren. "Does

each planet in the Arc have its own Central Control, or is it one with local branches?"

"How long have you got?" said Saki with a chuckle. "Each has its own, but with a common unifying umbrella. Some activities, like waste management, are largely independent, so the unified part is modest and more for information, technique, and technology sharing. With other activities, such as foreign relations, the unified part is bigger than the local part. Does that make sense?"

"Sort of."

Ren couldn't say with any confidence who was actually in charge. It still looked as though this hidden clique manufactured a popular belief in a non-existent freedom. He knew that these ideas were imbued with preconceived paranoia and were a reaction against many of the phrases used by Oso-Rae and Saki. It was hard to judge something that remained invisible. Bitter experience had taught him to fear the worst and celebrate anything even marginally better.

Despite Astrid's instructions, which gave him leeway to judge the situation for himself, he knew that he had strayed from the path in terms of duty to the Federation. Everything he had seen and heard so far would have once been enough for him to swing his axe without compunction, but he had no appetite for an invasion, and preventing it felt like the lesser of two evils.

He could now focus on the original goal: to understand the Arc. If they succeeded in avoiding catastrophic conflict, then this part of the mission would stand.

The steps ended at a bank of elevators, and from there they plunged downwards inside a slick, glassy box with a panoramic view of Eleuthera's interior. This was nothing like the smooth, carved form of Jericho's caverns, but rather a natural space, disordered and angular. That, and it was a hub of activity, teeming with people, structured, managed, engineered... far closer to a recognisable metropolis than anything they had seen on Kraken or Jericho.

Iora continued, "The demented geology of this moon provides vast numbers of these accidental interior spaces, all created long ago through tectonic shattering. Each is entirely unique, and in the early days, they provided natural spaces for humanity long before the surface was made useable. So, life originally developed underground in a model not unlike that of habitats.

"We also excavated caverns in the manner of Jericho, and Typhon, but there was no wish to despoil the surface. This was partly down to its natural beauty and partly due to the terraforming efforts. Waste was exported via gateways to an orbital location around Orcus. There it was gradually squirted out to create a new ring.

"It's odd to think of an artificially created planetary ring, but the truth is that one of those up there represents the guts of Eleuthera. Garbage in plain sight.

"Then finally, when the atmosphere became safe and stable, we just sort of opened the windows. The plan had always been to inhabit the surface eventually, but at some ill-defined point along the way, we became accustomed to our life interior, and we fell in love with the pristine world outside."

Their elevator glided to a halt at the cavern floor, where they exited directly into a plaza thick with commotion and hustle. This place was a world away from Hypatia's serenity and had an atmosphere more like San Cristobal. A thousand voices hummed and chattered.

Next to the elevators stood a station along with a boarding point for passenger drones. All about were shops, restaurants and kiosks, whilst in the plaza's centre stood a single local gateway. Hundreds of people flowed in and out of the station and through the square. Everything was pristine, clean and slick, which to Ren's cynical eye implied an insipid benevolence at odds with what a city should be.

Galleried walkways plastered the walls, rising from a couple of stories in places to forty or more at the highest points of the cavern. It was a collision of trapezoids, with every facet tiered, terraced and colonised. Levels were connected by stairways along with spectacular elevators. Drone traffic shuttled around in a contrarotating pattern, shot through with linear transit travelling at speed to more distant parts.

Here there was no spindle-sun on its daily migration. In its place was a simple glowing panel that spread a diffuse, shadowless light across everything.

"No spindle-sun?" asked Ren.

"The subtlety of day-night cycles is critical when maintaining an ecosystem. In Kakolem, there isn't nature beyond basic parkland. All we do is dim and brighten the cavern to create a cycle."

Parkland made up about half of the visible cavern floor and was composed of grasses, shrubs and a few trees, run through with a network of paths. Above, creepers dangled from balconies and galleries, some dropping several stories.

"Natural daylight cycles are complicated here. On a superficial level, we have a regular day-night cycle of thirty-five hours as the moon spins on its axis. However, one side of Eleuthera permanently faces Orcus and so receives plenty of reflected sunlight. This adds a softening effect to the cycle because the additional light adds most during our night and least during our day. We thus have no true night on one side of Eleuthera.

"Conversely, the other side permanently faces away from Orcus and never receives that reflected light. This means that one side is somewhat warmer than the other and experiences less extreme temperature variation. It creates complex weather systems."

Ren knew exactly what to ask now. He had been in the Arc for long enough to know what they always wanted to talk about.

"What does that mean for ecosystems on the surface?"

"Ha! Again, it's complicated. Truly nocturnal animals fare better on the side that faces away from Orcus, but most species adapt. If there is one thing that these planets, moons, and habitats have shown us, it is that life adapts in thousands of fabulous and often surprising ways. It instinctively, unstoppably moulds itself to its new surroundings. When we establish ecosystems, evolution occurs in violent bursts. Within a few dozen generations, the finches of Eleuthera became clearly distinct sub-species of those used to seed the populations."

Quoting something from the depths of memory, Ren said, "Obeying an inalienable law, things grow, growing riotous and strange in their impulse for growth."

"We need to keep moving. The intent is to trace August's route, but we will cut out the less relevant parts. This will allow us to cover his three days' journey in just one, all going well."

Ren now had sufficient access to the local mesh to navigate, use transport systems and find hostels. With this, he could theoretically have toured Eleuthera alone, but for now his work was with Oso-Rae and the tech team.

Strictly speaking, Ren was almost dispensable. It was they who knew the route August had followed, and they who had the volume of tools required for a wide-area search. But for the time being, his swarm was a relevant component of the investigation, and there was a trap to set.

They walked briskly across Kakolem to reach a second nexus at the far end. In some regards it was like any town, but in others it was thoroughly alien. It was too clean and weirdly calm. There was no graffiti, no beggars, and not one hint of that noxious underbelly of iniquity. These things were not desirable, of course, but there was something too immaculate about this place. Everything seemed plastic and lacklustre. It made him wonder whether his vision of humanity was over-associated with the many grey and messy layers of existence. A bland utopia was suspicious, as if some lump of dysfunction lay behind it. The metaphor was meeting someone with no known vices, who you can't help but suspect of having a well-hidden, darkly sordid secret.

As they walked, he learned more from Iora, not from a continuous lecture but from snippets of conversation. Ren was strangely fascinated by the story of Eleuthera's water.

The discoverers of this curious moon had been wowed by its exotic, alien beauty and tremendous potential for life. The problem was that it had pitifully little water, and that was an aching disappointment. This conundrum remained until a bright young engineer hatched a plan that earned her a boatload of kudos and a handsome bonus. Her scheme was to shamelessly violate Tinia, the next moon out beyond Eleuthera. There, beneath a kilometre of pack ice, lay another twenty of briny water. A series of vast, power-hungry gateways was opened between Tinia and the surface of Eleuthera, and the water simply flowed from one world to the other. More accurately, it 'blasted' across under a pressure drop of a hundred atmospheres. Tinia had been successfully milked, but the engineer, in a remorseful meltdown, quit her job, shaved her head, and moved to Typhon to become an experimental performance artist.

But what the hell do you do with gigatons of soupy brine? Salt was just part of the problem, as the water was deeply toxic in a variety of fun ways. Years of desalination and chemical sequestration were needed to make it suitable for seeding life. The toxic gunk was dumped back on Tinia, of course.

Decades passed, but finally Eleuthera had her lakes, rivers, and even glaciers, but not the grand, globe-spanning oceans of other worlds. It just didn't seem worth the effort. Water's one talent is its uncompromising search for the low ground. On Eleuthera, there were no vast, shallow basins, hence much of the water ended up in the calderas of ancient volcanoes, the depressions of meteor strikes, and in the deep crevasses of its cracked surface. She was left with innumerable small, circular fresh-water lakes, along with flooded canyons of staggering depth. Without great oceans, the Eleutherans hadn't bothered with marine habitats, instead focusing on their rivers and lakes. Anyway, Kraken had oceans in spades. They had once planned to create a few seas, but there was insufficient motivation, and frankly, it was too late now. People were satisfied with what they had and appreciated Eleuthera's unique identity.

At the opposite end of Kakolem, in the middle of a grand piazza, stood a second set of gateways. All four were domestic routes, but in true Arc style, none went directly from A to B, instead routing through remote hubs.

Prior to obtaining a mesh connection, Ren had been entirely reliant on locals for navigation. Now, with this new data feed, it was as though a blindfold had been removed. The gateways finally had names, and all onward routes went through hubs named Dax, Leon, Sfax and Acre. Onward destinations from each were neatly listed, some with descriptive names that hinted at their nature or purpose. Palapang Farms, Sendoru Forest Reserve and Lago Chico Glacier Park needed little explanation.

"One of these routes is coded differently. What's that all about?" asked Ren.

"That's a restricted Central Control destination. There are others in that category, such as military zones, sensitive research areas, and so on."

"How does the restriction work?"

"Actually, with most of them, there is no specific constraint on travelling the route, but there may be little that a visitor can do once they arrive. For example, Magdalena, the Central Control location shown here, has a reception and delivery point. Entry to the facility would require identification and appropriate permission… so you can go there, and yet you can't!"

"Doesn't it suggest that August would have figured such things out for himself and focused on the more accessible destinations?"

"It does, so our route will consider that."

The protocol was to go through each in turn. Starting with the Dax hub, they went through every sub-destination in rapid succession. At each, they spent a few minutes checking and measuring before releasing a few of their bee-like drones in tandem with a fraction of Ren's swarm. Moments later, they were back through to the hub and heading towards the next location. For Ren, with his quiet dread of gateways, this was a form of drawn-out torture.

It was an urgent mission but with a fleeting, flipbook style of tourism as an accidental side effect, like a photographic bus tour without narrative or explanation. One moment they were overlooking the glaciers of Lago Chico, and the next they were observing huge farms within brightly lit caverns.

Palapang Farms' caverns contained regiments of fields retreating to infinity. Crops were diverse, with groves of citrus and trestled rows of apple and pear trees, along with fields of cassava, capsicum and melons.

Lago Chico was a destination for day-trippers coming to hike, climb or stroll amongst nature. Several trails led away from the gateway towards forests and icefields. Much of Eleuthera's surface was off-limits, but this was one of a few exceptions where visitors were permitted. The gateway was the singular access point to Lago Chico, a wild basin fringed by three towering dead volcanos. Shadowy hollows below their peaks were nurseries for glacier formation.

Some seemed improbable targets for an attack, so they did not waste much time on them. That said, it was important to remember that an insertion would seek to control as many gateways as possible, whatever their purpose. It helped maximise the probability of securing the hidden hubs. The more access routes, the higher that probability. Seeker drones were delivered and they were on their way again.

After fourteen relentless hours, the day was finally done. Each and every significant hub on Eleuthera had been visited. All added up, they had walked twenty kilometres, covered hundreds using ground transport, and passed through thirty-four gateways, each twice. They finally returned to Kakolem, where Iora deposited them in the foyer of an unglamorous hotel before leaving for the night. Ren was exhausted, but his mind fizzed with sensory overload. Impressions from the frantic tour of this fantastical place were mashed together with anxiety.

Unable to rest, he soon found himself back in the lobby, heading out alone to explore. There was over an hour until he was due to meet Saki and Oso-Rae, and he was quietly thankful for the respite. Sometimes human company or conversation, or both, became a burden… actually quite regularly for Ren.

He explored the galleries of Kakolem in much the same way as he wandered the grimy streets of his home by night. Much reflected the universality of the human condition, and fifty years of isolation had not turned these people into aliens. They ate, they drank, they laughed, they argued and loved. The galleries nearest the cavern floor were devoted to shops, restaurants and social venues. Climbing higher, there were services and specialist shops. Yet higher were offices now closed for the night, and there the human traffic thinned to zero.

Ren was too physically drained to wander for long, so he found his way to Babylon, where he was due to meet his Arc friends. Yes, he realised 'friends' now seemed a fitting word, and that was something he had never felt or even allowed himself to consider in his work before. This gave him a contented glow tempered by a sense of treachery that he could neither justify nor shake off.

Babylon was as fabulous as the name implied, but instead of the expected extravagance, its glamour pivoted on a single, showy trick. A vast panel of glass, stretching a hundred metres across and twenty high, formed a window in the cavern wall. It was set high up on a cliff, gazing out over Eleuthera's savannah, a nocturnal scene illuminated only by the milky glow of Orcus's sphere.

A crisp maître d' escorted Ren to a table set flush up against the glass, where he took a seat alone, bathing in the opalescent nightscape. Rhythmic, tightly structured music played at the delicately precise volume that takes away silence without becoming noise. It was enough to shelter tables in bubbles of privacy whilst preserving conversation. He sipped a pleasant but overly sweet drink brought to him unrequested by a courteous waiter. This had been the way with people throughout the Arc. They had recognised him for the alien he was but maintained a respectful distance. Passing locals might do a double-take, but never stopped, stared or conversed unless approached.

He passed the time writing. It was not a moment for the wooden language of official reports; it was for anecdotes, observations, ideas, and the many little things he wanted to be able to recall.

After a time, Oso-Rae appeared on her own.

"Sorry, Saki had something to take care of… the data is coming in thick and fast. It's just us, I'm afraid."

She waved a waiter down and ordered for them both before stretching and reclining. She had figured out that Ren ate anything and everything, so it wasn't worth the effort to discuss options.

"Quite the view, eh?"

"If this is the standard here, I hope you never come to Marrakesh."

"I would love to swap places and go into the CPF."

"You would hate it."

"I genuinely don't know how I would feel about it all," said Oso-Rae. "I'm sure there would be moments of claustrophobia and shock, but I hope I'm capable of seeing the good."

"I have been to more places than you can imagine. There comes a point when you feel you have seen everything and you just want to be home. Endless novelty becomes exhausting, and it's quite sad when nothing can shock you. It leaves you jaded."

"Well, I hope never to reach that point. I don't want to go everywhere, but I want to get some sort of fix on what life is like outside my Archipelago."

"Do you think I have got a fix on what life is like here?" asked Ren.

"No, fair enough, but I need some reference point."

"At some point in the coming days or weeks," continued

Ren, "I will walk back through that gateway to Nuevo Mundo, and in that instant, I will be in a different world, both literally and metaphorically. From San Cristobal, I will head to Marrakesh, where I will be debriefed. If all goes to plan, it will be a highly 'vigorous' debrief. Our deed will be done, but I will still have to tell them my opinions of the Arc."

"You will, and I trust you will be kind to us."

"I still don't have my story in order, and I don't know how to fix that."

"My colleagues are sometimes clumsy and patronising. I hope that hasn't caused damage," said Oso-Rae.

"No, that's not the problem at all. I can see that they toe the party line, as do I much of the time. There are those who do it because they can't conceive of any other way of thinking and others whose job is to repeat standard credo. Some of the people I have met have indeed been arrogantly smug about the Arc's system and achievements, but it is hard to blame people who know nothing else."

"It's sad because it diminishes the message when people can't or won't be open about their or their system's failings."

Ren said, "It might help if you tell me what *you* would like to see change. That might tell me more than a year of investigation."

"I did explain some of it back on that beach, but I can elaborate if you want. First explain why you're helping us."

"We wouldn't have got this far if I didn't see reasons to help protect the Arc, but my loyalties don't turn overnight. Preventing an enormously stupid invasion doesn't mean that I am convinced by everything you do. Many things concern me, and a few of those have terrifying implications. That said, there are gaping holes in my understanding."

"And truth is hard to determine," declared Oso-Rae. "It's not this idealised, deterministic thing, but personal, ephemeral and elusive. A group conversation would never have illuminated it."

Ren had no wish to debate Oso-Rae's eccentric opinions about truth. She seemed about to go off-piste on another of her rants, so he steered the conversation back. "Now there are just the two of us, and we have both broken rank in our ways. Can I ask you about a couple of things that were left hanging?"

"Of course."

"That day in Viola Bay, they spoke of a woman who had left because she was not selected for pregnancy."

"Ah, that. I think I know why that troubles you. Procreation is a profound right that governments should stay away from, right? I can give you the official line, and I can give you mine. Which do you want first?"

"The official one, I guess."

"That is sort of theoretical," said Oso-Rae. "It revolves around an obsession with extrapolation ad infinitum. They always take an idea and then run a thought experiment to see where it lands up in ten, a hundred, a thousand, or a million years. This leads them to associate unlimited population growth with an absurd endpoint mired in misery, a ruined planet and mass extinction."

"And what would they say about the fundamental human right that so many other societies identify?"

"They would argue that obsessing about one right in isolation makes a mockery of other rights. The many deemed rights intersect and often conflict, so it is impossible to be pure and true to them all simultaneously. Therefore, you need some system, hopefully as kind a system as possible, to manage it."

"I struggle with the idea of a government dictating these basics, but would not be the first time in history," said Ren. "Anyway, some societies shrink. They don't always grow."

"That's true, but also irrelevant because they don't counterbalance the problem," said Oso-Rae. "So what do *you* do about population control?"

"Education and lifting people out of poverty are usually enough, but when that fails, there is always the option of exodus to new planets… and the galaxy is unknowably large. But that position is theoretical too."

"I can see the logic, but we don't wish humanity to become some pestilence snaking out into the galaxy."

"Our very existence could be deemed a form of pestilence. You use a value-laden word. I also wonder what it means as we move out into a lifeless universe."

"And if it isn't lifeless?"

Ren didn't answer, instead returning to his earlier question. "And how does your view differ from the official one?"

"I accept the arguments on a theoretical level, but the personal stories trouble me. I meant what I said about ensuring liberty by taking some small part of it away, but the invasion of bodies and minds does not fit so well with the spirit of our original mission."

Then, in the middle of this conversation, Oso-Rae paused, holding up a finger in that universal gesture that marked someone as dealing with some business in their implant. A moment later, she clapped her hands and said, "We're almost complete. They have identified equipment at dozens of key locations and, more critically, found a transmitting beacon. We can trace it."

Ren nodded and said, "Let the games begin."

"But look at this one…" said Oso-Rae whilst transmitting an image to him.

At first it was unclear what it showed, but as he zoomed in, Ren saw the tiny orb of a gateway hovering above the ground.

"Another one. That means there might be many more."

"It looks that way," answered Oso-Rae. "At least we know we can find them now."

By morning, several more sites with active beacons had been identified and cautious observation was underway. Continuing the operation in tandem with the tech teams served no further purpose. All that was left for Ren to do on Eleuthera was enact stage two of their plan. The ruse had to be seeded.

Oso-Rae and Ren made their way to the Sfax hub. From there, they were transported to a gateway at the head of the Orotelli Gorge, a geological eccentricity even by Eleuthera's high standards. Two giant tectonic slabs casually leant against each other, so forming a deep, V-shaped gulley. The gateway stood on a wide, grassy plain at the gorge's entrance and ahead of them, a well-travelled path led into the gloom towards the Orotelli facility where the stage had been set.

This was Ren's first glimpse of Arc military, a body he knew existed but that had not previously been revealed. He understood that this discretion was wrapped up in the Arc's tendency to hide away the things they found necessary but distasteful. The valley's head was enclosed by a security fence. Beyond it lay barracks, offices and depots. At the valley's knife-edge termination, a heavily guarded tunnel ran into the rock.

Their way forward was barred by the towering fence manned by a sentry. She tried to send them back down the path they had just travelled, but Oso-Rae's persistence forced the sentry to summon her superior. An awkward silence fell until they arrived, flustered and angry.

"Ren, could you give us a moment?"

He nodded and wandered off to the side, pretending to examine some flowers, but remaining just within earshot, recording it all.

"You can't bring him here."

"Why? He's an important guest."

"Look, I know who you are, and on your own, you would have clearance, but we're under the strictest instructions to keep Rub' al Khali under wraps. The public and outsiders are not permitted to learn that world exists or what we have found there."

"Right. I didn't know that gateway was here. I'm so sorry. We'll be on our way."

She winked at the colonel as if to say, "Thank you, you

played your role well."

And he *had* played his role well, for he was not a colonel at all, but an actor brought in just to deliver those few words.

And that was that. In a few seconds the seed had been sown, and their job on Eleuthera was done. Only an hour later, Ren was back in Hypatia, crafting a message to August, Imiko and Kani. The time was set for the following afternoon, and until then, he would hide from the snow and lounge by a fire.

"If things go to plan, I'll soon return and will need to explain all this in a way that Core can understand and hopefully cope with. Many Arc ideas are going to be a tough sell."

She said, "But our system has a purpose. Core accepts that some socio-political forces should be suppressed. A leader in power for decades will, without a shred of doubt, become a despot. Core understands this and should pay attention to our solution. Is it such a stretch for us to identify lethal tendencies and suppress them?"

"I accept the example of the despot, but I can't see how you can characterise nations in that way." Ren thought for a moment before elaborating. "People need identity, and the most comfortable forms stem from some blend of customs, history, nationality, language, race and religion."

"Those things are all different," snapped Oso-Rae, "and yet you stir them together in your encapsulation of the nation."

"True, but does that matter? Being more than a line on a map reinforces the state rather than detracting from it."

"It makes for a confused and easily manipulated definition of identity. People don't need a sense of self born from a national myth soaked in ideas of racial superiority and the celebration of brutal historic wars."

"Oh, Oso-Rae, you can be an extremist. If you do ever go to Core, you will need to tone it down."

"If you say so. Alternatively, they could just deal with me as I am."

Ren smiled. She had a point. He was fighting her on this

and yet, in defining his own identity, he had rejected his original nationality, both in its planetary form and also that of the nation within. He wondered about this hypocrisy but concluded that identity is a complex thing, and he had made a personal choice as opposed to obeying a dictum from above. That was a big distinction.

"Sorry, all this is based on what I have been taught," said Oso-Rae. "And yet it seems true that nationalism is in an impossibly close dance with barbarism."

"Or does it help avoid a descent into barbarism?" Ren still vaguely believed this but changed tack. "Look, let's not repeat the same debate. The real question is, how does Central Control manage it? Are you replacing one form of 'barbarism' with another? Do you use brutal methods to achieve this? Do you have a dark monolith of secret police? Do you send in the troops when new political bodies form?"

"The rotation of C-C personnel back to their caverns, sectors, and clans allows the system to monitor society closely without recourse to surveillance and trickery," said Oso-Rae. She was about to say more but stopped herself.

"Don't clan locals sometimes see you as giant snitches and so isolate you from anything radical?"

"That can happen."

"Are there no groups who meet in secret and spread the word through cloaked networks in back-streets and dens?" asked Ren.

"Yes, but they are generally easy to defuse. We can find reasons to move people around and in so doing neuter their subversive movements."

Ren paused and then said, "So, that connects to 'suppression of subversive influences,' which I remember from Saki's list of C-C activities. Oddly, we never discussed that one, but it seems closely linked."

"Sure, but that includes a bunch of other things too."

"It sounds to me as though Central Control can just throw

anything they like into that pot without having to answer to anyone."

Oso-Rae was ready for this line of questioning and slipped into a prepared argument. "You could say the same about any government. In Core, you find 'legitimate' ways to define subversive groups. You just don't like the words we use or the fact that we are open about it. In your leagues, these things have to be cloak and dagger. It's more legitimate to you when it is secret."

"It rolls back to the same issue – that non-elected government will begin to overstep given time. They always start to abuse their position."

With a hint of consternation, Oso-Rae said, "The government *is* elected here. You just don't like the manner of that election."

"Maybe that's true. Your leadership is selected through intellect, without even a nod to human decency or the forms of wisdom that don't award you top marks at school."

"Perhaps, but being smart doesn't preclude the possibility of decency and wisdom. Perhaps those that reach the top in Central Control have both. On the other hand, I might be deluding myself. And anyway, your leaders need neither intellect nor wisdom, just personal ambition and a knack for self-promotion." Just as Oso-Rae seemed to be building to some crescendo, she stopped herself and said, "We're repeating ourselves. Can we just leave this for now?"

Ren agreed. They were going around in circles.

"Next time you come, we're going dancing," she said. "Enough with all this talk."

"You're on."

Chapter 22

You're In for a Proper Beating

Palina had spent hours studying Kraken, in part as necessary preparation but also because that godlike eye made him feel immensely powerful.

The asteroid had been given a name: Avernus. It was far from official, but the mission's juvenile engineers liked to bestow names on their creations, and Palina actually quite liked it. In great antiquity 'Avernus' had been a name for the entrance to hell. Somehow it felt appropriate.

Around Kraken, fleets of drones had infiltrated the existing firmament of satellites, shadowing their orbits to be sure of discretion. Their cameras scrutinised the planet's surface, producing imagery of ridiculous resolution, even revealing the snowfinches in Hypatia's square.

Radiation sensors continued the delicate task of pinpointing gateway locations. This was a piece of cake if they were large, operational, and on the surface; their signatures practically lit up the sky. But with those that were idling, only occasionally open, or deep underground, the task was far more troublesome. It required time and patience.

Data was zapped back towards Avernus in occasional, erratic and tightly focused broadcast packets. This was far more restrained than continuous transmission and reduced the chances of interception.

Palina should perhaps have been running the operation from back in league space, since that was where the three missions' many threads came together, but increasingly he stationed himself on – or in – Avernus itself. It felt more tangible and immediate and also added a fiery tendril of genuine risk. If they were discovered or the gateway failed, that was it: seconds would instantly and irretrievably revert to decades, and he would be marooned. His only way home would be to surrender to the Arc and hope that they would find it in their hearts to return him. That sense of exposure added a hard edge to his determination.

Avernus was a frenetic hub of activity. In only a few days, Rubos's team had excavated thousands of cubic metres to create hangars, operational control rooms, and a far slicker power plant. Dozens of people now laboured in those spaces in a strict shift system to avoid long exposure to low-G. Hangars contained row upon row of orbital drop-out units like snarling pit bulls straining at the end of their leashes. Their purpose was to fall out of orbit into a planet's gravity well, where they would perform a host of military duties. Some flew, some walked, and others had no role but to deliver troops. Next to them stood squat boxes containing arrays of missiles, along with a range of non-lethal weapons.

The truth was that violence was not often the senders' modus operandi. Oddly, it was one of the few things that Core, the Hanseatics and Old Worlds had in common. Almost all of their work was in the realm of diplomacy, and where that failed, they used subterfuge, dirty tricks and manipulation. Sitting behind all that scheming endeavour were their military forces. Each league had their own behemoth of barely-utilised military. Somehow they still needed that threat as a spine behind everything else but chose not to use it. Even when violence was employed, it was usually non-lethal; disabling enemy installations, securing gateways, and knocking out physical and data infrastructures. Core cared more than anyone about this image. They had their self-proclaimed role as lofty guardians of the moral high ground to maintain, and shooting people didn't help. But Core had nothing to do with this mission.

Palina was hosting an update briefing in the conference room.

"Right, give me the big picture first," he instructed.

"We now have boots on the ground on all Arc planets, even Bathsheba, which was never expected or planned for. Beacons continue to spin up and many are well-established, particularly on Jericho and Kraken."

"Let's talk about Typhon," said Palina.

"We are confident that it's no longer their political capital," began Rubos. "Traffic is too low to support that notion. Gateway numbers and activity are modest. There are several connecting Typhon to Kraken, a few to intermediary hubs and about sixty used internally for local transport. The hubs along with the unknown destinations are our focus."

"But we're cross-referencing activity from the other missions, right?"

Data from the other Arc systems had been correlated with Kraken's. The mathematics were complex, particularly as these routes usually went via hidden hub junctions. Algorithms sat and studied the data until a correlation could be declared. It didn't require six sigma, just some hint of a correlation. Some of the hubs had been identified, but far from all.

Rubos nodded towards a subordinate, who took up the response.

"Yes, that data has been very helpful with the interplanetary links, except for the Karakorum system of course."

That was the insertion that had failed, thus completely isolating Bathsheba from Palina's mission.

"But, as mentioned before, there's good news from Bathsheba. A few beacons have spun up along with two gateways, so we can now consider it as a viable target too."

Palina smiled. They now had all the Arc planets.

"I'm frustrated we only know where a fraction of these hubs are," said Palina with a degree of petulance. "I need better results than that."

He was punishing his staff for the sake of it, as it could be obscenely hard to determine a hub's location. The correlation mathematics was second nature to him, but sometimes it was necessary to act as though he didn't understand and demand the world.

Palina also recognised that it was not always mission-critical to know the locations of these hubs. They existed for a blend of convenience and safety. The convenience part meant that they could be anywhere, so long as several were co-located. It was a matter of 'changing trains' efficiently. The safety part meant that they were defended against a variety of threats, some of which dictated that distance from population centres was desirable. He also knew that if a military force like his were to seize a gateway, it could generally infiltrate the hub too. The hosts then had to make a split-second judgement about killing the hub – a decision that might have staggering implications. Most commanders, whilst given the power to make such decisions, shat themselves in the moment and left them alive.

All that said, he desperately wanted to know the location of the other hubs. That would give them total control when the party finally started.

After an awkward silence, the subordinate continued, "There remains a huge challenge with gateways used less frequently or lacking correlating data from a second location. Of course, there are bound to be some that are dormant also."

"Which I assume makes them impossible to spot from radiation signatures," said Palina.

"Correct. Unless you're standing right next to them, anyway. However, we can always search for the supporting infrastructure."

Palina was keen to discover the destinations of those hidden gateways on Kraken and Typhon. The main domestic routes had all been confirmed via the cadences, rhythms and patterns of their activity, but some they might never find.

Had they been less concerned about revealing their presence, the team might have sent a swarm to monitor the uncertain gateways, perhaps even dip through for a recce and then back. But that was far too risky, so instead they resorted to satellite surveillance and the impatient wait for uplinks from agents on the ground. Frankly, without the latter, he would have to wait months or even years to be ready for a ground assault. With it, he could be ready in a matter of days.

"How about Kraken?" asked Palina.

"Human activity and infrastructure are relatively evenly spread. At first glance that makes everywhere appear equally important, but closer inspection has helped identify key locations."

"And the capital?"

"There are seven or eight centres of activity that are credible candidates for seats of government, but we now know that this place is key. The ground team's arrival there pretty much confirmed what we already knew."

A projection appeared showing satellite imagery of a mountain town with a still lake at its centre and a river tumbling down from the lip of a terminal moraine.

"It was called Juliaca on our older maps from before the coup, but it seems to have been renamed. The team on the ground call it 'Hypatia'. Gateway density is higher than anywhere else, and it doesn't follow the standard sector pattern. Most settlements are of modest size and surrounded by agriculture and forest. Juliaca – or Hypatia – sits in awkward terrain at high altitude with nothing but mountain peaks around it."

The town had been flagged as a conspicuous location within hours of arrival. Most critically, a series of inter-planet gateways stood in the cobbled square, and that alone said a great deal. Orbital sensors bore down on the town and monitored every corner, every street and every movement.

Beyond Hypatia, the team had identified a host of strategic targets including governmental hubs, administrative centres, military bases, and industrial sectors. A few were mysterious.

"Right, let's talk about orbital drop-out."

The bank of screens switched to a high-contrast view of rank upon rank of orbital drop-out units huddling low in the shadow of a crater's lip.

"We found a quiet spot on one of Kraken's moons. As you can see, our units are in place and can be on the surface in a matter of hours."

Even left exposed, they would have barely been visible, but as a precaution, they had been netted in the sandy-grey colours of the moon's surface.

"And do we have enough for all our targets?" asked Palina.

"It's one of those areas where we always want more than we have," replied Rubos. "But yes, by tomorrow all our units will be ready."

With one simple command, they would cast off their nets, lift, and blast across the hundred thousand kilometres to Kraken. In just a few hours, they could be screaming down through the atmosphere on glowing heat shields before gliding to their targets, shamelessly cracking the air with a volley of sonic booms. From utmost discretion to brazen fireworks.

The meeting over, Palina found himself alone in the conference room, his head swimming with tactical data. He knew that he was supposed to find moral satisfaction in avoiding conflict, or when that failed, in de-escalating with minimum harm. Those were the principles that he pretended and that he voiced publicly, but that was not the truth in his heart. Indeed, what mercenary really held those ideals dear? What he desired with a dark fervour was real conflict, and here he was with the keys to a ridiculous arsenal. God damn, this was going to be fun. The entire network would soon be armed, readied, and poised under the hair trigger beneath his finger.

Chapter 23

Ren Spins His Web

Ren lingered in a surreal limbo, his dreams withering and the rational, waking world still out of reach. Given the choice, he would have wallowed in the cold half-light for hours. Talk to no one. Go nowhere. He had returned to Hypatia bone-weary from the whirlwind of Eleuthera, exhausted by the physical effort and the mental struggle of adapting to his new purpose. He was accustomed to knowing which side he was on. There could be no more fundamental ingredient in a diplomat's identity. The new uncertainty was taking its toll.

He delved into emergency reserves of energy, eventually finding the sinew to haul himself from his bed. There he sat for a while, half-in, half-out, before standing. In the mirror, he faced a gaunt, shadowy, and hollow-eyed vision of himself. He practised a spectrum of facial expressions all the way from amusement to shock and surprise. There was an act to play out, and whilst he was good at playing a role, he wasn't an actor. The others would be here soon.

An hour later, they had arrived and were assembled. Despite everything, there was a genuine camaraderie between them, for they had travelled together and bonded over a unique shared experience. Were they truly the enemy? Ren knew that things are rarely black-and-white with character and ethics. Good goes hand-in-hand with the bad. The more that people stand out for their shining benevolence, the more likely it seems that they harbour dark, destructive thoughts or some malevolent dysfunction. This is the awkward nature of a moral existence. So no, he was not ready or willing to loathe these people, but he had chosen a path, and now had to let it play out.

They must have expected some grand speech. After all, he had summoned them from other planets just for this, but first, he wanted to hear them perform. He wanted to know what they sounded like faking normality when in truth they were seeding an invasion. He had known for some time that these three might not know what they were doing. They might be naïve and blindly following orders. It was possible that they had no idea about the insertions, but that was the kindest possible interpretation.

"Kani, tell us about Bathsheba."

"It's a genuinely fascinating place with a vibe quite distinct from Jericho and Kraken. It's obviously young, and there are caverns still under construction. Honestly, I can't get used to the smell of the place."

"Have you been to the surface?"

"Yes, but briefly and at the sun's peak. You don't wear a suit, but you do have to bundle up and bring a mask. It's extraordinary – a vast, sculpted, sandy wilderness."

"And inside?"

"Culturally it's recognisable – caverns, clans, and all that delusional hippie shit."

Kani hadn't spent long there, and after a cursory couple of days he continued on to Jericho. Ren suspected he knew why. Without an insertion mission to Bathsheba, there was little Kani could achieve there, as beacons would serve no purpose. Still, the group had to maintain the pretence of being equally interested in all of the Arc's planets, and a couple of days felt like enough to prove that point.

Not long after Kani left, August found his way to Bathsheba, and it was he who could do the real work of seeding gateways, which would eventually provide a way in.

Kani turned to Imiko and asked, "How about Typhon?"

"Similar," she said. "It's recognisably part of the Arc, but also different in many ways. There are caverns, clans, and Central Control hovers over everything. Of course, it's older and society evolved in a more conventional form before Arc philosophy became endemic. They have not re-purposed all caverns, so there are several dedicated to farming, industry and commerce. It's a mix."

"Eleuthera is worthy of its fame," began August. "You really have to go there to understand. No picture does it justice. It has a few things in common with Imiko's description of Typhon, except that it has a vast wilderness across its surface. The gas giant rules the sky like an imperious god."

"I have been there too," said Ren. "Frankly, I couldn't resist a visit. Everything that August says is bang on."

They talked for a while about the physical and cultural differences amongst the planets, until Ren finally steered the conversation to the point.

"Right, I asked you all to come because I wanted – or needed – to share something potentially important and see what thoughts you have about it. As mentioned earlier, I visited Eleuthera too. Its fame got the better of me."

Ren spun up his Eleutheran story gently. It began with a lavish description of a half-fictional tour of the planet. He simply glued together a careful selection of the locations visited, repainted as a leisurely tour as opposed to the frantic sprint of real experience. Finally, his account arrived at the Orotelli Gorge, and he dwelt for a while on a description of the military installation, assuming that would be of interest, but also because it amplified the site's importance. He needed a build-up.

"This is what I heard."

As he spoke, an audio file was transmitted directly to each of their implants. He knew that the recording would be far more impactful than a quote from his mouth. It would feel immediate and less like some manufactured tale.

Ren repeated, "We're under the strictest instructions to keep Rub' al Khali under wraps. The public and outsiders are not permitted to learn that world exists or what we have found there."

"It seems as though our Arc friends have a rather fat and juicy secret. Have any of you heard about this? Can you add anything at all to the story?"

They all shook their heads, visibly shocked.

"No, I hadn't heard a thing. This is huge," said August.

"Me neither," said Imiko, but then continued, "That said, there was a rumour of some discovery from decades ago before the coup. It was never clear or tangible, but there were certainly whispers. I have never heard that name before, though."

"The first sentence alone is striking enough. Just the fact of something important being held back means a great deal. But the second sentence reveals that the secret is a world of its own, so they have another planet they haven't told us about."

"And there's something they have found there that's important," echoed August.

"Yes, that last bit is the gold."

"What are we supposed to do with this?" asked Kani.

"That's a good question. For now, I simply wanted to discover if you had heard of anything like this, even hints. Challenging them at this moment won't achieve anything. We take this back with us and let our leagues decide what to do with it."

They all agreed, but then again, they would. At any rate, agreement was not the purpose here; it was laying bait. The gathering dispersed, and not one of them stayed in Hypatia for a second longer than necessary. They returned to their worlds at a sprint.

Chapter 24

Rub' al Khali

Nako Moon was at the door.

"Hello, Mr Markov."

When they were first introduced, Ren hadn't the first clue about Nako's importance. He had simply assumed that Moon was a smidgen more senior than Oso-Rae and Saki, but then again, their hierarchies were unfathomable. He didn't have the bearing, clothing or mannerisms of the sort of political royalty Ren was accustomed to.

"Mr Moon, what a privilege. I understand you are an important man."

"Not really. We have quite a flat organisation in Central Control. I just have a few extra responsibilities."

This was all nonsense, but what do you say to a statement like that?

"What can I do for you?"

"I would like to take you on a little journey."

"How fascinating. Now?"

"Now."

At the outset, their route was predictable, even familiar, but as Ren was about to discover, it would quickly take some deeply strange turns.

It began with the walk to Hypatia's square, a path that Ren could now navigate blindfolded, and then the gateway back to Eleuthera's Kakolem Cavern. So far, so boring. This time Ren was prepared, and he could pretend a nonchalance at the mind-blowing view of the gas giant's ghostly orb. He found it fascinating that Nako, one of the Arc's elite, travelled the conventional routes amongst the masses without protection or a security detail. Yes, people noticed him, but there was no adulation.

From there it was onwards to the Leon hub, and only then did things go off-piste. As with all the Arc hubs, several tunnels led away from a central core, each to its gateway via an obligatory series of pressure doors. They were all so similar that in Ren's brain, they had begun to blend into a single place. One branch of this hub complex was unmarked, unlabelled, and seemingly out of service, and yet this was the route they followed. Pressure doors hissed open and then closed, sealing them off from the rest of the complex. Then finally the idling gateway at the foot of the tunnel blossomed open to receive them.

For gateway travellers, there is a moment immediately after a transit when the brain performs a series of reality checks, subconsciously determining if something is not right. In just a few tenths of a second, indicators like gravity, light, smell and air pressure are scanned and then cross-referenced with other more subtle human sensations to determine what has changed. Experienced travellers could coalesce these root brain responses into a quick, instinctive planet identification. It wasn't always instant, as several sensations might be delayed until passing through a final pressure door, but gravity was one that could not be disguised, whichever side of a pressure door you were on. This was enough for Ren to be certain that he was still local. Nako appeared to read his mind.

"We're still on Eleuthera. The remainder of the journey is something we need to be discreet about, so excuse me in advance."

They stood within a hangar enclosure with ten flyers parked in neat rows. There was no sign of a security presence. For that matter, there wasn't another human soul in attendance. Whatever protocol allowed the gateway to open for Nako was all that was needed to restrict access. Why bother with guards when a sublime piece of technology can provide all the security required? This was technically true everywhere, but it was more common for sensitive locations to back this up with a display of defensive capability, intent and strength. The Arc, as always, was different.

One of the flyers sat ready for them, its bubble ajar, beckoning. Within moments, they were aboard and the capsule was sealed. Nako sent a discreet departure instruction, and the flyer was immediately aloft and accelerating. Daylight spilled into the hangar through a wide entrance slit, but as the flyer approached the exterior light, its bubble darkened to opacity. Only a few threads of light crept into the interior, enough to see one another in the gloom but nothing of the view outside.

"I see. This is a blindfold," said Ren.

"Yes, that's right. You'll understand in time."

Ren's feeling that things were going in a strange direction ratcheted up. A sublime sense of mystery was building, and he found himself basking in it. Nako was not willing to talk about what lay ahead, and a stilted attempt at ordinary conversation withered. They continued in silence until the craft began its descent.

"Oso-Rae took a liberty in telling you about our secret. However, it is what it is, and unless you were to have a nasty accident, the leagues will learn of it." Nako paused as if to emphasise what an 'accident' might mean. "Since the cat is partly out of the bag, we have decided to adapt to the new reality."

When the bubble's transparency returned, they were already parked in a new hangar, surrounded by equipment and a throng of people. It had the atmosphere of a slick, hypermodern laboratory. There was to be no easy path to the next gateway. Ren counted five sets of pressure and blast doors, and in the last chamber, they suffered an intrusive decontamination.

"Where the hell are you taking me, Nako?"

"You'll see," he laughed. "We're almost there. This is it now."

Finally, they approached the tiny orb of an idling gateway. Instead of blossoming open on their approach, they were obliged to wait for a scheduled departure time. A chime rang out, the gateway opened, and five people exited. Only once they were clear was traffic permitted inwards.

Nako went first, leaning forward and diving through as if plunging into a vertical swimming pool. Ren followed. This time, the reality slip hit with force, and he found himself cripplingly disoriented. His brain seemed unable to process the change. Gravity was gone. His first footstep, designed for nothing more than supporting his own weight, thrust him up towards the ceiling in a backward spin. He was caught by netting positioned just for this purpose. Nako laughed and helped to haul him down.

"Thanks for the warning."

"Sorry, I thought you might find it amusing."

Despite a lifetime of travelling between the stars, Ren never before experienced zero-G. Yes, he had been on moons with fractional gravity, but he had never needed to go into real outer space. The absence of gravity could only mean one of two things. Either they were very far from any planet, or in orbit around one. The answer came with Nako's next statement.

"We're in an orbital station about five hundred kilometres up. I'm afraid you'll have to learn to haul yourself around using the handholds."

All the safety layers and pressure control were on the other side, presumably to save space in the station. The gateway had

Archipelago

already shrunk back down to near invisibility behind them as they waited to be processed through a reception desk manned by a ridiculously cheerful attendant.

"Welcome, Nako. Welcome, Mr. Ren. It is an honour to have you both here."

Why did they keep calling him 'Mr Ren'? It was surely a quirk of formality or translation.

"Thank you. I haven't been back here in many years, but it looks just the same."

"Will you be going straight to the viewing deck?"

"Yes, that's the plan, and then we are heading down. Thank you."

Beyond was an interior crawling with personnel. Most were seated at banks of screens carpeted with the hieroglyphs of obscure data. Others were on the move, sailing about in zero-G with practised ease. In the centre of the room stood a circular arena displaying a detailed holographic representation of a planet.

"Follow me."

Nako was heading in the direction of an antechamber that stood on the far side of the room beyond the hologram. Ren's embarrassment at his clumsy, tumbling entry was softened by the fact that Nako, this magisterial figure from the Gang of Twelve, was equally incompetent without gravity.

The antechamber turned out to be a viewing deck: a large, mostly empty room with an array of comfortable seats and one transparent wall. Ren was no expert, but he was surprised it was possible to create such a huge window straight onto the vacuum of space.

And the view. The sight through the window was of a singularly curious planet. He knew at once that he had never seen this place before. Planets are always unique and strangely memorable simply for their colour gamut and textural qualities.

"Welcome to the Rub' al Khali."

"All I know is that name."

"We discovered this shortly before the coup and have kept it… erm… under wraps, you could say."

"Are we in Arc space?"

"We are about twenty light-years out from Bathsheba. It's hard to say where Arc space ends. There isn't exactly a line on a map."

The planet's surface drifted past, filling the field of view through the glass of the viewing deck. An absence of gravity does strange things to your sense of orientation. He knew full well they were looking down at a planet's surface, but the orientation of seats and window gave the sensation of looking ahead, as if at a stage. There was no true or correct interpretation of up, down or ahead, so Ren just let his subconscious decide for itself.

The view below was of a vast yellow desert, decorated with towering dunes that flowed one to the next like calligraphy. Looking closer, the colours were more complex than simple 'yellow.' Light-coloured sand was streaked with ginger, marmalade and rusty clay tones. The darker shades lay in the hollows, whilst the palest tipped the crests and slip faces.

"We gave it this name because of the desert and the dunes. They cover much of the surface, constantly shifting and migrating. It was the name of a famous desert on the dead planet."

"Why the secrecy? What's so special?"

"You'll see."

The dunes rolled past below, gradually reducing in height until they disappeared altogether, the terrain transitioning to a simple, arid plateau. In the distance a coastline was visible. Within moments it had rolled up to meet them, and then they were out over the water. This was the peculiarity of watching a planet from low orbit: hundreds of kilometres slipped past in a few seconds, but to the observer, it felt like dreamy slow-motion.

"It's approximately two-thirds land and one-third ocean.

By our standards, the ocean is a weird, briny mess and transforming it would take centuries. But the reality is that we couldn't conceive of doing that."

"It isn't the first time a world has been discovered with a challenging surface. You could burrow inside until the terraforming is complete. Like Eleuthera."

He continued, "But you're being more than vague about why I'm here."

Nako remained silent.

They were sliding into the planet's shadow, and beyond the ocean was an inky black. A distant, feeble moon provided just enough reflected light for the surface to remain dimly visible.

"Look carefully," said Nako.

Ren stared dutifully at the blackness, and at first, he saw nothing at all. Then suddenly his eye snapped towards something in the periphery of his vision. It was gone before his brain could register, but a second later, lights flicked on in the water below, blazing like a fairground ride. A phosphorescent glow streaked out in snaking dendrites from a central point. Light pulsed down the lengths of these arms in bands of blue, pink, and green. It seemed part octopus and part lightning strike. Then his brain registered that there were more — hundreds of them, pulsing for a few seconds and then resting like a flock of synchronised fireflies.

"What the hell am I looking at?"

"It's life, Ren. Alien life."

He turned and stared at Nako.

"You understand why showing works better than telling."

"I do now. Bloody hell. What is its nature?"

"It's hard to find appropriate language. Our library of words for flora and fauna just doesn't apply here. Up close, those are gelatinous threads kilometres long that spread from a central hub like some vast, deep-sea starfish."

Nako continued, "The Arc team treads very carefully. Generally, we stay up here in orbit to avoid the risk of contamination."

"Our form of life might damage theirs, or vice versa. Is that what you mean?"

"Precisely. That said, it appears that we don't poison one another. However, immediate death is not the only measure of damage. Some ill effects might not become apparent straight away. The simple introduction of a bacterium, or any one of our microorganisms, might have untold consequences."

"So, why the secrecy? Why not share this until now?"

"In the beginning, we trusted ourselves better than anyone else to walk softly. Our entire ethos is guardianship, so it is natural to extend that to alien life. There was no prospect of us bulldozing our way in, but we worried that others would have behaved like a drunken tyrannosaur in a rose garden.

"In many ways, we always knew that it was wrong of us to keep this from you, but we didn't trust others – you, the Hanseatics and the Old Worlds – to be careful or respectful of this discovery. It was a delicate matter and a huge responsibility. We couldn't risk you clumsily bearing down on this, or worse, fighting over it."

Ren was annoyed at this accusation but restrained himself. "I think we're better than that, but I acknowledge your caution."

"The tragedy is that after all these decades, we still understand very little. We stare at their structure through microscopes and see no double helixes, no enzymes, no amino acids or proteins. They remain baffling, and it feels as though we have barely started."

"Surely we wouldn't expect alien life to have these characteristics." Ren's words came out as half question, half statement.

"Well, we might or we might not. There has been no reference point until now."

"Fair enough."

"We don't know if there is any sentience. Nor do we understand their chemical mechanisms or the origin of the phosphorescence. Honestly, after all these years, we have started to feel a bit stupid. We lack the language or mindset to unravel the mysteries of this place."

"And you think we can bring fresh eyes to the problem?"

"Yes. At least, it makes sense to try. Our science has reached a dead end, and we probably need some help to decrypt it. If I'm being honest, this also gives us some leverage in negotiating a new deal with Core, so sending you home with this is part of a strategy."

Nako paused and then said, "We're not done yet. You only have half the story. I'm taking you down."

Ren blinked.

"We have no gateway access to the surface because that would require us to build a power plant down there… something we aren't ready to do."

It was not Arc style to display technical prowess with showy toys and machines. Their tech was almost always hidden away in tunnels and behind closed doors, almost as if they were ashamed of it. But the craft that carried them down into the planet's gravity well was a slick little beauty and knew it. It had the smooth form of an elongated ovoid with a long, curving window at the front, as if a neat wedge had been chopped out and the gap filled with glass. The rear had a single, large vent for some propulsion mechanism. Tiny flight surfaces protruded like the fins of a pufferfish.

They were strapped in along with two others from the orbiting research station who sat up front.

"Our pilots?"

"No, our guides. Only a gen-4 can pilot this thing."

"I'm Kuyo, a research scientist based on Hibiscus."

"That's the name of the station," explained Nako.

"And I'm Loai. Engineering."

"I'm…" started Ren.

Kuyo cut him off, saying, "We know who you are." The

words were accompanied by a wide grin to make it clear that it was meant as kindness. "Neither of us exactly lives on the station. Everyone returns to gravity at the end of their shift, as a break helps support bone density, organ health and all that."

He must have travelled hundreds of times between worlds, and in so doing traversed thousands of light-years, but to this point, he had never set foot in a spacecraft. Gateways always did the job. When he stopped to think about it, it was remarkable how completely they had erased the ancient world's expectation of how space travel would work. Actual interstellar travel was an entirely robotic activity for carrying gateways to new worlds. It was not the domain of men, except for a handful of eccentric, wealthy thrill-seekers.

There was one other group who could be considered members of the space-travelling fraternity. These were the rich, narcissistic weirdos who deliberately slept aboard vessels travelling at large fractions of the speed of light. It didn't slow ageing in a true experiential sense, but it did when compared to the ordinary mortals – friends, colleagues and family – following conventional lives around them. 'Oh, I just use a great face cream, darling.' Everyone had to be in on the act because it was essentially impossible to disguise several days' disappearance for a night of relativistic sleep. People.

Airlocks closed, and a quiet thrum permeated the craft as systems began to spin up. This was followed by a gentle, almost soundless decoupling from the orbital station. Directional thrusters fired briefly, just enough to build some distance between the craft and the station. Then the big thrusters burned, triggering an orbital deceleration and the ruin of its centripetal equilibrium with the planet. With just a few seconds push from the thrusters, atmospheric entry became an unrecoverable certainty. That job done, her nose tipped up away from the planet so that the thrusters could continue to slow angular velocity whilst also preparing to counter a plunge towards the planet's surface.

The classical glowing heatshield of frictional atmospheric

entry wasn't the only way of doing things. If you had the propellant available, which a craft carrying a gateway always did, it was simpler and less risky to gradually match velocity with the atmosphere whilst simultaneously dropping down to the surface. Following this approach, Ren's initial view was of a rapidly retreating orbital station, but then it pivoted out into space so that the thruster could point down at the planet and power a controlled descent. The blackness of space shifted to dark indigo as the first wisps of stratosphere enveloped them, and then slowly transitioned to a perfect, searing blue as they descended into atmosphere proper.

"We had a conundrum when designing this system," said Nako. "We needed matter for reaction mass to drive the engines. The thing about reaction mass is that it has to originate somewhere, but since we are dumping vast amounts of the stuff into Rub' al Khali's atmosphere, we needed to be sure it was uncontaminated. Where's it from again?"

The question was directed towards the pair up front and Kuyo answered, "It's mined robotically from a big icy blob about two AU from here."

"Icy blob? Is that the technical name?"

"It's an accurate description," said Loai.

"That must be the oddest pairing of gateways ever conceived."

"I'm sure there are stranger ones."

Ren said, "There is a tycoon on Nuevo Mundo who is said to have a pair of gateways simply to allow a mountain stream from another planet to flow through his house."

"Wow. I don't want to meet that person."

Their ability to hold this conversation at an ordinary volume, even with an active engine burn, was testament to the smoothness of entry. That, in turn, was down to the craft's exquisite engineering and the meticulous care of the gen-4 mind driving it. A second wonder of its design was the ability to switch between blisteringly high-velocity plasma and low-velocity bulk thrust. The former could be used high above the surface and only required tiny amounts of matter because it was flung out at three hundred kilometres per second. The latter was used close to the surface so that they didn't scorch it with plasma fire. On 'hot' mode, only a hundred kilogrammes of reaction mass was sufficient to reduce this twelve-tonne craft with an orbital velocity of ten thousand kilometres an hour, to a standstill, and that took just five minutes. In that time, it would be halfway down to the planet's surface.

After six minutes, plasma thrust cut out, and for a moment the only sound was of wind whistling past whilst the craft reoriented horizontally. The fins of control surfaces extended before thrust restarted. They were now in ordinary atmospheric flight, gently descending as they powered forward over open water.

To Ren's utter surprise, his overwhelming sensation was that this could be anywhere. It was nothing more than the surface of a sea with a cloudless blue sky above. Even the ocean surface looked like any other, with low waves, swirling currents and scattered white horses. How could the alien look so ordinary?

The craft's altitude stabilised only a few metres above the ocean surface as it swept forwards towards the coast.

"The starfish can't be seen from the air in daylight," said Kuyo. "Their tendrils lie well under the surface. It was quite a challenge getting close without having any kind of technical base on the surface."

"They call them starfish for want of a better word," added Nako.

Ren asked, "Are they the only living thing in the oceans?"

"Ha! No, there's plenty of diversity down there, from the microscopic through to the mega-scale like the starfish."

Approaching the coast, they slowed further, coming to a standstill hovering just above ground, balanced on a column of air driven from a fan turbine in the craft's underbelly.

The shoreline and entire littoral zone was abnormal and disquieting. Across the rocks lay a bulbous crust as if formed from inter-woven plates of fungus. At the shoreline, and presumably onwards under the water's surface, it was tightly packed and multi-tiered, but inland it dissipated into smaller mounds before fizzling out altogether. Beyond that lay sand and the dunes' foothills. The parabolic outer surfaces of these growths were nut-brown and veined with coloured tendrils.

Unmapped depths of the psyche harbour an ability to decide, quite independently of reason, whether a new experience engenders safety or danger. Fight or flight is settled in microseconds, even before a conscious thought has formed. A sense of unease emerged from those layers of Ren's psyche. It was an odd response as there was nothing explicitly threatening in these forms. In fact, they looked like nothing at all.

Ren recognised the fear and wondered whether the cause was not the objects themselves but the wider situation; the complexity of processing a new reality of alien life and the massive reality shift that went with it.

"What is it?" asked Ren.

"That's harder to answer than you might think. It's difficult to know if we are looking at many individuals or an extended, highly connected mega-entity." Nako, clearly saddened by their failures, continued, "I think you would be disappointed to know how little we have learned in fifty years. It feels as though we are looking at the whole problem from the wrong angle. It's like trying to read a book without any concept of a written language."

"How many people know about this?"

"It's not public knowledge in the Arc, but there is a whole semi-secret Central Control department devoted to the problem. That's bound to be a little leaky. Some people just want to leave it alone for the rest of time, perhaps with orbital monitoring. Others are determined to understand more."

"Which camp do you fall in?"

"If this were the tenth example of alien life we had come across, I might argue for isolation. However, this is the first, and we need to know what's out there."

"But you probe cautiously."

"Perhaps too cautiously."

The craft pivoted parallel to the shore and then sped along the coast just above the water. Rub' al Khali's discovery was without doubt momentous, but Ren was strangely disappointed by the blandness of its landscape.

"Does it not extend inland?" asked Ren.

"No. It seems that whatever life exists here is dependent on the ocean. It hasn't figured out how to leave it… yet."

"I have to ask the dumb question. Is it sentient?" It didn't look it, but Ren had to ask.

"We don't know how to answer that. There is motion that responds to us and a few other factors that could imply sentience, but on the other hand, a sunflower tracks the sun's passage across the sky."

"I'm thinking about what it might mean to leave this place alone and watch over it. Do we become guardians or gods?"

"Guardians, of course. Don't be melodramatic… but… okay, there's more. This gets complicated." Nako turned to face Ren, searching for a way to start. "When we talk about The Reaching Out, we refer to the big diaspora as if it occurred abruptly from one day to the next, but the truth of it was something else entirely. It sputtered into life, and the beginning was stretched over a couple of hundred years, involving more failures than successes. Some of the earliest missions simply disappeared into the void."

Nako paused before continuing, "One, a privately funded cult with a craft dubbed Prayer for Light, had a particularly strange story, long thought to be apocryphal. On reaching their first system, Wolf, they found nothing more than rocky moons. Their disappointment, blended with an existing certainty in their specialness, led them to sever the gateway link and disappear. Decades later, on arriving at that system by other means, they were nowhere to be seen, but it became evident that they had continued outwards. There was a small, abandoned subterranean town, a dead gateway and the destruction of all records. They wanted to disappear, and disappear they did.

"Look over there," instructed Nako. The craft had begun to rise and turn inland.

Ren strained his eyes, trying to make sense of patterns halfway to the horizon between the coast and a distant mountain range. Acknowledging the impossibility of seeing that far, a screen came to life, displaying the distant scene for what it was. Ren's mouth fell open.

A town stood before them. It had roads and buildings of all sizes including a structure that could only be a temple. All about it were verdant fields, which continued in a broad circle around the town before halting abruptly at the desert.

Nako continued his tale. "It turns out that the Prayer for Light mission found its way here almost fifteen hundred years ago. From what we can tell, some early event ruined their connection to the technology that brought them here. Their understanding of tech unravelled completely, and they became something akin to a medieval society. Any notion of where they came from was forgotten or deliberately deleted from their histories."

Ren finally found his voice and asked, "Have you spoken to them?"

"No. We didn't know if it was the right thing to do. We had this alien life form to protect and study, and we had to keep our distance for that reason."

"At least it proves that we and it aren't mutually toxic."

"True, but there's more to contamination than just falling over dead." After a pause, Nako continued, "We began to wonder if it was right to disturb their innocent little kingdom. They appear to know nothing of the worlds beyond."

"Ha! When I asked if you were guardians or gods you told me not to be melodramatic. Can you give me the same answer now?"

Nako looked defeated. "No, but it's not out of a wish to patronise these people. We just don't know what's right, and in that state of indecision we have drifted for decade after decade."

He fell into silence, and it seemed that with that, they were done. The craft gained altitude, at first under normal thrust. Then, as the sky began to darken into the indigo of stratosphere, it angled up and gunned the plasma. They were in orbit and docking in the time it took Ren to take the elevator from his apartment to the streets of Super Paradise.

Back in Hypatia, Nako walked Ren the last few steps to his house and stopped at the door.

"I know this is a lot to absorb. We at least know that life is not unique to us. It's also clear that life comes in extravagantly different forms which defy understanding. Beyond that, we don't know much."

Genuinely interested, Ren asked, "What has the discovery changed?"

"It hasn't changed much in terms of how we run our lives, but it has changed how we approach the idea of colonisation. The universe is no longer an infinite blank canvas.

"We will have to tread more carefully as we continue out into the uncharted void. We can't simply assume that everything out there will be ripe for colonisation, so we will have to stay well away from some discoveries."

"To my mind, leaving the colony ignorant and marooned is an ethical minefield," said Ren.

"Maybe, but even if we were to explain the truth to them, we could not allow them to leave the planet until we understand that it is safe to do so."

Ren knew this was true. Going forever onwards and outwards in search of fresh territory might have new constraints. On the other hand, it was just one planet amongst hundreds discovered so far.

They said goodbye, and Ren went inside and straight to his bed. He finally got the rest he needed, but his dreams were riddled with visions of pulsating phosphorescence.

Chapter 25

Astrid Swims with Sharks

A strid strode purposefully from the gateway down to the beach fringing the atoll's lagoon. After pausing to kick off her shoes, she continued on into the shallow water. She had arrived well in advance of the others, just to experience this and because she enjoyed the thrill of knowing that she was a hundred trillion kilometres from another human.

She swam, not purposefully in the way of those who seek exercise, just luxuriating in the warm embrace of water. She arched her back, eyes closed, and floated for a few moments, wondering about what she was going to say.

From a great height, the island seemed forlorn and inconsequential in a vast expanse of ocean. On this day, the surrounding seas were calmer, and no surf broke across the reef's rim. Instead, all that revealed the transition from lagoon to deep ocean were the graded shades of blue. The mottled, shifting teals of the lagoon mingled with darker peacock tones where the coral shelf started to drop off. Beyond was the blackened indigo of proper ocean, flecked with white horseheads, even on a calm day.

The news of Rub' al Khali had provided justification for meeting again. Strictly speaking, Astrid didn't *need* to speak to them, but the reality of this new planet had upped the ante. Perhaps she might learn something of their thinking and, with a little luck, discover why General Banz was involved.

Beyond the clearing, gateways leapt into life and the three magnificent rogues strode through. Astrid shook water from her hair, hung a beach dress over her still-wet frame and sauntered up to join them in the circle.

"Enjoying yourself, Astrid?" asked Mu Rosa with acidic sarcasm.

"Well, if I am going to cross half the populated systems just to meet you clowns, I'm going to have a swim. Look at this place."

"Yeah. Don't care."

Virsenko removed his jacket and with deliberate precision, folded it and lay it on a chair.

"So, what do you all make of the this?" asked Astrid.

"The Archipelago remains intact and functioning," said Virsenko. "They still adhere to those ideas that caused the coup in the first place. If anything, they seem even more entrenched than before."

"Look, I'm busy, you're busy," snapped Astrid. "Let's get to the point. I'm referring to this 'Rub' al Khali.'"

"Well, it's another illegal act by the Arc," said Virsenko. "In addition to the coup, we now see that they broke the ILISA."

He was referring to the *Inter-League Information Sharing Agreement,* which had been established hundreds of years before between the planetary leagues. It encompassed 'profound events' that might be seen to 'impact humanity as a whole.' In increasing order of vagueness, the three arms to this agreement were 'alien contact,' a 'discovery of import to humanity at large' and 'existential threat.' By hiding the Rub' al Khali, the Arc had probably broken this agreement.

Astrid recognised that the ILISA contained a degree of absurdity. In any real scenario, there might be too much riding on it to assume that information would be shared. It was the kind of thing that was happily added to inter-league agreements in the full knowledge that it could be ignored in a live situation. But nobody could say that out loud, because they all pretended to adhere to it.

There had always been rumours of some secret hanging in the background, and it helped to explain the level of attention given to the Archipelago. Astrid wondered if this was the driving force behind their insertion. Was this the real reason that she was standing here in the company of this gallery of narcissistic, scheming clowns? It was not that the Arc was insignificant, but it did not seem worthy of an insertion mission without some other motivating factor.

It suddenly occurred to Astrid that the knowledge of some deep secret in the Arc might always have been the principal motivation for this insertion. She wondered whether Mu Rosa and Virsenko even admitted that to each other.

That old secret had gained substance. The Arc had a whole new world that they had kept in the shadows, and it had a name: the Rub' al Khali. What gold waited for them at the end of that rainbow? Astrid's worry was that she could not easily stop the insertion, and if she interfered and failed, Core would surely be entirely isolated from it.

"Who knew of this before yesterday? How significant is it?" asked Astrid as calmly as she could.

It was not a question with an expected answer, at least not an honest or straightforward one, but she felt it was necessary to go through the motions. They took their turns lying.

Banz opened, "I was vaguely aware of those old rumours, and now we have confirmation. However, we shouldn't devote too much of our attention to rumours. It is better to focus on tangible facts."

Then attention turned to Virsenko, who said, "I was aware of it too, but we never put much store in gossip or tales. The Congregation of Populated Systems has a hundred such rumours, and they generally turn out to be the fabrication of conspiracy theorists. Could it be important? Yes, but let's not get carried away with something that has nothing more than a name."

"Exactly," added Mu Rosa. "There just isn't enough substance for it to influence us. It will have to be a discussion point in future negotiations, but beyond that, there's nothing to act on. So I agree with General Banz and Premier Virsenko... a rare event, I should add."

Astrid considered the prolific body language of glances, crossed arms and tiny gestures. These collectively told her more about the situation than their dismissive replies. She was now certain that the Rub' al Khali, whatever it proved to be, was their biggest motivation in this game. It was also evident that Banz was in a steamy threesome with Virsenko and Mu Rosa. Sometimes this sort of fishing was too easy. Even great powers can reveal their hands via simple plays.

She had already put a plan in place to detain Banz and isolate Helsingor should events kick off.

"Thank you all for your candour. I must have got carried away with it, and I'm thankful you're not giving it more credibility than it currently justifies. Let's focus on the mission."

None of them lingered. Mu Rosa, Virsenko and Banz walked to their gateways and were gone, leaving Astrid alone. She looked out to sea and thought, *An attempt to achieve good by force is like an attempt to provide a man with a picture gallery at the price of cutting out his eyes. Our patience and wisdom achieve more than our force.*

They were broken fragments of quotation from somewhere, but she didn't know whose words they were. Something in the core of her scheming mind still held on to principle. She smiled sadly, feeling foolish for clinging to threads of idealism in these byzantine corridors of power.

There was no way to truly cooperate with this group, as they were vipers to the last. They were clearly withholding far more than they were telling her, so she would have to let them go about their business and she about hers. Alone on the beach, Astrid waded back into the shallows.

Stingrays patrolled the lagoon floor whilst tiny silver fish leapt and glittered in the sunlight. Terns continued their artful darting and diving, catching fish as the first breath of an afternoon breeze caught the palms' upper leaves.

Astrid swam once more and then lingered on the beach, feeling the crispening salt against her skin as she dried. Grains of shell stuck to her calves as if glued there. Still damp from her swim, she returned to the clearing, took one last look back, and departed through the gateway's black sphere.

Chapter 26

Orbital Hide and Seek

Gradually, over days and weeks, the planted motes of microtech began to evolve. Their nascent forms were barely capable of anything beyond a primal impulse for growth. But deep within the crystalline form of their memories, they carried potential for vast complexity.

Oso-Rae had developed a dark fascination with all this curious alchemy and spent long hours studying its evolution. On this afternoon, her attention was on a beacon, now highly evolved, that had been planted in Hypatia by Kani – quite brazenly – just off to the side of the square.

Ren had explained that the location would have been dictated by Kani, since the motes themselves were little larger than pollen, incapable of locomotion and, in this rudimentary state, far too stupid to select a discreet spot for themselves.

She remembered the moment, days before, when Kani had walked away from the square, feigning a desire to look at the view down the valley. He had sat on a flat rock, gazing into the distance. She now knew he had used that moment to let fly this fleck of technology. With a signal from his implant it woke and set to work.

Safely ensconced in a little crack in the rock, it mined basic minerals. Armed with those and the array of knowledge in its memory banks, it created a better version of itself. This improved variant was able to make more sense of the encoded instructions it carried, and it used those subroutines to build an even more advanced iteration. Three days later, it was on version four, and with that had reached intellectual maturity. All that remained was to build the tools it needed for the remainder of its duties.

Like a queen ant, it let loose a private army of workers, each extraordinarily dumb on its own but capable of doing a specific job very well. With that army at work, further materials were mined and more evolved remote tools established.

It was around then that the Arc team had first identified this beacon. They watched cautiously as a ring of tiny cameras sprouted and began to stare out at the town. A passer-by would have thought little of these cameras since they looked for all the world like rock-dwelling xerophytic plants. But Oso-Rae was no passer-by, and took an oddly personal interest in staring back at them, marvelling at the irony of subverting their purpose. She took delight in the vanity of its tireless dedication to discretion... but then she tamed those smug sentiments and turned her thoughts to the wonders of their technology and how far behind the leagues her Archipelago trailed. Was there any chance of the Arc surviving in the shadow of these great leagues and their awesome capability?

The discovery of the first beacon actively broadcasting on Eleuthera had been the real key. Arc technicians established their own monitoring equipment that worked doubly hard to remain invisible. The Arc peered at the invaders' tech, whilst the latter stared right back without seeing a thing or knowing it was being scrutinised. There had been an urgency to find them all before their cameras and sensors were established enough to know that they might be being watched. This was the beauty of the insect-like drones deployed by the Arc. They could buzz around, casually evaluating the beacons' state of evolution. If young enough, they established local monitoring, otherwise they maintained their distance and determined what they could from there. The worst-case scenario would be for them to transmit an 'I'm busted' message to the insertion units. That would destroy the surprise and change the balance of power.

More cameras looked up at the sky and began to identify stars and the paths of satellites. With this, the beacon could establish perfect positional information and proceed to the crucial next step. It was here that the Arc's technical teams focused their efforts.

The beacon might have eyes, ears, and a private army of worker ants, but it had no voice, no way of reaching out to its masters. Creating a voice loud enough to reach out beyond the planet was no trivial task, so this step had taken days to complete.

Over this period Oso-Rae regularly returned to the scene, watching as a concavity formed in the rock. At the centre of this perfect little parabola was an antenna with the capacity to transmit and receive telemetry.

It waited and listened, tirelessly monitoring the constellation of satellites passing overhead. Finally, at just the right moment, it received the 'ping' it sought. This contact message lasted a microsecond and would seem innocent to any other listener, but it was unique enough to establish with certainty that it had made formal contact. Some hours later, as the satellite swung past on its next orbit, a reply was transmitted and a confirmation returned. The handshake was complete.

From that point on, the beacon and satellite swapped data in short, compressed bursts on each orbit. It was tight beam and used a part of the electromagnetic spectrum that nobody bothered much with.

The Arc team could study the transmissions but could not decrypt them. Then again, that wasn't really the point. What was important was not *what* was being transmitted but *where* it was being sent. Microburst transmissions were studied and triangulated, allowing them to identify the orbital destinations. Armed with that data, they began to monitor the insertion units hidden in the firmament of satellites, and, in turn, attempt to triangulate the remote destinations of their comms.

None of this was easy, but in the Juliet-II system they had it all. The invaders' base had been detected deep within one of Jericho's moons. A robotic mission was soon delivered and anchored to the moon's surface, whereupon it burrowed down to hide in the fine dust of a crater's floor. Once settled, mining machines dropped through the crust to seek out the invader's lair, sequestering the plasma of boiled rock as it went. The final approach was feather-light. A tiny hole was opened – just enough to take a peek inside and determine if the location was discreet enough to continue. Some abandoned their journey there, but others found entry points.

On Jericho at least, the Arc mission was poised with an exposed blade over the invader's Achilles heel. They had mined the gateway power and control circuitry. With that, they had the power to kill the only escape route.

But the other systems were proving more elusive. The low-albedo asteroid in Hypnos space, where Palina sat and plotted, remained obscure. Eleuthera was an even bigger mystery. Where could they possibly be hiding out in the midst of Orcus's raging sea of radiation?

If and when the Arc finally discovered the remaining bases, they would have to throw caution to the wind. Cruising out using conventional physics was not an option if they wanted to get there in good time, so a series of gateways was scattered through the systems to stand by. Hopefully one would be close enough.

Across the Arc, August's micro-gateways were also sparking into life. The one Ren had first discovered was still nothing more than a tiny orb, but it remained busy with the delicate process of parasitically attaching itself to Arc power. When that was done, it too would be ready.

Dozens more beacons and micro-gateways gradually joined the party, springing to life in a haphazard pattern that matched the visitors' march across planets. Little by little they began to declare their readiness. The invader's network was spinning up, and the Arc was hot on their heels.

Oso-Rae marvelled at this technology but also detested the insidious way it had infiltrated and infected her worlds. She knew that the Arc, with Ren's help, had a chance of sabotaging the attack, but luck had to be on their side.

Chapter 27

A Siren Pierces the Stillness

It was a fine winter's morning in Hypatia when the attack came. The sky was a high-altitude midnight blue. Shadows stood long and dark in thin, dustless air. The sun's rays penetrated straight and unscattered, rendering the town in sharp contrast. A patchwork of light clouds dotted the Western horizon. From the mountains, a brisk breeze flowed, sweeping away the winter sun's meagre warmth.

Ren was still unused to life at high altitude, and the thin air muddled his brain. He repeatedly forgot to breathe deeply enough and then had to recover with a series of deep, desperate inhalations. He was lost in thought, wandering the streets towards the top of town, just below the scree fields. The snow was mostly gone, now only clinging to a few shadowy hollows and the darker alleys. He was out walking just for the sake of it. It was a way to clear the mind and think through events. Few people experience revelatory moments, and Ren's more useful ideas always stemmed from stewing on thoughts and allowing conclusions to gradually distil out over the course of days. Walking seemed to greatly help the distillation process.

Even if this mad operation went to plan, he faced a deeply uncertain future. The many-branched tree of possible outcomes presented none where he would be seen as a hero – not that he wanted that – but more importantly, few that would allow him to be entirely honest about his role. Someone would be bound to throw him under the bus, whether he had aimed to do right for External Affairs and Core Planets or not. It wasn't clear if he could return to CEA work, but then again, it wasn't clear that he wanted to either.

He would certainly try to craft a story such that he appeared as an innocent bystander. It shouldn't be too hard to pretend that the Arc figured it out without his help. But that felt naïve.

Maybe it didn't matter. If everything went to crap, he would end up in the Arc for the rest of his days. Perhaps that wouldn't be such a bad outcome, but the truth was he didn't belong here. He was deeply affected by the undeniable beauty of their planets, but Ren's essence still felt unchangeably urban. His libertarian sensibilities would never sit well with all their intrusive controls.

A siren abruptly pierced the stillness. This was expected. The resident population had been discreetly prepared for this seemingly inevitable event, and many had returned to their sectors. They had departed in dribs and drabs and by as many diverse routes as possible so as not to arouse suspicion. A more public exodus would have attracted the notice of those staring down from orbit. Now there was only a skeleton crew present in Hypatia, enough to give the semblance of normality whilst minimising risk to the populace. The military was present, but discreetly, pretending to be ordinary citizens but poised for possible guerrilla action.

Arching his head up, Ren saw dozens of white streaks falling out of the stratosphere. At the foot of each was a glowing heatshield, happily ablating energy from the friction of entry. As the heatshields darkened, their job done, they fell away, and the drop-out units powered forward in normal flight towards their destinations. One cluster approached Hypatia, whilst others targeted a host of distant locations.

Then came the cracks from a volley of sonic booms. The

units were upon them, their engines howling like distressed animals.

Ren seemed to suddenly wake up, setting off at a sprint towards the town centre. As he approached, a new gateway blossomed to the side of the square. This was the one he had discovered days ago: the first of August's payload to have been found. The Arc team allowed it to open for a few moments before killing its power supply. Pretending that they were reacting in the moment was a necessary part of the act. Killing it any earlier would have proved that they knew too much. Ren watched in awe as a vehicle that had begun to emerge was sliced clean in half.

He arrived at the recently improvised HQ to join Nako Moon and the others. All had their heads arched upwards, watching three dark gunmetal blocks appear over the square. To Ren's non-military eye, they didn't look much like flying craft at all, more like crudely streamlined shipping containers. There was not one shred of beauty in their forms, just a commanding impression of power and capability. Stubby wings looked pointlessly ornamental. Every angle and every surface screamed danger.

The three craft hovered briefly on columns of air driven from vertical thrusters, before dropping down to settle on the cobbles of the square. Hatchways opened even before their sharp, articulated feet had made contact. From the first poured a column of troops in combat gear. They formed a cordon around the square and angled weapons outwards towards the town. The second produced a multi-legged machine, a giant spider adorned with weapon turrets. It appeared from a hatchway and then scampered around the square with a creepy motion blending insect with machine. The sharp points of its eight legs clanked against stone cobbles beneath its body. Even from Ren's distant viewpoint, he could hear the tinny clacks of its footsteps. The third craft contained a large drone that swept upwards to take up position a few hundred metres above them. There it hung, watching, waiting.

Within sixty seconds, all motion had ceased, and a crisp, metallic tension gripped the winter air. There was no sound, no further action, and a surprising stillness settled over everything. Sparrows were already returning to the square. A single soldier scanned the ground with a handheld device.

Hypatia's gateways had been seized, and all was quiet for a time.

Nako turned to Ren and, with magnificent calm, said, "The games begin."

Ren only nodded in response and sent his swarm out towards the faceless invaders. The Arc's military response would take time... in theory. But all this had been prepared days ago, and they would fly in at the appropriate moment and take up positions at a cautious distance. They didn't need conflict to win, but had to at least appear to be playing the game. The truth of it was that the military was already here, but in the shadows.

Despite ample mental preparation, the moment when it came felt profoundly surreal to Ren. It was a chunk of fiction sandwiched between strata of reality. The burst of military action was not a sight often witnessed in this age of dialogue.

A small group approached the drop-out team's cordon. They, and groups like them across the Arc planets, had been coached about when to arrive and what to say. It was easy to play out the role expected of them because they felt genuine fear. No pretence was required. From a safe distance, questions were barked.

"Who are you?"

"What do you want?"

"Where have you come from?"

"Why are you doing this?"

There was no word of reply, nor one shred of acknowledgement. Masked and helmeted troops simply faced ahead, their features hidden behind visors. Behind them, the lone soldier with the scanner completed her work, whereupon a machine was brought out and anchored to the ground.

Awakening, it immediately began burrowing into the rock beneath the square. A hellish, grating howl permeated the town as it descended. One half of that strange machine stayed at the surface, whilst the other half dropped into the hole it was creating. Rock cuttings were spat out in a perfect parabola to accumulate in a conical heap outside the cordon.

It was burrowing down to access Hypatia's gateway control equipment. The Arc's gateways might stand eccentrically naked in squares and forest clearings, but they weren't magic, and there was no escaping the need for power and control. There was nowhere for it to hide except somewhere under the square.

Ren had prepared and practised his part in the plan. His swarm flooded the invaders' perimeter. It would infiltrate, record, monitor and then cycle back to him in a continuous flow.

Of Hypatia's indigenous gateways, only two had been open when the attack came. These had quickly shrunk down to join the others as idling marbles. Moments later, three more had shut off altogether. Pressing that kill switch was a huge decision as it permanently destroyed a gateway coupling, leaving an inert, useless pile of metal and ceramics. Creating a replacement meant starting from scratch with a new coupled pair and then transporting them to the entry and exit points. That was one thing for a domestic route but quite another for an interplanetary one. The first could be done in days, whereas the second might be a matter of years or even decades. It was a very rare act to deliberately kill an interplanetary route.

They soon discovered that the invaders hadn't relied on August's gateway. Shortly after the burrowing machine had completed its work, a brand new one swelled open, evidently carried here with the landing craft.

Ren joined Saki and Nako at a vast bank of screens delivering a live feed of the invasion from all corners of the Archipelago. Gateways were spinning up and opening in each of the Arc's planets and habitats.

"Look," said Saki. "They're actually taking the hard way

in."

Ren followed Saki's gaze and saw a hailstorm of cutting machines rain down and begin pummelling their way into the habitats' bowels. Jericho and Typhon would have been a devil of a challenge without August's gateways, but the invaders clearly hadn't wanted to rely on them entirely. Slicing through hundreds of metres of rock to reach the cavern spaces within could not be done either subtly or quickly.

"It seems that subtlety no longer counts for much," replied Ren.

"Yes, but it's fascinating to study the psychology of an invasion you knew was coming," said Saki.

Their plan was nuanced. If the Arc had been wholly acquiescent, it would have been suspicious, but if they had responded too violently, they would have pointlessly lost lives. The answer had been a weirdly muted response from the Arc military.

Ren knew that this would have been the one massive uncertainty for the invaders. Until the attack, they would have had little idea of what the extent and speed of the Arc reaction would be. Now, minutes after orbital drop-out, there had been an almost absurdly minimal response. Nothing had stood in the way of their arrival. The only riposte to gateway seizures had been a handful of muted volleys. This disturbing puzzle would be sure to engender more anxiety than celebration.

"Have you got anything yet?" asked Nako.

"No. It will take a while," replied Ren. "But I'm through their gateway, so I think it might be time to move."

His microtech was profoundly useful but its Achilles heel was speed. The individual motes were slow both in motion and their capacity to build a detailed picture.

"Okay, let's get you moving," said Nako.

A gateway opened just long enough for him to step from Kraken to Eleuthera. There he joined Oso-Rae, who was with the team outside Kakolem cavern. Ahead of them stood the showy gateway where he had first arrived on Eleuthera. It now stood cocooned within a bubble of military equipment, all silhouetted against the gas giant's milky cloud tops.

"Ren," said Oso-Rae, her voice shaking with stress. "Look at this."

"Just a minute..." began Ren before letting the sentence fizzle out, his mind distracted by the act of dispatching his swarm.

Within moments the motes would be in amongst the invaders and gathering data. Then they would dip through their gateways and start rummaging around in the secret spaces behind the scenes. All this was key to the success of their planned counteroffensive. The location of the invaders' bases wasn't yet certain, at least not all of them. Jericho was absolutely clear, and for that they were thankful, but it still left two other systems to pin down. They had ideas, but Ren's swarm would return data that could provide clues or perhaps even clarity.

"They're preparing," she continued. "Something big is coming through."

He watched as a lithe, eight-legged machine broke the cordon and sprinted down towards the bowels of Kakolem. Like the one that strutted around Hypatia's square, it had an arachnid form with pointed metal feet that clattered against stone.

Eleuthera was quite different to Kraken, as it was half-in, half-out, so to speak: part habitat, part planet. There were a hundred ways of gaining entry without industrial-scale tunnelling, and this was one of them.

Control room feeds tracked the machine as it progressed into the cavern. At the elevator banks, it just carried on running, bursting through barriers into open cavern space. At first, it dropped like a stone towards the cavern floor, but then came the ear-splitting roar of engines. Legs were pulled in tight against its fuselage, thrust generated lift, and it hurtled forward into Kakolem. Its trajectory stabilised into horizontal flight only a few metres above the cavern floor. Hot on its tail, a second machine dropped straight down from the elevator bank to secure the lone gateway in the plaza.

It had been one thing to prepare Hypatia, a Central Control location, for the attack, but it had been impossible to achieve the same with whole planetary populations. In Kakolem, there had been less forewarning and preparation, so chaos and fear reigned. This population had never known war, had no known aggressors, and could have little conception of a long-planned insertion. The utter mystery of purpose and identity was as terrifying as the physical fact of invasion.

As it swept down the cavern, thruster blast shattered windows, sent tables and chairs flying, and shredded the park. A rolling wave of exhaust tore bushes from the ground and scattered loose objects like leaves in a storm. Interior spaces like Kakolem had none of the intrinsic strength of surface towns. There was no reason to design for storms, deluges, hail or snowdrifts, so the structures were essentially flimsy. People were blown to the ground and huddled in corners, whimpering.

"I hope they judged this right," said Oso-Rae. "What if we have just accidentally surrendered?"

"I understand your fear, but it's a good plan," said Ren. "That's assuming we have properly estimated their capability."

In forty seconds flat, it had screamed down to the cavern's far end, where it settled by the cluster of gateways leading to Dax, Leon, Sfax and Acre hubs. Turrets pivoted and turned, measuring, mapping, patrolling. A handful of troops spilled out of its belly to take up positions around the gateway complex's periphery. The machine sat poised on its eight legs as if ready to pounce.

Three of the gateways had closed but Sfax remained open at full aperture. Half of the landing team sprinted through to secure the hub. Gaining control of as many of these as possible would be critical to the invaders' operation. Too few would lead to a protracted stalemate.

"I should go back," said Ren.

"Right, I'll open the gateway now," she replied.

This was the only approach they could come up with. He would have to dip back and forth between Hypatia and Eleuthera, gathering up his swarm, interpreting their data and then dispatching them once again. Back and forth. Sortie after sortie.

A flood of telemetry surged into the Arc's control HQ. There it was processed by a gen-4 tactical mind before being sprayed onto screens in crisp infographics. Ren couldn't interpret it all, but he understood enough to know that it was a mixed bag. There were successes and there were failures, but enough of the latter to make the invaders confident of victory.

The events Ren witnessed in Hypatia were mirrored in every corner of the Arc in a genuinely impressive display of planning and synchronisation. At least eighty of the micro-gateways had spun up, but only half of those had survived the first few hours of the attack. Still, those that remained had transformed the invaders' access to the Arc.

A media broadcast from Central Control was delivered in a tone that subtly balanced anger and calm. It stated plainly that this was an invasion, undoubtedly sponsored by other leagues, most probably Core Planets or the Hanseatic League.

They had secured many of the critical gateways. That was the big story. That was the key to everything. Then again, without a military riposte, this was inevitable. Prior to the attack, Ren had listened to the debate with fascination. The decision was to make them believe they had succeeded but for the reality to be a marginal success: not enough for them to break out the champagne.

Ren saw something of the Arc'ers in their plan. It was in many ways reckless but also designed to do minimal harm. Managing his swarm only required half his attention, and with the rest he watched and listened as the operation played out.

One critical story was that of the intermediary hubs.

Controlling these did more than disable the Arc transportation system, it also gave the invaders the capacity to move around Arc space using indigenous infrastructure whilst pinning the Arc'ers in place. Here the statistics told a more muted story. Most gateways had closed in the first moments of the attack. A handful had remained open, and troops had hurled themselves through those. It was enough to control some of the hubs, but fewer than they would have wanted.

"They have secured the trunk route between Kraken and Bathsheba," said Nako. "It's a key interplanetary link, particularly as they don't have insertion hardware around the latter. But we have prevented them from controlling most others, at least for now."

Saki continued, "They'll believe they have the numbers to call it a success and avoid a drawn-out siege or an escalation."

"Agreed," said Nako. "All we need is for them to hold onto that belief if we are to avoid worse violence."

Not that their job was done yet. The invaders still had a long way to go until they secured Jericho and Typhon. August's gateways had done much of the work on both planets, but a few critical installations remained deep within. Burrowing machines continued to sink through the rocky crust towards those buried spaces.

As telemetry from the Orotelli Valley arrived, it became abundantly clear that the Rub' al Khali ruse had worked. Staggering volumes of the invaders' hardware showered down on this remote, heavily guarded valley. Half aimed straight for the main tunnel entrance leading to the cavern within. The remaining half adopted peripheral locations to overpower the encampment. At the tunnel entrance, a few units took up defensive positions, whilst others scrambled in through the entrance.

Defensive emplacements in the cliffs were neatly destroyed, even as they rotated to face this sudden threat. The invaders were in and amongst them in moments, and by then it was too late. Their defensive capability looked outwards and was useless against a threat from within the compound. Orotelli had been entirely subdued with barely a shot fired. It was an immaculate operation... at least that's how it appeared.

Units penetrating the tunnel found themselves in a large cavern. Defensive blast doors slammed shut behind them, the trigger for their closure coming seconds too late. The black sphere of Orotelli's precious gateway stood naked in the cavern's centre. Although still open, it was not yet won. Beyond lay an intermediary hub, and only that would lead to the prize the invaders so desired. They ploughed headlong through the gateway to face whatever lay beyond.

"How is it looking?" asked Ren.

"I think the balance is right," began Saki. "It hasn't been a complete, riotously successful rout. Still, they'll believe that the operation has gone well and that they have done enough."

"And Orotelli?"

"They secured the gateway and the hub that lies beyond, but they're stuck at that point, just as planned. The Rub' al Khali and its secrets remain tantalisingly out of reach."

Nako added, "We've also managed to waste a fair percentage of their resources elsewhere."

Many of the invaders' units had captured gateways that simply closed and winked off for good. Those dejected teams found themselves ridiculously guarding nothing more than a patch of grass or an irrelevant town square.

Ren's latest sortie on Kraken had returned, and a picture was emerging from the mists of data. It wouldn't be long before he discovered the location of the invaders' base in the Hypnos system, so he turned his attention back to Heimdall and Eleuthera. The gateway opened once again, and he stepped through.

Chapter 28

Nako and Palina Exchange Pleasantries

Only a day had passed since the invasion: a tiny, inconsequential drop of time when set against the decades of preparation, but Palina's impatience was palpable. He would not be drawn into a lengthy standoff, nor could they permit them the opportunity to regroup, so he was determined to force the pace. Other than a half-hearted skirmish on Bathsheba, the Arc had been docile and uncommunicative. Most probably they were in a state of shock. Palina was sure that they would still be speculating about both the identity of their attackers and their purpose. The absence of a military response implied an understanding that they faced a capable invader. Firing back impulsively might bring fire and brimstone down upon them. It didn't matter now. It was time for parley.

By morning, Rubos's team had opened their final gateway down to the Arc planets, and they could now move around fluidly. Palina now prepared for his grand arrival. Straightening the creases in his uniform and donning dark glasses, he walked through the gateway into Hypatia's square.

The shift into Kraken's gravity almost caused him to trip, but he caught himself and narrowly avoided an embarrassing, stumbling arrival. A local lieutenant saluted him and opened a path out through their security cordon. There he stood waiting, with arms folded and a broad smile across his face. The message was clear: "come and talk to me." Palina's uniform and arrogant demeanour made his status clear.

An hour later, Nako Moon and Commander Palina stood face to face in Hypatia's tree-lined avenue.

They were finally talking. Nako arrived alone, and they exchanged bizarrely polite pleasantries before walking a short distance away to speak amongst the trees of the main avenue. They were in the open but could speak discreetly.

Nako smiled and said, "You are aware that we could fight you but have chosen not to."

"I don't think you'll do that. Your entire interplanetary society fails without the gateways that we now control."

"You don't have them all," said Nako, still smiling.

"We have enough."

"So, what do you want?"

"I want two things. One is to know what you have on the other side of the Orotelli gateway. What is Rub' al Khali? What have you found?"

"Oh, you mean you got stuck in the hub? What a shame for you. That must be frustrating."

Palina quietly bristled. He was shocked at this man's humoured cockiness in the face of an invasion. Although what he said was true: they had secured the hub, but the other gateways within remained tightly shut. For now, they had control but no prospect of progressing further.

"And the second thing?" asked Nako.

Commander Palina had prepared his answer long before. "To have a permanent physical base on all five planets. We now have our own access points into three of these systems. On Jericho, we will also require control of the gateway to Nuevo Mundo."

"Who do you represent?"

"I represent several parties with an interest in this. I'm not at liberty to discuss details."

"Okay then. Shall I hazard a guess at a little ménage-a-trois between the Hanseatic League, the Old Worlds and Helsingor?"

That stung Palina. There should be no way for Nako Moon to have knowledge of this precise brew. Palina himself had had to theorize about the identity of some of the forces behind the plot he commanded. He was a mercenary and wore no uniform of government or state. His organisation shunned insignia. Nako had made a small statement, but it changed the landscape of the conversation. The Arc was not wondering about his identity. A new disquiet swelled within him.

"Why are you doing this?"

"We require embassies and corporate access. Our companies will have the right to begin recovering their losses and to operate in the Arc."

"So, just that, then? Are you sure you wouldn't like a back rub and a medal too?"

The sarcasm irritated Palina, so he fired back in the same tone. "Sure, why not?"

In truth, Palina was increasingly puzzled by Nako's nonchalance and calm. Everything about this situation dictated that he should have been riddled with anxiety, but instead he displayed the emotion of a granite boulder. Why had Central Control delivered this one man to him? It may have been his ego talking, but he had hoped to face an array of generals and ministers. He had envisaged a rich drama in which he delivered explosive demands and watched them gasp. He had even planned the perfect moment to remove his dark glasses for impact.

"Come with me. We are going for a little walk," said Nako.

"Where are we going?"

"You asked to see the Orotelli gateway. Let's go."

Palina blinked.

They could have been there in seconds by way of his

sparkling new gateways, but there wasn't a snowball's chance in hell of him allowing Nako to travel through the secret spaces of his moons and asteroids. Instead, they relied on domestic routes. Orotelli's isolation, set against the confused state of gateway control, forced an awkward cooperation to open an unencumbered path to Eleuthera. From there, it took one final gateway and then a short hop in a flyer to reach Orotelli. In the forty minutes all this took, the team in the valley prepared for their arrival. Their flyer was waved through to land, and the way ahead was clear.

The base lay in a green and pleasant glade. Anywhere in the galaxy outside the Arc, this would have been deemed an eccentric and pointless affectation for a military site. Here, different priorities seeped into every walk of life. In the gloom of the valley's depths, ferns, mosses, and other shade-loving species covered the ground and coated the rocks. Torrents of water tumbled down from above before disappearing into boulders and re-emerging as a bubbling brook. All was mistily damp.

Palina and Nako, an odd pair by any measure, walked together in silence to the tunnel entrance guarded by troops in dark fatigues. After two hundred metres, the tunnel terminated in a hangar with a single gateway standing open. Without breaking their stride, the pair approached the orb and passed through to the intermediary hub where Palina's team had hit a wall. Only one of the hub's spoked tunnels led to a dormant gateway. The others were dusty dead ends.

"Your people control the far end and are evidently not in a hurry to open it," said Palina.

Instead of replying, Nako sent an implant instruction. Commands were issued, buttons were pressed, and power surged. Within a moment, the gateway began to open.

"Shall we?"

Palina was troubled. This seemed pathetically effortless, and that made him sense that something was not right. He hadn't had to delve into his ample store of threats. There had been no escalation of any sort, and yet Nako was casually walking him to the prize. It seemed too easy. It *was* too easy.

Putting aside his unease, driven by a desperate desire to know more, Palina continued through behind Nako. Bright light. Cool wind. He found himself blinking in Kraken's winter sun. They were back in Hypatia, and Nako was smiling.

"Sorry, Commander, but Orotelli was a dummy... a blind. I'm afraid you will have to try harder. Sorry for all the theatre, but I quite enjoyed it, didn't you?"

The situation had turned upside-down in a moment, and Palina had been made to look ridiculous. He was purple with fury, that rigid, professional façade in tatters.

"That was childish. We are here to stay and we'll find your secrets."

"Not if there aren't any. Even so, come with me. We certainly do need to find our way out of this."

Nako led Palina to the rough ground at the side of the square and picked his way over rocks and low scrub to a flat rock. There he reached down and picked up one of the tiny, camouflaged cameras – a fragment of the trail of microtech left behind by the others. He held it between thumb and forefinger before Palina's face.

"The interesting thing about these little fellows is that they left a trail."

Palina didn't say a word at first, but his face and body language spoke for him. Finally, he said, "So what? What are you doing?"

"Walk with me one last time. Let's negotiate an end to it."

Nako and Palina sat across from each other at a table designed for twenty. They were alone.

"I would like you to watch this," said Nako, suddenly deadly serious.

A large screen flicked on, and they were presented with a view split into three panels. Each showed one of Palina's hidden operational bases. One was the little asteroid near Kraken where Palina had based his operations and from where he had departed for Hypatia. A second showed the moon in distant orbit around Orcus where Eleuthera's operation was based, and the third showed Jericho's dusty moon.

Palina just stared. He was struggling to process the implications and couldn't fathom what his next move should be. Every step he had taken today had amplified his unease. Now that unease had blossomed into full panic. Nako's cockiness had started the slide, and when he correctly identified the powers behind the insertions, it went further south. The juvenile trick with the gateway, the knowledge of his surveillance site, and now this… it was going horribly wrong.

As they stared at the screen, a flash appeared, and the asteroid began to fall apart in graceful slow motion. It was cracked in two. A searing light enveloped the broken shards, and the screen went white for a moment, the camera's sensor overwhelmed by light from the blast. Simultaneously, explosions erupted deep within the two moons. On each, an area of the surface liquefied, dimpled and cracked. Rock and dust ballooned outwards before gravity took hold and pulled it back down again, leaving brand-new craters.

"When I said we should negotiate an end to this, I feel it might be a bit one-sided. Checkmate."

Palina knew then that he was done for. Fighting their way out was an absurd idea, meaning that they were immediately and completely at the Arc's mercy. He couldn't quite absorb the irony of it. Here he was using control of gateways to win a battle, and that very tool of war had been used against him.

"This is done now. The gateways are all dead. People have perished, but fewer than if we had allowed this to become a weaponised conflict. You and all of your people are trapped and this is over."

Every word of this was true. He would not beg to be returned home, but he might have to beg for his people. He thought of the many souls he knew well who now lay dead, entombed for eternity inside moons or frozen in space.

"Please address your staff and request that they stand down and await instructions. Can you get that message to all planets? Do this now to buy a return journey for your people."

There was nothing left to say. Palina sent the command, loosened his collar, and started planning for his retirement. Perhaps he could travel or grow roses.

Part IV

Chapter 29

Ren Drifts Home

Only Ren was free. The hundreds who had made landfall on the Arc planets were detained in camps. Despite everything, Palina was startlingly calm. He had quickly discovered a serene resignation to the prospect of a radically different future. Perhaps he even relished the idea of a new beginning doing something far from military service. Of course, that depended on him obtaining passage out of the Arc and getting off lightly with a dishonourable discharge. Neither of those things was in any way guaranteed.

There were four camps, one on each of the invaded planets. Nobody had been moved between them, so the invaders remained where they had been when their missions and pride were ruined. A few more had been mopped up from orbital positions, but there were no survivors from the destroyed bases. Treatment was adequate, the camps were generous, and the food was excellent, if a little peculiar. The singular piece of cruelty shown was an ongoing silence about their fate.

The insertion hardware remaining intact had been gathered up to be dissected by Arc engineers. At the moment of surrender, many systems had been scuttled, so much of it was now useless puddles of molten goo. August, Imiko, Kani and Palina were in solitary detention, as they were receiving a special kind of interview that cared little for the conventional boundaries of war.

The fact of it was that they had little to tell that wasn't now abundantly clear. The others had admitted their roles and could say with simple honesty that they were under orders. None of them had explicitly known about the insertion missions, but all had guessed.

Ren sat with Oso-Rae and Saki in the little house in Hypatia. The snow was back with a vengeance, now accompanied by a bellowing winter storm. Wind howled, and visibility reached no further than the tip of an outstretched hand.

"What happens to you on your return to Core?" asked Saki.

"That depends on what my people know," replied Ren.

"Not a thing... yet. Well, the leagues know that their insertion gateways are dead, so probably assume the worst, particularly as they were killed simultaneously. We see no great hurry to return people from the insertion teams. The longer we wait, the longer we have to interrogate them and dissect their surviving hardware. As soon as we start talking, we will come under pressure to return them."

"So, what's the plan?" asked Ren.

Oso-Rae answered, "We'll open the gateway and send you back on your own in about a week. That gives us sufficient time to plan our formal statements and demands. You will carry those back to External Affairs personally."

"I'm not looking forward to that. Astrid might have my back, but she might also have no choice but to throw me under the bus."

"You don't need to tell them that you helped us," said Oso-Rae. "Arguably, we might have succeeded without your help."

"Oh, that's between me, Astrid and a brick wall, but there's a chance I will be exposed. It's difficult to maintain a perfectly consistent story under questioning."

"Who is this famous Astrid?" asked Saki.

"I suppose she's my version of your Nako Moon, although she's far more ferocious and perhaps the most impatient woman in the known universe. So, I sit in a storm in Hypatia for a week?"

"Not necessarily. You have a few days, during which time you can go wherever you want. After that, we will regroup here. We'll need a couple of days to get back to the Jericho gateway, and also some time to prep you for the big conversations in Core."

"I will head back to Eleuthera, then. It's unlikely that I will set foot in the Arc again after this week, so I should use my time well."

He began by returning to Kakolem. The view of Orcus hadn't become boring. Would it ever? He spent some minutes just staring at its globe, now a slender crescent. The dark side was sheathed in green aurorae towards the poles, and vast electrical storms riddled the equator, their filigree patterns flickering.

The descent to the cavern floor triggered a new unease. In their eyes, he would surely be seen as complicit with the invaders who had brought fear and havoc to this world only two days before. As a harsh reminder, there was still twisted metal and shattered glass at the elevators. Why hadn't this occurred to him until this moment? But his unease proved misplaced, and all those he passed proved exaggeratedly courteous. The only explanation for this was that the populace had been made aware of his role. Otherwise, he would have been treated with disdain at best and aggression at worst. This would make his wanderings through Eleuthera easier but weaken his claim to innocent involvement.

A clean-up operation was in full swing. Parkland was being replanted, and debris was long gone. The two insectile machines had disappeared, but gouges marked the ground where metal feet had scratched and grasped. Everything else seemed relatively normal. Throngs of people were on the move, and the multi-layered traffic cruised and spun.

He stopped for a moment in the middle of the square and gazed around. This was his first truly free moment in the Arc. So far, he had been on a mission – always being led, always being told where to go, what to look at and what to think about it. The only exceptions were a few solitary strolls around Hypatia, but even there he had been in work mode and inhibited by other pressures. Now he was a tourist with a world at his disposal.

He would find a bar. In characteristic style, inexplicable to anyone else, and despite the hour, Ren decided that the best thing to do with this magical moment was have a drink. To that end, he wandered the tiers of shops and stalls, seeing if instinct and serendipity would provide a destination.

It wasn't easy, but find a bar he did and a fine one at that. They weren't quite open yet, and staff were still polishing and sweeping, but with kind respect for this unexpected newfound celebrity, they ushered him in. There were tables, bar stools, and a few sheltered alcoves. As the only customer, he chose to sit at the bar.

"Welcome, Mr Ren," said a barman.

He was tall, lanky, and dressed in a patterned sarong with a wide-necked top.

"Thank you. How do you know my name?"

"Oh, we know plenty about all this now."

"Good. I think. At least I'm not in trouble."

"We heard you helped us. I'm very happy to meet you."

This was the first Arc citizen who had not been carefully selected and presented on a plate, but Ren wanted a quiet drink, not an interview.

"What'll you have?"

"What have you got?"

The drinks were explained. Many things seemed to be

universal, even after decades of isolation. He started with a beer.

"Tell me about your life."

"My name is Zafi, and I'm from here… well, not here exactly, because people don't live in Kakolem. I'm from Palolem next door."

"And how did you come to work here?"

"Oh, I chose this path long ago and have always done it."

"I like the idea of all jobs being a long path to perfection; that everything can be a vocation. Where I come from, this kind of work is something people do temporarily on their journey to something else."

"That's strange. It takes a lifetime to master trades like mine."

Ren spent another two hours there, talking occasionally but not incessantly. He discovered a little about ordinary life on Eleuthera. In many ways, he learned far more from this one exchange than he had in all the long sessions with Central Control. Anecdote and casual experience usually trump formal sources when finding the essence of a place.

Eventually, in a merry but far-from-drunken state, he left the bar and continued down the cavern to the Sfax hub access. After the chaos, not all had returned to normal operation, so options were limited. No longer on a mission for External Affairs, he thought hard about what he *wanted* to do, rather than what he *ought* to do. Instead of jungle, savannah or temperate forest, he chose the rich broth of humanity.

That decision told Ren plenty about his own identity. He turned left when a more sensible mind would have turned right, and he found himself in Erruscal, Eleuthera's largest town. The two caverns were separated by five thousand kilometres or five minutes, depending on how you chose to measure things. Ren hated himself a little. With all Eleuthera's beauty at his fingertips, he was being shallow and self-serving.

The truth was, he had been wrestling with conflicted feelings about the Arc for days. On little more than instinct, he had quite possibly betrayed Core's best interests. But that didn't mean that he was convinced by Arc philosophy. It wasn't just that there were deep flaws with the human condition here – these issues might take years to unravel – it was also that he couldn't place a human on the same stone as a toad… and judge them equally. He certainly hadn't chosen this path because he saw the Arc as superior, nor to shit on the Hanseatics. Instead, he had acted because he could no longer stomach the old methods. The cause of his diligent service remained edgily intact, but something had changed.

Kakolem and Erruscal had transformed Ren's preconceptions about the Arc. The other towns had been modest and wrapped in a pastoral conceit. Erruscal was different – a thrumming urban creature that leapt straight into your lap and lovingly snuggled into your chin. This place was full of recognisable humans living recognisable lives. Eleuthera had helped him claw back from what had been a bleak vision of the Arc, one that judged humanity to be just another dot in the sweep of domains, kingdoms and phyla.

Ren stood in an expansive concourse in the midst of this fabulous new place. Foot traffic streamed past him as if he were an inert bollard. He had seconds to decide whether to subdue his happy intoxication with the one remaining pink pill he carried, or recklessly dive headlong in. This was the tipping point, as one more drink would change the momentum of the day altogether. His ability to make reasonable decisions would be subverted. Ren was accustomed to leading a sensible life on the job for months at a time and then putting that aside on his return. Then, safely ensconced in his private sphere, he could play by different rules. He swallowed the pill.

Waiting for sober clarity to course through him, he thought about how the alternate path might have played out. What would have happened if he had put sense aside and walked towards Erruscal's bars? He could imagine waking ten hours later with his face stuck to a glutinous pillow. His head would be burning, his mouth dry, and his mind a tangle of remorse.

The night would come back to him via that cruel form of memory that clings to the embarrassing and tosses aside the pleasurable or factual. A hangover was easily fixed, but remorse would linger.

There were those who used these pills all the time to enable a lifestyle burning the candle at both ends. For a while, they managed a diligent working life whilst still partying late, day after day, night after night. It would work for a few weeks, perhaps months, but in the end, they would be ruined – burned-out shells with a life of therapy and illness awaiting them. Ren just wasn't that stupid.

At that moment, he understood that he was not in the mindset for parties or tourism, so he turned around and marched back to the gateway and on to Kakolem. There, he walked the arcades for a while, ate a simple meal, and checked into a hotel, where he slept deeply and in great comfort. Many travellers never achieve a decent night's sleep in a strange bed in some foreign land, but this was not true for Ren. For him, the opposite applied. He preferred the surreal dislocation of waking in a strange place.

The very next morning, he was back in Hypatia in his lodge opposite a confused Oso-Rae.

"It was impossible. Too much has happened, and uncertainty lies ahead. I couldn't relax."

"I understand. We can start for Jericho in two days. Until then, you'll be here in the snow."

"Can you take me back to Viola Bay?"

By the afternoon they were on the seafront, watching boats bobbing in the harbour. Ren had spent time alone with his aunt – it still felt odd to be wielding the word 'aunt.' It had been mildly moving but muted. The culture gap was so vast that it proved difficult to engage deeply. Ren didn't really understand her world and didn't to try overly hard to explain his. In the end, it was simpler to stick with simple reminiscence and private anecdotes about his mother. He took his leave vowing to return and keep in touch, but he wasn't entirely sure that would happen.

Now he was back to being the exhausting inquisitor with Oso-Rae. It was a final attempt to consolidate his understanding before returning to face the music.

"I'm missing something. It isn't just ecology, pods, sectors and clans. There's something else at work here. The Arc has some distinctive view of the universe I haven't been able to put my finger on."

"What are you asking?"

"What else makes the Arc mentality distinctive?"

They had reached the end of the paved edge of the harbour wall and were picking their way through mountains of lobster pots and heaped nets. Beyond was a narrow path that climbed from the bay upwards toward the bluff, where the flyer had parked on their first visit.

Oso-Rae thought a while before saying, "We are in a complex dance between humanity's savage heart and the veneer of society. Elsewhere, these two forces are in tense, often violent opposition. People are tightly policed and tied up in an encyclopaedia of laws. We do things differently here."

"What do you do differently and why?"

"I suppose we have modified our expectations of mankind."

"What expectations?" asked Ren.

"Since we see humanity as just another species, we have more realistic expectations. One should expect a degree of animalistic behaviour from animals. We understand that people are ruled by biology, deep instinct and the heart. The logical brain is often a supporting actor."

"Is it not dangerous to be so dismissive of rationality? Thought leads to enlightenment, and that, in turn, shows us the path out of barbarism."

"I think it's more dangerous to pretend we're something we are not."

"It also seems to be an odd idea from a society founded by an intellectual elite," said Ren. "It also sounds like a dangerously slippery slope."

"I don't see it as such an obvious conflict. It isn't anti-intellectual to recognise ourselves for what we are. Many societies think that they can re-wire humanity via social policy, whereas we think that people are just people and will only change over millennia, and even then in ways that can't be easily coerced by social policy."

"That's a disturbing idea, as you could use it to dismiss enlightened thought, forgive all sorts of awful behaviour, and give people an excuse not to strive for a better society."

"I'm not trying to convince you," said Oso-Rae. "What I'm saying is in response to your question. I do think that most societies attempt to hammer in ethics before the childish mind can comprehend them. Children learn far more from example and experience than they do from lectures in the codex of morality."

"But you police people's minds," replied Ren impatiently. "You use implants to monitor your people. I don't know if I can ever get past that."

"We do, but it's a gen-6 mind that absorbs all the data and then very occasionally suggests intervention. We don't have *people* observing and listening."

"I remember the story of the man in Viola Bay. So, if someone has a proclivity or tendency that is incompatible with society, you can re-educate. God, what do you do? Cut out a chunk of their frontal lobe?"

"Is it not helpful to have something in place to stop the worst?" answered Oso-Rae innocently. "We agree that the best way to ensure liberty in societies of this scale is to take small pieces of it away. We both do it; you with your endless laws and we with this."

"Maybe that's true, but the Arc seems conflicted as a society that claims to be libertarian."

"Fair enough, but to my mind, by protecting ourselves against the very worst transgressions, it becomes possible to remove a plethora of restrictions for everyone else. But you don't seek new ideas, do you, Ren? You have given up on the idea of betterment."

"That could be true. Either I'm cynical or realistic," he replied.

Oso-Rae said, "There's another thing, Ren. Most communities in the Arc are empaths. Some data from our implants is shared across the community, and you don't get a choice if you're within the sector. It's quite normal for us to leak thoughts or emotions within our groups, so giving us a form of hive sensitivity."

"I can't believe this hasn't been mentioned before, nor that I didn't see it."

"In truth, we knew this would be an awkward topic for you, so we didn't want to broach it too soon. Not every community does it and many only in a mild way. Here in Viola Bay, key raw emotions such as anger, sadness and joy are visible, but we stop there. In other communities they go much further. Imagine how complex it is to broadcast lust or the desire for violence."

"I really, really can't imagine that. This is bound to become a major point of debate in our future relations. The privacy of an implant is utterly non-negotiable in Core. But then again, you don't seek membership, only contact."

They had reached the top of the bluff and were both out of breath from the steep climb. Standing side by side, they gazed out at the expanse of ocean in silence. Its immensity and power had the effect of making all these conversations seem silly. Ren imagined how it might be living a life in a humble house by the water, watching the sea's endless moods and mutations, and never having a debate like this again.

"There's more," said Oso-Rae. "The Gang of Twelve are highly enhanced. They're entwined with the gen-6s that monitor society at large. They can sense and read the texture of thoughts across the Arc's billions of inhabitants."

Somewhere deep within, Ren had already begun to suspect this, but it was still a shock to hear it spelled out. It instantly made the Bureau a pariah. He may have solved one problem by torching the invasion, but another one loomed with this newly empowered Archipelago and their deified oligarchy.

"You know that's going to be a huge problem going forward, don't you?" asked Ren. It breaks every rule in the book."

Oso-Rae just spread her hands as if to say, *don't ask me.*

Briefings complete, Ren chose to spend his remaining time on a languid, solitary return to the Rose Cavern. He had no urge to seek out the new or the thrilling. Instead, he would retrace their original path in reverse, because it is remarkable how different a place can seem from another angle. Each road wends its way through an entirely different land when travelled in the other direction. If anything, he sought the mundane, the mediocrity of everyday life, and the calm simplicity of being in a place without urgency or grand purpose.

The experience of travel is an entirely different beast when acted out alone, without anyone telling you where to look, what to think, where to stop or whom to converse with. All these decisions can be made on momentary instinct.

In Taskala Caverns, he stopped for a while at the falls, where divers continued to plunge down the cliff face. He soaked in the glorious warmth of the spindle-sun and watched them, entranced by both their skill and the joy it brought. Then, ignoring the absence of a path, he worked his way down to the cliff's foot, where he sat on a narrow ledge with his feet in the water, and with divers thumping into the sea beside him.

It was only then that he remembered precisely what Oso-Rae had said the day before. She had clearly spoken of a *gen-6* mind that patrolled the population's thoughts. But a gen-6 didn't exist, at least not in Core. Had they really achieved something that all the other planets and trans-planetary corporates had failed at?

The sea route to El Borj was served by a shuttle boat service that ran regularly from the pier. So, with a few minutes to spare, he dried his feet and wandered over to wait. People greeted him kindly by name but did not press further to make conversation. That suited him perfectly. Within seconds of departure, the launch rose from the water on the hidden wing of a hydrofoil. Ren laid his chin on the gunwale and watched mesmerised as the water slipped past at fifty knots.

After stopping at a few Taskala towns en route, the boat arrived at the familiar marina below El Borj. He thanked the boatman and strolled along the dock a little way. Acting on a whim, he struck out across the desert towards the green smudge of a wadi. Massively misjudging scale and distance, he arrived forty minutes later, sweaty and scratched to hell by desiccated, thorny bushes. Their spikes were so obscenely sharp that even a starving goat would think twice before gnawing on them.

The wadi was just the oasis he had hoped for. It was lush, green, well-shaded, and nestled in a moistness that contrasted sharply with the surrounding land. Amongst and between the greenery lay a network of irrigation ditches, cross-hatched in a neat grid. Between them grew a host of crops, largely tended by robotic farm machines. This was striking, as the Arc'ers preferred to give the impression of some pastoral dreamscape in which simple, earthy people laboured in the fields and ate their own produce. It didn't make it all a lie; it would have been quite absurd to discard technology in a world so underpinned by it. The disconcerting part was that his earlier journey was evidently a hyper-designed series of tableaux. If the Arc was so high-functioning, why did they feel such a need for propaganda? Those practised, polished lies had been the favoured tool of dysfunctional states and broken ideologies since the dawn of time.

In the pools and irrigation ditches, tadpoles swarmed amongst shoals of tiny fish. Somewhere beneath his feet, in a dark tunnel, the river must be passing on its subterranean route to the sea. A little of its water was siphoned off and brought to the surface to create this. Ren couldn't decide if it was beautiful or an absurd pastiche.

He spent a while in a blissful daze at a café table in a shady corner of El Borj's square. His thoughts failed to coalesce into meaningful new ideas, so instead Ren passed the time watching locals scurry about on their daily meanderings. He drank a sweet, milkless tea and quietly wondered about the cliché of this. It was evident that aspects of El Borj reflected a form of desert aesthetic, which seemed strange because that people and its culture existed thousands of years ago on a dead planet that no longer mattered. Over the centuries, the ethnicities had blurred beyond recognition, as had cultural traditions. Diverse new peoples had emerged on different worlds, and the memories of ancient cultural birthplaces were long forgotten. Yet, here in El Borj, all this must have been manufactured. Was this the choice of the people or that of some cynical designer, imposing a culture on them?

It was true that the ways, languages, and aesthetics of cultures rolled on through the centuries, transported about by the threads of memory and the arcs of great migrations. The arrival of a people on some distant planet often engendered a new urgency for recreating the past and reviving tradition. These are the deepest forces of identity at play. Cultures collided like galaxies, slicing through one another and then spinning off in new directions, their forms changed but often still recognisable. The question of how real this culture was had no easy answer, nor one that particularly mattered if it delivered a binding identity.

Putting aside the overly sweet tea, he walked through the market to absorb the mercantile life. This time, looking more intimately at the stalls than he had on the first visit, he was struck by a new vision. In addition to the vibrance and colour, there was austerity. Certainly, there were heaps of fruit, vegetables, fish and olives, but beyond that, it seemed meagre.

He wondered if this was a forced economy or a happily accepted one? Did he need the madness of a shop like Party Time with its many floors of frivolous tat? On the other hand, was this sobriety something imposed? He was discovering many questions as he walked but continued in silence. The truth was, he couldn't face the conversations anymore.

He lingered in El Borj until midday, walking the winding, confused backstreets reminiscent of an ancient souk or kasbah. On a conventional planet, the sun would be at its peak overhead at midday. Indeed, that was the essential, technical definition of the word. On Jericho things were different, and the spindle-sun was still far away, halfway along its migration. Shadows were long, and shade was plentiful between the town's solid walls. It remained hot, but not as unbearably stifling as when the spindle-sun lay above them. Life alternated between pairs of days; a fierce evening and morning followed by a refreshingly cool and gentle period. This was cavern life.

Leaving El Borj presented Ren with a quandary. Should he find an alternative route back and discover new places, or should he continue to retrace the route in reverse? His data feed remained rudimentary, but it was enough to navigate the transport system. A decision made, he boarded the train to Wakaba, in the heart of Kawazu's tropical pod.

A little over a day later, Ren approached the Rose Cavern on his final train journey in the Arc. The previous two days had been dreamy and surreal. He had spent hours wandering the streets of Wakaba, learning what he could about their life, habits, culture and ways. A simple hotel was easily found, and with that secured, he walked deep into the farmland and forest fringes. Again, he saw robotics helping to till the land, snip, trim, pluck, sow and harvest. Had he simply not noticed this before, or had it been deliberately hidden away for their passing? They were discreet machines of organic form, so perhaps easy to miss against the land. He might never know the answer to that question.

The ground beneath their feet was damp from overnight rain, and the heavy scent of wet soil filled the air. Central Control had left this final stage of the departure in Oso-Rae's hands, so it was just the two of them who followed the path up to the head of Rose Cavern. Nako Moon had thanked him and said goodbye back at the lake. Ren wondered at this powerful man, one of the Gang of Twelve. There was a simple humility to his being, and instinct told Ren that this was no cynical act to conceal a dictatorial heart. But he still didn't know what these people were capable of, and great horrors can be enacted by kindly souls on private missions to do what seems right to them.

For a long while, they walked arm-in-arm in silence. In this final approach, the forest's incidental music was enough. Ren was now more attuned to the discrete sounds that combined to form the cavern's soundscape. Its gilded stars were the tropical birds, some with pleasant melodies played out in nearby branches, and others with great, penetrating calls travelling far through the canopy. Then there were the diverse chirps of grasshoppers and cicadas in the grasses and meadows, along with the buzz and whir of wings. Layered through it all were the occasional croaks of frogs and the endless drip-drip-drip of rainwater from countless branches.

Ren paused when he came upon the dark lake where he had first stopped all those weeks ago. It had been the first moment when he had stood alone and exchanged words with Oso-Rae, but now it felt like a lifetime ago. Only tens of days had passed; a brief period in that specific version of time as measured by clocks and calendars. But the flow of life's experience does not always obey that mechanistic measure. Time passes in bursts and surges, accelerating and decelerating around you. At times it marches ahead of the calendar, and at others, it lags behind.

Oso-Rae and Ren entered the forest clearing where he had first arrived, blinking and anxious, into Jericho's light.

"Good luck, Ren."

"Goodbye, Oso-Rae. I don't know if we will meet again,

but thank you for everything."

"I suspect we will."

They didn't linger over a drawn-out farewell. Enough had been said, and the walk up the Rose Cavern had provided time for closure. The final moment was mired in awkwardness, neither knowing whether to treat the other as a counterpart, colleague or friend.

Oso-Rae sent a command, and the gateway blossomed. Ren nodded, bowed in the style of the Arc, and stepped through with all the confidence he could muster.

Chapter 30

Two Storms Brew

Astrid chose to meet on the island again for a reason. It is said that the ocean has a thousand faces, and each visit reinforced this ancient metaphor. These were the brooding hours that foreshadow a monster tropical cyclone. Winds were building, skies loomed dark, and the earth was lashed by ferocious squalls.

A persistent wind kept the palms bent and straining, their fronds outstretched like streamers. Massive waves boiled and foamed at the reef. It was a wonder where all those fragile fish hid when five-metre breakers hurled themselves at the coral wall. The ocean seemed to lose its translucence altogether, becoming instead a form of liquid iron, streaked with white spray.

Even the lagoon was a rough, dark cauldron, barely recognisable from the pristine cozumel glass where Astrid had bathed three weeks before. The shore was covered in a carpet of foam whipped up by the turbulence. Birds ignored the fuss, seeming entirely relaxed, cocky even, on the wing, despite the wind.

The arriving storm added a useful slice of drama… for she had a point to make, and wasn't afraid to apply some tricks to influence mood, response and outcome. She had rarely felt more entirely in control.

Mu Rosa stepped through, looked around her, and said, "What the fuck, Astrid? Do you know how much this suit cost? Now it's going to get covered in crap."

"I don't think you'll be too worried about your suit when we're done."

"Darling, I'll send you my cleaning bill."

Mu Rosa was talking nonsense, of course. She didn't care what clothes cost, nor did she even know how they got cleaned. Other people worried about that. It didn't even enter her mind.

Moments later, Banz, Volse and Virsenko appeared in quick succession through their respective gateways. They too were momentarily thrown by the building storm's ferocity but quickly shrugged it off. They were accustomed to Astrid's eccentricities.

A simple tarpaulin strung over the clearing provided meagre protection from the squalls but at least kept their faces dry.

Astrid skipped the conventional greetings. "As you know, Ren Markov has returned alone from the Arc, and we have had a little talk. Actually quite a big talk.

"I'll get straight to the point. Would you like an update on your invasion?"

That sentence turned the tables so immediately and entirely that they were momentarily at a loss. The three looked at each other. Mu Rosa obstinately held on to her pride, but it was now blended with anger. Banz closed his eyes briefly and then flicked them open again. That was all he needed to recover his composure. Virsenko didn't even blink. He seemed made of stone.

"The Arc found all of the insertion bases and killed them in a simultaneous action sometime after the drop-out occurred. Your ground teams are detained, and the negotiation of their release is in my hands."

"Why you?" said Mu Rosa angrily. "We all had a stake in this mission. You can't cut us out."

"Oh, stop. Kani and Imiko are detained, as is August," said Astrid. She delivered the last line while locking eyes with Banz. "The tech they delivered was tracked, and they have all confessed their roles and loyalties. Furthermore, just because the insertion troops were without insignia, it doesn't mean that they can't be identified under questioning. Commander Palina has been extremely helpful, although you may find him a changed man."

Denial was pointless, and each of them was now angling to reposition and adapt to the new factual landscape. General Banz had turned visibly pale. At least Mu Rosa and Virsenko could run home with their tails between their legs, but he was royally screwed.

"Are you going to throw me into the lagoon?" asked Banz wearily.

"I'm sorely tempted."

Mu Rosa finally said, "None of us was involved with the decision to send the missions all those years ago. All we did was inherit the fact of their existence."

Casting aside the last threads of denial, Virsenko added, "We had very high confidence levels that the Arc was hiding something important, and we were correct. They had no right to hide that."

"And you thought that this was the way to obtain it?"

"They committed an act of piracy against the Hanseatic companies, so this represented a fair and measured response," explained Mu Rosa.

"How lovely that you cling on to your absurd justifications," replied Astrid. "An eye for an eye. Piracy for piracy.

"Let's move on and talk about the implications for you. I'll start with Director Mu Rosa and Premier Virsenko, since your leagues are in no way under my jurisdiction. You will evidently do what you will. There is, however, the question of whether you want your people back and what you want from a future relationship with both Core Planets and the Archipelago."

She continued, "The message from the Arc for both of your Leagues is that they will grudgingly put the incident aside in exchange for writing off all real or deemed debts."

"Nonsense. I can't agree to that," spat Mu Rosa.

"The same goes for us," added Virsenko. "Anyway, there is little to negotiate, as they have nothing we need if they are not intending to repay us."

With victorious glee, Astrid said, "Fine. Then contact me in due course regarding the return of your people. Oh, and do get in touch if you would like to be involved in an information share on the alien discovery at Rub' al Khali. I have details now, and I will share them with anyone willing to play by my rules."

Astrid dropped that bombshell quietly, without emphasis, and then carried on as if nothing had happened. Mu Rosa smiled a wry smile and deflated, suddenly looking small and fragile in her stiff designer clothes. Her entire game was gone, and she would have to make a judgement call as to whether to accept defeat and come back crawling on her knees, or remain proud and forgo the offering. This was not the moment for that decision, so there was only an exit remaining.

"Volse and I will discuss the remainder alone with Banz, since he is nominally under our jurisdiction."

Virsenko and Mu Rosa nodded but said nothing more. They walked up to the gateways, which expanded as they approached and then snapped closed behind them.

It could so easily have been Banz leaving with them. Helsingor's government had been on the cusp of announcing the shift of allegiance when the insertion gateways went quiet. At that moment, the deal stopped dead in its tracks. There was no longer a transaction. Had it occurred a day later, they would have been outside Core and a new member of the Hanseatic League. Now everyone needed to rethink the deal in the context of this new world order.

Astrid turned to Banz.

"The fallout from this will be vast and far-reaching. Core's integrity is in danger, as is the relationship between our leagues. You have contributed to undermining that. Perhaps we have a problem of balkanised power and dual allegiances. On the other hand, maybe you're just a self-serving narcissist."

"Astrid, don't patronise," said Banz. "You don't own the CPF. There are forces at play that you can't coerce. Even when we are united, there will always be a struggle for power between planets, just as there is an instinctive struggle for power between people... for that is our nature."

"Alian, please don't lecture me about human nature. Of all people here, *we* were supposed to be working together."

"I didn't believe that there was a diplomatic path through this," he replied. "I had Core's best interests at heart."

"Bravo. There will be a hearing to determine that. I think I know which way that will go, don't you?

"The implication for UCoM is that a demilitarised zone will have to be maintained. In addition, they will be obliged to accept an Arc unit into the fold. Keep your friends close and your enemies closer. That seems to be their thinking. Those terms are all your fault. The implications for Helsingor will take time to unravel, don't you think?

"For now we are done here and you are free to leave."

Volse accompanied Banz back to the gateway, leaving Astrid alone. She chose to stay back for a few moments to take a breath before hurling herself back into the alternative maelstrom of politics. There was a storm arriving, both here and in relations between the great leagues. They had stirred a hornet's nest. Ren's actions had flung it all open, and that would have consequences. The fallout was going to be spectacular.

Straining at its limits, the tarpaulin finally gave up. It disconnected itself from three corners and then furled itself into the trunk of a supporting palm. Sometimes objects that look simple turn out to be quite the opposite. Now, facing the full force of the elements, she surrendered and walked back to her gateway.

From high above, the island normally appeared as a tiny dot in the sea's vast expanse. But on this day it was obscured by the creamy whirlpool of a storm a thousand kilometres across. At its heart lay that peculiar little eye – an island of tranquillity that serves only to guarantee that worse is to come.

Chapter 31

A Quiet Evening in Lafayette

I t was a sultry evening in the Lafayette Cavern. Flaming lanterns had been lit all about the grounds. One long row swept down from the house and across its lawns, illuminating the path down to the gateway and the water's edge. Insects fussed about the lights, drawn by that insatiable biological urge. In the darker shadows amongst the trees, fireflies sparkled.

Anli Sikinen had the floor. She had been in this gang for twenty years and had just one remaining until retirement and a return to an ordinary life on her home planet of Bathsheba. The retirement would be from the Gang of Twelve, but, should she choose to, she might continue her professional role in the department she had headed all these years. It could be hard to accept a demotion and see one of your underlings not only become your boss but also take a seat in the Lafayette Cavern. In truth, Anli hadn't yet decided if she would continue in the Terraforming Department or sit out her twilight years in peaceful retirement.

There was a vague hierarchy within the twelve, but it had little meaning beyond deciding who spoke first. With twenty years under her belt, Anli was the longest-serving member, and for this alone she opened the discussion.

"We are alone again in our little Archipelago. The last of their personnel have now been returned through the gateway to Nuevo Mundo, which has closed for two weeks while both parties process the situation."

The next to speak was Maae De Ri. She headed the Department of Ecology, and that inevitably made her more entrenched, defensive and risk-averse. Throughout this process, she had taken a more conservative and isolationist stance. Maae was not at odds with the others, but was certainly made more anxious by these events.

"In that period, we have to decide whether to revert to our happy isolation or take on a role in the Congregation of Populated Systems."

"No, we have debated this before," replied Anli, "and sending Mr. Markov back with the Rub' al Khali has set our path in stone."

"We could still change our minds and leave it at this. It would be easy to hide the gateway."

Nako had made up his mind. Admittedly, the head of Foreign Affairs was bound to have a position that favoured sustained contact, or any contact, for that matter. Through fifty years of isolation, it sounded to many like a splendidly pointless department, despite its role in the governance of affairs between the Arc's planets.

"I disagree. If we stay closed, they will send a flotilla of new missions to our systems, along with any within easy reach of us. They will rain fire down upon us and will find Rub' of their own accord; there are only so many places it could be. I know that remains decades away, but we will increasingly live in fear as the clock ticks down."

Maae's was not a lone voice. It was built from the ocean of thoughts from those within her organisation and tempered by the sentiments of billions in society at large. All of this seethed through her. It was the awareness of billions of minds, a sensation that no human could conceive of until they had experienced it: simultaneously empowering, terrifying and humbling.

Maae replied, "That's true, but for the record, let it be known that I think this course of action was not my first choice."

"Understood."

The conversation then flitted around amongst the twelve.

"We can use Rub' to control the relationship, certainly for a few years. We'll drag out the negotiation and use that time to gauge them, understand their motivations, and build a diplomatic policy."

"What did the Hanseatic League decide?"

"They have accepted the debt write-off but in return insist on equal access to the discovery. They also demand a satellite office for Genesis and two other trans-planetary corporates."

"We can allow that, can't we?"

"Yes, we can pretend to let them lobby us and completely waste their time."

"Are you not worried about them inserting surveillance technology that we can't recognise or find?"

"Yes, but I'm hoping that External Affairs will help us counter threats of that type. I don't think that we should suddenly trust them or treat them as a best friend, but I do think that we can cautiously cooperate."

"But watch our backs."

"Agreed. Can we vote on that one? Who accepts the corporate offices?"

Ten hands went up, and two remained down.

"Carried."

"And the Old Worlds?"

"They're still mute on the subject, but I reckon they'll follow where the Hanseatics go."

The debate continued, guided by a gen-5 mind that kept

them on topic and approximately on schedule. Their words were spirited but respectful and kind. This was not a forum for arguments or raised voices. They didn't come to this as ideological combatants, more as relatives at an extended family gathering.

Several more points were discussed and a handful of new motions carried. All through this, the gen-5 recorded every word spoken and registered the voting processes. It wasn't as secretive as some liked to believe. A fair portion, admittedly in a condensed form, would be disseminated to their departments as memos and new instructions. Parts would be delivered to the press. Some secrecy was useful because it added to the mystique of Lafayette and the Gang.

The Jericho gateway would remain open. All arrivals would be delivered to the Rose Cavern and would walk its long forest path as a standard initiation into the Arc. The job of making outsiders understand their ways would require a sustained effort, and the added theatre of arrival seemed like a fine start.

For the foreseeable future, visitors would be strictly limited, both in number and in purpose. The first exchanges would comprise diplomatic teams, specialists for Rub' al Khali, and groups of ecologists, although it was not yet clear if Core cared about the latter.

The debate was calm, but Maae looked forlorn and defeated. Nako attempted to provide encouragement.

"Maae, there are some amazing opportunities that we can now grasp. There are missing species of Cetacea – blue whales, narwhal, and others – that we will have the opportunity to introduce. What excites me most is that scientists from the other leagues have developed techniques for returning extinct species to existence."

She turned towards him and stared, blinking. "How?"

"I don't know the details, but I do know that it's limited to species that went extinct post-genome-mapping. We can arrange for them to send people who have been involved with that project."

She looked at the floor, thrilled by the possibilities but already mulling the difficult existential issues it raised. How do you introduce a Siberian tiger to an ecology where new apex predators have been positioned to inhabit that niche? Can they only do it on new planets? What does it mean to bring a species back from the dead? Still, Nako's words had helped, and she was warming to the idea.

He had one more thing on his mind. "I for one am grateful to Ren Markov for his role in this. As a small gesture, I would like to offer him freedom of movement through the Arc."

"Has that been requested?"

"No. I had hoped to present it as a simple gift. He may need a bolt-hole if certain forces turn against him."

The motion was carried easily, and they turned to one final topic.

"What's our backup plan? What do we do if Core or the other Leagues become problematic? Once they have what they want from Rub' al Khali, we lose leverage. They have a history of being, ummm… overbearing."

"I can't see them reverting to bullying and subversion, but from now on we keep rigid control over any connecting gateways into Arc space. We should stick to the one linking Jericho to Nuevo Mundo and maintain kill switches for emergencies. We now know how to detect these micro-gateways, so they will not be able to sneak new ones in."

"If I may, it seems a pertinent moment to raise something new."

The speaker was Amza. He headed up the Department of Expeditions, which sent exploratory missions out to new star systems. They had reached out so far that the word "archipelago" was beginning to seem absurd. Their expanse of explored space was now more like a cone shape than a ball, extending outwards from Alegra towards the galaxy's rim.

"I would have been ready to announce this in a few days

anyway, but these circumstances encourage me to speed through normal protocol. My department is still figuring things out as we speak, but we recently reached beta-Faustus, which is in the outer limits of any explored zone, let alone ours. It seems likely that we have found something there that changes everything."

Amza had the room's unbridled attention as he started to tell his story. He had little more than the limited initial facts of beta-Faustus, but he spun it out because it was worthy of a story. It became evident that they had a topic that could easily fill another hour, so the gen-5 mind was instructed to permit this modification to the agenda.

Eventually, the discussion ended, and Nako poured himself a whiskey before taking a seat at an ageing white piano. He began to play, and the others sat in silence and listened. The villa stood alone in its puddle of light, framed by the lawns, swamp and shadowy forest.

Chapter 32

Reflection

Ren returned to Super Paradise and its familiar, sordid streets. Out of habit more than any true urge, he set forth into this den of iniquity. The first stop was a simple choice, barely a choice at all: a cavernous club near his apartment called Soy Capitan! He felt more than a fraction of self-loathing for setting foot there, but entered nonetheless. It was tawdry, but the beer was cheap, and most importantly, it was honest about itself. Tonight it seemed aggressively loud. It grated. The array of gyrating professional go-go dancers, normally a semi-ironic distraction, was now an irritating presence. They seemed more animalistic, sweaty and crude than he remembered. Even in the kindly, dull-red lighting of the club, they looked second-rate. This was a one-beer stop at the best of times, but tonight he swallowed it quickly and returned to the swirling streets.

Stop number two was The Nameless, an explosively energetic live-music venue with passably talented acts. He often opted for a place like this early in the evening while still warming up and not quite ready to communicate with other humans. The trick was to stay on the periphery of the throng near the stage, where he could go unnoticed and avoid unwanted advances.

The night simply didn't lift off in the way he anticipated. Ren drifted from bar to bar, never pausing for more than one drink and consistently avoiding conversation. Eventually, realising that the evening was going nowhere, he made his way to the Silver Arcade and the quiet familiarity of the Only God Forgives.

"Ren! You skanky mutherfucka. Where have you been?"

"Suiiki. You cock-juggling thunder-cunt. I've been at work."

"Where this time? Let me guess, you'd tell me, but then you'd have to kill me."

"Yeah. Actually, that's probably true this time. For once it's genuinely secret."

"Thank you, Ren! Finally, you confess."

"It's not like that, but this last mission ended up in cloud cuckoo land."

"I'll get you drunk, and then you'll talk," said Suiiki following with a slightly crazed laugh.

"You better get me very drunk."

He was far happier here in Suiiki's quiet, elegant bar. Somehow the rest of Super Paradise's frenetic urgency wasn't clicking for him. The techno-pace of this crazy place was jarring after weeks in the Arc's laid-back quietude. It was inevitable but still disorienting. But it was not only that; he was more aware than ever that he had no deep friendships or community. Would he really grow old here, staggering between bars, sitting alone bathed in the eternal neon glow?

Sitting there watching Suiiki polish glasses, Ren felt a surprising urge surface. Some thoughts appear from nowhere but then latch onto your consciousness like an alligator's jaw. From one moment to the next, he found himself obsessively dwelling on his childhood in Palau. This was a place he hadn't visited in years, had little remaining empathy for, and where, for the longest time, he had never expected to return. The urge evolved beyond a simple thought and then crystallised into a solid certainty. He would return to Palau the next day.

There was no clear plan, no agenda, nor any rigid purpose behind the trip. Instead, Ren was obeying some arcane instinct. He was one of life's drifters, and such people, though generally happy with their path, occasionally fall into the arms of a peculiar nostalgia that reaches out insidiously from the galleries and hallways of memory.

The morning's journey had been simple enough, and he found himself quite at ease passing through the two gateways required to reach Malakal. There was no avoiding that disconcerting reality slip, but the lurking anxiety was absent, at least for now.

Palau had few domestic gateways, so from the capital Malakal, he relied on old-fashioned ground transportation to get him to Prospect, the provincial town of his birth. A rickety, noisy train from another century hauled him out of the capital at a speed that seemed comically lackadaisical when compared to the slick, tunnelled routes on Marrakesh. Still, it was faster than that mad contraption on Jericho, and speed was not of the essence. This journey allowed for open windows and a carriage filled with the pungent scents of Palau's farm country.

Mile after mile of low, rolling hills slipped by in the haze of mid-afternoon. Saffron fields of wheat stretched to the horizon without fences or hedges to reveal their boundaries. Only local farmers understood the mysteries of where their land stopped and their neighbour's began. A breeze painted swirling, shifting patterns on the wheat as if a vast shoal of fish were sweeping across the landscape just below the surface.

Ren surveyed all this from an entirely different perspective to that of his blinkered youth. Back then, he had been annoyed by its redneck banality. His eye had found not one shred of beauty in these fields, so from a young age, he had looked towards cities instead. The simple, bucolic serenity and humble charm of Palau had been invisible. He might even have felt betrayed by his future self for suddenly finding beauty here, just as a teen might feel betrayed by their middle-aged self who had discarded youthful ideals and taken up gardening, golf or bridge.

In his youth, this train journey to Malakal would have him buried in a book, oblivious to the immense skies. Age, separation and the power of recent experience had given Ren a different way of seeing things. Now he sat gazing outwards, mesmerised for most of the afternoon whilst the train rattled on.

Prospect was considered a 'provincial town' but Ren had always thought of it as a 'muddy backwater.' Whichever words you chose, the town was just big enough to allow him to remain invisible. He spent three days in a modest pensione, and during that time, he wandered the streets, visited old haunts and ate well. In restaurants, he ordered the local classics and chewed slowly, finding layers of flavour he had forgotten existed. It was farmers' fare – solid, filling and not all that refined, but it was just what he wanted. He sat and read the local paper from cover to cover, marvelling at its stubborn refusal to look beyond local issues. Palau was a microcosm, but it was unpretentious and honest.

One day he paid a visit to his parents' graves, which stood in a well-tended cemetery towards the outskirts of town. To his distress, he felt almost psychopathically cold walking up to it. There was a complete absence of the feelings he was supposed to have, and that disturbed him. Their lives together – his old life here – felt like a mirage or a scene from a forgotten movie. After fifteen minutes sitting at the graves, something finally snapped, and a wave of grief surged through him. Later, his composure recovered, he finally understood something of the catharsis of grief. It was something that had not revealed itself until this day, having sat somewhere inside him like a cold stone all these years.

The revelation revealed itself slowly as his remaining time in Prospect wound down. The smells, flavours and the accent's musical lilt struck him more than on any previous trip, but Prospect was still never going to be his place. With that abrupt realisation, any further attempt at enthusiasm for Prospect melted away. Most of his brain was already on the train out, and the rest was packing its bags. He didn't need a shrink to tell him that he was searching for roots, for belonging and for identity. Super Paradise was a place he parked his hat, not a home in any real sense. His entire adult life had been with External Affairs, but that relationship had eroded his spirit and principles. It had been necessary to come back here to lay ghosts to rest and make certain that his heart did not belong in Palau. That job was done. It didn't. The problem was that it did not belong in Super Paradise either, nor did it lie with External Affairs, but at least a plan was forming.

The very day of his return, he resigned. Astrid hadn't even tried to talk him out of it, because she knew he had already left the fold. The truth was that he had now become an awkward presence, since nobody quite understood what had occurred in the Arc and why he had been the only one to leave unencumbered and with permanent permission to return. Nobody could prove it, but in some quarters he was thought to be a traitor.

Not long after, he packed up his apartment, terminated his lease and said a handful of goodbyes. It was a revealing but cheerless fact that Suiiki was the only person here that he would miss. Even that little bastard was more of an acquaintance than a friend. He sat there, surrounded by a handful of boxes, and realised that in deciding to leave, he had acted in the right spirit but rashly. It was all very well to choose to move on, but it helps to have a new destination in mind.

He conjured a representation of Marrakesh's globe and allowed that visualisation to slowly rotate. Next, he added layers to screen out remote farming country, the frozen poles and the many industrial wastelands, thus blanking three-quarters of the planet. With the remaining patchwork edition of Marrakesh still spinning, he began to zoom in to places that appeared interesting from afar. He took a virtual tour along the waterfront in Monte Alto and perused restaurant reviews in Jacqueville. He was naturally drawn towards the sleepier seaside towns close to the equator… towns full of life but tempered by tranquillity.

Finally, he settled on Apollo Bay, a low-rise, timber-framed community of about ten thousand souls. It was the nearest that Marrakesh got to a holiday town on the sea, and that gave it a little more vibrancy and diversity than places like Prospect. A house was available to rent on the seafront, and he snapped it up without ever having visited the town or even the region.

Two days later, he arrived at Apollo Bay's quaint station. There was no gateway for hundreds of kilometres, but that was now irrelevant. He walked the half-hour from the station to his new home, travelling light because his few belongings would be delivered in time. The town's streets were wide, dusty, devoid of traffic and overhung with leafy trees. He could not yet see the ocean, but a light breeze carried the tang of sea air, and the murmur of distant waves was unmistakable.

The house was wooden clapboard with peeling blue paint, white shuttered windows and a covered veranda. It was enclosed by a garden, but not of the formal type that required maintenance. The few succulents, xerophytes and palms would surely look after themselves. It lay a few hundred metres beyond a long beachside boulevard of seasonal restaurants and bars. The beach was of fine sand, and the water was clear enough, but it was nothing like the exotic beauty of renowned destinations on other planets. That said, it was a million miles from Super Paradise, and, more critically, it was everything he had hoped it would be.

That first evening, he went out in search of a new favoured haunt. At the very least, he needed to find somewhere offering simple, familiar comfort to replace Suiiki's. He was determined to begin a new life here with the right foot forward.

***

Weeks later, Ren was awake late, reclining with a whiskey on his veranda and waiting for dawn to gather. There was a sense of déjà vu but not of repetition. The shadow of melancholia had been absent these past weeks since returning from the Arc, and in particular since moving here, but he had a decision to make. On his lap sat a contract awaiting his signature.

He wondered if Astrid was still battling the dragons that their actions had set loose. In theory, he should have felt some pride in his achievement. Instead of acting as agent provocateur, sowing the seeds of chaos, he had achieved something decent… something that by most measures would make the Congregation of Populated Systems better. The Arc had taught him something about himself. He had never really done his job with External Affairs out of faith in the system, but more for the joy of the game and the intellectual satisfaction. Maybe that made him shallow, but still, it is better to know yourself than pretend a nobility that is not there. It certainly made him better at his job, because he found practical solutions unencumbered by the mental cage of those who can only view the world through the lenses of faith and ideology.

His debates with Oso-Rae had been swordplay as opposed to some desperate need to proselytise. He thought that the same was true of her, despite the energy she brought. Perhaps that was at the heart of their playful dialogue. Parry and riposte.

All that said, there was now an ember of belief in a better future. He did hope that Core could learn something from the Archipelago, and he was equally certain that they needed to adapt and veer away from the march towards absolutism. It wasn't the end of history for either of them.

These were other people's concerns now. He had walked away from all of that for good. The contract in front of him was for the purchase of one of the seaside bars along the boulevard. He would disconnect from the news feeds and make his community here. An identity can be built, and he would build his around this simple neighbourhood in Apollo Bay. He signed.

In recent weeks, Core and the Arc had plugged their data systems together, permitting a rush of private comms between individuals. Families separated decades ago were reunited, and tears flowed like the Antipili Falls. Many had even started to imagine a day when they could meet relatives whose existence had just been revealed.

The new communication system had delivered a surprise. Sitting unopened was a message from Oso-Rae. He was waiting for the right moment to open it. Perhaps tomorrow.

References

In this book, I make indirect reference to several writers and political theorists from history. Some of their words appear as direct quotes, and others are more disguised. I never directly attribute their words, as that would be disorienting in a work of science fiction. It is not my intent to present their thoughts as my own, and so, for completeness, these are the writers whose works are referenced in the book:

Jean-Jacques Rousseau, Pierre-Joseph Proudhon, Niccolò Machiavelli, Samuel Johnston, Edmund Burke, Hannah Arrendt, Emma Goldman, Baruch Spinoza

Acknowledgements

I would like to thank those who have helped in the writing of this work. In particular, I would like to thank my editors, Joe Pierson and Elizabeth Thurmond.

I also owe a great debt to my beta readers, Atalanti, Claudia, Fay, Jasmine, Matthew and Giancarlo, all of whom helped a great deal with their feedback

.

Archipelago

Printed in Great Britain
by Amazon